ULTIMATE BETRAYAL

ULTIMATE BETRAYAL

Bil Holton

Liberty Publishing Group
Durham, North Carolina

Liberty Publishing Group
Attn: Author, Bil Holton
1405 Autumn Ridge Drive
Durham, NC 27712

ISBN: 978-1-983095-06-9
Library of Congress Control Number: 2016913195

Chapter One

So help me—so help me, God. I'm going to pull the trigger."

"Clarence! No! Please no. Don't do that," Pamela pleaded, wincing as she held the phone to her ear.

"Give me one good reason why I shouldn't end my miserable life."

Pamela's bickering thoughts forced her eyes shut.

"Because ... because we can ... "

"We can what?" he shouted.

"We can work this thing out," she recovered, trying her best to marshal her composure.

"Don't even try that. You've already told me it's over. You reminded me again five minutes ago."

"I told you we could still be friends. We could ... "

"Friends!" he yelled. "I don't want to be just friends. I love you, Pamela. Don't you understand that?"

"People who love one another are faithful to each other. How dare you say you love me when you ... "

"I told you I was sorry. How many more times do I have to say it? I made a mistake—okay? It ... it just happened."

"Clarence, I don't want your apology. You can't apologize for the inexcusable. Your affair with her was simply a product of your own arrogance. Yes! You made a mistake all right. You chose lust over love and expected me to tolerate it."

"I told you it won't happen again."

"You're right. It won't happen again, because I'm not putting myself in a position to get hurt again."

"See. You still don't get it, do you?" he blasted. "If you had been there, I would never have let her into my room. I had a bad day that day and she listened. She was there for me. That's more than I can say for you. Your work was more important than me."

Pamela's mouth flung open in disbelief as she wrestled with his absurdity.

"What a terrible thing to say. You know I work for a living. I can't follow you around the country and watch you play football."

"I make more than enough money for both of us," he bellowed.

"And you remind me of that every chance you get. That's one of the things we never worked out. I love what I do, Clarence. You have always made me feel that what I do is silly ... that it's unimportant. I may never make as much money as you, but I'm making a living doing something I enjoy."

"So am I. I love football."

"So where do you think that leaves us?"

"With me holding a gun to my head," Clarence replied.

Pamela bit her lip and hesitated before she chanced a reply. Clarence took advantage of her pause.

"I'm sitting here holding this .38 caliber pistol to my head, wondering why I haven't fired it yet."

Pamela stiffened again in response to his suicide threat.

"Why haven't you?" she asked, realizing she was entering risky territory.

When he didn't respond immediately, she became agitated.

"Clarence, why are you putting us both through this? I don't want you to hurt yourself. I'm still willing to be friends, but we've got a lot to consider before we even think about continuing our relationship."

"On your terms or mine?"

"What do you mean?" she asked, finding it difficult to justify further conversation.

"Are we going to settle this your way or my way?"

"I was hoping we could reach a mutual agreement."

She listened to his labored sigh.

"Such as?" he replied, purposefully blunting his own input.

Pamela bit her lower lip as she moved slowly to the side of the sofa.

"When you called me, you said you would do anything to get me back."

"That's right. Anything."

"Then why are you threatening to kill yourself?"

"Because you don't want me anymore. I make one mistake and you want to throw me away."

"It was a pretty serious mistake, Clarence. We were engaged to be married."

"I told you I'm sorry."

Pamela huffed her resentment.

"I would like us to remain friends ... but ... "

"But the marriage is off, right?" he countered.

She held her breath and then let it out.

"As it stands right now ... yes."

Click!

She heard him cock the trigger.

"It'll take time to work things out," Pamela pleaded. "Please don't force things like this. You're asking me to promise something I can't ... "

"Can't or won't? I don't want time to be friends. I want time to be your husband. I want you to forgive me."

Pamela frowned.

"I want to forgive you, too. You really hurt me, Clarence ..."

"But you don't want me to be your husband, do you?"

"No. You've pretty much destroyed any chances of that happening."

"Then there's nothing left for me to live for, is there, you unforgiving hussy? You think just because you've got the body and looks that you can treat a man any way you want ... you ... ."

"Once upon a time, this body and my looks were just for you!" she interrupted. ""I enjoyed looking good for you. You obviously grew tired of me or you wouldn't have done what you did. Looks didn't have anything to do with it. It wouldn't have mattered what I looked like, how thin or heavy I was, how rich or poor I was, or how over-sexed or under-sexed I was. People like you think only of themselves and what they want for the moment. You didn't care if you hurt me. And as for your high opinion of me, what did you just call me ... a hussy? I never did anything to you that justifies that label."

"You left me."

"No. You left me when you had the affair ... and now you want to blame me for your own bad judgment."

"You sound like you don't care what happens to me," he teased.

Pamela gritted her teeth, but held her tongue.

"How are you going to feel when I commit suicide because of you? I'm begging you to take me back. Please! Are you going to save my life?"

"Why, you manipulative hyena. You're enjoying this, aren't you?"

"I'm begging you. Say yes or I'm going to splatter my brains all over this room."

"If you promise to get counseling, I'll consider taking you back."

"You really are a hussy. You know that?"

"Clarence. What you did can't be repaired just like that. It'll take time. And if you want to continue this conversation, you'd better clean up your language."

"Then stop acting like a little hussy. Thanks to you my time's running out."

"If you want to take your life, I can't save it. Nobody can. If you insist on calling me names, I'm going to hang up."

"I'm going to put the gun in my mouth."

"Clarence. Please stop this or I'm going to hang up."

"Okay!"

"Okay what?"

Bang!

The sound of the gun blast drove the phone from her ear as she screamed in horror. When she heard the gun drop to the floor, followed by what sounded like his lifeless body falling to the floor, she screamed again. She fumbled with the phone before she brought the receiver back to her ear.

"Clar ... Clarence!"

She listened, hyperventilating her fear.

"Clarence!" she yelled through disbelieving lips.

Oh, my God. He's shot himself.

She listened for any sound. Any indication of life. Anything that might tell her he botched his own assassination.

"Clarence! Please come to the phone if you can."

She pressed the phone to her cheek to erase the rush of air from the furnace, which announced another cycle of warmth through the vent at her feet.

Please tell me you didn't do this. Please tell me ...

She lowered the phone as she sank onto the chair. Her trembling fingers allowed the phone to fall into her lap before she could catch it.

Damn you for doing this to me. Damn you for making me witness your vulgar act of cowardice.

Pamela suddenly felt the urge to vomit and barely reached the bathroom before she emptied herself. She hugged the commode seat for support until she felt she could stand to retrieve a washcloth to whip her mouth.

Then she pulled a towel off its hanger to wipe her face, and leaned against the sink to regain her composure.

The sound of the gun blast rifled through her emotions, sending her fist crashing against the sink.

"I hate you for doing this to me," she said aloud, kneeling over the commode again in response to a nauseous lump in her throat.

She readied herself for another unpleasant reunion with the toilet, but managed to avoid the need for the sour deposit.

"I've got to call someone," she instructed herself. "I've got to report ... report his death."

She stood beside the sink and dampened a cloth again to wipe her face and neck.

Her soulful glance into the mirror showed the affects of just having witnessed a suicide. She was as white as a sheet and her unsteady legs struggled to support her weight.

This is unreal, she announced to herself as she made her way to her cell phone, which was in her purse tucked beneath her desk. She couldn't use the office phone because Clarence's phone was still live. *I've just heard a man shoot himself.*

She picked up the phone and listened, hoping her pilgrimage to the bathroom had somehow altered reality and that he would be on the phone, arrogant, but alive.

Still no sound.

"Clarence! Clarence!"

She listened again and then picked up her cell phone to make the dreaded emergency call.

"If he's just wounded himself, maybe I've got time to get help. I'll never forgive myself," she chastised herself as she sat in the office chair to keep herself from fainting.

Her finger flew across the phone screen, calling up the app for the 911 emergency number as she took a deep breath.

As soon as the 911 operator announced herself, Pamela explained who she was and speeded up her report so much the operator had to slow her down.

"Ms. Justice, first, give me the name and location of the victim."

"Clarence Blount."

"Clarence Blount?" the operator repeated. "And where is he?"

"At his home in San Francisco. I think. His address is 4824 Pacific Avenue. It's near Navato ... just across the bridge ... The Golden Gate Bridge. You've got to hurry. You've got to get someone there. He may still be alive," Pamela accelerated her words again.

"All right, Pamela. I'm having paramedics dispatched to that address, but I want you to stay on the phone and tell me everything you can about it."

"He shot himself while I was on the phone with him. I ... "

"Ms. Justice ... Pamela ... I want you to calm down. Okay?"

"Do you have Mr. Blount's phone number?" asked the operator, sounding mechanical, but efficient.

Pamela gave it to her.

"I'm going to give this information to the operator next to me, but Pamela, I want you to stay on the phone. Okay?"

"Okay," Pamela repeated shivering her obedience.

In a few moments the operator was back.

"Pamela?"

"Yes, I'm here."

"We've already notified the San Francisco police. I need you to help me clear up a few details. Can you do that?"

"Yes, I think so."

"Do you want someone there with you? A relative ... or a friend?"

"No, I'm okay."

"You've had quite a shock. I'd be happy to call someone for you."

"No. That's okay."

"If you change your mind, let me know."

"I will." Pamela assured her as she glanced at the office phone sandwiched between the Rolodex and the laptop on her desk. "I've still got an open line," she told the operator.

"I beg your pardon?" replied the confused 911 operator. "You mustn't hang up."

Pamela would have chuckled if she weren't so upset, but she let her jaw drop instead.

"No, I mean my connection with Clarence's home phone. I've got that line open, too."

"You've still got an open connection between the residences?" exclaimed the operator.

"Yes. He wasn't able to hang up."

"That's okay. You're doing just fine, Pamela. Leave the office phone line open. Okay?"

Pamela sat beside the desk holding both phones, but with her cell phone to her ear.

"Leave the office phone open," came the operator's hurried direction. "Pamela, listen to Mr. Blount's connection and tell me if you hear anything."

Pamela lowered the cell phone and raised the business phone to her ear. She narrowed her eyes to improve her hearing and listened intently for a few moments.

"Yes, I hear something," she said excitedly. "It ... it sounds like ticking. A clock I think," she blunted her own sentence realizing she wasn't speaking into the cell phone.

She repeated on the cell phone what she'd said into the office phone, so the operator could hear.

"The clock is the only thing you hear."

"Yes, just the clock," Pamela confirmed, not knowing whether to feel relieved or disappointed. "I didn't hear it before. I ..."

"Pamela, that's okay. You ... wait ... hold on. I've just gotten word that the San Francisco police are at the Pacific Avenue residence. Stay on the ..."

Pamela quickly exchanged phones, silencing the 911 operator's voice.

She could hear what sounded like muffled voices in Clarence's room along with the ever-present ticking of the clock.

She exchanged phones again, running into a mild, but firm reprimand from the operator.

"I hear voices. The police are in his townhouse," exclaimed Pamela.

"Pamela. Ms. Justice ... Pamela!" crowed the operator. "The San Francisco police want to speak to you. Keep both lines open ... Don't hang up. But speak to them. They're on your office phone."

Pamela exchanged the phones, placing her cell phone on her desk.

She lifted the office phone to her ear.

"Hello.

"Ms. Justice?"

"Yes, this is she."

"This is Sergeant Anderson of the SFPD. Are you the one who reported a possible suicide?"

Pamela swallowed hard and sensed that her throat was dry. Her first attempt to speak produced a cough.

"Yes. Yes I am."

"Well, we're here at Mr. Blount's apartment."

Pamela began to hyperventilate as she struggled to get her words out.

"Is he ... is he ... ? I heard him shoot himself. I ... "

"Ms. Justice. Mr. Blount is standing right here. You couldn't have heard a suicide."

A stupefied look jumped on her face, and her mouth flung open.

"Ms. Justice, are you still there? Did you hear what I said?"

Her eyes darted across the surface of her desk top as she tried to get hold of herself.

"You mean ... he's ... alive?"

"He's standing right here in front of me."

"He ... he didn't shoot himself?"

"Here. He wants to talk to you."

Her knees suddenly felt weak, sending her back onto the edge of the desk.

"Pamela, what's wrong with you? Are you crazy? You told these people I committed suicide? Look, I've put up with your threats and lies all I'm going to. I don't want you calling here again. I should have hung up on you this time, but I figured you needed the catharsis so I laid the phone down. But to say I shot myself over you ... you need to get a grip on yourself. You need to get a life. But most of all, you need to leave me alone."

He slammed the phone down, sending her phone from her ear.

I can't believe this. He didn't shoot himself. It was all just a game. A horrible manipulative game.

"You jerk!" She raised the phone to throw it across the floor, but, screamed her vehemence instead.

She bridled her anger when she spied the cell phone lying face up on her desk.

Oh dear, she heard me scream.

Apologetic hands grabbed the phone and lifted it to her ear. She could hear the woman's frantic voice pleading with her to get back on the phone.

"Operator ... operator. I'm back. I'm sorry I frightened you. I ... he's okay. He didn't shoot himself. I guess you heard."

"I just wanted to make sure you were all right. You sound distressed."

"Yes ... well ... It doesn't matter anymore," Pamela whispered. "He's ... he's playing games with me."

"Ms. Justice, are you sure you're okay? Do you need me to call someone?"

"No," Pamela replied, letting out a sigh. "I'm sorry I bothered you."

"No bother at all. That's what we're here for. I can tell by your call you believed you were reporting someone's death. We're glad your friend is okay."

"Friend! That jerk's no friend ... Am I in trouble? You know, for calling in a false alarm?"

"I don't think you have to worry about that. You seem sincere. If we need to clear up any details, the watch commander will probably call you. Most of our calls don't end this happily. If you're sure you're okay, we need to clear this line, Ms. Justice."

"Yes. I'm ... that's fine. Thank you, operator."

"Good-bye then."

"Good-bye."

Her lips tightened as she placed the phone on its base.

That common, no good piece of trash. He deliberately manufactured his suicide to harass me. I definitely made the right decision to end our relationship.

She raised herself from her desk and plucked the business phone from the desktop.

"I'm not going to be intimidated again by that moron," she hissed, as she picked up speed walking toward the kitchen.

She spied the Halloween candy on the counter and realized it was Halloween night.

"Of course. It fits him perfectly. His troll-like behavior was perfect for tonight. He's put a whole new meaning on trick-or-treat."

Pamela grabbed a piece of candy and headed toward her bathroom.

A long shower will wash his stench off. Then I'll call Karen to see if I can pay her an early holiday visit.

It was Pamela's practice to contact her sister whenever she felt wounded by relationships. Both Karen and Geoffrey, her childhood friend, would take turns consoling her, repairing the hurts, soothing the emotional wounds.

She pulled her clothes off and wrapped herself in one of the huge bath towels her grandparents bought her. Then she did a proper job on the candy.

Intuition took her back to the calendar in her office.

My schedule's too full between now and Thanksgiving. But that week after Thanksgiving looks good. I'll see if I can get to Asheville then, and celebrate the holiday a little late with Karen. Maybe Geoffrey will help me decide what to do.

Pamela penciled in the Asheville trip and reversed her steps to the bathroom.

Geoffrey's a cop who ought to be a psychologist, she praised him to herself. *There's no doubt in my mind he can put Humpty Dumpty back together again.*

She turned on the shower and flung the towel over the glass shower stall.

She felt soiled by the whole episode with Clarence and wanted to be cleansed by the warm water.

Her troubled steps carried her into the shower and separated her from the harsh realities of a few moments before.

"Ummm," she said softly as the warm water cascaded over her. "I'm going to wash him right out of my life."

Tonight will be fun serving the trick or treaters in the neighborhood.

She tilted her water soaked head toward the skylight above the shower.

The sky is beautiful. I'm going to put my frustrations behind me and turn tonight into an Oktoberfest. He can't intimidate me without my consent. And I'm not giving it anymore!

CHAPTER TWO

*I*t had been over a month since his fake suicide call. Clarence had called on Thanksgiving Day just to harass her, and again just last night. As soon as she realized it was him, she let the phone ring.

That's the problem with cell phones, she complained to herself. *They follow you wherever you go—including Asheville! Why can't he just leave me alone? He picks the holidays to grandstand his contempt for me. I wish he had pulled the trigger.*

"What am I saying?" she chastised herself aloud, as she laced up her running shoes. "I don't wish that way out for anyone, not even Clarence. I can't let him form outposts in my mind."

Pamela shot a quick glance at Hans, her sister's lovable four-year-old German Shepherd. He stood protectively at her side, facing into the raw, icy wind that encircled them. His wet nose quivered constantly, as a plethora of odors reached his nostrils.

"Thanks, young fella, for escorting me this morning," she addressed the obedient canine. "It's great to have such good company."

When she gave him a couple of quick pats on the head, Hans let out a small yelp and moved impatiently in a clockwise motion around her.

"Just a minute, fella," she said encouragingly. "I'm almost ready."

Hans voiced another impatient plea as she pulled her second glove over well-manicured fingers. When she finally opened the door, Pamela's eyes narrowed into emerald slits underneath dark lashes in response to a refrigerated blast of air that hit her in the face.

Hans continued his doleful recital by barking his impatience.

A mere apology will not suffice, she reasoned. *No more delays. He's ready to go.*

"Okay, okay, Rudolph. I know you want to get this show on the road. But in a couple of weeks it'll be Christmas. And I'm the one with the red nose," she teased. Her levity at his antics spiraled into laughter as she reacted to his latest series of playful yelps.

Encouraged by her mild protest, Hans barked again and lunged forward, sending the nylon lease into a perfectly straight umbilical cord.

Pulled off balance by his exuberance, Pamela staggered momentarily to regain her footing on a pavement spotted with icy patches.

"Hans," she said agitatedly. "Stop it. No! What's gotten into you? Now, come on, take it easy. You're going to make me fall."

Obedient to the tone of her voice, Hans sat on the icy pavement and waited for her direction.

"I'm sorry, boy," she apologized. "After all, I'm the one who got us up at seven-fifteen on the coldest morning they've had in Asheville this winter. And for what? A thirty-minute jog. I ought to have my head examined."

Hans looked at her disciple-like, pitching his massive head from side-to-side as if he understood her.

"I promised Karen we'd be back around eight-fifteen or eight-thirty," she told Hans, referring to the hastily scribbled note she'd left on the kitchen counter for her sister to find. "So we'd better get started."

Hans lunged forward immediately, prompted by her advance.

Leading Hans from behind as she jogged down the icy sidewalk, she remembered the conversation she'd had the night before with Karen about going out this morning. There had been a couple of robberies downtown and a woman was attacked in broad daylight. She was forced at knife point into her car, driven near Riverside Cemetery, and then beaten and raped.

The holidays, it seems, brings out the best, and unfortunately the worse, in people, she reminded herself, believing Clarence to be the chief Grinch. She glanced at Hans admiringly. *I'm safe with you around, aren't I, fella? You won't let anything happen to me, will you?*

Her thoughts took her to her current painful situation. She was spending Christmas at her sister's before leaving for Europe. She was flying to Brussels, Belgium the day after Christmas to start a six-month consulting contract as a multi-cultural meeting facilitator with NATO. The real reason for her accepting the contract was more personal than professional.

She had ended her emotionally and physically devastating relationship with Clarence at Halloween, but her abusive fiancé was making it difficult for her to remain in Raleigh, North Carolina, where she lived. His threats were escalating, and she was getting little help from the Raleigh police. Despite her precautions, he had shown up in Raleigh, breached her security several times, and left dead bouquets of flowers and taunting notes in her house.

The restraining order she served on him only intensified his relentless harassment. Fear for her life and concern for the safety of her family and friends prompted her to take evasive action. Only her immediate family knew about the overseas assignment.

Her reverie was interrupted suddenly by the harsh voice of a woman, who clucked mild irritation at her.

"Watch where you're going, young lady, or whoever you are. You can't tell these days. You almost knocked me down." Then she cursed at Pamela and raised her fist in self-righteous defiance.

Pamela slowed her pace almost to a stop and turned toward her accuser to make amends, but saw that the woman, quite happy in her tirade, was still shouting obscenities at both her and Hans, who stood, wagging his tail, pleased at the commotion. Pamela proffered a quick apology and wheeled around, giving Hans more slack. They continued their trek up the icy street which was sprinkled with dozens of skeletal trees whose branches and trunks glistened with the light layer of ice that had fallen overnight.

The streets were desolate and, judging by the reception she just received at the last corner, uninviting. Only an occasional pale yellow light emanated from the snow-speckled windows of the houses that lined the streets.

Not many people up this early on a Saturday morning, she observed, a wry smile cracking her face.

There was a decided iciness to the arid gusts. December had ushered in the foulest of weather.

"Hans, old boy, most people dream of white Christmases. I think it's really a wish for more time off of work. Who in their right minds thinks this kind of weather warms up the holidays?"

The unpleasant sensation she experienced earlier with the agitated woman returned, sending a chill through her. There was an edge to the atmosphere that had nothing to do with the weather. The morning felt diabolical, as if it had something unpleasant in store for her.

Suddenly Hans pulled hard on the leash, pivoting her around to face him. Pamela slipped on a patch of ice and clung to the taught lease for support.

"Hans! What have you found?" she demanded agitatedly.

Oblivious to Pamela's mild reprimand, Hans was occupied with the discovery of a recently-discharged excrement deposited just off the sidewalk by a canine relative. Pamela had just missed stepping in it moments earlier as she jogged down the sidewalk.

"No, Hans, no!" she shouted disdainfully, pulling him away from the fecal waste. Ignoring his brief objection, she pulled on the leash again. "Enough of this dilly-dallying," she remonstrated. "Stay away from that."

When Pamela pulled on his leash a third time, Hans surrendered, satisfied with his abbreviated visit.

"Owners who let their pets defecate on public walks should have their irresponsible noses rubbed in it," she said aloud. "Isn't that right, boy?"

Hans signaled his innocent approval by trotting a few paces ahead of her, looking for something else to catch his fancy.

§   §   §   §   §   §

"You piece of shit," the hung over driver screamed as he bent down to retrieve the car keys he dropped. He went ballistic when he dropped the keys again, allowing the obscenities to come uncensored.

His three passengers, heavily clothed, scarved, and booted for winter weather, watched—amused at his clumsy attempts to hold onto the keys.

Suddenly the driver slipped and fell, cursing the trio of passengers and the keys for their insolence.

"Let me help you," said his wife as she inched closer to him.

He ignored her and shouted a few more expletives at the insubordinate keys, which ricocheted off the icy curb and slid next to the front tire.

"Come here, damn you," he ordered the keys. It was early in the morning and he was still suffering the effects of too much partying the night before. He used the door handle to pull himself up beside the car and pointed the key at the lock.

"That's the wrong key. Here, let me do it," his wife volunteered, placing her gloved hand over his.

"Get outta my way," he slurred, pushing his wife aside. "If I want your help, I'll ask for it. Otherwise stay the hell outta my way."

She grabbed the car to balance herself, recoiling in waxen silence from his vehement outburst. The faces of the other two passengers turned as ashen as the endless tones of grey that blanketed the landscape around them, giving the trio a ghostlike appearance under the designer clothing they wore.

"I think you'd better drive," the alcoholic's wife said to one of the others.

"Like hell he will," hissed the drunkard.

"You're not in any shape to drive," his wife challenged.

"The hell I'm not!"

"You can't even unlock the door. Just how do you expect to drive?"

"There! It's unlocked," he praised himself, pretending he didn't hear her.

Despite another impotent rash of protestations criticizing his driving ability, the driver stubbornly threw himself behind the steering wheel, inadvertently locking the car when his elbow bumped the electronic lock. He angrily unlocked the car again and ordered the passengers to get in. Without exception, all three confederates flew into the sedan, taking their places without so much as a word between them.

§   §   §   §   §   §

Karen hastily snaked out of her nightclothes, ran her fingers through her shoulder length auburn hair, and then shook her head from side to side as if to complete the aeration that busy fingers had only begun. Nonchalantly, she rifled quickly through her middle dresser drawer and retrieved her favorite red sweater. She quickly pulled it over her head and arms simultaneously, allowing it to cascade down over small but round, upstanding breasts, unconfined by a bra.

A pair of knee-less blue jeans was draped across the antique oak and hickory rocker in the corner. She loved the sense of freedom she felt when she wore them. So without hesitation, she confidently sheathed herself in jeans that were loose-fitting, and purposefully air-conditioned.

It's funny, or maybe not so funny, Karen thought, as she gazed intently at her reflection in the beveled mirror attached to the back of the antique oak dresser. *I spruce myself up whenever Pamela visits. She has that affect on me.*

She glanced at the photo of Pamela on her bureau.

"You've always been the pretty one, Sis," she addressed the photo aloud. "But you've never made me feel less than beautiful. Sometimes you make me think I really am beautiful. Maybe that's why I step up my looks when you're here."

She playfully tugged at the collar of the sweater, a gift from Pamela, and smiled wryly, catching her reflection again in the mirror. Normally, Saturday mornings found her snuggled in one of her sweat shirts, inexpensive trophies rescued mainly from yard sales or flea markets. Occasionally she would purchase one at half-priced sales proffered routinely from the proliferation of shops which sprung up like weeds throughout the town. Merchants competing for customers lowered their prices, keeping her in sweatshirts, music books, and house plants.

The muted roar of the furnace coming alive brought her attention to her bare feet, which were beginning to get cold the longer she stood on the bare hardwood floor. One final scrutiny of her hair yielded a perfunctory tussle to fluff the left side a little more. Satisfied, she flew quietly over to other large dresser and confiscated a pair of woolen socks. Her small but strong hands, artist's hands, made short work of pulling her socks over appreciative feet. She glanced around the room, and her blue eyes squinted momentarily to focus on the numbers on the clock face.

"Seven forty-five," she whispered to herself. "I've probably got enough time to give Hans a walk, start the coffee, and get out the tree ornaments before Sis wakes up." She'd purposely neglected the tree, hoping Pamela would want to help trim it when she arrived.

She extinguished the Santa Claus night light in the hallway, and glanced at the door to Pamela's room. It was shut. She paused, listening for any sound that might indicate activity. Except for the rush of the air from the furnace forcing its way through the overhead vents, and an occasional chorus from tenacious birds broadcasting the start of a new day, there was no evidence of anyone else up.

Content that her movements had not disturbed her sister's sleep, Karen retreated quietly down the stairs, skipping over the third step from the top, which usually announced anyone's passage by creaking loudly.

CHAPTER THREE

There was a decided spring to Pamela's confident step as she rounded the next corner to begin her descent toward McDowell Street. She passed an untenanted section of Reed Street. The old houses that once lined the right side of the street had been torn down, leaving vacant lots to punctuate her path.

As she stepped carefully over a clump of sooty ice, she slipped on a patch of black ice, too gelid to be water, yet too clear to be seen. Arms flailing and legs scrambling, she made quite a scene as she struggled toward a spastic recovery.

Hans came to life and circled her, barking and wagging his tail, wanting to join in on the fun. He liked her new game and interpreted her less than graceful moves as part of the fun. In her valiant effort to stabilize herself while holding on to his leash, she was thrown off balance completely when Hans bolted toward her. Down she went, legs going north and arms going south. She hit the pavement hard, banging her right elbow on the frozen sidewalk.

"Damn it," she yelled. Then she moaned as she held her injured elbow and attempted to sit up.

Hans was on her in a flash, jumping her from behind, his paws landing on both of her shoulders.

His attempt to lick her face was met with vociferous disapproval as Pamela raised her voice, "Hans, No! I'm hurt, I think I've cracked my elbow."

When she registered her complain, Hans buried his wet muzzle in her neck and face in an attempt to console her.

"It's okay, boy," Pamela encouraged, rubbing her elbow. Then she reached over to pet Hans, "Good boy," she continued, "I'm okay. Oh, no," she added painfully. "I think I've broken a nail." When she pulled off her glove she confirmed her suspicion. The tip of the nail on her ring finger had broken off, leaving an exposed jagged edge.

Her momentary disappointment turned to laughter as Hans accelerated his licks, moving in at every opportunity to wash her face. The harsh coldness of the pavement finally forced Pamela to her feet, slowly at first, then with a modicum of stability as she lifted herself cautiously from the icy patch.

Still rubbing her elbow, she began to walk, then jog, regaining her disciplined step. She continued her trek, lifting her eyes occasionally to scan the ashen sky and gaze at the bleak landscape as she moved down the ice-encrusted streets that stretched out before her.

The pain began to subside in her elbow and she was able to move her arms in rhythm with her stride. The crunching of her patterned footsteps on the frozen streets and sidewalks, and an occasional jingle of Hans' identification tag were the only sounds in the early morning air.

She could see the McDowell Street Bridge through the mass of skeletal trees, made anorexic with the loss of foliage. The scenery was brushed in savage grays and painted with innumerable hues of ashen charcoal. Forgetting the murkiness of her surroundings for a moment, Pamela's eyes turned into jade slits, as she peered once more through the sparsely endowed treetops to catch a better glimpse of the bridge.

"We'll cross the bridge," she told Hans, referring to the McDowell Street Bridge. "That's as far as I'll take us this morning. I told Karen we'd only be out half an hour, so we'll make the bridge our turn-around point."

As she approached McDowell Street and the majestic entrance to the Biltmore Estate, she glanced at the shops along the street. Their storefront windows were filled with displays and their exteriors were adorned with Christmas lights that crawled up corners and crept across the eaves, framing each shop with hundreds of multicolored lights. The storeowners' holiday spirit spilled onto the ice-laden tree limbs and hearty shrubbery that proudly bore sprays of Christmas lights and garlands.

She made her way through streets spotted with ice and lined with oaks and hemlocks and hickories, and came upon a beautiful cluster of gnarled rhododendrons, long-time residents of Asheville. Most were ten to twelve feet high, spilling their dark green foliage fifteen or more feet into yards punctuated with an assortment of azaleas, junipers and cedars.

Pamela's breath came out in short, white puffs of air, visible in the frigid coldness, as she jogged steadily toward their destination—the McDowell Street Bridge. Another cold blast hit her, and she gasped as she spoke once more to her faithful companion. "Hans, what have I gotten us into this morning?"

§　　§　　§　　§　　§　　§

He took another defiant sip of coffee.

"Are you satisfied now? I'm drinking coffee."

"I'd feel better if you'd let someone else drive," his wife petitioned cautiously.

"That way you could give the coffee a chance to work," pleaded the woman in the back seat.

"You two are enjoying this, aren't you?" retorted the driver as he swerved into the curb and back out into the street again.

"If that skid was on purpose, you idiot, it wasn't funny," hissed his wife. "And no, we're not enjoying the ride. You've got a hangover and I'd prefer someone else to drive."

"This holiday trip was my treat and I intend to fulfill my civic duty by staying behind the wheel."

"Then stay on the road, damn it," shouted his wife, who threw her hands on the dash as he ran onto the curb and ricocheted off a packed mound of crusty ice before settling back on the street.

"Oops! Must have hit an icy patch."

"That does it," blasted his wife. "Stop the car. You're going to let someone else drive before you hurt somebody."

She reached over to grab the steering wheel, but her husband blocked her move with his right arm, spilling his coffee.

"I told you it was a patch of ice. Anybody would have skidded into the curb. Now look what you've done. You made me spill my coffee."

Suddenly the car spun out of control, sending them toward an icy embankment.

Both women screamed as the car completed its three-sixty spiral, skidding to a stop that left it facing toward its original line of travel.

"Everyone all right?" questioned the male passenger in the rear seat as he straightened himself.

"Yes, I'm fine," whispered the blond beside him.

"I think I'm okay," replied the driver's exasperated wife.

"Here," snapped her husband as he threw his half empty cup of coffee at her. "You need this more than I do."

Coffee spewed from the small opening in the lid of the cup before the top came off, sending the rest of it over his wife's coat, the car door, and the dash.

"Why, you common son-of-a ... "

"Don't you dare say it. You didn't get burned, did you?" mediated the male passenger.

She threw him a befuddled look.

"I don't believe he did that. He threw a hot cup of coffee at me."

"It was either that or shutting you up with my fist," countered the driver, leering at her.

"All right. That's enough, you two. I think we've all had enough excitement for one day. How 'bout it, old boy? Suppose I drive home. Looks like you two could use a little space between you."

"I could use something to get these coffee stains off my coat," his wife said, trying her best to keep her composure.

"Probably the only thing open this early are service stations," chimed the blonde-haired woman.

"Then that'll have to do. This is a brand new coat. I hope you haven't ruined it, you jerk."

"Okay," soothed the male passenger. "I'll see if I can find us a service station. Come on, old boy. We're only a few blocks from the Biltmore entrance. I think there's a service station near there."

"Then let's not keep the lady waiting," teased the hungover driver as he floored the accelerator.

"What are you doing?" his wife yelled. "I thought you were going to let him drive."

"You want the stains off your over-priced coat, and he wants to drive. So why waste time? You'll both get your wishes in a couple of minutes."

He silenced the screaming tires by lifting his foot off the accelerator, allowing the car to slow almost to a stop. Then he inched the car forward.

"See, I'm fine. I promise to keep it under a hundred until we get to the bridge.

None of the passengers challenged him. All of them kept their contempt to themselves.

§   §   §   §   §   §

Tentative steps took Pamela across the paved entrance to the Biltmore Estate. The sidewalk was dry except for a few patches of ice. She paused to catch her breath, and gazed at the ornate entrance to the estate. It reminded Pamela of the interesting tidbits Karen had shared with her—information she'd picked up while doing some interior design consulting at the Estate. She recalled that the two-hundred and fifty room French Renaissance-type chateau was built for George Washington Vanderbilt, and it had seventy-five acres of formal gardens designed by Frederick Law Olmsted, the same man who designed New York's Central Park. Visitors the world over paid homage to its splendor. Each year hundreds of thousands of tourists came to see the Festival of Flowers, the Victorian Celebration of Spring, and the Christmas Candlelight Tours, all lavishly sponsored by the estate.

The gardens are natural magnets, she thought, *attracting tourists who speak dozens of languages, yet share paraphernalia common to tourists all over the world: cameras, maps, guide books, bags filled with souvenirs, clothing decorated with the names and pictures of places they've been.* She smiled at her appraisal. *Oh, and inquisitive stares, a nervousness with unfamiliar currency, and fingers pointing in all directions. Can't forget about that.*

She unceremoniously bent down to give Hans a quick, vigorous rub. Cupping his massive head in her gloved hands, Pamela rubbed Hans' ears and brought his muzzle up level with her own face. Dog lover and obedient canine were lost in each other's gaze for a moment, each drinking in the other's affection both feeling the effects of a frigid blast of air, fierce and raw as it introduced itself to exposed skin. Even Hans seemed pinched by the cold.

Suddenly she caught something coming toward them out of the corner of her eye. A lone figure, silhouetted against the slate mist and light gray sky which enveloped the bridge, was moving steadily toward them. Her full attention was riveted toward the solitary jogger whose easy stride was all too familiar to her. And the hat, a cap, a light blue cap protected his head.

"Geoffrey," she shouted in recognition, and then waved her acknowledgement while bringing her other hand up to shield her eyes from a burst of frigid air. "Hans, it's Geoffrey! What a wonderful surprise. Geoffrey, it's me, Pamela!"

Geoffrey returned her salutation with a wave of his own and slowed his pace to compensate for the slope ahead of him as he shortened the distance between them.

Pamela's four-legged protector steadied himself. His gaze steeled on Geoffrey, Hans publicized his recognition by wagging his tail vigorously.

Pamela shivered. The blast of air that just slapped her face seemed like a warning. She felt the strongest urge to shout for Geoffrey to hurry. There was nothing observable to justify her alarm. And she wasn't going to embarrass herself by over-reacting in typical female fashion to a feeling, an intuition that had no basis in reality. She quickly dismissed her uneasiness and instead began to slowly jog up the bridge to meet him.

CHAPTER FOUR

ans! Here, boy," Karen called, expecting his obedience. A lightning fast surveillance of the kitchen convinced her Hans wasn't there, so she wheeled around quickly and took an unscheduled tour of the living room.

It was a fairly large room, an area in which Karen's artistic and musical preferences were apparent everywhere. Her piano, an old Wurlitzer, was a graduation present from her grandparents. The brass music stand, a recent addition, occupied a permanent place next to the old piano ever since its arrival.

Bookcases, repositories of songbooks, musical awards, instruments of all types and sizes and her collection of metronomes, bore silent witness to the extent of her melodious talents and interests. Windows and doors intersected the walls, emphatically displaying their wide oak facings and lacquered surfaces, but there was a spaciousness and a warmth which balanced the austerity and asceticism characterized by Karen's simple tastes and preference for understated and unpretentious furnishings. The result was a cacophony of oak, walnut, and pine furniture, all from different eras, uncoordinated, but filled with character.

"Not in his favorite corner," she whispered to herself. "Where could he be?"

"Hans!" she flushed "don't do this to me."

Intuition told her to check the kitchen again and another thought surfaced just as quickly that he might be upstairs rooming with Pamela. That realization comforted her. After all, Hans had taken to Pamela, especially the ear rubs which melted him into voluntary submission. She decided to recheck the kitchen first. That's where his food dish was.

She stood for a moment framed by the massive doorway as her eyes shot across the kitchen. She noticed a piece of her favorite note paper taped to the coffee pot. There was something scribbled on it, in large lettering, cursive style. She recognized the handwriting immediately, and a look of relief slipped onto her face as she read the message. Abbreviated, bulleted, and to the point, it read:

> *Good morning, Sis,*
> *Decided to go jogging.*
> *Took Hans*
> *Keep the coffee hot*
> *ETA- eight-fifteen to eight-thirty*
> *Call Geoffrey. See if he'll join us for lunch.*
> > *Luv, P*

> *P. S. I'll help you trim the Christmas tree*
> *before we hit the shops.*

She breathed a sigh of relief, sending her tense lips into a smile as she glanced at the clock over the sink.

"Seven-fifty-five," she said aloud. "That gives me half an hour to start unboxing the Christmas tree ornaments and grab a cup of that coffee Pamela brought with her last night."

"Hazelnut Cream and Peppermint Candy," she said half aloud as she moved toward the refrigerator. "I think I'll try the Peppermint Candy first. It has a candy cane taste that's hard to resist."

She took the half-pound bag of coffee out of the freezer, peeled back the folds that sealed in the freshness, and with some ceremony, held the open bag up to her nose. Not getting the aromatic kick she anticipated, she retreated to the grinder dumped a couple of scoops of coffee beans into its wide mouth, capped it tightly, and with a whimsical smile pushed the button, sending the brown nuggets to their inexorable fate. Her anticipation mounted as she removed the plastic cap on the grinder exposing the rich aroma of freshly-ground coffee. She inhaled slowly, savoring the caffeinated moment. "Um ... mm! I love the smell of freshly-ground coffee," she whispered aloud.

A few minutes later she carried her coffee mug into the living room, took a sip, then set it down on the raised stone lip of the hearth. It tasted as good as the inaugural cup she'd enjoyed the night before, when Pamela presented her with a small electric coffee bean grinder as a birthday gift, celebrating her thirty-five years on the planet.

"What a treat," she chimed aloud, "a peppermint jump-start."

She licked her lips after the next sip and then shook her head slowly, savoring the gourmet blend's wet residue on her lips.

"Outstanding," she cheered, and then busied herself by plucking the first set of tree lights from the box marked "Tree Ornaments."

§   §   §   §   §   §

Pamela's eyes were glued on Geoffrey, his silhouetted figure becoming more recognizable as their steps brought them closer together. She found, to her surprise, that she was gawking as she admired the ease of his descent. His carriage was that of someone used to running.

Geoffrey Fitzgerald Collins, III, was a policeman who was the product of a law enforcement family. His six-foot four inch frame was powerfully built, forged by the crucible of flesh meeting iron six days a week in gymnasiums designed to tear musculature down just to build it up again. His massive chest, held superb by a narrow waist and carried by muscular thighs and calves, won him a place on last year's national law enforcement Hard Bodies Calendar, sponsored by Gold's Gym.

His stately features were bordered by well-groomed blond hair, and his eyes were slate gray, set deep in sockets above well-formed cheeks. Prominent and warrior-like, they added to his vital and energetic appearance. His perfect set of teeth, magnificently showcased a smile so completely intoxicating that he could mesmerize—instantly—anyone caught in his charismatic presence.

Locked in a prolonged moment of reverie, Pamela hadn't noticed Hans' strong pull of the leash as he struggled to free himself to greet Geoffrey. Her gaze dropped down to Hans as she became aware of his dilemma. She stopped jogging and unhooked the leash from his collar, sending Hans racing toward Geoffrey, who was only a few meters away. Hans stutter-stepped at the start, slipping on a patch of black ice, but regained his momentum and was on Geoffrey in seconds.

"Come here, fella," Geoffrey coaxed, as he slowed to a walk and patted his hand against his thigh. Then he looked at Pamela and grinned his welcome.

"What a nice surprise," Pamela squealed. "I didn't expect to see you until tonight."

"You're as beautiful as ever," he said affectionately, his rich baritone voice filling the morning air. "Am I seeing you tonight?"

"You'd better, silly. Hasn't Karen called you this morning?" Geoffrey looked at his watch.

"It's only five after eight. I doubt she'd call this early. Besides, I left my apartment over an hour ago. I wish I had known you were going to be out this morning."

" I didn't decide myself until I woke up."

Geoffrey's sigh was followed by an attempt to catch his breath.

As he reached down to pet Hans, the dog reared up on his hind feet and placed his icy paws on Geoffrey's nylon jacket.

Tail wagging like a metronome out of control, Hans capitalized on every opportunity to lick Geoffrey in the face.

"Slowing down in your old age, huh?" Pamela teased.

"I've been jogging since seven," he countered good-naturedly.

"Poor baby," she bantered.

"And it's been a cold jog at that. The wind's been brutal since I left the protection of the buildings."

"Yes, I know. I was beginning to wonder if it's worth it."

"Me, too!"

"Bad idea, huh?" she winced.

"Not if there's a hug involved," he smiled.

She took a couple of steps toward him, but before they could embrace a strong gust of icy wind caused each of them to take a step sideways. As soon as they steadied themselves their eyes met, acknowledging their mutual lunacy for jogging on the coldest day of the year.

He cupped her head in his gloved hands, placing them around the outside of her hood, and then pulled her to him. At the same time, he repositioned himself so he could shield her from the icy blasts of air that seemed to come with renewed vigor.

"I see you've been shopping," His quick wink was allied with a comedic smile.

"Shopping?" she repeated, not catching his curve.

"Your suit," he asserted, and squeezed her hooded neck for emphasis. "It's new, isn't it?"

"Oh, yes, do you like it?" She rallied innocently, placing her hands on her hips as she posed mannequin-like for his approval. Her attempt at modeling invited his good-natured teasing as he grabbed her again and proceeded to give her a playful head rub.

"Yes, I like it, you silly girl," he chided playfully. "It looks good on you. Those are your favorite colors, aren't they?"

Her sweat suit was forest green, sprinkled with a touch of gray and mauve and slashed with a couple of well-placed ribbons of Confederate gray, which punctuated the suit, giving it a graceful yet streamlined look. It was perfect for Pamela's naturally slim, athletic build. Its dark green color complemented the brilliant lights coming from her eyes, making them appear more jade than emerald.

Her shoulder-length hair was pulled into a ponytail, which stuck out of the opening in the back of the mauve ball cap she tucked under the hood. The cap had gray lettering on it which read Civilized Leadership—the name of her Raleigh-based company.

Pamela nodded. "I bought it in Chicago. I had some work up there at a decent wage and decided to leave some of my hard-earned money in the windy city."

Geoffrey laughed. "Nothing wrong with that." He hesitated, then changed the subject. "Looks like we've got a windy city of our own. Suppose we grab some breakfast at Karen's place."

Pamela consented immediately, sliding her arm through his. She had not noticed until this moment how extremely treacherous the surface of the bridge had become. A light mist covered the macadam with large pockets of black ice, which blanketed the entire surface of the bridge from top to bottom.

After they took a few tentative steps, Pamela stopped and asked, "Would you mind ... " She hesitated, then looked directly into Geoffrey's eyes. "Do you mind listening to a sob story on the way back?"

"We've had these chats before, young lady." He looked at her with a hint of concern. "You don't have to apologize. And yes, of course I'm happy to listen to anything you have to say."

Pamela shot him a grateful look.

"I'm so lucky to have you."

"I feel the same way about you." Geoffrey tossed her one of his patented smiles. "You want to talk about ass hole, right?"

"Geoffrey!"

"Oops. Did I say that?" he pretended embarrassment by placing his hand over his heart. "Forgive me. You want to talk about what's-his-name."

Pamela raised her eyebrows and tightened her chapped lips.

"Clarence is still harassing me."

"He can't leave well enough alone, can he?"

"I should have listened to you from the very beginning," Pamela confessed.

"Stop shoulding on yourself."

"What?" She gave him the most incredulous look.

"I said, stop shoulding on yourself. If you should do anything at all, you should listen to your own heart, Pam. Listen to that inner voice deep within you that knows what's best for you. Trust your intuition." He squeezed her arm, for emphasis. "There's someone out there in the same predicament as you. He's looking for a woman of your qualities. He's Mr. Right."

Geoffrey smiled again, but remained absolutely serious.

"And he will be the kind of guy that will truly love you, Pam. You'll know it because he'll treat you right. He'll be compatible with you in all of the important things. Like communication. And sexuality. And finances. And interests. He'll respect you. And he won't be threatened by your independence, intellect, or beauty." He paused, waiting for his thoughts to catch up. "And most of all, Pam, he'll find you permanently irresistible. And he'll be a man of character."

Her gaze rested on his face with great intensity.

"I wish I could believe that," Pamela spoke softly. "I don't think Mr. Right exists."

Geoffrey sent her a frown.

"That's part of the problem with women."

Pamela shot him a puzzled expression.

"Oh, you don't say, Dr. Freud."

"Oh, but I do say," Geoffrey pulled her close to him so that they faced each other. "Most women think Mr. Right is a fantasy. So they settle for less. And when they settle for less ..."

"They get somebody like Clarence," she interrupted.

"You got it." Geoffrey agreed. "He's got money, looks, and an NFL contract. So you thought ... "

"He was Mr. Right," she finished his sentence.

"Yep. You were looking for Mr. Perfect, not Mr. Right."

"And I found Mr. Wrong. Dead wrong!"

Geoffrey rolled his eyes.

"Well, you're lucky. You've got a chance to right a wrong. Right?"

Pamela nodded her agreement.

Just then Geoffrey stiffened. Pamela could see that he was looking over her shoulder. His eyes were riveted on something behind her.

In the split second it took Geoffrey's consciousness to move from Pamela to Hans and then to something as yet unnamed behind them, it was too late.

Everything appeared to transpire in slow motion. Geoffrey had only hesitated a fraction of a second. His lightning fast comprehension of the danger they were in sent him into a flurry of evasive action.

"Run, Pam, run!" he screamed instinctively, as he lunged forward convulsively and grabbed Pamela's left arm at the elbow, flinging her in front of him with considerable force.

Pamela winced and let out a scream as Geoffrey's vice-like grip sent shooting pains down her arm.

She staggered again, gripped in panic, trying to find purchase with her feet, only to slip again. As each foot failed to take hold, her weight and momentum carried both of them off balance, sending her left leg skewed sideways as she went down on one knee hard on the ice, so that she heard her knee crack.

Pamela cried out. The pain, sharp and excruciating, traveled up her leg, paralyzing her for a moment. Her heart was pounding so hard she was sure her chest would burst. She held on to Geoffrey for dear life as she felt his strong pull.

Geoffrey's body blocked her view up the bridge, but his evasive actions told her they were in serious trouble.

Then she heard it. Metal against concrete. Broken glass.

"Oh, my God!" she screamed. Chills streaked up her spine.

Unbridled terror spread across her face as her eyes surreptitiously found his eyes. His entire countenance was one of urgency and action, yet devoid of fear. His decisiveness reassured her, if only for a moment. Thoughts and emotions melded into a numbing buzz. Her own terror rendered her obedient to Geoffrey's evasive movements.

Pamela was transfixed, chagrin washed over her face. Her peaceful Saturday morning rendezvous was being torn asunder. She let out another full-throated scream, and suddenly realized that the roaring sensation in her head was much louder than the mere rise in internal blood pressure.

Not fifty feet from them was a black Mercedes, skidding toward them out of control. It was traveling very fast and would be upon them any second.

Terror immobilized her.

The driver saw them as soon as he crested the bridge. His reaction time, dulled by the effects of a hangover, was too slow, putting him too close to the joggers for any reasonable abortive action.

"Shit!"

The look of discomfort on his contorted face turned to mortification when he realized the finality of the event he had carelessly set in motion.

"Shit, shit!"

His passengers reeled in horror as the Benz hydroplaned over the ice, slamming into the cement railing, sending sparks resembling hundreds of tracer bullets along the passenger side windows.

"For Christ sake, hit the brakes," came a panicked voice from the back seat.

"We're on ice, you idiot," hissed the driver who was holding on to the steering wheel for dear life. "I can't stop," he lamented, "it's no use. Shit!"

The backseat passenger wished he had insisted on taking over the driving responsibilities when they left the service station. Now he was experiencing the consequences of his cowardice.

The driver shuddered as he stared helplessly at the two people struggling to free themselves from the path of his car.

Pamela was yanked to her feet, whiplashed by Geoffrey's Herculean strength, as he pulled her to him. In a matter of seconds the car would be upon them. Incredibly, Geoffrey ended their retreat and flung her in front of him, cradling her in his arms.

She could feel the power of his tense embrace.

The two friends clung to each other in a frenzied tangle of desperation and resignation, facing the out-of-control metallic missile that rocketed toward them.

Reacting on an impulse driven by her instincts for survival, Pamela tried to extricate herself from Geoffrey's bizarre incarceration. But his strength denied her flight. Escape was impossible. Waxen, she chanced an incredulous glance at his chiseled face. His gaze was cemented on every contorted movement of the oncoming car. Hans stood beside them barking at the oncoming car.

Suddenly Pamela shrieked. She understood what Geoffrey was going to do.

"No, Geoffrey," she gasped. "My God, no!"

Fully aware now of how this thing would play itself out, she closed her eyes, resigned to her fate.

"We're going to die," she whispered, but her cry was vaporized by the sound of concrete meeting obstinate metal and glass.

His eyes still riveted on the projectile, Geoffrey said softly, but loudly enough for Pamela to hear, "Trust me."

An instant later, just before impact, he inched his left foot up against the curbing to give himself the leverage he needed.

In the odd stillness of the moment just before the Mercedes bulldozed into them, screeching in its own metallic agony as it scraped along the thick cement railings toward them, Pamela felt Geoffrey tighten his grip. Then she heard him whisper as calmly and as clearly as she had ever heard him, "I love you, Babe."

Another voice shrieked, but it was inaudible to Geoffrey and Pamela. It came from one of the passengers in the car. "We're going to die! Oh, my God, we're going to die!"

"Shut up!" came a venomous reply from the driver as the Mercedes continued its lethal slide along the cement railing.

Geoffrey flung Pamela away from him just before impact, with such force that he lifted her off the pavement. Airborne and dazed by his heroic act of sacrifice, she heard his gut-wrenching groan as he attempted to leap over the hood. The car sent kisses of sparks as it gauged and ripped it way along the railing and struck him with the force of a locomotive, sending him over the cement abutment and into the ravine twenty feet below.

A few feet away, Pamela hit the pavement hard, cracking her elbow again as she fell. A panicked look in Geoffrey's direction caused her to gasp. The battered car had careened off the abutment and was headed directly at her. Before she could get out of its path, the underside of the vehicle passed over her, pinning her in its accelerated slither. She was caught under it for thirty or so feet before it left her behind. It completed its scything down the bridge, and coasted to a gliding stop at the base of the bridge.

The occupants remained seated, in stunned amazement.

"Anybody hurt?" queried the agitated, but somewhat shaken voice of the driver.

"No, I'm okay."

"Me, too."

"Yes, thank God," came the third reply. "Oh, my God, what have we done?"

"Stay in the car," the driver commanded, in a tone that demanded obedience.

As he stumbled out of the lacerated Benz, he inched his way toward Pamela's body. She was lying on her side, one leg twisted over the other. Her left arm, elbow up, hung at her side. She was motionless, sprawled like a toy doll that had been thoughtlessly dumped at the side of the road.

As he took a few steps closer, his bloodshot eyes caught a glimpse of something approaching him from the base of the bridge. Then he heard a growl that almost sent his heart into fibrillation.

A dog, a large dog with an attitude, was headed his way.

Sensing his peril, he quickly retreated, stepping back into his car. Testing the car's capacity to move and finding it drivable, he sped off despite the objections of his horrified passengers. The car slid past Hans as he advanced tentatively toward Pamela's broken body. He sensed her predicament and whined his concern. Then he began to lick the blood off her face and neck.

Pamela's injuries made her oblivious to Hans' loving attempts to resuscitate her. Her whole body seemed glaciated, numbed, cemented to the surface of the street. She sensed she was lying in her own blood, yet she felt no need to move ... no sense of fear—only an odd acceptance.

Part of her seemed to burn. *How strange,* she thought, as she began to lose consciousness, *how very strange.* An odd mixture of fire and ice seemed to be taking control, washing over her, numbing her.

Another chilling sensation drowned her senses, liberating her. She could feel herself slipping away. A peacefulness made its presence known, slowly at first, but evolving steadily, slowed only by the passage of time. A gentle lessening of the need for struggle touched her senses. *Can't move,* she sensed. *No need to try.*

Her eyes glazed over, dimmed by the dual impacts of car and pavement, harsh co-conspirators when it came to damaging flesh. Her beautiful emerald eyes lost their radiance. Their light was extinguished as her eyes slowly drifted shut, sending her into darkness. Oblivion welcomed her to its fathomless depths.

CHAPTER FIVE

All right, that's enough! You've made your point," he exploded, half slurring, half spitting as he launched a venomous counterattack from his cramped position in the back seat. "You've taken over my driving responsibilities. So let me be. You can all go to hell," he blasted.

His rage filled the interior of the car, giving it an air of combustibility.

"That's one place we won't go with you, you drunken buffoon," came his wife's scornful reply as she pushed away from him. She was repelled as much by the latest edition of his verbal abuse as from the scent of alcohol mixed with vomit that she noticed on his clothes.

His cockeyed smile extinguished a caustic slur that started to leave his foul mouth. The look in his bloodshot slits for eyes held her rebelliousness in check just long enough for him to rebut her angry reply with a well-timed, repugnant belch.

"Oh, how very adult of you," she said disdainfully. "That would be the perfect opening remark in your speech next week. Give 'em a great big belch. Just barf it out ... "

"Shut up," he cut in sharply. "Just shut the hell up."

"No, I won't shut up. You're the one who ought to shut that filthy mouth of yours."

His wild, spastic attempt to slap her across the face missed, sending a plethora of nasty expletives from his lips, unintelligible for the most part as he began to get wound up again.

"That's enough. I've heard enough," the driver said trying to hold his irritation in check. "We've got a major problem here," he announced, marshaling his composure to cool his rage. "You've left us with a considerable public relations problem. It'll call for some serious damage control."

"Damage control," screamed the drunkard's wife from the back seat. "We've killed ... " she paused to catch her breath, "he's killed two people and you call that damage control?"

The driver frowned his disapproval. "What would you call it?" he leveled convulsively.

"Murder," she screamed hysterically. "Second degree murder. Manslaughter, on two counts. Maybe even premeditated murder. What would you call it?"

"It was an accident. Wasn't it?" came the meek little voice in the passenger's side of the front seat.

"We left the scene, brainless," snorted the drunkard. "That's called a bump-and-run. Do you know the penalty for ... "

"That was more than a bump-and-run, you idiot," interrupted is wife. "It was a hit-and-run ... Kill and run!"

"Shut up!" the driver usurped his authority once again. His anger caused him to hit the brakes too hard, catapulting the two in the back hard against the leather backs of the front seats, as he brought the Mercedes to a sliding stop along the side of the road.

"What's the matter with you people?" he scoffed. "This kind of verbal karate is getting us nowhere." He twisted in his seat and placed his arm over the back of the driver's seat, fixing his gaze on the drunkard who straightened himself up in his seat. "Not one more word out of you until you get a decent tongue in your mouth."

"He'll need more than a bath to clean up his language," his wife fumed. "His filth goes more than skin deep." Then, tauntingly, she placed her finger and thumb over her nose and spewed, "Of course, a bath would be a good place to start."

"Aw, come on," lamented the driver, trying his best to diffuse hostilities. "Let's all chill out. Okay?"

There was a lengthy, unpleasant pause as the driver traded eye contact with everyone present.

The drunk in the back seat stilled himself, sensing that immediate compliance was in his best interest. Trying to summon the dignity he lacked, the dullard straightened himself as best he could. He decided to remove his soiled sweater over his head in a feeble attempt to extricate himself from his smelly garments.

"What are you doing?" yelled his wife as she reached over to arrest his ridiculous attempt at disrobement. "Just how much do you plan to take off?"

"Shut up," he hissed, spewing spittle over the inside fabric of his expensive sweater.

His recoil against her attempt to free him from his self-imposed straight jacket only succeeded in stretching the arms of his sweater in such a fashion that his elbows were caught, suspended above his head. His entanglement gave him the appearance of a headless ogre from a fairy tale or rock music video. He sat there as befuddled as he was embarrassed.

Her second attempt to free him from his self-inflicted bondage met with the same results, so she settled back in her seat and crossed her arms defensively.

"Go ahead, be that way," she rebuffed sourly. "You're just cutting off your nose to spite your face."

Wordlessly, he leaned back in his seat, arms still suspended over his head. He was exhausted, frustrated at his ineptitude to free himself.

The driver forced a smile. "Now guys, we can't just leave him in suspended inebriation like that," he pleaded, laughing at his assessment of the drunkard's predicament.

His attempt at comic relief brought nervous laughter from the others, which lightened the tension. Even the drunkard cracked a covert smile under his Coogi head wrap.

The young woman in the front seat motioned for his wife to unravel him. "Have a little pity," she pleaded. "I think we've ridiculed him enough."

"Yeah, have a little pity," mimicked the alcoholic.

"Are you going to let me help you?"

"Have pity on the poor lost soul who can't find his way out of a sweater."

"Is that a yes?"

The woman in the front seat intervened again. "She wants to help you. Tell her yes, for Pete's sake."

"For whose sake?" he driveled. "Oh, for my sake," he corrected himself. "Yes, for Pete's sake ... for my sake—for everybody's sake, help me see the light."

While the antics in the back seat were coming to a peaceful conclusion, the driver restarted the car and headed cautiously down the road.

"I didn't realize he was in such bad shape this morning, did you?" petitioned the blonde.

"No, I didn't. Or I would never have allowed him to drive."

"It's not your fault," she consoled. "He's a hard man to say no to, especially when he's been drinking."

The driver nodded his agreement. "Just the same, I should have driven. I knew he had a hangover, but I let him drive anyway," he repeated apologetically.

"What's going to happen now?" she asked, training her frightened eyes on him.

"We've got to get him home, and hide this car. They'll be looking for us."

"Then you're not going back?"

He threw her a mournful glance, then shook his head. "No, we're not going back."

"I didn't think so," she sighed, redirecting her gaze to the road ahead.

The driver remembered he hadn't turned the radio on when he assumed chauffeuring responsibilities shortly after they left the scene of the accident.

He punched the power button for the radio and tapped the seek button until an Asheville station announced itself: *... and that's the news at the top of the hour. Stay tuned for Asheville weather coming up just after this word from our sponsor.*

His eyes darted to the clock on the dash panel: 08:13.

"Just missed the news," he announced fretfully. "Maybe they'll air the accident later, in a special bulletin or something."

"Yeah, maybe in an APB," hissed the alcoholic's wife, still feeling the slights of a few moments ago.

"Let's hope not, my dear. Not while I'm driving the get-away car."

"Do you think anyone saw us?" asked the alcoholic, beginning to shake off the effects of a night of celebration.

"I don't know. It's hard to say. We were out fairly early. Most people sleep late on Saturday. Even if they were up, the weather probably kept them indoors."

"I wish we had stayed indoors, too," voiced his wife, her misgivings apparent.

"I wish I hadn't been such an idiot. I should have let you drive. We wouldn't be in this fix if I had."

"Do I hear an apology—a touch of conscience?" chastised his wife.

"Let's not start that again," the driver pleaded.

"Alcohol and driving don't mix," volunteered the blonde.

The tact of her remark was lost on the alcoholic who glared at her, the fire in his eyes glowing red. His dagger-like stare prompted his wife to touch his arm in an attempt to quell another confrontation. She made eye contact with him and shook her head, hoping he'd take the hint. Her peacekeeping was successful.

He breathed deeply and slumped back in the seat, combat weary and thankful that he was being spirited away from public embarrassment.

"This could be a career stopper," he confessed, in intoxicated garrulousness.

"And very well may be," added the driver. "Leaving the scene of a fatal accident wasn't a very smart thing to do."

"I didn't even see them until it was too late. Drinking or not drinking, I couldn't have stopped on the ice. Besides, I've always been able to hold my liquor," he rambled, ignoring his wife's rueful stare. "What else could I have done?"

"You could have laid off the brakes, for one thing," corrected his wife. "They don't work on ice."

"You should have stopped and helped those people." Another indictment came from the blonde in the front seat.

"Oh, sure, and what would I have told the police, 'Pardon me, officer, but I was drunk at the time and decided to run over two people.'"

"Stop it!" demanded his wife. "Your sarcasm isn't helping matters one iota."

"And neither are your self-righteous attacks," interjected the driver. "If we had stopped, his career would have stopped. They would have locked him up and thrown away the key. And, heaven help me for saying it, he may have been right about the accident. Sober or hung over, he may not have been able to stop. There were icy patches all over that bridge. It might have ended the same way no matter who was behind the wheel."

The alcoholic nodded, but didn't take his eyes off the floorboard.

Both women grimaced their disbelief. But neither dared to speak. In each case they stifled their outrage, realizing they were helpless confederates.

Determined to present his most pragmatic face, the driver continued, addressing the drunkard's wife. "You said it before. They would have charged him with manslaughter on two counts. The state of North Carolina would have prosecuted him with malice. It's one of the toughest states in the country on DUI's. One thing's for certain," he continued, an air of objectivity evident, "we're involved ... we're all involved, whether we like it or not, in a hit-and-run. That means we're all guilty." He emphasized his comments by banging his hand on the steering wheel. "We're all accessories before and after the fact."

His next appraising glance at the blonde caught her weeping. Her hands cupped her face, and tears streamed unabated down her cheeks.

Disconsolate, he brushed a tear back from his own reddened eyes, and announced in a voice filled with emotion, "If we're lucky enough to get away with this," he stopped to reconsider his last statement. "If by the grace of God ... ," he paused again, "if we survive this damnable mess you've gotten us into ... damn you! ... " He cut himself off and gazed scornfully in the mirror at the alcoholic.

"Damn you for implicating us." He took another deep breath. "You promise us now—you give us your word that you will seek immediate help in some sort of alcoholic rehabilitation center, alcoholics anonymous, detox center or whatever. Or so help me I'll turn around right now and take your pathetic alcoholic ass to the Asheville police before you can say Pepto Bismal."

Before the repentant alcoholic could respond, the group's attention was drawn to an announcement on the radio:

We interrupt your regularly scheduled programming to bring you this special announcement ...

CHAPTER SIX

*Y*ou bet I want him shot," Officer Holland hissed disdainfully as he wheeled around to confront the unofficial animal rights crusader. "What's wrong with you?" he bellowed. "You know police protocol."

The young fireman recoiled as if he had been struck. When his eyes met the officer's angry gaze, he averted his eyes quickly in a conciliatory gesture.

"You don't have to kill the dog," he arbitrated softly. "Jake Detrick's here, and he ... "

"Where's Petrie?" the indignant officer's searing voice cut him short.

"Petrie ... somebody get me Petrie," raved the officer, spittle spewing from his tense lips.

As head of the STEPP unit traffic response team, he knew the verdict was already in. Human life came first. The dog was protecting its injured master and was not letting anyone close, including the paramedics. So the dog must be destroyed.

"Petrie," Officer Holland exploded, causing the veins in his neck to protrude. "Shoot the damn dog now!" He aborted eye contact with the fireman and focused on Officer Petrie, who unholstered his revolver, a 9 mm Browning.

"Hold on, children," came a voice behind them. "I'll take care of it." Jake Detrick's voice, although tinted with a veneer of cordiality, was firm enough to command attention.

He moved briskly past the assassination party and stepped confidently toward the anxious dog.

Measuring Jake's calculated advance, one tentative step at a time, Hans lowered his head and exposed vicious teeth. Edging closer to Pamela, he assumed a defiant stance.

Speaking to the animal in a soft soothing lilt, Jake halted his own advance and stopped about twenty-five feet from the animal. Thirty years as a nature center employee taught him a little about animal behavior, particularly frightened or wounded animals.

This one means business, Jake thought to himself. He softened the perimeter as much as he could, and his instincts told him to end the standoff before anyone got hurt. He had taken the precaution to cock the bolt-action rifle moments earlier, and was glad he had. One disconcerting sound, one threatening move, and the dog would pounce on him.

Hans' ears laid straight back, and his eyes, black holes of volcanic anger, were set above menacing white teeth that showed themselves ready to tear the intruder to shreds, given the slightest provocation.

As Jake slowly raised the rifle, he saw the dog's eyes narrow with rage. Jake kept the rifle steady as Hans watched. With rehearsed detachment, Jake took the safety off and aimed at Hans' left shoulder.

When Hans saw Jake depress the trigger, his natural instincts look over. His sudden lunge was met with Jake's expert marksmanship. It was over in a matter of seconds.

Seizing on the unexpected turn of events, Officer Holland ordered everyone into action.

As the paramedics raced to Pamela's side, Jake cradled the unconscious animal in his arms. The tranquilizer had taken effect.

"That was an act of decency, Jake," one of the volunteer firemen praised him.

Another, a police officer, gave Jake a hearty pat on the back.

Officer Holland met Jake's smile with one of his own as he walked up to him.

"Thanks, Jake," congratulated Officer Holland. His irascibility had evaporated the moment Jake tranquilized the dog.

Jake shook his head. He always enjoyed upstaging Asheville's finest, particularly when it came to animal rights.

"I didn't know you were here," Holland said, in a conciliatory tone as he followed Jake to his Blazer. Hoping for more of a response from Jake, he opened the tailgate for him and waited. He knew Jake wasn't the talkative sort. And Jake could be downright uncommunicative at times.

Jake carefully placed Hans in the compartment designed to transport injured animals and then sat on the tailgate facing Officer Holland.

"Actually, I'm the one who called it in," he spoke, breaking the silence. "I was on my way to work and saw the damnable mess. I'd have had him down before the first response team arrived, if I hadn't misplaced the tranquilizer darts." Jake let out an embarrassed smile.

"Well, I'm glad you were here."

"Me, too."

"I would have had to destroy him."

"I know. Let's hope she makes out just as well," Jake changed the subject and nodded at the paramedics who surrounded Pamela.

"Yeah," nodded Officer Holland sympathetically as he pulled his collar up higher on his neck to shield himself from the cold.

Almost as an afterthought, he asked Jake, "Say, look, do I need to ask you any questions? About this?" he purposefully trailed off, and gestured toward the accident scene.

"I didn't see a thing," came Jake's immediate reply. "When I drove up, she was lying in the middle of the road ... " he paused, pointing to Hans, " ... ably guarded by this beautiful animal."

"Well, if I need you ... "

"You'll know where to find me," Jake cut in.

"Catch you later."

"Oh, wait a minute," Jake spoke hastily.

Officer Holland wheeled around, halted by Jake's apparent urgency.

Jake was scribbling something on a note pad. Then he looked up and handed it to Officer Holland.

"Here's the address and phone number off the dog tag. Thought you might need it." Then he quickly added, "When you find the owner, let 'em know I've got the dog ... Hans ... tell 'em I've got Hans. I'm taking him over to Mast's Animal Hospital. They're the best around."

"Good. Glad you thought of checking the tag. Should make it easier to locate kinfolk."

Jake closed the tailgate and started around the Blazer to open the driver's side door.

Officer Holland pushed the slip of paper in his pocket and waved good-bye to Jake. Then he maneuvered through the cadre of emergency vehicles toward his cruiser parked a few feet away.

Fanned around him, at various intervals, was a phalanx of rescue crews and policemen who busied themselves with their respective emergency responsibilities. The glare of red and blue lights flashed across the broken ice patches, creating small islands of glistening color that disappeared, only to reappear as the obedient strobes recycled their silent alarms.

Suddenly there was a flurry of activity near the base of the bridge. Rescue personnel scampered down the bridge toward the Biltmore entrance, carrying their medical paraphernalia.

Out of his car now, Officer Holland stood leaning against the open door. A patrolman, sealed in his dark blue jacket, stutter-stepped his way across the ice. He was shouting breathlessly and unintelligibly. Officer Holland's ear caught one of the words, made distinct by the calm that followed an icy blast of air. His face went suddenly pale.

Body ... did I hear that right? Another body? The news sent chills up his spine.

Another apprehensive cry fell from the patrolman's lips as he gasped, trying to catch his breath. "We've found another body."

"What?" asked Officer Holland, surprise flashing across his face.

"Another body," repeated the patrolman. Then the patrolman hesitated clearing his throat. "Uh, I'm sorry to have to tell you, but it's Collins, sir."

The words hit Officer Holland like a sledgehammer. "Collins? Geoffrey Collins ... Lieutenant Collins?" he asked incredulously.

"Yes sir. Lieutenant Collins."

"Is he ... "

"No sir, he's not dead," he interrupted, "but the Lieutenant's in real bad shape." He pointed to the bridge. "He must have been knocked over the railing over there after he was hit. There's evidence of car paint and glass embedded in the cement." He paused, letting out a sigh that was filled with misgivings. "And blood, sir ... all over the cement railing."

Officer Holland rubbed his temples with his fingers, while visions of Lieutenant Geoffrey Fitzgerald Collins, III flashed through his mind. Geoffrey Collins, a policeman who was the son of a policeman, a product of a law enforcement family, was revered by many and respected by all, law-abiding citizens and criminals alike.

With his good looks, outgoing personality, and endless energy, Geoffrey had an uncanny ability to win friends and influence people—engineer or salesperson, man or woman, CEO or custodian, Democrat or Republican, drug dealer or victim. He was one of the best on the force.

"Why Geoffrey? Damn it, what was he doing here at this ungodly hour anyway?" Officer Holland slammed his fist into his thigh for emphasis.

In the midst of his emotion over the discovery of Geoffrey's body, Officer Holland's attention was diverted suddenly to the paramedics on the bridge who were lifting Pamela into the ambulance. One of them fastened a clear plastic mask over her face and another held a plastic bag of fluid connected by a thin tube to her arm. The looks that registered on the paramedic's faces gave silent testimony to the life-threatening nature of her injuries.

Officer Holland made eye contact with one of the paramedics, who gave a thumbs-up sign followed by extending his outstretched hand in a waffling motion.

Alive, Officer Holland thought to himself, *but barely.* Then he redirected his attention to the patrolman who was waiting impatiently to report more about the discovery of Geoffrey.

"That's why we searched for another body," he picked up where he'd left off.

"What?" responded Officer Holland awkwardly.

"When we saw the blood on the railing. And then we found this ball cap over there ... "

"Ball cap?"

"We found this ball cap over there," the patrolman repeated and held up a Carolina Tar Heel ball cap while pointing to the scarred cement railing some fifty feet away.

"It didn't match the color of clothing she was wearing," he confirmed. "We found her cap lying under her."

The two officers walked toward the chest-high railing.

"Good thing you noticed the caps," mumbled Officer Holland. "You think he went over the abutment here?"

"Yes, sir! It's the only spot where the blood is mixed with the chipped concrete."

He led Officer Holland to the place where Geoffrey fell over the railing.

"Incredible," said Officer Holland, shaking his head. "He must have fallen fifteen, twenty feet."

"Not many people could have survived a fall like that," deduced the patrolman.

Officer Holland nodded, mildly sedated by his comment. He watched the rescue teams attend to Officer Collins in the ravine below.

By the looks of it, he may wish he'd never survived the fall. Officer Holland kept his prognosis to himself.

The paramedics strapped the critically injured officer onto a stretcher and started up the ravine.

He knew by the way the paramedics handled the victim that Lt. Collins had suffered serious head, neck, and back injuries.

"He's broken up pretty badly, isn't he?" lamented the patrolman. "I'm amazed he's still alive."

"Anybody called his father, yet?"

"No, I don't believe so," volunteered the patrolman.

"I'll take care of it," Officer Holland acquiesced. Then he thought to himself, *the old man probably knows already. He keeps his police scanner on all the time.*

As they watched the paramedics carry Geoffrey over the uneven ground toward the ambulance, the two officers moved along the railing toward the base of the bridge.

They continued watching as the paramedics loaded Geoffrey into the second ambulance. The one carrying Pamela had already left.

"You got anything for me?" Officer Holland asked.

"Not much. Pieces of metal. Glass, black paint."

"Any witnesses?" A distinct investigative tone characterized Officer Holland's voice.

A policeman is down, maybe dying. And an innocent woman, apparently out for a walk, is fighting for her life, he thought to himself.

The patrolman shook his head and frowned, "Don't know of any yet."

"Institute a door to door."

"Already in motion," confirmed the patrolman, nodding his head in the direction of a small group of people standing near the Biltmore entrance. The entrance was packed with on-lookers who had nothing better to do on a Saturday morning.

"Clear the area as soon as you can."

"Yes, sir."

"I want to find out who did this."

"We will, sir."

"Do we know who the young woman is?"

"Yes, sir," answered the patrolman. "They found her driver's license in her sweat suit. She's Pamela Anne Justice from Raleigh. We've got a call out now, trying to contact her next of kin." He paused, embarrassed at his assumption. "I mean ... her family. We're trying to get hold of her family."

Officer Holland accepted his amendment and took out the note Jake had given him.

"Here," he announced with detached authority, "looks like we've got an Asheville address and a Raleigh address. Check 'em both out."

As he watched the retreating officer, Officer Holland wearily shook his head. Twenty-five years on the force had taught him a couple of things about criminals. Most refuse to take responsibility for their actions, placing their own insecurities over human life. Others use their weaknesses as an excuse to stay weak by exploiting others.

"Whoever you are," he turned his head toward the summit of the bridge. "No matter how far you've run, it won't be far enough. I'm not going to let you get away with this."

He made another pilgrimage over to the cement railing and looked at the cuts and scrapes, blood, and black paint that blemished its rough surface.

Accident graffiti, he thought sadly. *The kind of defacement you never get used to.*

§　　§　　§　　§　　§　　§

The voice on the other end of the phone was Ted Collins, Geoffrey's father. His initial reaction was one of relief at finding her home. Then he cleared his throat and spoken quietly.

"Karen, honey, I've got some bad news. It's Geoffrey. He's been in an accident. I don't know how else to say it. I still monitor 911 calls on my scanner. Old habits are heard to break," he said, as he voiced a nervous addendum.

Still unable to speak, Karen pressed the phone closer to her ear. She braced herself for the upsetting news. Currents of fear washed through her with such fury that she thought she would explode.

"The precinct called me seven or eight minutes after the first response team arrived on the scene," Ted reported. He paused, not certain how to proceed. "They found Geoffrey lying in a ravine, twenty feet under the McDowell Street Bridge."

"No! Oh, no. Wha ... What happened?" Karen screamed. "Is he dead?"

"I don't think so. But it's pretty serious."

A rising feeling of nausea swept through Karen. She leaned against the kitchen counter, the small of her back pressed hard against the lip of the counter top. Goose flesh quickly migrated up both of her arms and then engulfed her entire body.

"Honey, there's more. I hate to tell you this, but they found Pamela on the bridge," Ted choked as he shared the terrible news.

Another shriek from Karen sent Ted's phone away from his ringing ear.

"Karen, listen to me. They've taken her to the hospital, too."

"Is she ... ?"

"She's alive. I don't know how much alive, but she's alive."

Karen broke down numbed by the horrible news. She struggled to keep from fainting.

"Karen ... Karen, they're going to be all right," he spoke softly through the mouth piece. "They've got to be all right. You've got to get a hold of yourself. Karen, are you listening to me? Take a few deep breaths. Karen. Karen! Do you ... "

"Yes ... yes I hear you."

"Good. Now I need you to listen to me."

Ted heard her labored breathing begin to settle. Then a sudden gasp from Karen caused Ted to hesitate before he spoke again.

"Hans! What about Hans?"

"He's okay. He's ... "

"Hans!" she cut in apprehensively. "Ted, what's happened to Hans?"

"Karen, you've got to get control of yourself," he lashed out firmly. He could hear her attempts to slow her breathing again. "He's okay. He was tranquilized at the scene."

"What!"

"He's being taken good care of, Karen," he reassured her.

He used her name again. Well-schooled for situations like this, after a lifetime of police work, Ted knew that using someone's name produced a calming influence.

"Karen, honey. We'll pick up Hans later. Right now our first objective is to find out how those kids are. Are you with me?"

She shook her head affirmatively.

"Karen!"

"Yes, yes. I'm sorry, Ted," she apologized, realizing he couldn't see her. She felt herself overcome by a mild case of nervous hilarity. "I heard you," she snorted. "I was nodding my head but," another uncontrollable snicker erupted. "You couldn't see me, of course. I'm sorry. I'm with you. I'm sorry."

"That's okay, honey. This horrible thing has frayed me, too. Look, we've got to get to the hospital."

"I'll meet you there."

"No, Karen. I think it would be better if ... "

"Oh, wait, Ted," Karen shrieked, half talking to herself and half talking to him. Her voice was frantic. "I've got to call Gramma and Grampa. They'll ... "

"Karen, I'm going to tranquilize you like they did Hans if you don't get hold of yourself."

At the mention of Hans' name again, she asked "Hans! What about Hans?"

"He's at the Mast's. We'll pick him up later." Ted could feel her nervousness through the phone connection.

"Karen. Karen!"

"I'm here. I think I'm here," she paused. "I'm sorry, Ted. You must be sick with worry, too, about Geoffrey." She inhaled deeply. "Okay, I'm in control now. I'll wait for you here."

"That's my girl. I'll call George and Constance as soon as we hang up. Okay? You collect some things you think Pamela will need. You know, cosmetics, toiletries, a few clothes. I'm ten minutes from you. I'll pick you up soon."

Ted mentioned the personal items as a distraction to give her something to do. He knew she was in no condition to drive, or talk to grandparents in Raleigh who would fire a hundred questions at her.

Conscious of her emotional state, he consoled, "Karen, it's going to be all right. Now, hang in there, okay? I'll see you in a few minutes."

§　　§　　§　　§　　§　　§

By the time George Lee called Karen's number, he was greeted by a series of unanswered rings that signaled his granddaughter's absence. He frowned as he hung up the phone.

"Must have just missed her," he lamented. "Ted said he was leaving immediately to pick her up."

This is one time, he thought to himself, *I wish Karen had decided to become a part of the Twenty-first Century. Most people have cell phones, e-mail, texting or Twitter. But, no, not*

Karen! It would have been nice to have left her a message, our flight number, estimated time of arrival ...

Constance cut into his thoughts, jolting him out of his rumination. "We'll have to stop by the bank on our way to the airport. I'm short of cash, and I think I took your last forty yesterday when I picked up your blood pressure medicine. Oh, couldn't you get her?"

George shook his head.

"Ted's probably already picked her up."

George nodded his head this time, but Constance had already left the room to continue her preparations for their unexpected flight to Asheville.

"You packed yet?" Constance persisted, her voice somewhat muffled by the two layers of rooms between them.

"Haven't started."

"George!"

"I've got a couple more calls to make and then I'll attend to it." He defended. The tone of his voice signaled a mild reprimand. Either Constance didn't hear him or she simply ignored the comment, because George heard no reply.

He quickly made arrangements with a trusted neighbor for newspaper and mail pick-ups and then trekked through the condominium, stopping at the appropriate receptacles, unplugging appliances, TV, coffee pot, toaster, and so on, until he disconnected everything on his mental checklist.

Each room was a tribute to his wife's exquisite tastes in furniture and décor: Broyhill sofa and chairs, transitional Fontana with coordinating accent pillows, Eden House bedroom furniture, 18th Century style pieces in a cherry veneer, elegantly carved and surrounded by stately mirrors and night stands. His own oil paintings dressed in custom-made gold frames adorned many of the walls throughout, giving each room an added warmth and charm.

The cocoon of soft light from the glow of a lamp caught his attention as he passed the entrance to the study. The quick detour to douse the lights turned into a nostalgic moment that George found he wasn't prepared for. Corralled between the lamp and the rolodex on his desk was a portrait of the four of them, Constance, the two granddaughters and himself, which he had presented last February as Valentine's Day gifts to the three women in his life. Pamela, radiant and smiling, was wearing the amethyst Angora sweater they'd given her for her birthday. Both Constance and Karen, one wearing pink, the other lilac, flanked Pamela making the photo very special.

George attempted a smile, but his despondence censored it. He quickly brushed away a tear as Constance appeared at the door to the study.

"Honey," she asked, the urgency in her voice surrendering to concern for him, "are you all right?"

George looked up, and pressing his lips together in a tight line, gave her a disconsolate nod that told her he was not all right. Before she could say anything, he picked up the family portrait and held it toward her.

"If I had taken your advice and agreed to fly to Asheville a day early, we'd all have been at Golden Corral eating breakfast by now, instead of ... " he trailed off, unable to continue.

George had insisted on being present at an emergency Board meeting at the church on Friday night, which precluded their leaving early to visit the girls. No one disagreed with him about that. The girls knew he took his church work seriously, and Constance was proud of his leadership role. Still, guilt snaked its way into his thoughts and now tore at his heart.

Constance was at his side and put her arm around him.

"Our being there wouldn't have made any difference."

"Yes, it would have. We would have all made the pilgrimage to Golden Corral and pigged out on the breakfast buffet. Pamela would have had her two glasses of orange juice for starters. Karen would have ensured we sat near a window. You'd have made sure we got coffee."

"And you would have encouraged her to go jogging before we left. You know you would have," she interrupted.

George shot her a mournful glance. He knew she was right, but George was the kind of person who assumed responsibility for everything. When the girls' parents died in a plane crash, Constance kept the girls while he flew to the crash site in Peru to accompany the remains back home. Etched in his memory forever was the wreckage-strewn crash site, all six miles of it.

She remembered the melancholy look on his tired face, and how dispirited he seemed, when she and the girls met him on his return flight to Raleigh-Durham. He had lost eight pounds in two weeks, not so much from the change in diet, but from his self-imposed fasting. His distress over the deaths of their daughter and son-in-law had kept him from eating.

Ted's call this morning had taken George's appetite, reminding Constance of his inclination to fast when he got upset.

George's voice cut into her thoughts. "Maybe her conditioning helped her. She's got your passion for exercise."

"She's in tremendous shape. Maybe that'll count for something," Constance agreed.

She looked sympathetically at George's drawn face, then back at the photograph George had handed her. Staring at the happy faces in the picture took her thoughts back to the girl's childhood.

After the plane crash, the Lee's had adopted both girls and raised them as if they were their own. Pamela was six when her parents died, and she was unsettlingly mature in accepting their deaths. Karen, a fourth grader, fell into incredulous despair, missing a month of her classes, yet miraculously managing to pass. She had let it all out. But Pamela internalized all of the fury, the confusion, the rage, the anger at her parents for abandoning them.

Constance remembered the thing that stole many-a-night's restful sleep from Pamela was the fact that she hadn't said a proper good-bye to her parents. She'd been angry at them because their flight from the Raleigh-Durham Airport made it impossible for them to attend one of her swim meets.

The Justices seldom missed the girls' extra-curricular school activities. In this instance her parents were members of a tour, and had to meet up-line connections so they could join the rest of the tour group in Miami.

The evening before they left for their trip, her parents attended Karen's piano recital. Pamela saw their unavailability the next morning for her swim meet as invisible support. A typical six-year-old, she pouted, using all of the ploys most children use when they don't get their way. She topped it off by reciprocating her parents' good-byes with a temper tantrum she designed especially for the occasion. She met their hugs and kissed with stiff, incorrigible silence.

Karen intervened, using her influence as Pamela's older sister to appoint herself as peacemaker. When her parents called to announce their safe arrival in Lima, the plan was for Pamela to ask for immediate clemency, blaming temporary insanity for her foul mood and then shower her parents with the verbal bouquets of love and kisses, mentioning, of course, her need for a few souvenirs.

When the call came early the next morning, it would not be from the girls' parents. Both girls sat in stunned silence as their grandfather listened to a representative from the airlines confirm the deaths of both of their parents.

It would soon become evident that there was another casualty of the plane crash. Pamela Ann Justice would bury, along with her deceased parents, her own innocence and capacity for intimacy. The young, spoiled carefree little first grader had become an orphaned second grader. And in her place was a youngster who would fear intimacy and suffer the unfortunate pangs of abandonment and guilt for many years to come.

Both girls were provided therapy, a precautionary measure that both Constance and George were thankful they had the wisdom to initiate and finance.

Pamela had grown into her looks at a young age, leaping past the awkward years in one bound it seemed, never needing braces, a padded bra, school tutors, or eye ware.

Her sister, Karen, was more dependent, requiring two years of braces, followed by a year of retainers. She wore extended-wear contacts and needed an army of math tutors throughout high school.

Karen was a typical teenager while her sister seemed to by-pass the normal things teens do.

Pamela's high school and collegiate years were filled with academic and athletic achievements. She graduated cum laude in Business Administration from N. C. State University, was an outstanding ballroom dancer, and paced the women's swim team to two national titles.

Pamela Anne Justice wasn't interested in many of the young men who pursued her. Piqued, yet fascinated, unable to believe that she preferred to remain so proudly unavailable, her suitors chased her, even fought over her to prove their worth. She remained a mystery to her suitors, an enigma, a young woman stampeded after, yet illusive. To many a disappointed young boy, her glossy radiance was wasted on family and friends and swim meets.

She was infuriatingly aloof. Admirers wanted to make an impression on her, alter her views to prove she was malleable, influence her, make love to her. A kiss from her was rare and boys craving any selfish experience with her remained frustrated beyond their imaginations.

"Honey, are you all right?" George's voice snapped Constance out of her reverie.

"Yes, I was just remembering their childhood. It's so long ago, but it all went by so fast. They surely are different, aren't they?"

Both George and Constance stood staring at the photograph, each reflecting on the two girls they had raised so lovingly.

The sisters were as different as the geography they inhabited, one nested comfortably in rhododendron-studded woodlands, the other, more cosmopolitan, flitted through the Piedmont's industrial, steel and glass forests.

Pamela was five feet seven, athletically built, and three years yonger than Karen. Her face was delicately square, framed with shoulder-length, jet black hair, silken and shimmering. Her eyes gleamed as emerald as tropical forests, punctuated by their brightness and intensity. A slightly curved nose with just the right touch of slenderness complimented a delicately curved mouth that dimpled at each end when she smiled. Her lips were full and sensual. Long perfect teeth, very white, were without blemish as was her beautiful face, proportioned like a model's, photogenic and alluring.

Her figure was tantalizingly curvaceous with a buxomness that turned many a man's attention in her direction. She was aware of their philandering stares as they scrutinized her every curve and movement, of their flirtatious winks and lustful glances. But she was aware that her beauty was an asset as well as a liability.

Although generous, sometimes to a fault, she disapproved of anyone or any organization, which she considered to be a professional beggar. She enjoyed a reputation as an astute business woman, one capable of helping companies engineer highly successful quality improvement programs. The one area which gave her the most grief, and tears, was romance. She was hesitant about romantic love. Love demands vulnerability and submission. She decided long ago that she would only submit to her work. She dated men occasionally, only to be reminded of their selfishness. Her most recent romantic entanglement left her empty, angry and hurt. It was the latest episode that took her to Asheville, to mend, to heal, and forget.

Her sister Karen, on the other hand, had no real enduring interest in money or the politics of employment. To the uninitiated, she seemed vulnerable, possessing only an ordinary means of livelihood by teaching piano or voice and producing an occasional sculpture or painting to ease her financial woes. Her personal survival technology was aesthetic and spiritual, with art and music her twin compasses.

Her artistic abilities were her safety net. She moved through each life circumstance with childlike faith, but she had the positively arresting quality of refusing to take life too seriously. She was always in baptism and resurrection, celebrating the unknown, welcoming novelty.

Karen's sixty-four inches in height had a firm foundation. She was slightly over-weight, but far from being obese. She was well-proportioned and graceful. Her small round face was covered with a light dusting of girlish freckles that kept her womanliness concealed, taking off the years instead of adding them. Eyes as azure as Carolina skies, beamed as brightly as the stars that graced the heavens. There was something slightly pioneer-like about her, almost colonial, an earthiness, most probably due to the lingering influence of growing up in Asheville.

Constance squeezed George's arm. "Remember when Pamela left the utility firm to start her own business?"

George smiled knowingly, and nodded. A glimmer of light that wasn't there before danced in his eyes.

"She did the only thing any self-respecting young woman would do when faced with such a conglomeration of incompetent bureaucrats dressed in data clothes, who paraded around lamely through anesthetized corridors, marching to conformity and playing the tune called mediocrity. She quit and started her own business."

"Don't hold back George, tell me what you really think."

Weak smiles cut across both of their faces, lessening the tension, if only for a few moments.

George collected himself. "She really has done well, hasn't she?"

"Yes, darling, she has."

"She loves doing what she does. Most people can't say that, you know. Both of our granddaughters enjoy what they do. Karen, her music and art. Pamela her consulting work."

"Oh, George," Constance's voice cracked and tears formed at her eyelids. "Do you think she'll be all right?"

The severity of his expression did not change. His concern, unalterable, was etched deeply across his face, but he spoke softly and with a confidence that was reassuring somehow.

"Let's hope so. Let's pray so." He paused, swallowed hard and took a deep breath before he continued. "I suppose we'd best be going if we want to catch that flight. We have another granddaughter waiting for us. She needs us, too."

The noise of the busy capital city greeted the Lees as they exited the warmth of the condo. Engrossed in their concern for Pamela, they were immune to the discordant shrillness of a city coming to life on Saturday morning. Even the wind, tinged with rawness and accompanied by flurries that swept across the unprotected parking lot in front of them, seemed to have no noticeable effect on their despondency.

Chapter Seven

Jake Detrick was well-known in Western Carolina for his love of animals. Even as a youngster, he had 'the knack' as they called it, of connecting on a positively primal level with all animals. He spoke their language and animals, domesticated or wild, healthy or hurt, trusted him.

He made national headlines when the story broke of his heroism in saving a stray cat from a burning building. Witnesses saw the courageous feline rush into a burning warehouse, set aflame by an arsonist, to rescue her family of five small kittens. She hauled the first four to safety one at a time through a small hole in the basement window. Singed and soot-covered, she had gone back in for the fifth kitten.

Jake was one of the by-standers who witnessed her unbelievable feat of courage. When he realized it took her too long to reappear, Jake broke through the plastic-tape barriers the fire department used to seal the perimeter and rushed into the inferno. He stumbled out a few harrowing moments later carrying the charred feline and her kitten.

Although she was blinded by the fire, the gutsy cat accounted for her young by pressing her own sightless head onto each of her kitten's faces.

Jake found homes for the kittens. Hundreds of people wanted them. He kept the heroic mother and named her Backdraft, in honor of her courage and for the sudden blast of fire that destroyed her eyesight.

So in his usual sort of proprietary way, Jake made certain Hans was well cared for as the effects of the tranquilizer dart wore off. He drove across town to billet the dog at the Blue Ridge Veterinary Clinic because Mark Mast was a friend and veterinarian he trusted. They had roomed together when they attended the vet school at N. C. State University some fifteen years before. Mark finished, Jake didn't. It was as much a question of finances as it was brains, and Mark had both. Jake, on the other hand, was more inclined to capture animals in the wild than on laminated pages of textbooks.

An attendant took Hans, freeing Jake to loiter a bit while he waited for Mark's wife, Lisa, who was on the phone.

The Masts had repaired, vaccinated, and delivered every conceivable kind of domesticated animal known to man since they opened the clinic. Both husband and wife carried the bite marks and scars to prove it.

Anyone, he thought, *who deals with animals has been tattooed a time or two by a frightened animal who was generous with fang or claw.*

He proudly wore his own battle scars. Several years back a confused raccoon had bitten off the end of Jake's little finger on his right hand when Jake attempted to corral him. Fortunately, the critter wasn't rabid, only frightened. He also bore the insignia of a wounded grizzly that crushed a few of his ribs and ripped nearly a pound of flesh away. The indention was still noticeable whenever he took his shirt off. Still he loved animals, calling them the only honest beings on the planet.

Lisa answered another phone call from a desperate pet owner, Jake guessed by the way the conversation was going. So he walked over to one of the front windows to occupy himself with the beautiful winter scenery until she got off the phone.

They're a great couple, he ruminated as he stared out of the frost-pinched window.

He remembered she was a transplanted surfer from Morehead City. Her unusually generous smile complemented her nature, and her self-confidence was so strong it needed no connotation other than the radiant lights that danced symphonies in her eyes. She was slightly built, although she appeared taller due to a full head of gorgeous auburn hair which was well-groomed and puffed out. Her round face was brightened by hazel eyes that always shined brilliantly, above full, voluptuous lips.

Although she wasn't what he considered a gorgeous woman, there was something about her that was strikingly pleasant to the eye.

He turned to face her and thought, *Maybe it's the way she uses that smile to disarm impatient pet owners when they try to bamboozle her with well-rehearsed attempts to excuse their lackadaisical care of their pets—like the one she's talking to now. Or perhaps it's her furious gaze whenever she witnesses the mistreatment of any animal. Or maybe it's that all-knowing look accompanied by a half-concealed smirk whenever she deals with the conceited little 'pup' that's just bounded through the front door.*

A young boy suddenly blitzed into the waiting room.

Jake adopted a veneer of serious cordiality as he gazed intently at the Mast's nine-year-old son, Hennessey. The youngster was carrying a pair of roller blades and looking as obnoxious as always.

Jake called him Hennessey, the Menace.

Hennessey shot a quick glance over in Jake's direction, but the blank look that registered in the boy's eyes told Jake the youngster hadn't recognized him.

Evidently he's mistaken me for one of his parent's customers, someone to ignore—a non-person, Jake smiled to himself.

"Hennessey, say 'hi' to Mr. Detrick," Lisa instructed, cupping her hand over the receiver in an attempt to force good manners on her son. She tilted her head toward Jake.

"Hello there, partner," came Jake's immediate reply.

"Hi," Hennessey fired softly and then darted his eyes back to his mother.

Jake dismissed the boy's lack of social graces with a slight grin.

"Your appointment's set for three fifteen this afternoon, Mrs. Blevins. We'll see you then ... Thanks ... Good-bye."

The boy's mother hung up the receiver and eyed the two of them.

"I'm going with Jimmy to the movie this afternoon. His parents are taking us. Harrison Ford and Brad Pitt are starring."

"I thought you weren't going to go."

"Mom, I didn't know Brad was co-starring."

"Mr. Pitt to you," Lisa corrected, as she lovingly tapped the bill of his rainbow-colored cap, a much worn Jeff Gordon souvenir.

"Mr. Pitt, Mr. Brad Pitt," Hennessey mimicked, throwing her a nasty look, then pulling back to avoid her hug. "Mr. this, Mr. that. Nobody says that anymore."

She smiled, then raised a critical eyebrow to emphasize that his antics weren't appreciated.

"Well, can I?"

"Can you what?"

"You know."

"If you mean, 'May I go'—Yes you may. Provided ... provided, young man, that I call Mr. Wilson to make sure it's okay," she admonished as she grabbed his arm, halting his hasty retreat.

"Aw, Mom, you always want to do that. I'm not a baby anymore," he hissed ingratiatingly. Then he punctuated his usual unpleasantness by kicking the baseboard under the counter.

Jake stood there, casual and relaxed, leaning against the front counter, relieved that his children were grown. He found himself sadistically amused at the child's antics.

"We've had this conversation before, young man," she said sharply.

"But, Mom ... "

"No call, no movie."

Hennessey frowned his disappointment. He started to speak, but paused, searching for the appropriate retort. It came in the form of retaliation.

"All right then, I won't go! Might as well be cooped up in some damn prison somewhere."

"Hennessey! You know we don't allow that kind of language around here. I will not excuse that kind of filthy talk."

"I'm sorry."

"We're past sorry, young man. Until you choose to speak responsibly in public I feel uncomfortable allowing you to go to a public place."

"Aw, Mom. Jimmy's father is going to be there."

"I'm not going to subject Mr. Wilson to your foul mouth. We don't use profanity and I won't allow my son to embarrass me in public—like a movie theatre. Sit in that chair, young man, until I've finished my conversation with Mr. Detrick," she raised her voice, pointing to a waiting room chair in the corner.

Hennessey flat-footed his way over to the chair. He made certain he dragged his roller blades along the floor all the way over to the chair. Then he slouched over one of the wooden chair arms and intentionally dangled his feet through the rungs of the other arm.

Jake smiled and thought to himself, *This kid's negotiation skills are in serious need of repair, and so are his manners.*

Lisa shot Jake a quick wink, then tossed a critical gaze in Hennessey's direction. Satisfied with his silent compliance, she re-established eye contact with Jake.

"I'm sorry about that."

Jake glanced at Hennessey.

"That's okay. Hennessey's wearing his obnoxious hat. It's all part of growing up."

"I suppose so. I hope it's sooner than later."

Jake threw her an amused look.

"You need to call the Center?"

"Yeah, I guess so. I told them I'd be in around ten o'clock. I was hoping to see Mark before I left, though."

"I'm sorry. It's taking him longer to get here than I thought. I guess the weather isn't helping."

"That's okay. Tell 'em I'll call him a little later."

"Okay, Mom, you can call," Hennessey interrupted.

His mother's icy stare vaporized his attempt to make amends.

He started to complain, but thought better of it and sank further down into his chair.

Hennessey knew enough to remain silent, but showed his defiance by dropping the roller blades, letting them crash to the floor with a flourish.

Unsympathetic to his cause, both Lisa and Jake ignored the youngster and continued their conversation.

"We'll take good care of Hans. Don't worry about that."

Jake smiled his appreciation.

"You'll let Karen know he's here?" she repeated a question she'd asked him previously.

"You mean the dog's owner?" Jake asked.

"Yes, Karen Justice. She's Hans' owner."

"I've already taken care of that. Officer Holland is going to notify her."

"How are the young woman and the police officer?"

"I don't know. From what I saw, they'll need our prayers."

"Oh, that's too bad."

Jake tightened his lips and nodded his farewell as he made his way to the door. Stopping at the door, he heard Hennessey squeak out another arrogant conciliatory attempt.

"Mom, I said you could call."

Not that she needs the help, Jake told himself, as he wheeled around to confront the obnoxious nine-year-old.

Something within him refused to sanction the youngster's insolence. He decided he wouldn't let it go unnoticed. *Silence is consent,* he reminded himself. *And I'm not consenting.*

"Hennessey." The words were out before he could blunt them. "Those fellas you want to see at the movie ... those actors ... " Jake steeled his gaze on the youngster, who looked at him with renewed interest.

"Both of them have mothers, don't they? Or is that something a boy your age keeps track of?"

Jake lowered himself to a semi-squat. Resting his hands on both knees, he faced Hennessey squarely. Hennessey shrugged as Jake continued.

"You don't become an international star ... or anything else ... without discipline or character ... you know what I mean by discipline?"

Sensing a lecture, Hennessey dropped his eyes.

"How 'bout character? You understand what I mean by character?"

Hennessey threw him a sheepish look.

Jake tilted his head and studied the boy for a moment. He decided elaboration wasn't necessary or appropriate.

"And you don't develop discipline or character without listening to your parents," instructed Jake. Then he gave Hennessey a playful tussle on his cap, forcing the youngster to straighten his cap.

"Son," he insisted, placing his hand on the boy's shoulder. "You're really a good kid ... I can see that ... I can tell that about people."

Hennessey chanced a quick glance into Jake's penetratingly insightful eyes and found his own soul laid bare. Escape was impossible, but saving face might be possible. He could sense Jake knew more about him than anyone should outside his parents.

Does he know about the video game I borrowed from Steven and didn't return? Hennessey thought. He fidgeted nervously. *Does he know I snuck a few cigarettes at school?* He didn't know why, but he believed the man wearing the khaki uniform who was so effectively blocking his escape, knew everything about him.

Jake's tone was soft and cordial, but firm enough to keep Hennessey glued to his chair. Until now, Jake had never voiced his disapproval openly.

Hennessey renewed his fidgeting regime, but remained quiet.

"You seem to be a nine-year-old who thinks he's too old to listen to his mother."

Hennessey pulled back slightly. He didn't like where this was headed. Jake knelt on one knee beside Hennessey and resumed his uncontested reproof.

Lisa remained attentively silent.

"Hennessey, you will never be too big, or too old, or too rich to listen to your mother. The moment you think you are is the time you need to listen to her the most."

Jake paused, waiting for another thought to surface. "Do you think you're too big to listen to your mother?"

"No sir," Hennessey spoke, as if the words were leaden weights.

"Too old?"

"No sir."

"Too rich?"

The youngster grinned. "Definitely no, sir!"

Jake extinguished the smile he felt coming.

"Then it's especially important to listen to your mom in public. People judge you, Hennessey, by the way you behave in public. And they judge parents by their children's behavior. Now I know you didn't mean to be unkind to your mother, did you?"

"No, sir."

Jake gave the boy's cap another tussle and lightly squeezed his neck.

"Then apologize to your mother and tell her how much you love her."

Hennessey hesitated.

"Go on. It's something Brad Pitt would do."

His embarrassment was complete. Hennessey meandered toward his mother's outstretched arms. Although he succumbed perfunctorily to her embrace, he felt relieved to be free of Jake's penetrating gaze.

The two adults exchanged winks.

Hennessey murmured an apology and then retreated from behind the counter to retrieve his roller blades.

Jake corralled him one more time and pulled the cap from his head, holding it ransom until Hennessey reached for it. Using the cap as a magnet Jake pulled the youngster closer until he snared him in his arms. Then in an unmistakably authoritative tone, Jake whispered into Hennessey's ear, "I'm your mother's friend, and I respect and love both your mother and your dad."

Jake's glance at Lisa carried Hennessey's eyes with it.

"They're good people," he continued. "And they deserve your love and respect." He squeezed Hennessey's arm lightly.

"So if you ever curse your mother in my presence again, I'll turn you over my knee and whip the do-winding snot out of you! You got that?"

Hennessey's chin fell and he stood frozen to the floor. His eyes stayed locked onto Jake's steel gaze. A shiver sliced through him, imperceptible, yet nonetheless there.

As Jake stood, he placed the cap on Hennessey's head. Retracing his steps toward the door, he shot a respectful glance at Lisa.

"Forgive me for overstepping my bounds here."

She waved his apology off, and glanced at Hennessey, who hadn't decided whether it was okay to move or remain frozen. Then she made eye contact with Jake again.

"Hennessey and I have an understanding," he reported charitably and invited her eyes to join his as he glanced in Hennessey's direction. "Isn't that right, son?"

Hennessey nodded.

Jake smiled his approval and then changed the subject quickly. "Thanks for boarding that German Shepherd."

Lisa smiled. "We've treated Hans since he was a pup. We'll take good care of him."

"I have no doubt about that. I hope the two young people who were run over receive just as good a treatment."

"Me, too. It's not a very good way to spend the holidays, is it?"

Jake shook his head.

"No. No it isn't. My heart goes out to their families."

"I almost feel guilty now, spending a healthy Christmas with my family."

"Don't you dare feel guilty about that," Jake reprimanded her sympathetically. "It's not your fault. When people hurt people, we all feel responsible. I suppose that's because we're all connected somehow. We feel each other's pain ... and hunger ... and loss. But that doesn't mean we have to beat ourselves up over it."

"I know you're right, but it still makes it hard to celebrate when you know someone's going through a bad time."

"Sobering, isn't it. And it's particularly tough when you care about people. But you can't take responsibility for everything that happens."

"But we can care for their pets, can't we?"

"Yep. You got that right."

"And pray for their owners."

"Right again."

Jake pulled the door open.

"Merry Christmas, Lisa. And you, too, son."

"Merry Christmas, Jake," Lisa replied as she stood next to her son.

"Merry Christmas, Mr. Detrick," Hennessey spoke softly as he repositioned his cap over his eyes.

Jake politely tipped his hat and winked at the two of them as he pulled the door closed securely behind him.

CHAPTER EIGHT

*K*aren saw them as soon as they swept through the swinging doors at the end of the hall. George, one inch over six feet tall, in his late seventies was striding in a most dignified manner. Product of old money, he was a curious amalgam of old North State gentleness, international sophistication, and homespun common sense. Adept in all the social graces, he complemented the savoir faire of his wife, who was well-connected politically and socially. Well-groomed regardless of the circumstance or activity, his flawless attire was neither flashy nor cluttered with designer labels. His preference for fine clothes was one of the few indulgences he allowed himself.

At seventy-two, Constance had none of the usual infirmities associated with a woman her age, nor any loss of grace or poise. Her vibrancy and vitality mirrored those same qualities in her husband. Totally in command of her faculties, she was courageous and dignified.

Most of all Karen admired her for her strength of character, her integrity, her devotion to George and to her and Pamela.

Constance was dressed in a simple yet elegant dark business suit, with traditional two button closure and notched collar. Its severity was softened quite nicely by the egg shell whiteness of the silk kerchief in the jacket pocket, and complemented by the expensive cameo pin perched on her lapel.

Her majestic silver hair was a coil around her head, exposing a widow's peak above a face etched with concern. Her oval face, with prominent cheekbones and conservative make-up, was alert and animated and there was a hint of resoluteness in her firm chin. But even from a distance her eyes showed signs of stress and her tightened lips couldn't conceal her anxiety.

George's concern mounted as they drew closer to Karen, who was encased in a dim light emanating from the waiting area. His eyes strained to get a better glimpse of her.

They came together, grim smiles and aching hearts, sharing a distress that mere words were powerless to explain. The three of them threw their arms around each other and stood firm in their mournful solidarity. For a few gut-wrenching moments, no one spoke.

"How is she?" Constance asked, finding the courage to speak.

Her question jettisoned the group apart slightly, although they held on to each other, siphoning every morsel of strength from their union.

"They've taken her ... " Karen broke off, trying to regain her composure. She exhaled a wearisome sigh. "She's in surgery. She's been in there over four hours."

Constance closed her eyes in despair.

"Do you know the extent of her injuries?" George asked, rushing his question. He struggled to remain calm, to sound coherent.

"I ... No! Not really. She's still unconscious. She has multiple injuries. Some are very serious. They told me she's in critical but stable condition." Karen reported, stopping to catch her breath.

George and Constance stood motionless. Their eyes were riveted to her weary face.

"They asked me to call next of kin," Karen lamented.

"Then they don't expect her to live, do they?" Constance's voice cracked, and her hands automatically covered her mouth.

"We don't know that," George followed, tension mounting in his voice. "Let's not jump to conclusions."

Karen bit her lip and tried not to cry. "The surgeon looked worried when he spoke to me an hour ago. I'm so scared.."

"I know, dear, we all are."

Karen clutched the ball cap she was holding even tighter. Something deep inside her told her if she could hold onto Pamela's cap, she could hold onto Pamela. Bloodstains were spattered across the bill and nearly blotted out the letters except for "C" and "Lea" which were printed on the cap. A policeman gave Pamela's hat to Karen, along with his well wishes, as he left the hospital.

Constance hugged Karen tighter.

"I'm glad you're here," Karen said, as she reciprocated her grandmother's lengthy embrace.

"We are, too, honey," said George, squeezing her arm. "We are, too."

"You said you saw the doctor an hour ago?" George questioned.

"Yes, Close to an hour ago."

"Well, I want to see him."

"Calm down, now George," Constance warned.

"She's not going to die, is she?" Karen asked, as she maintained a white knuckled grip on Pamela's hat.

Constance let out a sharp gasp.

"Is that's Pamela's hat?" she whispered sorrowfully. She was struck by the searing reality of the horror her granddaughter experienced earlier that morning when her young body was crushed beneath the oncoming car. "It's Pamela's cap, isn't it?" she whispered, as her hands automatically reached out for the bloody cap.

Karen handed Constance the cap. The thought of what the surgeons were doing to her sister at that very moment sent chills through her.

How awful, she shuddered. *How positively ghoulish ...*

Constance eyed the bloodstained cap tearfully.

My granddaughter's beautiful head was in this cap a few hours ago, Constance agonized to herself. **I can't believe this is happening.**

"George, I can't believe this is happening!" she repeated aloud.

George put his arms around both women and spoke with such conviction they thought his statement must be true.

"She will be all right—however this thing turns out. We're all going to get through this. I promise you that."

As he spoke, he saw a doctor dressed in light blue surgical garb exit from an elevator and head toward them. The doctor's demeanor indicated a hint of recognition as he made eye contact with the threesome. But the doctor's solemn expression caused George to stiffen.

"I think this is the doctor," Karen announced, struggling to lift her voice above a hoarse whisper.

The women peeled away from each other, their red eyes concentrated on the figure that had veered to the right to avoid bumping into a middle-aged man in the hall.

The surgeon stopped in front of them. "Mr. and Mrs. Justice?"

"These are my grandparents," Karen announced for clarity's sake, "Mr. and Mrs. George Lee. I'm Pamela's sister, Karen Justice. You met me earlier."

"We're the Lees," chimed Constance absentmindedly, offering clarification that wasn't necessary.

The surgeon nodded.

Well, folks," he began slowly. "She made it through surgery and is in the recovery room. I must be perfectly honest with you, her condition is grave. The next twenty-four hours will tell. We'll probably have to operate on her right arm again, but we need to get her stabilized first.

His announcement was followed by simultaneous gasps from the women.

"Your granddaughter's a tough young lady. We've done all we can right now ... "

"When can we see her?" George interrupted.

The doctor paused and then placed his hand on George's shoulder. Without missing another beat he described Pamela's condition: her fractured ribs, one of which punctured a lung, her broken pelvis and right leg, her mangled right arm, her loss of blood and lowered body temperature, a concussion which left her unconscious. He did not mention the numerous lacerations, cuts and bruises which covered fifty percent of her body.

The horrified family stood there pathetically, looking like doleful extras in a tragic play waiting to speak their lines. Held in the clutches of his forceful commentary, all three tried to comprehend what had happened. Numbed by disbelief and immobilized by anguish, they held onto each other. Each pronouncement spiked their hearts with inconsolable pain and fear. But they listened to the surgeon's ghastly report. Their trepidation mounted, fearful of what he would say next, yet they felt a need to hear his prognosis in detail.

"She will be in recovery for several hours and then we'll move her to intensive care. You'll be able to see her then."

Their absorption in the surgeon's prognosis was so complete that they were only dimly aware of the hustle and bustle of the orderlies and nurses in the hospital corridors. None of them heard the mournful wail of an ambulance as it approached the emergency room entrance, signaling the anxious arrival of another injured person.

Employing his most clinical tone, the surgeon continued, "We have guarded optimism she will recover. We expect that she will regain consciousness soon. Just when, I can't say. Maybe a couple of days, a week, a month, maybe longer. It's hard to say." He paused and purposefully made eye contact with George. "May I be frank with you?"

George drew himself up to his full height and took a deep breath. "It seems to me you already have."

The doctor aborted a nervous smile and pointed to a small room nearby that was empty. "Perhaps we'd better step into that room. There's something else I need to share."

With hesitant steps, the nervous trio followed the doctor into the empty room.

"I think you need to know that there is a possibility we may have to amputate her right arm."

Constance staggered her dismay and fell back against George, who found his own legs weakened by the surgeon's repulsive prognosis. Karen stood motionless, and then muffled a strangled sob.

"Amputate her ... arm?" Karen asked, finding it difficult to articulate the words.

The surgeon nodded. "In a few more days we'll know for sure ... but I feel I need to prepare you ... she will probably lose her arm."

"How much of it?" George gulped his question.

Constance shot a horrified glance at George, surprised at his uncharacteristic detachment. It was all she could do to suppress the urge to scream.

"Doctor," George pressed. His face was flushed. He tried his best not to vomit. "How much?"

"If we have to amputate ... it'll be from the shoulder down ... I'm sorry."

His words crushed them. Both women let out torturous gasps. George winced, but held his head erect and remained motionless.

"It's going to be several hours before you can see her. She made it through the initial surgery, be encouraged by that. Now the rest is up to her. We'll call you when you can see her and, of course, we'll keep you informed. I suggest you get some rest. If you can, try to grab something to eat."

"Yes ... thank you, doctor. Thank you ... but I suspect we'll stay right here. We'll want to see her as soon as we can."

"I understand."

George shook the surgeon's hand before the doctor took his leave. The shaken family watched as the surgeon walked quickly toward one of the nurses in the surgical area.

Constance used a handkerchief to do a proper job on the mucus and tears that smeared her face while Karen slid stiffly into one of the chairs in the waiting area, too overcome with shock to speak. She sat trance-like, letting her tears flow unchecked down her face and onto her sweater.

Constance stood next to her, still cradling Pamela's bloody cap in her hands.

Karen stood up and without saying a word headed toward the restroom.

"Karen, honey, are you all right?" Constance asked.

She nodded.

"I'll be right back." She walked over to her grandmother and whispered in her ear. "I think my period's started."

"Aw, honey, I'm sorry. Do you need ... ?"

"It's all right, I'm prepared."

The Lees steadied their gaze on their granddaughter as she walked down the hallway. Constance leaned her head on George's shoulder and closed her eyes. When the tears came, they gushed freely down her husband's shoulder.

§ § § § § §

Karen hadn't been in the restroom more than a few minutes when Ted Collins entered the surgical waiting room to find George and Constance sitting on a low-backed sofa near a window. Both looked haggard and as Ted closed the distance between them, he slowed his pace to avoid intruding too quickly.

The waiting room looked alien, unreal, and offensive in its clutter. Magazines and papers, temporary distractions which gave nervous hands and aching hearts something to hide behind, were strewn all over the waiting area.

The pale green vinyl sofa and chairs would have seemed a bit understated to Ted if not for their drabness and lack of warmth that complemented the dullness of the room quite well.

He eased himself into their silence.

"George ... Constance, how is she?"

"Ted ... how's Geoffrey? My God, George ... we forgot all about dear Geoffrey."

George's attempt to stand was greeted by Ted's firm hand on his shoulder, accompanied by a light downward push to keep him seated. Ted crumpled into the chair adjacent to them.

Constance absorbed every bit of agony out of Ted's look before she attempted to speak.

"How is he, Ted?" she asked. Then not wanting to sound too clinical added, "He is going to be okay, isn't he?"

Overcome by despair, Ted exploded into uncontrollable cries of agony.

The Lees could not hold back their own tears.

"I'm sorry," he apologized. "I'm sorry guys."

"That's all right," Constance consoled, in her most maternal tone. "Let it all out."

Ted's sobs were interrupted by his attempts to mop up the tears and clear his nose with his handkerchief. He finally raised himself higher in the chair and shot a lightning quick glance around the waiting room to see if he had an audience other than the Lees. Satisfied that he hadn't embarrassed himself publicly, he collected himself and faced the Lees squarely.

"I'm sorry, I don't know what got into me."

"Concern for your son," assured George, giving Ted a pat on the shoulder.

Constance shook her head in agreement.

"I don't normally do that. Cry like that, I mean."

"This isn't a normal day, my friend," George counseled, "you needn't feel embarrassed.

Constance found herself nodding her consent again. Lost momentarily in her own thoughts, she remembered, *George has always been good at this sort of thing. When the girls' parents died, he was the strong one, the glue that held the family together. He'll see all of us through this crisis.* The sound of Ted's voice brought her back to the reality of the moment.

"He's paralyzed from the waist down ... he may never be able to walk again."

Shock registered on both George and Constance's faces as they exchanged swift and disquieted glances. Although Constance forced back the tears, she couldn't censor the gasp that lifted from her throat.

"Oh, Ted," Constance said, reaching out to touch his hand.

Ted started to elaborate, but blunted his explanation when he saw Karen gliding slowly into the room.

Both George and Constance followed his gaze to where Karen stood and waited for her to join them.

She forced a tight smile and searched each of their eyes for the slightest hint of Geoffrey's condition.

"He's alive," came George's assurance.

Both Constance and Ted gave weary smiles, each exhaling fully to vent the pressure they had felt all morning.

"Thank God," whispered Karen. She moved her grandmother's tweed overcoat and black leather handbag over to the next chair. Karen exhaustedly slid down beside Ted, who hugged her immediately.

Ted quickly repeated what he told the Lees a short while before.

Bludgeoned by Ted's description of Geoffrey's injuries, Karen's resonating wail filled the waiting room.

I'm going to wake up and find this has all been a dream, she tried to convince herself.

"Can I see him? Is he conscious?" Karen asked.

"Yes, he's conscious. Thank God for that small miracle. Yes, you can see him as soon as they say we can go back in. They asked me to leave so they could make a few adjustments in his bedding."

"He must be so frightened. Oh, Ted, I still can't believe it."

"How ... How's Pamela?" Ted asked, this time repositioning himself in his chair so that he sat straight.

George told him what they learned from the surgeon, including what they learned about her arm.

"Oh, no, I hope they won't have to do that," Ted reacted sympathetically. "Let's pray they don't have to do that," he repeated and then grew silent.

Constance watched the three of them with growing consternation, darting her eyes first to one of them and then to another. Her grief-weathered face made her whole demeanor appear even more solemn.

"I can't imagine how anyone, any rational, God fearing human being could drive away like that, and leave someone to die," George said slowly, laboriously.

For the first time in his dignified life, George felt the desire to smash something, or someone. The driver of the car that struck the kids was the primary candidate of his mounting rage. The idea that anyone could be so inhuman enraged him to the point of vigilantism.

"It takes an uncaring, reprehensible jerk to do something like that," Ted echoed.

Karen made no attempt to camouflage her anger as she launched her own vigorous assault on the unknown assailant.

"They'd better find that loathsome coward before I do. That's all I can say."

"Karen!" admonished Constance. A look of astonishment jumped on her face.

George raised his eyebrows and, except for a preemptive smirk that danced briefly around his mouth, said nothing.

Karen's searing cynicism erupted again, but from a more philosophical view.

"I'm as serious as a heart attack!" she leveled caustically. She lifted Pamela's bloodstained cap from her grandmother's lap, and with a knot of anger in her throat choked out another flammable innuendo.

"I swear, with every ounce of my being, that coward is going to get a piece of me. So the police had better ... "

Constance cut into her tirade, "Karen, darling ... "

"I mean it," came Karen's swift retort.

Ted gave her a fatherly embrace, and then cradled her tear-stained face in his palms. He tilted her head forward and kissed her forehead through her bangs.

"I know you do. I know," he consoled, kissing her forehead again. He gave her another consoling hug and held her cheeks in his palms so he could look into her eyes.

Every wrathful curve of her eyebrows expressed her contempt for the driver who left all of their lives in such a tangle. Karen reached up in an unconscious display of vanity and brushed away a strand of her hair that had fallen across her face. Her eyes were still riveted on Ted.

You think I'm kidding, she thought to herself. *You see me as the mild-mannered artist. But somebody's just messed up my sister. And if she dies ... and if Geoffrey doesn't recover, I'm going to kill whoever did this!*

She bit her lip, forcing back a comment that she was sure would meet with disapproval. Instead she bowed to an instinct that was a surer guide than reason itself, and greeted Ted's affectionate gaze with a smile.

Ted released her and leaned back on the sofa. He felt leaden. His sigh prompted Karen to stand so she could join her grandfather at the window.

George peeled back the mini-blinds, tattered out of alignment by a distressed predecessor who made a similar pilgrimage to the window. George sighed heavily, clouding the window pane with his breath.

Karen could see it was snowing again. As each tiny crystal flake bombarded the window, it disappeared into rivulets down the glass. She saw George press his weary head against the window, and guessed that its coolness might comfort him somehow.

"Miss Justice. Miss Karen Justice ... "

The foursome turned their attention quickly in the direction of a young hospital volunteer holding the phone in the waiting room. She looked quite official and antiseptically clean. She held the phone out toward Karen, who she guessed was the benefactor of the call.

"It's a Mr. Detrick for you."

"Detrick?" murmured Karen, sending her a puzzled expression. "I don't know any Mr. Detrick," she said as she accepted the receiver. She shot a bewildered glance at George as she brought the phone to her ear.

Jake Detrick introduced himself as one of the rescue team members and then asked nervously after Pamela and Geoffrey.

"They're both still in recovery. My sister is unconscious," Karen amended her report by adding that Geoffrey would probably be paralyzed from the waist down.

There was a slight pause on the other end of the line and then Jake sent his heartfelt prayers.

"The thing I called about," he began, "is your dog, Hans. He's at ... "

"Hans!" she sliced into his sentence, realizing she had not given Hans a thought since arriving at the hospital.

"How do you know about Hans?" she asked suspiciously.

"He's okay. He's just fine."

"I know ... I ... oh, yes, I remember now ... the police told us someone saved him. Was that you?"

"I work at the nature center in Swannanoa," Jake began again and recounted how he was first on the scene and tranquilized her dog to save him from being shot.

"So, you saved Hans," Karen shouted, feeling energized by his news. Her enthusiasm perked up the others who watched her become more animated by the minute.

"Where is he?"

"That's why I'm calling."

"Where ... is, do you have him?" she trailed, her emotions getting the best of her.

"No, but I've boarded him in the best hotel in town."

Karen's look of puzzlement returned for an instant. "Hotel?" she questioned.

Jake told her about the boarding arrangements he made with the Masts and assured her she didn't have to worry about Hans.

"The Masts—they're my veterinarians," Karen squealed.

"I know, Lisa Mast told me. I couldn't just leave him there without your knowing where he was ... and I wanted to check on your sister. It is your sister isn't? And the young fella, too."

"Yes, she's my sister and Geoffrey is my ... our friend."

"Your dog was under sedation. I had to use a fairly high dose ... he was so hyper. I called Lisa just before I reached you and she says he's doing fine."

"Thank you, Mr. Detrick. Thank you so very much."

"I just didn't want you to have worry about your dog. You've got enough to worry about. Oh, and you don't have to worry about the boarding costs, either. It's all taken care of."

"Thank you, Mr. Detrick. Thank you very much. It's very good of you to call."

Karen expressed her appreciation on behalf of the family, then hung up. She announced to the others, "What a nice man. How about that? He took the time to call. He's really thoughtful. He insisted on taking care of the boarding fees and associated costs for Hans. He said he had already taken care of it and for me not to worry about repaying him. Isn't that incredible?"

"We'll have to send him a special thanks," protracted Constance. "We must return kindness with kindness."

George shot a nervous glance in the direction of a doctor who was headed their way. He could see him through the steel and glass enclosure that framed the room.

In the short conversation that followed, the surgeon prepared them for their visit.

"Be prepared for a shock. She's decorated with tubes and covered with surgical bandages. You'll find her surrounded by tons of monitoring equipment. I'm telling you this so you'll know what to expect."

The surgeon updated them on Pamela's condition. "She is still unconscious but we've been able to stabilize her. We drilled a tiny hole in her skull to relieve the pressure and are monitoring the pressure inside her head. As I told you before, the preliminary surgery on her right arm was successful, but I'm doubtful that it can be saved. The punctured lung is a concern, but we're monitoring that, as well. The next couple of days will tell us what we need to know. As for now, she is in critical, but stable, condition."

The doctor looked at the four of them and made it clear that only two visitors were allowed at a time.

George turned to invite Ted, feeling he was part of the family. But Ted waved him off. Karen waved her visit off too.

"I'll stay in the waiting room," Ted announced. "They're supposed to tell me when I can see Geoffrey again. I'll visit Pamela after you've had a chance to see her. I won't be leaving the hospital, anyway—not with the kids in such danger."

From their positions just outside the surgical waiting area, Ted and Karen watched the two of them follow the surgeon down the corridor.

A lone tear found its way down George's cheek as he focused on Constance as she walked down the dimly-lit corridor. Her heels echoed sharply as she nervously crossed the tiled floor on her way to her granddaughter's cubical.

CHAPTER NINE

*P*amela was lying face up in a cocoon of soft light. Her eyes were closed and her face wore the lacerations and cuts from the accident. She looked peaceful in spite of the preponderance of coils of plastic tubing that snaked their way around her frail body. A clear tube coming from the respirator poked through her parted lips and another fed up her nose. More tubes hung in clusters from bottles and bags positioned above her like silent sentinels rationing out life-saving liquids a drop at a time.

A light blue valve was slotted into her jugular, terminating a clear plastic tube held secure by a patch of flesh-colored tape. The tape pulled her skin tightly around the incision.

Oh, dear, I'm going to faint, Constance thought.

The tape's pinching her neck, George said to himself. *It's going to bruise her.*

His compassionate eyes surveyed the electrodes attached to her temples, chest and arms. The attachments were fastened with the same flesh-colored tape.

She'll bruise, he repeated to himself. Then he quickly dismissed his absurd concern for her bruises, realizing there were more important things to worry about.

Constance inadvertently placed her hand over her own throat when she saw the incision at her granddaughter's throat.

"The white bandages covering her head," explained an attending nurse, "are there to prevent infection. We change them periodically."

Both of the Lees paused after they took a few more languished steps toward Pamela. Smitten by the graveness of her condition, they clung to each other, needing one another's strength.

A forest of hospital equipment stood between them and their embattered granddaughter. Officious nurses, antiseptic in their watch, fussed over her. The nurses were masterful at exacting readings from the machines.

One of the nurses edged closer to the twosome and diligently explained the substance of the electronic messages that spewed across computer screens lighted by quivering lines, some blinking, others racing across display panels repetitively, silently.

The respirator made a loud hissing sound as it created a quick, inhaled breath and forced an upward motion of Pamela's chest. Then it deflated just as rapidly as it belched air from its mechanical core.

Constance squeezed George's hand as they moved toward their granddaughter.

"Oh, Pamela, my darling, my dear, dear child. You've been through such a ... " Constance trailed off, unable to continue.

George slid an arm around Constance's waist just in time to catch her before her legs buckled.

"You okay, honey?"

"Oh, George, I expected to ... but I didn't think ... I didn't expect ... "

"Do you want to go?"

"No! Heavens no ... I ... no. I don't want to leave her."

He fixed his gaze on Pamela's angelic face. "You'll take very good care of her, won't you?" he addressed one of the nurses who brushed by them, apparently to check the fluid level in one of the bags. He spoke without looking at her, so it took the nurse a few seconds to realize he was addressing her.

"The best of care," she assured him after a quick preliminary nod. "We'll take very good care of her." The nurse glanced at one of the monitors and busied herself pushing several buttons before she spoke again. "She's a strong young woman. And she's holding her own."

George started to say something in order to continue the conversation, but found it difficult to put two syllables together. The buzz and hiss of the gadgetry, accompanied by the dutiful activities of the nurse, took his power of speech away.

A technician appeared, accompanied by a perfunctory knock on the door. One of the nurses waived him in and announced that they would have to leave for a few moments while the technician drew a vial of Pamela's blood.

George hesitated, thinking to himself, *she's lost several pints of blood already and they want to take more? That seems cruel somehow.* He recovered quickly and assisted Constance in a dignified retreat.

The nurse gave Constance a light touch on her arm. "I promise. I'll call you back as soon as we've finished."

Constance answered with a weary smile and shot another quick glance at Pamela before she followed George out into the corridor.

"I'll let you go back in," George volunteered, giving Constance a soft, encouraging hug. "I'll see if Karen wants to go in."

"Oh, no, you don't have to do that. I'll let her substitute for me," Constance replied.

"That's okay, honey. Karen wants to see her and I want to see how Geoffrey's doing. Maybe Ted's in with Geoffrey now," George guessed, as he headed toward the waiting area.

Ted saw him round the corner and walked to George from the nurses' station.

"How is she?"

"Well, she's holding her own. She's still unconscious," George lamented. "We had to step out for a few minutes, nurse's orders. They're drawing blood."

George pulled Karen to him and kissed her on the cheek. "She doesn't look like her picture in North Carolina Woman Magazine last month," George said, preparing her for what she was about to see. His levity surprised her as she wiped back a compensating tear.

"She'll look beautiful to me," Karen responded. "She's alive. We'll get a smile on that gorgeous face before too long."

"Are you all right?" Ted inquired as he looked anxiously at George.

"Yes, I'm okay," he said wearily, forcing a smile.

"I was able to see Geoffrey a little while ago," Ted informed him. And then he paused, finding it difficult to continue. "He looks pretty bad. I'm out here on nurse's orders, too. The doctor wants to see me, though, as soon as he examines my boy."

George turned to Karen.

"Look, I'll go with Ted to see Geoffrey. You go in to see Pamela. We'll meet back here to plan what to do with the rest of our evening."

George blew her a kiss. When he wheeled around to take his leave, he almost collided with an orderly who was able to side-step George's abrupt departure.

The two men glided wordlessly through the shadowy hall that was sheathed in dim lights and cluttered with hospital equipment.

Food carts and laundry hampers stood in the aisle appearing phantom-like from a distance, but recognizable nonetheless. George was struck by the habitual randomness of the clutter.

Hospital corridors are always strewn with orphaned equipment, he reminded himself. *And yet I can't help but feel a lingering sense of chaotic order. Someone knows the whereabouts of each piece of equipment, every cart, each soiled dust mop. I'm sure of it.*

George and Ted had been friends ever since the girls and Geoffrey were day care companions. Each knew how close

Pamela felt to Geoffrey, who was aware he was too protective for her independent streak, too deliberate for her impatience, too practical for her naiveté in regard to relationships with men. And both knew one's survival depended on the other.

If Pamela could have picked a brother, George thought to himself, *I bet he'd be just like Geoffrey.*

He stopped at one of the recessed windows along the hallway leading from one section of the hospital to another while Ted cleaned his eyeglasses. Peering out of the window to update himself on the weather, George spied several large clusters of rhododendrons which bordered one end of the solarium on the first floor. Snow and ice had flattened their immense foliage making the bushes more horizontal than erect. He admired their tenacity, but they were yielding patiently to the crush of eight inches of frozen water.

I wonder how much more pressure they can take before they snap? I wonder how much more the kids can take? How much we can take? He quizzed himself.

He was surprised that something Karen told him many years before about the history of rhododendrons popped into his mind.

Folklore had it that each June, rhododendrons bloom red from the blood of the Catawba Indians, ancient warriors who were killed in three legendary battles over a hundred years ago. They constantly warred against other tribes who sought to take Grandfather Mountain from them.

Rhododendrons will bloom red again this year, he prophesied sadly to himself. *The blood of these two innocent kids has consecrated the ground.*

He brushed away a tear with his forefinger as he turned from the window in response to Ted's movement down the hallway.

George tapped Ted's arm, and pointed to the men's room.

"I've got to make a pit stop. You go on."

Ted nodded and continued walking slowly down the hallway.

As George entered the men's room, he walked past a man who was exiting in a wheelchair. He immediately thought of Geoffrey. *Looks like Ted's son will graduate into a life of wheelchairs. Some graduation.* He watched the man wheel expertly down the hallway. I *wonder if Geoffrey will give himself a chance to accept his limitations?*

After George left the restroom, he was surprised to see Ted's solitary figure through the glass enclosures bordering the surgical waiting room door.

Looks like he was pushed out of Geoffrey's room again, George thought as he walked through the doorway.

Ted was crumpled in a chair and looked as if the weight of the world had settled on his sixty-seven-year-old shoulders.

"How is he? Did you see the doctor yet?" George asked. Not waiting for an answer, he continued, "What did he say?"

"They've found some internal bleeding. That's why they sent me back out. Said they'd call for me after the doctor saw him."

Ted gave George the most forlorn look.

"George, that s.o.b. really messed him up. If my son dies, I'm going to spend whatever days I have left tracking that creep down. He's not going to get away with it! I swear on my wife's grave!"

"Your son is going to survive this thing, Ted. He's a strong young man. And we've got to show him we're just as strong."

"It was probably the fall that broke his back," Ted added. He grabbed George's arm, as if to emphasize his plight. "If my boy doesn't make it, George, there won't be enough room on this planet for me and whoever did this. I mean it!"

George sighed, unsure what to say.

"I'd ... I ... I know how you feel. But whatever happens, I want you to remember we all have each other. By the grace of God, we'll get through this. Your son is strong. So is our granddaughter. So let's see both of them pulling through this. They haven't given up, and neither can we."

George stood beside Ted, who remained seated. He hadn't seen Ted this devastated since his wife, Marie, died of cancer. She was a branch manager at a local Bank for over twenty-five years and was planning to retire when Ted did. They were going to stay in Asheville, but decided to spend the winters in Florida. Her illness, of course, changed all of that.

Ted took an early retirement from the police force to spend as much time with Marie as he could during her final months. She died on her birthday, August 18, surrounded by those who loved her. He recalled Ted's appraisal of the local hospice volunteers who provided such excellent care for her that she was able to die a dignified death. Ted was so appreciative of their support through the bereavement process that he donated part of Marie's insurance money to hospice. Later he became a non-medical volunteer himself.

"Hungry?" George asked, tapping Ted's shoulder.

"No."

"Are you sure?"

Ted nodded.

"When's the last time you've eaten? Did you have anything this morning?"

"Oh, half a bowl of cereal ... some coffee ... a little orange juice, I think."

"It's almost four o'clock. You've got to have something," George insisted sympathetically.

"No, really. Thanks anyway."

"How 'bout something to drink?"

"I've had so much coffee my head hurts," Ted confessed, rubbing his temples a couple of times.

"That's because you haven't eaten, my friend," George replied mildly.

"Look, suppose I bring us both something from the canteen? One of those sandwiches wrapped in cellophane. Some chips, something to drink to tide us over."

"Okay, sure," Ted finally conceded. "That would be great."

"No, not great!" George mused, a smile creasing his lips. "We're talking hospital food here. Great is not an adjective I'd use to describe it!"

Ted forced a smile and then shook his head. George had always been good at taking the edge off of things.

"As long as it's edible then," Ted condescended, taking a stab at neutralizing his depression.

"What do you want to wash it down?"

Ted's pensiveness, coupled with a sudden urge for a drink, broadcast itself over his face.

"Now that you ask ... " he purposefully trailed off.

George took the hint.

"I don't think they serve mixed drinks here, old boy!" chimed George. "How 'bout something a little more tame?"

"As long as it's wet ... and cold."

George signaled his departure and vanished through the open door.

CHAPTER TEN

$\mathcal{S}$he felt unutterably weary as she sat beside her granddaughter's bed. It had been two weeks since the accident and Pamela still lay in a coma, although she was now breathing on her own.

Thank God I refused to let them amputate Pamela's arm, Constance thought to herself. *Her arm is coming along nicely now and will be as good as new after a few more operations.*

A convulsive shiver shot through her body as she remembered how close Pamela had come to losing her arm, from the shoulder down.

"I refused to let them amputate your arm, honey, and it's healing nicely. I defied medical opinion. You'd be proud of your sassy Gramma. I'm glad I disregarded the surgeon's eloquent attempts to persuade me to reconsider. Pamela, honey, I almost believed him when he said it was a necessary and prudent amputation. But I know you didn't want to lose your arm. I told them you'd been through enough, so they had better come up with something. And they did. Praise God, they did!"

She regretted her arguments with George. They had never argued with such hostility before. She couldn't remember a time when they had been so polarized over an issue.

"Our prayers have been answered, darling. You must wake up to see how nice your arm looks. It's healing perfectly."

She clasped Pamela's hand, the hand that wouldn't have been there if the surgeons had amputated. She squeezed it, allowing the pressure to communicate her presence. Pamela's long, manicured nails had been polished by a manicurist at Constance's request. Constance hoped that when Pamela regained consciousness, the new nail polish on her fingernails and her toenails would ease her shock at seeing her cuts and scars.

"I've alerted the nurses, darling, that as soon as they remove the head bandages, I want them to shampoo your hair, so I can brush it. I've got your make-up. It'll be nice to see color on your beautiful face again."

Constance knew Pamela was sensitive about her looks and would want a new make-over. The manicurist had talked to Pamela while she filed and polished her nails, commenting on how healthy her cuticles looked and how impressed she was that a working woman could manage to keep such long fingernails.

Constance and the manicurist exchanged views about the effects of positive symbols in depressed environments; for example, how the Jews scrawled etchings of butterflies and flowers on sterile prison walls as poignant reminders of how beautiful life can be and of the metamorphosis from darkness into the light. They discussed how murals painted on walls and small flower gardens, planted in poor neighborhoods, softened the harsh realities of inner city life. As ornaments of decency and love, they symbolized humanity's quest for balance and harmony instead of violence.

The conceptualizing helped Constance focus on something else besides Pamela's injuries. It lifted her spirits. George had even become interested and added his own, amazingly profound insights. Karen had been shopping that day, she remembered, and missed the discussion.

Karen enjoys discussions like that, she reminded herself. *She is quite knowledgeable on metaphysical subjects. She'd often been surprised at some of the things I've said.*

Her attention was drawn to Karen's CD player. The current selection was from Bette Midler's *Wind Beneath My Wings*.

"Karen says that's your favorite selection, dear. It's become one of mine, too. You're the wind beneath our wings, so please come back to us."

She noticed something out of place as she switched her focus from the CD player and then back to her granddaughter. A Kleenex tissue box, wedged between scores of get-well cards, was empty.

"Karen has emptied that tissue box again. Pamela, honey, you're going to have to get well soon or your sister will bankrupt us buying Kleenex."

She looked at Pamela, hoping to see her come to life.

"Just a little smile, honey. Give me a beautiful smile so I know you're listening."

She waited nervously for a sign.

"That's okay, darling. I know you can hear me."

She waited again, unwinding her hands.

When nothing happened, Constance peeked at her watch. George and Karen would be joining her for lunch in a couple of hours. The family agreed on round-the-clock shifts until Pamela regained consciousness. The hospital staff had graciously accommodated their request for twenty-four hour vigilance and Karen rewarded the staff with a batch of homemade cookies or a cake twice a week. Her sugar cookies and fruitcakes were hits with the nursing staff, and so were her cheese balls.

The chorus of Midler's song *Wind Beneath My Wings* brought Constance's attention back to her granddaughter.

Constance squeezed Pamela's hand gently and then stood, watching her granddaughter intently.

"The medical staff has explained to us that comatose patients are still connected with the world around them somehow," she whispered aloud. "Patients have regained consciousness and recounted conversations that took place in their rooms while they were unconscious. The doctors say your improvement is phenomenal. We know you want to come back to us, Pamela. And it's almost Christmas."

As she released Pamela's hand, she whispered compassionately, "I'm not leaving, my dear. I just need to stretch these old theatrical legs a little. This old retired professional dancer needs to walk around the room and get the kinks out."

She took a few unsure steps as one of her knees buckled before she could steady herself.

"You've sat too long in one place, old girl," she chided herself.

A web of wrinkles divided her eyebrows as she fell into deep thought. *I don't know how much more any of us can endure the formality of hospital visits, fretful sleep, if it comes at all, and the endless hours of waiting for you to come back to us.*

Impatience snapped at her. Impatience for the cure, not for Pamela's unseen struggle to regain consciousness. Impatience for the medical profession's inability to bring her back. Impatience for the police investigative efforts, unproductive and unencouraging.

They haven't produced even one lead, one iota of evidence that identifies the criminal responsible for Pamela's coma and for Geoffrey's paralysis, her thoughts continued.

Constance, that's not fair, she criticized herself. *Officer Holland is confident he'll apprehend the driver. He's even made several strong pleas on the local and statewide news channels and in the newspaper and Internet for help in finding the one responsible for the hit-and-run.*

She walked over to the window and directed her gaze through the venetian blinds which she'd opened the night before. It was a ritual she adopted on the first night. George had positioned the cot for her so she would be greeted by the shimmering orb of golden morning light as it cut its way into the room through the open blinds.

"Darling, it's beautiful outside. I know how much you like the out-of-doors. It looks like we're going to have a white Christmas."

She stood reverently by the window, her hands clasped, nervous fingers intertwined. Her knuckles whitened with the tension of a lengthy vigilance, and she decided to pray. Her faith inextinguishable, she moved her lips in prayer:

"In the name of the living Christ, I affirm in this moment of need, that what is perfect and right will manifest for my granddaughter. I give thanks for the strength all of us have expressed in dealing with her accident and for the wonderful team of surgeons and nurses who are caring for her. I declare her highest and best good as she aligns her human self with her Christ Self. I see every cell, each atom, and every molecule in her body expressing its health and wholeness.

"I forgive those who are responsible for doing this terrible thing. And I bless both of these two wonderful kids. They have so much to offer, I ... "

She sighed heavily before she continued:

"I erase the anger and hatred from my heart and declare good will come from this. I also lift up George and Karen ... and Ted. I see each of them safe and healthy and surrounded with white light.

"And if one of these kids should die ... I know that there is no geography in Spirit."

She trailed off, squeezing her hands tighter. She looked up through watery eyes toward the ceiling, and cried out in a voice filled with resolve:

"I declare in this now moment that we—the medical team, the kids, and us—can work all things together for good. And so it is!"

§　　§　　§　　§　　§　　§

George pulled a book from the shelf and settled back into the chair near the fireplace. He had given the book to Karen as a gift. It was a paperback about General Robert E. Lee entitled *From Battlefield to Boardroom: Leadership Lessons of Robert*

E. Lee. He used his copy as a daily devotional, reading the leadership wisdom of Lee over and over again, digesting each phrase and bit of insightful commentary with thoughtfulness and thoroughness. He found the most remote passages inspirational. Written by a management consultant from Raleigh, it seemed to capture the essence of General Lee as a military leader and as a man. He had also given a copy to Pamela, who included quotes from it in her leadership training programs.

He noticed yellow highlighting over some of the text. "Good," he whispered. Karen has actually read this.

He turned to page forty as his favorite Lee quote:

> *Toil and trust. We often see only the ebb of*
> *the advancing wave and are thus*
> *discouraged. It is history that*
> *teaches us to hope.*

He found comfort again in that short passage. He had always admired the General for his religious convictions and for his uncompromised character and integrity. And now the southern gentleman spoke to him from the words of the text, consoling him with timeless wisdom and eternal hope.

George shivered, suddenly aware of the coldness in his arms and legs.

"Must be a cracked window that's causing a draft."

A quick glance around the room verified all the windows were shut.

He rubbed his arms through his sweater and then rose, not swiftly, but purposefully, and picked up the iron poker. He drove it with some calculation into the burning logs that smoldered like burned out heaters in a sea of molten orange ash in the fireplace.

Every once in a while he would poke fiercely at the irregular cylinders of charred wood as if to vent his rage at the one who had taken the joy out of their Christmas.

The charred remains glowed red and orange and spat miniature meteors of light back at him through the screen that separated the inferno from the carpet. He renewed his efforts to stoke the fire, partly because he was cold, but mostly because he was agitated at the whole situation. His granddaughter had been in a coma now for nineteen days.

The long embers retreated easily with each swift poke, falling apart in the bed of flowing coals that blanketed the super-heated grate. His drawn face was illuminated with their pyric glow, which was reflected to each of the pear-shaped teardrops that fell from his moist eyes.

He almost didn't hear Karen's announcement from the kitchen, which came at precisely the same time as embers spewed from the fireplace, sending dozens of specks of flaming ashes through the screen, creating the effect of a miniature fireworks display.

"Ten minutes," Karen repeated, when she got no response from her grandfather.

"What was that you said, honey?"

"The pies should be ready in ten minutes," she repeated a third time, "I have to leave them in an extra ten minutes, the fillings aren't quite done."

As he sat deciding whether to continue reading or simply enjoy what was left of the fire before they went to the hospital, he felt Hans' cool wet muzzle against his hand.

"What's up, fella?"

Hans stood while George stroked his ears and gave him a few light pats on his massive head. Having won George's attention, Hans lost no time begging for more affection by forcing his way on to George's lap with his front paws. He positioned himself so his eyes were level with those of his visitor.

"Oh, I see," taunted George. "You want to go out."

Hans barked.

George raised his eyebrows and tilted his head, sending Hans' tail wagging.

Hans pleaded one more time by letting out another irrepressible howl.

"What are you two doing in there?" boomed Karen lightheartedly from the kitchen.

"We're negotiating."

His comment coaxed Karen to the doorway. She had a dishtowel in her hands and a confused look on her face, which prompted a quick wink from George.

"I think he wants to go outside, and I'm not sure I want to just yet. He's got two competitors for my time, the warm fire and the Lee book."

"So you're negotiating!"

"I think he's trying to drum up support."

George laughed as Hans retreated toward Karen, giving George time to evict himself from the chair.

"Suppose I take him out," volunteered Karen, as she renewed her efforts to dry her hands on the dishtowel.

"No, no, I don't mind. You've got things to do," George replied as he headed toward her. "Besides, I've got to earn my keep," he added, smiling broadly. He leaned over to kiss her on the forehead as he grabbed his coat off the hook.

"Oh, Grampa. You don't need to take him out. Let me do it."

"No, I really want to. Come on, boy," ordered George as he retrieved the leash from its perch on a small hook near the refrigerator. "I've been sedentary too long today." Both he and the dog vanished through the outside kitchen door.

For some reason Karen remembered the trip to the veterinarian's three weeks before. Hans, washed, perfumed and fed, had greeted them with the excitement of a costumed child who races home proudly with a full bag of Halloween booty.

He had been so glad to see them. His overnight stay at the vet's was only the second time he had bunked anywhere without Karen. The only other time was when he was fixed, and because his appointment had been scheduled for late afternoon, he stayed overnight at the Mast Veterinary Clinic.

That was Karen's first experience with the Masts, four years ago today. She was impressed with the special care they gave Hans as a pup. As any dog owner knows, veterinarians who win the trust and confidence of frightened pets usually convert the pet owners, too. Karen was a believer. She felt Hans could not have been in better hands all these years.

That sentiment brought her attention to the calendar hanging on the side of the refrigerator. It was the type that displayed nature scenes on the top half and calendar squares on the bottom. The scene for December showed a family of Pandas frolicking in the snow. One of the young Pandas was turned slightly sideways on his back and seemed to be playfully pushing against the front legs of a huge Panda who Karen decided was the mother since both the youngsters seemed to hover close to her.

Each of the one-inch squares beginning with December 2 through today's date, December 21, had been tagged with a bright yellow smiley face. The faces indicated the number of days both Pamela and Geoffrey had been in the hospital. She used the smiley faces instead of X's because the colorful faces were positive symbols. The X's seemed inappropriate—like deletions rather than restoration.

Whatever is happening to you internally, Sis, has to be acknowledged externally. You're still alive and your struggle must be rewarded. You are being restored, not deleted, she told her sister, *so the smiley faces are the things to use.*

She touched the square marked December 21 and placed her hand over the smiley face. "Today's the day. Today is the day you come back to us. Right, God?" she whispered prayerfully.

She lifted up another quick prayer, silently this time. She believed that a sister's whispered prayers from home could reach a sister's silent, ceramic coma in the hospital. Pear shaped tears ran down her face, prompting her to retrieve a tissue from the box near the phone. She took care of her runny nose and wiped another trickle of tears away, smearing her make-up.

Applying make-up was a practice she had incorporated only since Pamela's accident. Painting her face and plastering her eyelashes and brows were only high priorities when Pamela visited. George referred to her makeover as sympathy make-up. She remembered a conversation between her grandparents late one evening at the hospital.

The three of them were in Pamela's hospital room. Her grandparents, thinking she was asleep, quietly discussed her newly acquired make-up habit. Their secretive appraisal was loving and generally complimentary. George had said she looked mature and sophisticated—he had even described her as womanly. He told Constance he believed she wore the make-up to imitate Pamela. The cosmetics, he said, bonded the sisters somehow. He was sure Karen found strength in the connection.

"You're probably right, Grampa," she said aloud, half to herself and half to her absentee sister, as she gently touched the smiley face on the calendar again.

"I do want you to get well. And I want you to see all the cosmetics I've bought for myself. They're not as expensive as yours ... drugstore variety, you know, but effective just the same.

She was jolted back from her reverie by the obnoxious wail of the oven timer.

"The pies!"

She punched the alarm off and quickly took the pies from the oven. Using the old padded gloves she bought at a yard sale, she placed both pies on top of the stove to cool. She untied her apron, gave it a quick toss onto one of the kitchen chairs, and retreated from the heat of the kitchen.

"I must be bright and cheery for Sis when she awakens," she said aloud, calling upon her reserve. Her cheerfulness had been an act before. Today was different. She believed she might have something to cheer about soon.

"Today's the day," she repeated, raising her voice almost to the point of a cheer as she ran upstairs to her bedroom. She opened her sweater drawer and chose the one Pamela gave her last Christmas. She threw on some make-up and tussled her hair with her fingertips.

"Ready," she celebrated.

She skipped two steps at a time and leaped into the living room. Then she decided to take another look at the Christmas tree before they left for the hospital.

The tree is perfect, just the right size, Karen congratulated herself. She had potted it the night before, and admired how stately it looked in its skirted tree stand between the front picture window and the fireplace.

"Water," she shouted aloud. "I forgot to water the tree last night," she repeated as she flew into the kitchen to retrieve a pitcher from under the sink cabinet.

Having poured what she considered to be the right amount of water on the tree ball, Karen stepped back. She tilted her head to one side, placed her thumb against one corner of her mouth and her index finger across the top of her lips as she studied the six-foot fir.

Her gaze carried her eyes up the ornamented boughs of the tree to the angel at the top. It was a beautiful figurine dressed in white lace and sprinkled generously with miniature stars. The delicate lines of the angel seemed to blur as she tried to focus on it. First she squinted as she concentrated, and then blinked a few times to focus on the luminous quality emanating from the angel. She discovered that the figurine's brilliance was produced by a ribbon of light that sent its shimmering radiance dancing through the skylight mounted directly above the tree.

"Please, God," Karen pleaded, her voice light as a whisper. "Please have mercy on my sister ... and Geoffrey. And if there are a couple of unassigned guardian angels up there this Christmas," she paused, "please send them to help my sister and Geoffrey."

Karen addressed the angel at the top of the tree. "You are in charge of the Nativity, of new birth ... and promise. You are supposed to protect us. Help us. Bring us tidings of great joy. Well, we're waiting. We'd like a little joy around here. And I'm sure there are other families out there that want loved ones home for Christmas, too. I'm praying for them, too."

Karen was so immersed in her conversation with the Christmas tree angel that she didn't hear George lead Hans through the door in the kitchen.

George had even announced his arrival by explaining why they were a little late, but Karen was caught in the acoustics of her prayer.

George walked to the doorway leading to the living room. He started to speak, but suppressed his own comment and kept Hans tethered at his side.

Karen stood in front of the tree with her back to them. He listened respectfully as she continued to address the angel perched a foot above her at the top of the tree.

"Remember Dr. Theo Chase, the cardiologist from Charlotte? He had a rough Christmas one year."

Not expecting the ornamental angel to speak, she continued. "He was awakened by someone who knocked on his door at two o'clock on Christmas morning. When he opened it he found, to his surprise, a little girl seven or eight years old, I think. She was poorly dressed and deeply upset. She told him her mother was having a heart attack and pleaded with him to come with her. It was a bitterly cold, snowy night, but the doctor decided to accompany her to her house, which was only a few blocks away. He telephoned the hospital and instructed the ambulance to meet him at the little girl's house."

Karen continued as if she were having a conversation with an adult.

"He found the mother desperately ill, but still conscious. As he attended to her, he complimented the woman on the intelligence and resourcefulness of her brave little girl. The woman seemed perplexed and then angry. She finally told him that her daughter had died six months before. The cardiologist was flabbergasted. So he described the little girl in every detail. She told him he had accurately described her daughter all right, but her daughter could not have been the one to call for help that night. Her daughter was dead. Was this the work of a Christmas angel?"

An impatient stir by Hans caused Karen to wheel around facing them.

"You have the most angelic look on your face," George praised.

Hans barked his excitement. The look in his eyes beamed his undisguised longing for a quick reunion with his master.

"It's only been fifteen minutes since you've seen me, fella."

That's what I like about dogs, Karen thought. *They're always glad to see you, even if there's only been a few minutes' separation.*

"You're back," she addressed George.

"Yes, a little sooner than I expected."

"You heard me praying to the angel then?"

George nodded, making no attempt to conceal the smile which crept onto his lips.

"Well, I ... "

"No need to explain," he dismissed her attempt at an apology. "I've talked to angels many times."

"You have?"

He nodded his agreement and then leaned down to liberate Hans, who was already at the limits of his patience.

"I spoke to them about Pamela."

"I had no idea you believed in angels."

Reprieved from the leash, Hans bolted over to Karen, and gave her a few complimentary licks. Once he got the attention he expected, he shot back past George and into the kitchen to visit his ceramic watering hole.

The sound of Hans' dog tag rang out rhythmically against the side of the dish as he drank his fill.

"Yes, I believe in angels," George responded in his most clerical tone. Karen's raised eyebrows were a signal for him to continue.

"Angels belong to a uniquely different dimension of reality. Limited as we humans are to natural order, we can scarcely comprehend their presence. The fact that angels are mentioned in all the world's religions and have been painted and sculpted by thousands of artists who portray their characteristics with remarkable consistency, convinces me they are real and should be taken seriously."

Karen's eyes brightened.

"They are messengers from the multiverse, from a higher, more divine state of being," George added.

"There you go again, Grampa, spouting Unity theology." She teased. But then she continued, "Is that their chief purpose, as messengers?"

"As Christed beings, assigned to help us while we're in 'skin school,' they are just an affirmation, an affirmative prayer, a visualization away."

"Can we see them?"

"Many people do."

"Have you ever seen one?"

"Three."

Karen's face lit up. "Three?"

"Yes! Your grandmother, Pamela, and you," George smiled.

"Oh, Grampa."

"You're not talking to a theologian or a pope or a minister, but I can tell you from my own experience that I believe angels exist and their primary purpose is to provide guidance for us in human affairs. Many people believe, and your Grandmother and I are two of them, that angels could very well be more highly evolved intra-dimensional aspects of us. They are ambassadors, process champions, to use one of Pamela's terms, to help us successfully matriculate through this 'skin school' experience. And that school has many classes."

"What do you mean—classes?"

"Oh, let's see. The class called honesty, or the one called duty or commitment. Free speech, or love thy neighbor, or the care of your body, or the class called answering tough religious questions from your granddaughter."

"Which class are we going through now?" Karen asked, implicitly buying this explanation. Its spin was making more sense than she had realized at first.

As George settled back into his chair, she sank childlike into his steadily glowing words.

"In addition to answering tough religious questions from your granddaughter, I'd say we're experiencing the school of sometimes terrible things happen to good people," he guessed. "It's a school I don't want to visit too often."

"What are we supposed to learn from it? I mean if Pamela ... suppose she doesn't recover. What if she ... ?"

"Dies?" George finished her question.

Karen tightened her lips and nodded, a twinge of pain stinging her face.

"I don't even want to think about her dying. Geoffrey either. But if the worst happens, we have to realize that although we are spiritual beings in human form, we don't know all of the answers yet. The cures are there. We just need to find them. We need to stop spending so much money on war and spend it on health care and ways to help people."

Karen looked endearingly confused.

"Suppose physical death itself is a cure!" George summarized, looking directly into Karen's penetrating gaze.

Her chin dropped slightly and her mouth opened to speak words that never came.

"We just have to have faith, honey," he consoled, giving her a fatherly embrace. "I hope both kids recover. We'll just have to wait and see, and pray, affirming their highest and best."

Karen shook her head and a smile creased her face. "With a little help from our friends—those heavenly process champions. Right?"

"Right."

George lightly kissed her cheek. "Well, we'd best be going. Your grandmother is expecting us."

Karen picked up the travel bag that contained Pamela's belongings. Then she walked purposefully into the living room and retrieved her boots, which her grandfather had deposited sometime earlier near the hearth. She pulled each boot on rather decisively, enjoying the sensation of warmth each radiated from her feet up her calve through her jeans. She smiled her satisfaction at her grandfather's thoughtfulness.

"Grampa, you done good. They feel wonderful!"

George smiled and winked his approval.

Hans settled in his place on the rug near the glowing ashes in the fireplace. Somehow he sensed he would be left behind.

Poor dear, Karen thought, *he knows we're leaving. Dogs are creatures of habit,* she reasoned, *so they probably catch on to routines faster than most people.* That last thought struck her as funny. *There I go again, subscribing human qualities to a mere animal.* It produced a little chuckle that faded as she grew more melancholy. They were going to the hospital again.

She sighed heavily as she slipped into her ski coat, poking her scarf in as she inched the zipper toward her chin. She slapped the bright red wool cap on her head with a flourish and glanced at George, who was closing the brass and glass windows on the hearth.

As he straightened, she could see the effect of three weeks of stress and fatigue as he rose slowly, arthritically. But his eyes had not lost their glow. And there was a sense of duty etched on his weathered face.

To her surprise, and then to her amusement, he stopped before he got to the dining room door and retraced his steps. A quick wink told Karen something was up.

George went over to her baby grand piano and dashed off a reverent version of *I'll Be Home for Christmas*.

Karen felt the tears come.

"Yes, God. Let Pamela come home for Christmas," she whispered aloud.

"Life must go on, in spite of accidents, and Asheville winters, and concussions, and anger, and fear and ... a rusty pianist at the keyboard," George chimed.

"I love you, Grandpa." Her salute was in words, admiration in her eyes.

"I love you, too, honey. Well, we'd best be going." He slid himself into his coat and left it unbuttoned.

"I'll make a quick call to Constance to let her know we're on our way. It's right at twelve o'clock and I don't want her to think we've forgotten about lunch."

"Sorry old boy," Karen addressed Hans as she gave him a quick pat on the head and then made a quick exit behind George.

§　§　§　§　§　§

"Oh, hi, honey, everything okay?"

"Yes, we're leaving now. How is our granddaughter?"

"Still no change, outwardly. I thought I saw her move last night. But it must have been my imagination. She's been quiet ever since. The doctor was in this morning and said she's doing fine. He was encouraging. They've been very good here. The care continues to be excellent."

"Good. Karen just pasted another smiley face on the calendar this morning. It could be today, you know."

There was no immediate reply on the other end of the line.

"Constance, are you all right?"

"I'm fine. I've prayed so hard. Every day, in my mind, I see her sit up and smile at me. Oh, George what are going to do if ... ?"

"We're going to hang in there together and see her highest and best," he interrupted. "She's going to pull through this. And so are we. Both kids are resilient. All I know is the ultimate cure comes from love, not logic." He paused to catch his breath. "Have you heard any news about Geoffrey today?"

"Ted was in at 9:15, just after Dr. Schoenberg left. Geoffrey's had a setback."

"Oh, no—what happened?"

"He developed blood clots in both of his legs."

"Oh, my God, how serious?"

"They've got him on blood thinner. I think it's Heparin. I'm not sure. They said that's not unusual, the blood clots, I mean. Young active men who get laid up by an accident are at risk of developing blood clots."

"I didn't know that."

"The doctors found the clots in time. Ted says the thinner should control the clots long enough for them to dissolve. We can thank God for small miracles. He'll be on the intravenous blood thinner for at least two weeks. Then they'll put him on Coumadin for at least six months."

"That boy has been through enough hell. I'm so sorry to hear he had clots. How's Ted holding up?"

"Okay, but the blood clots rocked him a little. He said to thank you for your phone call last night. It helped fortify him for the bad news he got today. I invited him to eat with us, but he said he's tired.

"The pot of vegetable soup Karen took over a few nights ago has been his sole nutritional source. I chastised him for his eating habits, but you know how Ted is ... how men are."

George laughed. He usually thought of something to say in response to Constance's banter when it was too late to be funny. However, this time he thought of something cute.

"Tell me how men are, Dr. Philipia," he bantered suggesting a female imitation of Dr. Phil.

Constance laughed heartily.

It was good to hear her laugh again. It was the first time she had given herself permission to lighten up since they arrived in Asheville. With his usual diplomacy, George changed the subject.

"I've got the cleanser, moisturizer, foundation, blush and lip gloss you asked me to bring. Anything else?"

"Lipstick. Bring her favorite. Very Berrie."

"Oh, Okay, Very Berrie," he repeated and smiled wryly. "We'll have to pick that up on the way. The names those manufacturers come up with these days. What's the difference between lipstick and lip gloss?"

He felt Constance smile on her end of the phone.

"Lipstick is the color, lip gloss is the shine."

"Oh."

"Some women wear one or the other. Other women wear both. Pamela wears both."

"Very Berric lipstick coming right up. Anything else?"

"Yes, but you're already in the car."

"We're stopping for lipstick."

"Okay, I could use some Tylenol. I've got another one of those pesky headaches. Buy a small container of Tylenol. No. Wait. Just pick up some at the hospital when you get here. I'll keep them in my purse." She paused briefly and then added, "I wish I had told you to bring that crossword puzzle book I started. I feel like working on that some more."

"Karen's already thought of that. She's brought the Dickens book, too.

"A Christmas Carol?"

"Yep!"

"She's earned her wings."

"Anything else? Last call."

"Just you two. I believe I have a luncheon date with two very special people."

His smile came to her.

"And we look forward to dining with a very special lady. See you in a few."

"Not a minute longer, mind you. You don't want to keep Dr. Philipia waiting."

George chuckled. "The good doctor, maybe—my sassy wife, never."

"Drive carefully. I love you."

"Ditto."

CHAPTER ELEVEN

Christmas Eve resembled a frozen tempest from Siberia. The rogue progeny of some massive nor'easter had descended on the western part of the state, extending north to Virginia and Pennsylvania and then through Maryland and Jersey northward. The Chicago area and the Mid West were buried two days before. The Poconos were under siege with twenty-eight to thirty inches, and Philadelphia was buried under eighteen to twenty inches. It was a slow-moving storm, promising accumulations from eighteen inches to twenty-four in Asheville, which already had accumulations of six to twelve inches.

George stood at the hospital room window, its blinds open in horizontal slits to allow light in. He watched the snow fall in small flakes, tossed about by gusts of wind that carried them like tiny missiles across the parking lot. A nicely dressed couple was having considerable trouble with a recalcitrant umbrella that seemed determined to invert itself with each gust of wind. Someone else had slipped in the snow and was being helped up. The parking lots were accessible, but Mother Nature's white crystalline "storm troops" outnumbered maintenance crews and covered the parking lot with another two to three inches of white stuff every ninety seconds.

Karen leaned against the other side of the window, in silent vigil, watching the same scene unfold.

The Styrofoam coffee cup in her hand was uncovered, sending small whiffs of steam rising from her cup. The last half dozen cups had been bitter and scalding, so she stirred the coffee a few times with the wooden stick before taking a cautious sip.

George watched her reaction as she jerked her head back after burning her lips again on the scalding liquid.

"Too hot, again?"

"At least it's wet ... and caffeinated ... and it gives my nervous fingers a focus."

George smiled. He had stopped drinking it for that very reason. He tilted his head, directing Karen's attention to her grandmother who was asleep in the chair.

Karen smiled broadly, and then whispered softly, "She has to be zonked."

"I know, she's only left the hospital a couple of hours each day in the past three and a half weeks. I don't know how she does it. She's an extraordinary woman."

Their conversation had not gone unnoticed, since Constance had only closed her eyes momentarily, resting them from the strain caused by working too many hours on crossword puzzles. She used the puzzles to distance herself from the stress of the interminable waiting.

Constance was managing reasonably well by her own standards. Her antennae remained constantly alert for any sound in the room, particularly when she had her eyes shut. She didn't want to miss any kinesthetic nuance or technological glitch that signaled a change in Pamela's condition.

Fully aware of the watchful eyes of her audience, she repositioned herself in her chair and laid the puzzle book aside.

"I'm not asleep," Constance reported. "Just resting my eyes."

Both her watchful roommates gave her patronizing smiles. And George added a raised eyebrow to punctuate his suspicions.

"Resting your eyes, huh?"

"You looked like you were asleep to me," teased Karen.

"Think what you want, you two," Constance grinned. "I was just resting my eyes."

Her vigilant eye caught something out of place. She leaned forward and gently pressed down a loose piece of tape that had come unstuck from one of the catheters in Pamela's arm. Her eyes darted up at the battery of electronic gadgets that encircled her granddaughter. Her critical eye carried out a perfunctory, but systematic check as she scanned the screen, valves, and fluid levels, to make sure nothing out of the ordinary had happened while she dozed. Logically, she knew it was all computerized and that alarms would sound the nurses' station just down the hall if anything went wrong, but she had to see for herself.

Both George and Karen turned toward the window again, just in time to see a snowplow sweep into the main entrance to the hospital, pushing the snow aside as it chased the flakes off the driveway.

"Looks like we're in for a white Christmas," Karen predicted.

George nodded.

"That will make two white Christmases in a row," she added.

George nodded again.

"Here in Asheville, that is. You-all didn't get any snow at all in Raleigh last year, did you?"

"No, and you can keep all of the white stuff here, young lady."

"We don't want any of it," Constance interjected.

Karen smiled and peered out the window again.

Unapprehending the world outside, her embattered sister lay silently fighting for her life, buried in the privacy of her coma. It had been over four torturous weeks since her accident and her improvement had come in micro measurements, but it had come nonetheless. Her food was still being delivered through a plastic tube. And three times a day a physical therapist expertly worked her limbs and massaged her muscles like an athletic trainer to prevent her muscles and joints from wasting away. The manicurist had been in again and the doctor had removed the bandages from her head. The portions of her hair that had been shaved to allow the doctors to treat her head wounds sprouted new growth. X-rays showed her pelvis and leg injuries to be on the mend, too.

Constance felt like quite the nurse. Both she and George had become increasingly proficient in assisting the therapist in keeping Pamela's limbs limber and well-circulated. She had also assumed responsibility for cleaning Pamela's mouth, eyes, and ears, and changing the urine bag when it got full. She even enjoyed washing the scars on Pamela's legs and hip since the doctors had taken the stitches out.

George turned toward Constance.

"Can I get you anything, dear?"

Constance halted her advance toward Pamela only long enough to give her reply. "No thanks. I'm fine."

As George watched Constance wipe a trickle of saliva from the corner of Pamela's mouth, he remembered something she said to one of the nurses a few day before. He couldn't remember exactly how it came up, but the subject of Pamela's complete recovery had been discussed. The nurse indicated how impressed she was with Constance's caretaking. But the nurse had sounded a little too condescending. Constance thought the nurse meant she was over-doing it, that she was cleaning the patient's mouth out too much, combing her hair unnecessarily, or spending too much time in the room.

Constance was offended and took it upon herself to set the nurse straight. She had informed the wide-eyed nurse that every wipe, each touch, all of the hair brushing, every speck of lint removed from her granddaughter's hospital gown, each polished nail, including toe nails, every card read, each CD played, were absolutely necessary to show Pamela, on whatever level she could understand, that those who loved her wanted her back.

The more we communicate with her in words and actions, Constance had predicted, the more she will want to communicate with us—to come back to us.

They both knew that their granddaughter had one essential ingredient, one vital quality that would propel her beyond crisis. And that characteristic was an enormous capacity for survival—and the ability to choose life over death.

Her grandparents knew Pamela understood that death is the destruction of human physical form, not life itself. George remembered hearing Pamela say many times that 'we are divine beings stuck in the world in physical form. The world is the staging area for our transformation, our evolving selfhood. We owe it to ourselves to live fully, responsibly and lovingly—and to make our transition with dignity, pain-free, and in the presence of loved ones. In most cases, death itself is a choice.'

George could almost hear Pamela's voice as he recalled her quote, and thought, *Death isn't always a choice, dear Pamela. Sometimes situations determine if people live or die. Your parents, my daughter, and son-in-law, died when their plane crashed into a mountainside in Peru. The people on that plane did not have much of a choice. Bodies tend to disintegrate on impact when a plane goes down.*

His eyes began to well up with tears, prompted by the conversation he was having with himself. He began to give himself a pep talk instead.

Pamela's body has not been destroyed, he reflected earnestly. Her body is still intact. She will come back to us.

The sound of Karen's voice lifted George out of his mild trance.

"Gramma, Grampa, I've got to go now. I've got to stop by the Post Office and mail those letters, then run to the grocery store for some odds and ends: orange juice, napkins, and a few other things before it gets too bad out there."

George waited to see if Constance wanted to add anything to the list, like egg nog. Satisfied that she wasn't, he gave Karen a preemptory nod and added, "Egg nog would be great."

"Okay, honey, be careful," Constance cautioned as she kissed Karen on the cheek.

Karen grabbed her coat to go, but was detoured by one of her own thoughts. "Gramma, would you like to accompany me to the canteen for a cup of coffee on my way out? You could use a break and I need to ask you about an idea I have that involves Grampa."

Constance was about to decline her offer, but saw the common sense in it. George tossed Karen a wink and gave Constance a go-ahead smile.

In a few minutes he was alone and his thoughts turned to one of Karen's errands. He was so proud of her. She had done an extraordinary job contacting Pamela's clients, notifying them of her accident, and handling the cancellations of programs which would have to wait for her sister's recovery. For a young woman who was not a number cruncher, Karen had expedited the return of deposits and consulting fees with such dispatch that she had amazed everyone, including herself. She had flown to Raleigh a week before and collected anything that looked pending or important for Pamela's office files and desk: Rolodex®, calendar, phone log, accounts receivable, accounts payable, contracts pending, prospect list, telephone follow-up list, bank deposits.

She had returned to Asheville a new woman, business folders and brown leather attaché case in hand. Her weariness had dissipated completely, and vibrancy had returned to her face. She had become a self-appointed interim partner in her sister's business.

Pamela's clients were shocked at the news of her accident and most were gracious sin sending cards, large bouquets of flowers, and E-mail get-well wishes. A few had even visited the hospital, as testimony to the close relationship she had developed with them over the years. The Belgians were most hospitable, indicating they would postpone the training and teambuilding programs until Pamela could present them.

"Karen has done a masterful job for you, honey," George whispered, as he stood near Pamela's hospital bed. "She has taken care of all of the adminstrivia in your business while you've been away. The only work you'll have to do when you get home is get well."

Her room was filled with Christmas decorations, a small three foot artificial tree trimmed with get-well cards, a half dozen or so pots of red and gold artificial poinsettias, some holly and a Christmas stocking stuffed with her favorite make-up, soap, mouthwash, toothbrush, toothpaste, brush, shampoo and conditioner.

George reached down affectionately and smoothed his granddaughter's stylishly cut, surgically modified, jet black hair. It didn't need it, since Constance had just brushed it to perfection a few moments before. But George needed to feel her warmth, her ongoing life. The patches of shortened hair contrasted with her long silken strands and gave her the appearance of a punk rock star. In a poignant display of affection he leaned over and kissed the stubbles of hair spawned over the area claimed earlier by scalpel cuts and razor blade.

A deep flush migrated up his neck and spilled up to his cheeks, emotional preambles to tears that began to collect in the rim of his eyelids.

"It's Christmas Eve, young lady, and you still haven't wished us a Merry Christmas," he said, his voice quivering with emotion.

He paused, waiting for a miracle, then took a deep breath and forced himself to continue talking.

"Time for some Christmas aerobics," George announced, as he pushed up his shirt sleeves and pulled the chair Constance had used closer to the bed.

He began with the injured arm, the one with the pins in the elbow, and inclined it slightly from the wrist. He worked her fingers, separating them one by one, bending them, manipulating them into a loose fist, backward and forward, squeezing and massaging them ever go gently. Then he worked his way back up to the wrist, repeating the gyrations that he learned from the physical therapist.

He migrated to her elbow, steadying it with one hand, and lifted it just enough to rotate the upper arm at the shoulder. At the same time, he reduced the pressure on the elbow. The routine complete, it was time to move around to the other side, so he laid Pamela's arm gently at her side. He took a little longer with the other arm, giving it a few more bends and twists, since it was her good arm.

Next he moved to her lower extremities, but limited his physical manipulation to her feet and lower legs, so as not to re-injure her hip. Both he and Constance had relegated that sensitive tampering to the physical therapist. Her legs were slim and well-proportioned, and sinewy, the legs of a swimming champion turned runner. But he could feel a slight atrophy in both her calves.

Perhaps, he thought, *they are sleeping, too, waiting for Pamela to get in control of herself.*

Having completed his kinesthetic responsibilities, he moved back to the foot of her bed and looked intently at her comatose figure. Although a pinch of color was back in her face, she remained generally pale and helpless, uncommunicative except for the rise and fall of her chest as she breathed on her own.

Please, honey, come back to us. We need you. We're not a whole family without you.

He ached to see her move on her own, to be the beneficiary of one of her trademark smiles. His lips tightened as he remembered that someone out there was responsible for her condition. Marshaling his composure to cool his anger, he decided to pray.

"Because I have transcended my need for self-righteous malice, I forgive the one who did his best to take our granddaughter from us. We love her and want her back. I affirm her continued strength. And her restored health and wellbeing. And so it is!"

"It's Christmas Eve, ole body," he addressed himself aloud. "Must let the angels do their job."

He remembered the news of a few days before. Geoffrey supplied information to the police regarding the accident. The car that hit them was a Mercedes, an older model, an '80's model, black. Geoffrey believed it was occupied by three, maybe four people. A man was driving, but he did not see him well enough to make an identification. He knew the license plate was from North Carolina and that two of the letters were 'N.C.', but that's all he had time to make out, even with his trained investigative eye. But it gave the police something to work with after weeks of clueless investigation.

Officer Holland had dropped by a couple of times and offered his prayers to both families. He assured them the department was doing everything it could to apprehend those responsible.

George believed him. He was generally a good judge of character and Officer Holland seemed genuinely interested in solving this case, particularly since Geoffrey was one of their own.

"She's looking good today, Mr. Lee," a nurse entered, cutting into his thoughts.

"Yes, she is ... " George struggled, seeking the appropriate word. "She seems to have more color today. I've just finished giving her a workout."

"That's good, you keep working those muscles and reading to her," the nurse continued, as she busied herself monitoring the fluid levels in the clear plastic bags overhead and checking the valves which regulated the flow. Her eye spied a book lying next to Pamela's bed. "What's that you're reading her now?" She answered her own question, once she took a closer look. "*A Christmas Carol* by Charles Dickens," she read aloud.

"Reading it is a family tradition every year."

"Oh, isn't that nice. You're a close family, aren't you?" she asked, as she completed her scheduled checks. Then she turned to face him.

"We try to be," George hoped he sounded gracious.

"When you've been in the profession as long as I have, you can tell. You know, Mr. Lee, there are some families that only visit during regular visiting hours and some hardly visit at all. But you and your wife have been here every day ... and your other daughter, Karen. That's her name, right?"

George nodded, and decided not to make as issue out of her mistake about the girls' genealogy.

"She's been so nice to keep us well supplied with cookies and brownies. You have a wonderful family."

"Thank you," George threw her a gratified smile and then gave her a light appreciative touch on the arm.

"I'll be here 'till midnight, so I'll be checking in occasionally. Thought I'd give her a Christmas Eve bath later. You take care, Mr. Lee. I'll see you, or the Mrs. around nine."

She started toward the door and then stopped. Her eyes came to him as she spoke more slowly than was her custom.

"Mr. Lee, I've prayed for that sweet little thing every day." She touched the pin on her shoulder. "I rub my tiny guardian angel here and say a prayer for that beautiful daughter of yours every night just before I fall asleep. She's on our church prayer list, too. I hope you don't mind."

George shook his head." Thank you so much and, of course, we don't mind. How kind of you to include her in your prayers."

Satisfied she had expressed her feelings adequately and tactfully, she exchanged cordial smiles with George and turned to go. *Families like the Lees help make this job worthwhile,* she thought. *Intimate talks like these are such privileged encounters.*

She stopped again before she reached the doorway. "Mr. Lee," she said, pausing thoughtfully to give him time to make eye contact. "It's Christmas Eve." Having announced the obvious, she closed the distance between them.

"Do you mind if I give Pamela a Christmas gift now?" She had already decided her question was rhetorical because she reached up to unfasten the tiny brass guardian angel pin from her uniform.

Caught off guard but warmed by her generosity, George saw no need for protracted debate.

"You don't have to do that."

"No, please, I want to ... Mr. Lee. I would feel better if she wore it. I've wanted to give it to her since Sunday." Sensing his unspoken agreement, she fastened the angel on Pamela's hospital gown near her neckline.

"There now, Luke," She spoke softly, directing her valediction to the angel, "you take good care of her." She threw George a charitable glance and retraced her steps toward the doorway. He could see her take a tissue from her pocket and wipe her eyes just before she vanished down the hallway.

His eyes settled on the pin. "That's two angels," he began slowly, talking to himself out loud. "Where two or more are gathered together ... " he purposefully dampened his own words as he thought about the angel on the tree. Then, sparked by an insight, he walked briskly over to the book and sat down again beside Pamela's bed.

For as long as he could remember they had read this story to the girls. Both girls knew it by heart and could repeat the entire story almost verbatim. He turned to the bookmark that indicated where Constance had stopped reading earlier that afternoon. She had stopped at the place where the ghost of Christmas Future took Scrooge to Bob Cratchit's house. They had just finished the Christmas goose and were sitting in a circle around the hearth while Mrs. Cratchit prepared dessert.

George began reading aloud, his recitation a hymn:

"Merry Christmas to us all, my dears. May God bless us," Bob Cratchit proposed.

Which all the family re-echoed.

'God bless us, every one!' said Tiny Tim, weakly but proudly, as his little hands applauded the ceremony.

He sat close to his father's side upon the stool his father had made especially for him. His father pulled him up onto his lap, and silently dreaded the day Tiny Tim would be taken from them.

'Spirit,' said Scrooge, with an interest he hadn't shown before, 'tell me if Tiny Tim will live.'

'I see a vacant seat,' replied the ghost ... ."

George's voice trailed off. The implications of those few sentences tore at his heart. He wept uncontrollably and without embarrassment, as the tears flowed unabated down his cheeks and onto the worn pages of the book.

His tortured eyes fell upon the angel. "Tell me if my granddaughter will live ... will there be a vacant seat at ... ?"

The tears came again, bringing with them a loud gasp from his lips. He emptied the last four weeks of abysmal lows, fears, anger, hatred and depression into the cathartic moment.

He remembered something he'd told Karen earlier—suppose death itself is the cure. His sobs were the tears of a grandfather who wanted his granddaughter to live. He was not ready to let her go. *Modern medicine,* he agonized, is *hell-bent on cure and has no interest in the soul. It wants to eradicate all anomalies before it understands their relationship to the soul within. It abstracts the body into chemistries, organs and anatomies so that the spiritual self is hidden behind graphs, electronic displays, charts and numbers.* Another thought pierced his consciousness. *I shouldn't condemn the entire medical profession. There are some who treat body, mind and soul. Forgive me. I can't ... we can't do this alone.*

In his grief he did not notice Constance enter the room. Her initial concern about her husband's distress was vaporized in an instant. Her eyes were riveted on Pamela.

The movement was so slight that she dismissed it at first, believing she had imagined it. She thought she saw Pamela's head move to one side.

She took a few more tentative steps toward the bed, and thought she saw her granddaughter's finger twitch.

"George," she screamed, jolting him completely out of his chair.

As he stood, wiping his eyes with the back of his hands, he threw her the most confused look.

"She moved. I think I saw Pamela move."

She flew to the other side of the bed and mimicked George as he leaned closer to Pamela.

Nothing! Pamela's face was angelic, but motionless. The only movement was the top of her chest which rose and fell rhythmically with each breath she took. She had been breathing on her own for over two weeks. Constance's gazes met George's expectant look. Guarded hope was written across both of their faces.

George caught something out of the corner of his eye this time. Constance saw it, too.

"There!" Constance screamed jubilantly, pointing to Pamela's finger. "She moved her finger again."

George quickly glanced at the hoard of machines that monitored her vitals. The screen that monitored her heartbeat came to life. Pamela's heart rate had stayed constant at sixty-eight for almost a week. But now, he noticed, it was considerably higher. Eighty-nine, flicking to eighty-eight as he watched.

Constance found the monitor, too, and was becoming more animated by the moment. She grabbed Pamela's hand and began stroking her hair.

"Pamela, dear," she intoned, her voice rising to a higher pitch. "It's me. Your grandfather and I are right here, baby."

George looked around hurriedly. There were no nurses in sight. Another entreaty by Constance averted his attention to his granddaughter.

"Pamela!"

She squeezed Pamela's hand again, and George saw the monitor go crazy. Ninety-five, a hundred, a hundred and five ...

This time her name left George's lips.

"Pamela, honey?"

Constance straightened a little, trying to dislodge the crick in her lower back, but still held Pamela's hand firmly.

George peered into Pamela's face, scrutinizing every inch of her face for a sign, any sign of movement. He finally collected enough wits about him to summon a nurse. But before he could, the nurse who had given Pamela the angel pin and a young resident arrived at the door. The change in Pamela's heart rate had registered on one of the display monitors at the desk.

"We saw her move," came George's spontaneous report.

"She moved her head, I think ... and her hand," Constance amplified. She took a tentative step backward to allow the doctor access, but refused to release her hold on Pamela's hand.

"Squeeze her hand again," instructed the doctor in a heightened but definitely clinical tone. He took a penlight out of his white coat pocket and lifted one of Pamela's eyelids with his free hand. He switched on the light and peered into her left eye, watching for a reaction. Then he repeated the procedure on the other eye.

The nurse watched the monitors and rattled off the numbers with a cadence that was experienced and clerical: one hundred and fifteen, one hundred twenty-four."

"Say something to her again."

Constance raised her eyebrows and shot a quick look at George, whose eyes were locked onto Pamela's face. She swallowed and then shivered as she squeezed Pamela's hand again. For a split second, dumbfounded, she couldn't think of anything to say. Impatiently the intern looked up at her.

"Just say something. Anything! It doesn't matter what you say."

"Pamela. We're here, darling. It's time to wake up. We're right here, baby."

"Please, honey," George echoed, "we're waiting for you."

"Look! There!" the doctor emphasized.

Constance witnessed the flicker in her eye, too. She felt Pamela's hand constrict slightly. A noticeable gasp escaped Constance's lips and she rocked back and forth with excitement.

George beamed with relief.

"Her blood pressure is up to one-thirty," chorused the nurse.

Both of the Lee's shot quick glances in the doctor's direction, concern registering in each of their faces.

The doctor spoke quickly and calmly, cognizant of their distress. "Relax, it just means she's responding. It'll go back down."

Then he held his hand out to Constance. "May I ... ?"

Constance gave him Pamela's hand and watched as he held her eye open with his left hand.

"Pamela," he said, in an even tone, "Pamela Justice, I'm going to squeeze your hand now and I want you to squeeze as hard as you can. Okay?"

He squeezed and then relaxed his grip. Then he squeezed again, looking intently into her eye.

"There," he announced. "Good girl." He passed her hand back to Constance. "Now I want you to squeeze your grandmother's hand like you did mine."

Constance held her breath as she eased her granddaughter's hand into her own. She felt it! It was like the first, faint tentative kick of an infant in the womb. Deep in the unfathomed depths of the subterranean sleep imposed by the coma, something shimmered and was making its way to the surface.

"Keep calling her name," the doctor encouraged.

"Pamela, come back to us, Pamela, darling."

"Pamela!"

"Pamela, honey."

Pamela had the strangest floating sensation as she glided through the darkness. She was in a tunnel, some sort of sheath or cylinder. At the end she seemed to be moving forward, into a bright light. The purest and brightest she had ever seen. At the lower end, or at least that was the way she felt about it, was a much dimmer light. She sensed that she was equidistant from both points of contact with the light.

She had the greatest urge to move toward the bright light, but voices emanating from the dim region seemed familiar. She realized that whatever direction she traveled was a matter of choice. And then a thought entered her consciousness that effortlessly helped her reverse her direction. My family. What will they do without me? They need me.

She recognized the voices now. One was her Gramma's, the other distinctly her Grampa's . They were calling her name. She sensed a longing to be with them. Suddenly she felt herself moving at a more accelerated rate toward the dimmer of the two lights. The sensation was a pleasant one. She felt safe. Suddenly a strange humming noise rose in what she believed to be her ears, although she had no sensation of actually possessing ears per se.

"Pamela." Constance shouted. "You're back. Thank ... " her voice trailed off as she began weeping tears of joy.

"Yes, yes!" were the words that shot out of George's mouth, as he gave a huge sigh of relief. "Pamela, honey, we're here. We love you."

Pamela opened her eyes and offered a weak smile. Although she was still a little disoriented, she knew she was back amongst the living.

"Merry Christmas!" the doctor smiled. "Your Granddaughter has decided to come home for Christmas."

CHAPTER TWELVE

The scream Pamela had suppressed for so long tore from her twelve days after she regained consciousness. Two vases of cut flowers fell victim to her anger as she reached out blindly and swept them cleanly off the table in a single wrathful motion. She sat there tearfully, ripped by despair yet seething in anger, as she watched the contents of the vases spill onto the tiled floor. The wall near the table had also felt the effect of her outburst, its surface christened now with the treated water and a few flower fragments from the spent vases.

She let out such a sorrowful cry that anyone, friend or stranger, who heard it would be unable to resist being drawn to her, sympathetic to the gravity of her anguish.

Just then a nurse, trailed by an aide, burst through the closed door. One look at the patient, followed by a quick glance at the broken vases and scattered flowers, told them Pamela was in no immediate danger.

"Are you okay, dear?" asked the nurse, in a well-modulated voice. She appeared unperturbed, yet concerned.

The nurse's entreaty was drowned out by the intensity of Pamela's weeping. Both nurse and aide stood at Pamela's side.

"Pamela, honey, how can we help you?"

A long sigh that was his name came from Pamela's trembling lips. "Geof ... frey."

"Pamela," the nurse repeated her name, as she knelt down in front of her. She faced her patient directly so she could see into her eyes.

Pamela's face, clouded with a free-flowing grayness, lightened a little when she saw the nurse. The deep circles under Pamela's eyes, red-rimmed and swollen, were testimonies to her dishevelment. She recognized the nurse, but chose to remain wrapped in her own personal veil of melancholy.

"He won't be able to walk again," Pamela sobbed. "He can't run anymore ... and it's my fault."

"You mean that nice young man in Room 4098?" sympathized the nurse.

Pamela looked at her tearfully and nodded.

"Aw, honey, that's simply not true," the nurse consoled, brushing a few strands of hair out of Pamela's face.

Then the nurse averted her attention quickly to the aide. "Why don't you take care of the mess on the floor and I'll spend a few moments with her."

The aide dutifully obeyed, stooping over to pick up the broken glass and flowers, which had landed in pick-up-sticks fashion on the floor. Then she retrieved a handful of paper towels from the bath closet and made short work of the rest of the clean-up.

Meanwhile the nurse talked to Pamela, consoling her, mothering her. Hot tears welled heavily into Pamela's saddened eyes. They spilled out over their mascara-less rims, rolling onto the front of her pajamas in small splashes. She wept as sorrowfully as she had wept when her parents died. Now her torrents of tears were for her friend, her Geoffrey, the man who saved her life.

She brushed the tears from her cheeks with the back of her hand and reached for one of the tissues handed to her by the nurse. Fighting for control, Pamela took a deep breath and wiped the next installment of tears away with a flourish.

"When I saw him yesterday, I was fine," she lamented, fighting back the tears which flowed unabated in salty rivulets down her cheeks.

"I know it must have been quite a shock for you to see your friend in such a condition," soothed the nurse.

Pamela gave in to the sobs again, which began to diminish and slowly subside.

The nurse waited patiently. Empathetically.

"I was so proud of myself. I didn't break down like this in front of him yesterday," she replied triumphantly as she blew her nose.

"You are very courageous, my dear."

Pamela looked into the nurse's eyes.

"One of the most difficult things in life is to see someone you love in the hospital. And it makes it especially painful to know that they have become disabled as a result of their injuries," the nurse consoled.

Pamela bravely held back the tears.

"Sometimes life deals us blows. And it's hard to accept things that seem unfair," the nurse continued, the words falling out of her mouth softly and affectionately as she cupped Pamela's face in her hands. She trained her gaze directly into Pamela's eyes and held it there.

Her reflective manner told Pamela the nurse was about to say something very important. As the nurse opened her mouth to speak, Pamela looked intently into her compassionate brown eyes.

"You did not cause Geoffrey's paralysis any more than I did. The accident did. And the accident was caused by the driver of the car who hit him."

"But I slipped and hit my knee," wailed Pamela. "I couldn't run." She paused, then continued in a trembling voice, "Geoffrey could have gotten away if it hadn't been for me."

"Now listen here young lady," the nurse's tone was firm, with a faint touch of sympathetic irritation. "Wasn't it you who told me yesterday that Geoffrey said it wasn't your fault?"

"Yes," Pamela let out a whispered response. Her faint voice struggled to lift itself above her guilt.

"Why do you think he told you that?"

Pamela could do no more than shrug her shoulders and smile wryly in reply.

"Because he meant it," came the nurse's hurried response. She followed it quickly with another more philosophical comment, one she hoped would help put her patient's guilt to rest. "Because he wanted to make sure you were out of harm's way."

Pamela sat a little straighter and made one more pass at her nose with the tissue.

"It was an accident. A terrible accident in which two beautiful young people were seriously injured," she reaffirmed, pausing to search for the right words. "One of those people," she stopped herself in mid sentence and pressed her palms against Pamela's face, "was not injured as seriously as the other."

Pamela bit her lip, intent on holding back the flood of tears she knew would come unless she censored them.

The nurse smiled affectionately and continued. "You don't have to wear the guilt ... you don't have to take responsibility for something you didn't cause. Please don't do that to yourself."

With those words the nurse realized that her own eyes had manufactured a few tears. But she wore them proudly, neglecting to wipe them away.

The two sat facing each other in reverent silence. The nurse rested cross-legged on the floor in front of her young patient, and Pamela sat in her wheelchair.

Pamela was the first to speak after the long silence.

"Thank you, Sharon."

The nurse smiled.

Sighing heavily to dissipate some of the tension, Pamela began again. "You have helped me more than you know."

"Well, I don't know about that."

"No, you really have. It wouldn't have been the same coming from relatives or friends. I'd expect them to say that."

The nurse smiled affectionately and patted Pamela on her knee.

Pamela returned her smile.

"After all, what are nurses for if we can't help our patients feel better," she acknowledged in a failed attempt to camouflage her embarrassment.

"I just feel so depressed sometimes. I'll be feeling better—like I'm in control of myself, then all of a sudden, wham—it hits. Depression." At that moment, Pamela felt the tears well up in her eyes again. She reached up to wipe them away, and said, "See. Here I go again!"

Sharon patted her arm and said, "You know, honey, contrary to popular opinion, we allow our patients to be depressed here in the hospital."

Pamela threw her a puzzled look.

"But we need to set a time limit. So, you can go ahead and be depressed, but tell me, just how long would you like for your pity party?"

"You're going to allow me to be depressed?" Pamela asked, wearing a look of mock astonishment.

"Yes, but you have to decide how long you want this mood to last. Just how long do you think you will need for a good, deep and dark, anguished fit of depression?" Sharon teased melodiously. She wanted Pamela to regain the confidence and control the staff had admired in her since her arrival on their floor.

"You're serious."

"As serious as hemorrhoids."

Pamela made a face before she smiled.

"Well ... " Pamela thought for a moment, "give me thirty minutes, I guess."

She laughed nervously.

"Okay," Sharon confirmed. She quickly rose and moved toward the door. "Thirty minutes it is. Then I want to see you with a smile on your face." She threw Pamela a quick wink and swished out of the room authoritatively, triumphantly.

Waves of tears still made their appearance during the next thirty minutes, but Pamela took quick peeks at her watch. She did not want to extend the premeditated Pity Party past the end of her thirty-minute assignment.

When the nurse reappeared in the doorway half an hour later, she was met by a more composed Pamela, a young woman resolute in improving both physically and emotionally.

"How's it going?"

"I felt a little silly at first, but gave myself permission to cry and pout for half an hour."

"Good!"

"I felt like I was playing a game with myself. But I was in control of the game."

"That's my girl. And you're right. You are in control of how you feel. Now, is there anything you need?"

"No, thank you. You're an angel of mercy," Pamela cooed. The smile that curved her lips confirmed her improved spirits.

"I understand you're going home on Friday," the nurse said, changing the subject.

"Yes, and I can't wait. Just two days, ten hours ... " she said, looking at her watch, "and thirty-five minutes. But who's counting?" Pamela's voice was only upstaged by the sparkle in her eyes. Then she added quickly, as if she were accessing her own private file of information. "I'm going to stay here in Asheville with Karen for a couple of weeks to gather the strength I need, and then I'm going home to Raleigh. My grandparents want me closer to them ... They've moved my office downstairs ... I have my office in my home ... My physical therapy will continue there," she trailed off, pinched by the reality of the changes ahead. Looking a little more somber she faltered, "I've ... I've got to put my life back together."

"From what I've seen of you this past month," praised the nurse, "you'll do just fine. It's January fifth. You've been in here

... let's see ... since December second, that's a little over a month ... thirty-three days," she cut her own sentence short, and gave Pamela a playful wink. "But who's counting? Right?"

Her levity was accompanied by a telling grin from Pamela who was beginning to feel much better now.

"Sharon, you are truly an angel," Pamela repeated. Suddenly she jerked herself upright in her wheelchair and raised her hands to her pajama collar, to loosen a small brass charm.

"I want you to take this ... "

The nurse interrupted her, "Don't you even think about returning that pin."

"But you gave it to me so it could help me recover. I'm recovered."

"I gave it to you so you would be protected by a guardian angel."

"Oh, Sharon, I know ... and, oh, you know how much it means to me. Please don't take offense. It's a beautiful gift, but you should have it back," she petitioned, trying to save face.

"Oh, honey, I'm not upset" dismissed the nurse in a clearly sympathetic tone. "I don't want you to feel obligated to return it, that's all. I gave it to you to keep."

"I know," said Pamela. "And I feel it really is a guardian angel."

Then her face brightened and her eyebrows disappeared under her bangs.

"Look, I know what we can do, if it's okay with you ... there's a little girl, Ruthie, down in pediatrics that could use an angel. Do you know who I mean?"

The nurse threw a conspiratorial smile that beamed with delight.

"What a nice idea. She could be touched by an angel, too."

"You mean it?"

"Does a doctor need patients?" the nurse asked rhetorically.

Pamela bounded with delight, wheeling her wheelchair around only to moan a second later when she hit her elbow on the chair arm. "Oh-h-h," she winced, and then groaned in a mixture of moans and chuckles.

The nurse winced and puckered her lips, unintentionally mimicking Pamela's mild outcry.

"Are you okay?"

"Yes-s-s," Pamela assured her as she continued to rub her elbow.

The nurse laughed lightheartedly.

"What?" Pamela gave her a quizzical stare. "What?"

"This seems to be where I came in." She took a short breath and tried to appear serious. "Asking you if you were okay."

That brought a smile from Pamela, who became more animated. "Let's take it to her now." She spun the chair around and wheeled toward the door.

"Hold on there, hot rod," joked the nurse, "wait until I see if she's awake." With that word of caution, she vanished through the doorway and proceeded down the hall toward the elevator.

Pamela advanced through the doorway and out into the hall, but halted her own progress, waiting for the all-clear signal from Sharon.

It came within moments, when Sharon poked her head out of the elevator, gesturing for Pamela to follow her to the child's room.

"Here we go again, Luke," Pamela addressed the angel pin. "We're off to heal another one."

§   §   §   §   §   §

"Where is she?" asked Constance when she found that Pamela wasn't in her room.

George was about to ring for a nurse when he saw Sharon approaching them quietly down the hallway. Her white soft-soled shoes moved across the slick corridor floor with measured routineness.

"Sharon, where's ... ?"

The nurse moved her finger to her lips making a hush motion. George took the hint and ducked back inside Pamela's room, sensing Sharon's momentum would carry her inside as well.

She appeared shortly, blocking the doorway.

"Pamela is downstairs in pediatrics visiting a little girl who could use a guardian angel." Then she proceeded to explain why Pamela had gone. Satisfied that she had given a proper report, the nurse enthusiastically asked, "Are we still on?"

"You betcha," George confirmed as he threw her a mischievous wink. Acutely aware of his wife's eagerness, he glanced at Constance.

"You've taken care of the logistics?" Constance directed her query at Sharon. But the smile that enlivened her face softened her playful façade.

"We're all set at our end. As soon as I get the signal, we're in business," Sharon assured as she turned to go. In a few moments, she suddenly peeked back in. "There it is! Look." She pointed to an orderly who was pushing a hamper from the service elevator.

"I'll keep Pamela occupied long enough for you to get the package in here. She's downstairs in Room 2057. Mr. Lee, call down to let me know when you're ready. I'll answer the phone."

With that last piece of instruction, she was gone, making her way downstairs to pediatrics to the room Pamela was visiting.

A few minutes later, on a signal from George, Sharon informed Pamela that her grandparents and Karen had arrived.

When Pamela wheeled herself into her room, she was met with a reception that caught her completely off guard.

She burst out crying and immediately extended both of her arms forward.

"Hans!"

Her tears were tears of joy as she spied Hans sitting on the hospital bed, licking his muzzle and wagging his tail.

In an instant he leaped off the bed and landed with his two front paws on Pamela's lap.

There wasn't a dry eye in the room as all four conspirators watched girl and dog reunite.

"Hans," rejoiced Pamela, "You really are all right! You're really here!"

Hans let out a compensatory bark that brought hushes from everyone present, but Pamela.

Sharon peered out the door to see if Hans' chorus had attracted unwanted attention. Relieved that it hadn't, she moved back inside and closed the door again.

"How did you ... ?" Pamela started to ask, but Hans licked her in the mouth.

Karen explained how they smuggled Hans through hospital security.

"We sneaked him in using the freight elevator, and a loyal orderly spirited our canine contraband through the corridors and up to the fourth floor. We couldn't have done it without Sharon."

Pamela gave Sharon an admiring glance and returned her affections to Hans, who was quite pleased with the ruckus.

Suddenly Pamela addressed the whole group. "Geoffrey must see him, too!"

Her request was met initially with raised eyebrows and lowered jaws as a look of amazement jumped onto all of their faces.

"Oh, no," Constance was the first to recover. "We're in enough trouble."

"Please, oh, please."

When Hans barked again to register his vote, Sharon decided two votes were a majority in this case.

"The dog will have to be moved anyway. His howls will eventually allow the 'enemy' to locate our position. So ... "

"Shh-h-h. Be quiet, boy," Pamela whispered aloud. "We're going to see our jogging partner. Remember Geoffrey?"

"Honey, I don't know if this is a good idea," Constance fretted.

"The worst they can do is kick us out, and I've only got two more days anyway."

George motioned for both of them to lower their voices.

"Okay, okay!" Sharon capitulated. "Can you have him ready in five minutes?"

Hans was busying himself with a proper inspection of the wheelchair, sniffing and licking parts of the chair that interested him.

Pamela applauded. "Hans, we're going to see Geoffrey."

Hans looked at her, tilted his head to one side and let out a couple of muted yelps.

In a little while, Sharon gave a perfunctory knock at the door and then poked her worried head in.

"Come on," she said, "the coast is clear."

With a wave of her hand, Sharon led the group of co-conspirators down toward the elevator, followed by an orderly pushing a large hospital hamper. Geoffrey was about to receive a surprise visit.

CHAPTER THIRTEEN

esolve propelled her, and her tone was firm and detached.

"I can't believe you have the audacity to call me," Pamela spewed.

"I meant to call sooner. But my schedule has been unbelievable."

With surprising composure, she patiently waited for him to continue.

"Pamela, Darling, I ... "

"Stop right there Clarence," she interrupted. "When you left, you gave up the right to use such endearments."

"Pamela, Dar ... Excuse me, Pamela, will you let me speak?"

He had never experienced the new Pamela. He could feel the coldness in her voice, the sting of her words, her clipped manner. But there were a few things he wanted to say to remind her that no girl leaves him without his consent. "Give me five minutes."

"You've got two!" she severed his less than enthusiastic petition.

"Two? I can't ... I mean I can't ... "

"You're working just shy of a minute and a half!"

Her resolve was met with silence.

"Okay. Okay," he sputtered. "You've made it perfectly clear where you ... Look, I've learned from my mistakes. And she was a mistake."

"You see all women as mistakes," Pamela countered.

"I don't think I deserved that comment."

"You've got one minute."

"Now, Pamela, be nice."

There was an awkward silence.

"Look, I need to talk to you. One minute isn't enough," he bellowed.

"You're running out of time."

She prepared herself for what she knew would be a manipulative attempt to soften her. An abiding sadness blanketed her as she waited for his next pathetic rejoiner.

"You know how I abhor scenes," Clarence began.

"You abhor assertive women. Isn't that what you mean?"

"I asked you to give me half a chance. I'd like to explain," he countered in a rehearsed patronizing tone.

The sarcastic edge in his voice did not go unnoticed by Pamela, as she cut into his rationalization. "I think the explanation is very clear."

She was agitated with herself for allowing him to goad her into another ridiculous conversation. She swallowed hard and took a deep breath to control her anger.

"I'm trying to clarify it."

"You already have."

"Please, Pamela. Let me explain."

"Your time's up, creep!"

"Creep?"

"Perhaps you'd prefer something less complimentary?"

She waited him out.

"Contrary to popular opinion, I'm not the ogre you make me out to be," he challenged.

"I'm going to hang up now."

"No. No. Wait. Give me two more minutes. After all, you're the one who dumped me, you know," he challenged. His voice sounded a shade cooler.

"I found you in bed with another woman, you pontifical ape," she laughed. "What was I supposed to do, make believe it didn't happen?"

"I had hoped you'd forgiven me by now."

"For your infidelity? For your deceit? For your arrogance? Which one should I have forgiven?" She raised her voice again, incredulous at his insolence. She sighed heavily. "And for this phone call? Should I forgive you for this phone call?"

"I know, I'm sorry, I should have called sooner. But I was recovering from my own injuries."

"Oh, please! I'm not even going to ask about ... What is this ... One-upmanship on trauma?"

"Didn't you hear about my broken leg at the Super Bowl? I broke it in two places."

Pamela shook her head. "Too bad it wasn't your neck. Do you really expect me to believe you were injured? I know you, Clarence. That kind of stuff doesn't work anymore."

"No, really. I was laid up for six weeks."

"You're confusing me with someone who cares."

"I can fly in on the five-fifteen shuttle. You can pick me up at baggage claim, like you used to. Remember?"

There was a pregnant pause—a repugnant pause.

"We can make up for lost time. You want that, too, even though you may not know it now. Don't throw our love away just because I made one simple mistake. Pamela, darling. Pamela ... honey, I love you."

Pamela felt nauseous. But she was composed enough to launch a counter-attack with stinging sharpness.

"Save your money and your lies. Use your ticket to see a shrink. Better yet, buy a one-way ticket to Zaire ... or Belfast ... or Afghanistan."

"Now, Pamela, honey, I know you don't mean that. I love you. I want you to give me another chance."

"You have zero chance, Clarence. You're incapable of loving anyone but yourself."

"No, you're wrong about that. That was the old Clarence Blount. I'm a changed man."

Pamela shook her head, a tight curve forcing her lips into a stiff smile. She had had enough. Her accident had changed her life. It had caused her to reprioritize. She had concluded, after months of agonizing self-evaluation, that all she needed to do was to find her own depths, even if it meant facing every nightmarish shadow that lurked behind her.

"I know you don't believe it, but I've changed. I've really changed," Clarence petitioned.

Her broken body had given her time to heal her spirit ... to discover the real Pamela. Her thoughts drowned out his appeals as she thought to herself.

Everyone must pay attention to their inner wisdom, their own guide within. Without this source of wisdom, people are left with mere reason and logic and appearances as guides. Instead of seeking out personal odysseys, people prefer the shifting sands of opinion or policy or habit, which limit them to what they have been. People must be courageous enough to reclaim themselves. To uncover themselves. To express their inherent genius. They must become new and improved versions of themselves.

"Are you listening? Pamela? Are you there?"

She knew that Clarence represented one of the malevolent relationships robbing her life of joy, and she was not about to contaminate her new life with such a parasitic, diabolical influence.

Her thoughts worked rapidly for the appropriate words to terminate the conversation and eliminate any chance of Clarence's misunderstanding what she was about to say.

"Clarence," she said, pausing intentionally to control her response to his tasteless display of conceit.

"Yes, darling. I wondered if you were still there. You haven't said a word."

A protest sprung onto her rigid lips, but she remained resilient and focused. She rose from her chair in the living room and walked over to one of the front windows. She decided to stand for her farewell speech.

The heating vent under the front window sent a rush of heated air up the back of her legs and neck as it dutifully began its next cycle, oblivious to the emotional heat about to erupt in the room.

"Pamela, honey, say something."

"I loathe you. There must have been something good in you once upon a time; otherwise, I wouldn't have been attracted to you. But whatever it was must have been pushed out by your arrogance and pomposity."

Her tone was unmistakably flammable as she addressed the manipulative braggart on the other end of the phone.

"Now, Pamela," Clarence started to object.

"You saw me only as an object to be manipulated. Something to play with. An object to be tossed aside, discarded whenever I interfered with your next whim. Well, somewhere between the McDowell Street Bridge and the surgeon's scalpel, you ceased to exist for me."

"Pamela, honey."

"Let me finish," she flew into him. The tone and force of her voice demanded his unadulterated compliance.

"You are a taker, Clarence. You use people. You use people until you use them up," she blasted. She took a deep breath to slow herself down.

"When I first met you, you seemed interested in two things. Your NFL football career and me."

"Now, Pamela, I ... "

"I'm not finished yet," she warned, feeling more contemptuous and in control. His loathsomeness fueled her contempt. "Come to think of it, your interests were in exactly that order: football, then me. I don't know why I hadn't seen that before. Actually, I hadn't thought about it, but you've only really had one interest all along. Yourself. You sorry, pretentious, egotistical jerk."

"You forgot lonely," he injected with an evenness that would have disarmed her, had her guard been down.

"You really are a piece of work," she said, laughing bitterly.

"Thank you. Should I take that as a compliment?"

Pamela chuckled. "No, you simple-minded adulterer, it's an indictment."

"Adulterer!" he hissed. "Now look who's simple-minded. We weren't even married."

"I'd expect that coming from you." Her voice was cloaked with anger. "We were married emotionally ... and physically ... and spiritually, I thought. We were engaged," she blasted in a voice roughened with resentment. "An engagement means commitment. And commitment demands fidelity. You destroyed our love because it was easier to hurt me than face your own inadequacies, your own fears, your own selfishness, your own narcissism."

"Fear? What? What was I afraid of?"

"Intimacy ... commitment ... responsibility ... just to name a few!"

"Oh, come on, Pamela! How can you say that? I was good to you."

"Good to me? Good to me?" Pamela found her voice rising to a shrieking level. She took a deep breath to control her tone. It continued, cold and hard.

"You manipulated me. You saw me as an object ... a trophy ... something to be moved around, displayed. But when that object wanted something from you, you couldn't handle it. All I wanted was to be loved, Clarence."

He started to speak, but Pamela dowsed his feeble attempt to defend himself.

"You're not a very nice man, Clarence. You live in a world of testosterone and façade."

She halted her attack just long enough to catch her breath but not long enough for him to interrupt.

"Your arrogance will be the instrument of your undoing. It will lead to your ruin. You need help, Clarence. And I'm afraid," she said, pausing to correct herself, "no, I predict, your narcissism will destroy you, and anyone else foolish enough to hover blindly around you."

His silence confirmed her assessment.

"That's all I have to say, except I don't ever want to see or hear from you again. To use your expression, our relationship is history."

The uneasy cushion of silence was broken by a sinister laugh from his end.

Pamela almost hung the phone up, then wished she had.

"We finally agree on something," he began. "Quite frankly, I don't want to see you either. Who wants to hang around a cripple?"

Pamela recoiled, stunned that even he would stoop so low. His malicious defilement stung her.

She held back the tears that begged expression, refusing to give him the satisfaction of knowing he had wounded her.

"I won't dignify that remark with a response, except to say," she neutralized his bite, "I forgive you for your insensitivity, Clarence. I really do. I forgive you for your indecency. For the pain you must feel for your own inadequacies. For the hurt you cause people, especially people who love you."

She took a hurried breath and continued, "You need help, Clarence, and at this point I can give you neither help nor sympathy."

"Good-bye," she added. Not wanting to take a chance on another installment of his abuse, she quickly hung up the phone.

"I did it!" she squealed aloud. "Geoffrey will be so proud." A wide smile of self-congratulation streaked across her glowing face. She could hardly contain herself. "Yes!—I did it," she rejoiced.

She glanced at the clock.

"Three-fifteen," she noted aloud. "I've got to get ready for rehab. Gramma will be here shortly to pick me up."

Constance had insisted on chauffeuring Pamela to and from the clinic. Both George and Constance felt Pamela should take it slow. Go slow to go fast, George had reminded her. He read that somewhere in some Eastern philosophical writing. The ringing of the phone brought Pamela's thoughts back from the esoteric to the practical.

"That's probably Gramma," she whispered aloud as she eased her cell phone to her ear. Just as she was about to say hello, an icy voice sliced through her.

"Step out in traffic in front of me and I'll cripple you some more, bitch."

She stiffened as the words came at her. His searing callousness ripped her insides apart. Before she could respond, he continued.

"You think you're hot stuff, don't you? Well, watch your step, honey. I'm not through with you yet. I won't say good-bye now. I'll wait until the next time we meet."

Pamela closed her eyes and opened them just as Clarence hung up the phone. She let out a disbelieving sigh as she slowly lowered the cell phone to the top of the pillow.

Suddenly a chilling realization struck her. *This man was capable of more than emotional abuse. He's capable of assault.*

She tried to control a shiver that she felt coming, but couldn't short-circuit it.

He threatened me! He actually threatened my life, she announced to herself.

A long laborious sigh escaped her lips as she saw a teal-colored Taurus pull into the driveway.

That'll be Gramma. Get hold of yourself, girl, don't let her see you upset like this.

"Lord, please help me put that phone call behind me," she prayed aloud.

Pamela took a deep breath and closed her eyes. She planted a smile on her face and affirmed out loud, "I got rid of him, once and for all. I am in control. I feel terrific!" Then she grabbed her coat and headed for the door.

She waved to her grandmother as she pulled the door closed behind her, checking to be sure it was locked. She forced her thoughts away from the disturbing phone call and fast-forwarded to the upcoming therapy session that was next.

As she approached her ride, Pamela wondered how she would like the new physical therapist the clinic had assigned to her. He was replacing her original therapist, who relocated to another city, somewhere in the Southeast. The new therapist's name was Brad and he was the sort of good-looking guy who knew he was good-looking. She had seen him at the clinic, and she was looking forward to their first official meeting.

As Pamela slid into her seat, Constance greeted her with a warm smile and a quick hug.

"You look like you've had a good day."

Pamela hesitated, contemplating. "As a matter of fact, I have."

"Care to let me in on it?" proposed Constance, pleased to see Pamela out from under the veil of melancholy that had blanketed her for the past week.

"Maybe later," Pamela defined. "Let's just say I've kicked an old habit."

"Oh, good for you, honey," Constance praised, as she patted Pamela's leg, satisfied for now, at least, that her granddaughter was in good spirits.

A beam of sunlight cut through the car window, giving Pamela's hair a shimmering effervescence that lit up her face. The smile that inched its way across her beaming face was radiant. *Go slow to go fast,* she repeated to herself.

Her thoughts again centered on the young physical therapist she is about to meet. The curve of her smile extended a little.

CHAPTER FOURTEEN

One look into her eyes and Brad received her radiant smile. In his first appraising glance at her, he concluded quickly that to call her beautiful was too weak a description. *Striking is more like it,* he thought. *Peerless.*

Her face was delicately square, proportioned like a model's with lips full and sensual. Eyes as green as an emerald forest teeming with life, were punctuated with sparks of brightness and suggestive of something hidden just below a surface of intensity. His preliminary examination did not fail to notice her tantalizingly curvaceous figure that, he was certain, had turned many a man's attention in her direction. He could tell by her carriage that her black stretch leggings concealed long, well-formed legs.

His admiring gaze moved back up quickly to her sweatshirt, decorated with several appliquéd black and white pandas. He settled on her face again to meet her penetrating eyes, staring directly at him.

"Excuse me for staring at you. I'm so embarrassed."

Pamela smiled her amusement, granting him immediate and unconditional clemency.

"Suppose I begin again," he boyishly tried to recover.

Wanting to save what little face he had left, he stuck out his hand and introduced himself.

"Hi, I'm Brad Aikman. You must be Ms. Pamela Anne Justice." He kept his hand out, waiting for her to reciprocate.

"That simply will not do," she teased, as she completed the handshake.

Brad gave her a puzzled look. His lips started to form a response, but then retreated to their original shape.

"The formality, I mean," she bantered good-naturedly, taking pleasure in his befuddlement.

"Oh," he replied, grinning sheepishly. Although he tried to conceal his embarrassment, he knew enough about innocent foreplay to continue holding her hand.

"You may call me Pamela. I'll answer to that," she added. Thinking she would leave it at that, she found his awkwardness so endearing she decided to continue the fun. "Of course, if you prefer, Mr. Aikman, you may address me as Dr. Justice," she announced, pausing to catch his reaction. Satisfied she had thrown him a curve, she finished her sentence, "as was your predecessor's custom."

Brad gave her such an incredulous look that a mischievous smile slipped onto her face, making it impossible for her to keep a straight face.

"I'm kidding. You don't have to call me Dr. Justice. Pamela will do."

"Now, wait just one minute, young lady, that positively won't do ... the formality, I mean," he recovered, enjoying the emerging chemistry between them. "You called me Mr. Aikman."

Pamela mirrored his previous incredulous look. Then she raised an eyebrow, realizing for the first time that her hand was still wedged in his firm, but gentle grasp.

"Ms. Justice, Pamela, I mean, we had best begin your exercise or your time will be up before we've started." He checked his watch. "It's eleven ten, are you ready?"

When they released hands, the release was slow, as if some unconscious force required their touch to linger. As they walked toward the workout area, Brad reviewed her progress chart and discussed her rehabilitation activities. He praised her outstanding improvement and her more than modest advances in muscle strength and tone, range of motion, and stamina.

"My background is in sports medicine. So your rehabilitation will revolve around the concepts and regimens I use to recondition athletes."

"I see," Pamela said softly, pretending to understand.

He launched into a perfunctory stream of do's and don'ts, but stopped himself, realizing that Pamela was decidedly beyond the standard rhetoric reserved for most outpatients.

He was nervous with her standing so close, and was growing more uneasy by her proximity. He could smell her perfume—Opium, by Yves Saint Laurent, he guessed. He inadvertently brushed his arm against one of her breasts when he turned slightly to show her a notation on her chart.

Brad had the greatest urge to repeat the maneuver, but censored the counterfeit attempt. He did not want to offend the gorgeous creature positioned at his elbow.

She deserves my best behavior and my respect, he reminded himself. *The first touch was innocent enough,* his drifting thoughts concluded, *an accident. No use making either of us uneasy.*

Suddenly he realized he was explaining her workout schedule and thinking about her at the same time. He lost his train of thought and wasn't sure if what he was saying was making any sense at all. He chanced a quick glance at Pamela, who seemed quite content with his monologue.

There is something about her that makes you want to help her, he thought, feeling a bit unprofessional, *a desire to protect her, to make sure she is happy, to cover her mouth with kisses.* "What an understatement," he slipped aloud, catching himself too late.

"What?" Pamela asked, as surprise jumped on her face. "You think my long fingernails are an understatement?" She held up both of her hands, palms down, exposing well-manicured nails a full inch beyond her fingertips. The cherry-colored nail polish glistened as she turned her hands slightly back and forth.

"Oh, I'm sorry," he floundered, trying unsuccessfully to bridge the obvious misalignment in communication. "Did I say understated?" he asked, taking a stab at legitimacy.

Pamela gave him an amused nod. "I've been underpaid before, but never understated," she teased.

Brad winced.

They were sparring good-naturedly now and he knew she was a couple of moves ahead of him.

"Yes, you had mentioned the difficulty of my holding onto hand weights with these nails." She reminded him. Her deliciously mocking smile made her appear much more amused than agitated. She pushed her hands closer to his face and wiggled her fingers for emphasis.

Brad laughed heartily, prolonging his hilarity long enough to give himself time to think.

"No, they're beautiful," he recovered as he glanced at her nails. Then he admiringly held both of her hands, using his obligatory appraisal as an excuse to feel her warmth. "I was referring to the color of the hand weights!"

Pamela threw him a suspicious smile, but her eyes brightened, half with reserve and half in admiration for his skillful attempt to finagle his way out of another embarrassing moment.

"Hand weights?" she asked innocently.

"Yes, the hand weights," Brad grinned. "The color of the grips of the weights is certainly an understatement next to your nail polish." He paused, not certain if he had made any sense, but feeling pleased with himself for trying.

"Of course, the weight of the two-pound hand weights themselves may be an understatement," he added collaterally, hoping to reinforce his point. "They may be a bit light for you," he patronized playfully. "Perhaps you should start with three-pound weights—or even four," he winked, feeling his way around her sportive skepticism.

Pamela smiled approvingly and waited for the next tactful syllables to tumble out of his mouth.

"Let's see," he began again. "What does your chart say? Oh, yes," he ad-libbed, trying his best not to betray himself, "I see you're already up to five pounds, according to your chart."

She formed her lips into a contrived snoot.

"A bit understated, don't you think?" came Brad's swift retort, recognizing that she had seen through his little charade.

Joviality was in the air and both seemed pleased with the atmospherics.

Pamela stood with her back to the floor length mirrors and did not notice her host's wandering eyes.

He had caught her profile in the mirror and found himself admiring the view. Embarrassment carried his eyes to the floor.

Pamela's inquisitive eyebrows were her only indictment, as she waited patiently for him to continue his orientation.

He decided not to call attention to his momentary lapse in manners and instructed her to begin the first series of exercises.

She acquiesced obediently to his uncontested authority and busied herself with the routineness of stretching, bending, and tucking all of the appropriate parts of her anatomy.

As she stretched and began her first set of crunches, Pamela joined in the visual eavesdropping. She held her stare long enough to get a good look at him. She judged his height to be about six feet, maybe five eleven. His straight proud nose was set between two well-formed cheekbones with delicate shadows beneath that give his face a firm but aristocratic flare.

His smile was warm and congenial, adding an ineffable gentleness and cordiality to his over-all demeanor. There was a confidence in the determined lift of his head, yet she thought she detected a hint of vulnerability in his slate gray eyes. His athletic build was crowned by a head of golden hair that swept over his ears in blond sprays of shimmering echelon.

Her therapy, it seemed, was being undermined by stolen glances. *I like him,* she thought to herself. *He's able to mix the right amount of officiousness with tenderness and humor. He speaks softly and in clear sentences and seems more interested in me than the other physical therapist that stayed detached and had difficulty building and maintaining any degree of rapport. His sense of levity and warmth is definitely arresting.*

She ended her mental appraisal of him at the same time she ended her crunches. After a brief pause, she started her second set of sit-ups.

As she finished her last one, she sat up, placing her arms around the tops of her knees. The red lipsticked circle of her open mouth exhaled a controlled sigh as she enjoyed the break before her next set.

Her emerald gaze swept methodically around the room, lingering every now and then to assess the progress of someone else who labored at restoring health and mobility. One young boy, dressed in a Carolina Panther's sweat suit, stood at the railing. Evidently he was refusing to continue, because his therapist coaxed him in a manner consistent with a reprimand. Another patient, a woman in her sixties Pamela guessed, was being steadied as she walked slowly behind a wrap-around walker.

A half dozen or so people were walking around the track, some more briskly than others. Some were engaged in conversations while they walked, others were moving more quietly, yet just as purposefully. She recognized one of the walkers, an older white-haired man who always wore a Duke Blue Devil ball cap. He was moving with his usual gait, and with his characteristic limp, which didn't seem to slow his pace. His vitality reminded her of her Gramps, and she admired his drive.

Her unofficial reconnaissance fell upon Brad again, who was headed her way. Until now, he had been amicable, but she could see immediately that his face was etched with concern.

When he realized she noticed him, he attempted to conceal his consternation by turning his head, but his face was too readable to hide his thoughts.

"Let's take a quick trip over to the arm chair," he suggested, pointing to the apparatus wedged against one corner of the wall. His once confident voice seemed a little tentative as he addressed her.

"Anything wrong?" Pamela asked as she stuck her hand out for a lift.

"No," came his concise, if not slightly flippant answer. When he looked at her, he darted his eyes away from her inquiring gaze and then back again before he reached out to pull her up from her sitting position.

Pamela didn't pursue it, but it was evident that his joviality had evaporated. He seemed affable enough, but there was something amiss. His sudden change of attitude unsettled her, bringing an eerie sensation of nausea.

They stopped in front of the armchair, an exercise apparatus that looked like an elongated arm chair without a seat or legs. The arms protruded out from the frame and were about five feet high. Although she was fully aware of the procedure for using the chair, she listened patiently as Brad briefed her on the proper use of the equipment.

When he was satisfied that she understood, he helped her up so that her forearms rested horizontally on the arms and her feet dangled beneath her.

"I'd like you to push up slowly," he instructed, "by straightening your arms so you are supporting your weight with your arms. Then I want you to lower yourself just enough so you bend your elbows a little, then push yourself back up. Understand? How's that right arm?" he asked in a most decidedly clinical tone.

"Fine," she verified, and then added quickly, "of course, I guess we'll know more about that in a moment."

He shot her an encouraging look and then fixed his gaze on her arm as she initiated her first lift.

"That's good. Feel all right?"

Pamela smiled, then nodded.

"Okay, can you do three more?"

By the third push, Pamela found her arms wobbling as she tried to straighten them. Finally, out of sheer determination, she was able to push herself all the way up, extending her arms so they were straight.

"Bend the elbows just a little," he warned. "Don't lock them, remember?" Brad watched her move. His trained eye caught a hint of a reticence on her part to fully test the right elbow. Yet she moved with a grace that belied her injuries. His admiring gaze moved down to her forearms, then to her small wrists and hands, then to her slender fingers that griped the padded arms of the chair with such tightness that her knuckles had turned white.

"Relax," he whispered, then spoke a little louder. "Lower yourself now, that's all I want you to do."

"I want to try one more," she pleaded.

"No, that's enough for today. I don't want you to overdo it," he advised, as a smile creased his face. His affability was returning.

He kept his eyes on her as she lowered herself. She had a delicate toughness that heightened his admiration for her.

She chuckled, noting his swift change from solemness to gregariousness. Suddenly, a sensation of fainting weakness washed through her so completely that her arms buckled, sending her elbows crashing down on the padded chair arms.

But Brad was there. The muscles of his strong, lithe body uncoiled with explosive, yet precisely directed energy.

She felt his arms around her in an instant, cradling her from harm.

"I'm sorry," she apologized breathlessly, searching for his eyes. "Thank you," she followed, making no immediate attempt to free herself from his embrace, except to take her arms from around his neck as he stood her gently on the floor.

"I saw you start to tumble," Brad summarized as he gently loosened his hold on her. "Are you okay?"

She nodded, indicating that she was, and breathed a sigh of relief.

"How's your elbow?"

"Okay," she confirmed, and then validated its normality by bending it freely several times. "What's next?" she asked, as her face brightened.

"You want to continue?"

A broad triumphant smile was her answer. He shooed her toward the next apparatus and guided her through the next series of exercises.

Pamela could sense that he was more relaxed, but his reaction to something he had read in her chart still bothered her, so she decided to press for an answer.

"Brad," she queried innocently.

He fixed his eyes on her and raised an eyebrow in anticipation.

"You seem to be upset by something you read on my chart," she said, pausing to gauge his reaction.

It turned out to be only a slight tightening of his lips.

"Maybe I read you wrong or perhaps you were upset about something else, or maybe your distress had nothing to do with me," she continued breathlessly, squeezing out a stream of impressions. She let out a preemptory sigh. "If something on my chart bothers you, I want to know, otherwise ... "

"I feel I owe you an apology," Brad interrupted. He took a step toward her and placed his hand on her shoulder so that he stood slightly at an angle in front of her. After a slight hesitation, he looked at her. His eyes darted away, only for a moment, and then back again, finding her expectant gaze. "You are quite perceptive," he began. "I just read the medical report, the one that contained data about your accident last year in Asheville."

She tensed slightly, surprised at her own reaction to his mentioning the accident.

"I generally make it a practice to review a client's entire file so that I can design an treatment program that not only takes into account the injuries sustained, but a person's medical history, attitudes, outlook on life, and so on." He hesitated out of consideration for the mild shock that pinched her face. "When I read that it had been a hit-and-run, I wondered how anyone could leave the scene of an accident knowing someone was hurt." He shook his head and tightened his lips for emphasis. He looked away again momentarily before he reestablished eye contact.

Pamela managed to post a tentative smile before the tears filled their crescent rims under her eyes.

She graciously accepted the tissue he provided and used it to dry her eyes. "Thank you," Pamela said softly. "It's difficult for me to believe anyone could be so inhuman."

"I tend to get really agitated when people don't take responsibility for their actions, especially when those actions endanger someone else's life," he confessed. "Well, there I go again," he admitted, "spouting off, condemning society and upsetting my patients, all in the same conversation."

"No, it's okay—I'm glad you told me," Pamela replied diplomatically, "I was afraid I'd done something to offend you."

Brad was quick to explain. "No! No, of course not. It wasn't anything you did at all. When I see negligence on someone's part, negligence that ends up hurting someone, I generally get upset. I guess I'm especially sensitive to that kind of thing due to the business I'm in." He extended his arms outward and tilted his head toward the other patients in the workout area. "I know all about the long-term effects that accidents have on people's lives. I apologize again for upsetting you."

The lights in her eyes spoke her understanding.

"If you ever need to talk ... about ... you know ... your ... "

"Thanks, maybe some other time. I want to put all of that behind me. Life must go on, you know."

He gave her an admiring look. "Yes, you're right. It all comes down to that, doesn't it? The choice to go on," he interjected.

"People don't realize how important the power of choice is," she agreed, remembering something Geoffrey had told her. "It's one of the most," she accentuated by holding up her forefinger, making a gesture that indicated number one, "if not the most prized thing a person possesses. You cannot manage your life unless you manage yourself. And you can't manage yourself unless you manage your choices."

Brad lowered his gaze for an instant and nodded his head in agreement, lifted it, and found her eyes again. "That's good," he said, continuing to shake his head. "That's good. May I quote you on that?" he asked playfully, his smile eternally boyish.

"It's not mine to quote," she chimed, thinking of Geoffrey, "but you may use it anytime you want."

"I believe I will. There are a couple of patients of mine that need to hear good advice."

"Good," was all she could think to say as they walked across the now crowded workout room.

Brad could smell her sweet sweat and whiffs of her scented hair spray as he accompanied her to the cool-down area in the back of the room. Her long black ponytail fell to her shoulders in shimmering patterns of the blue-black silk as it moved rhythmically with her graceful stride.

He admired her toughness, her determination. She had caught his eye long before today, when she was working with David Young, her previous physical therapist. Normally he didn't eavesdrop on another therapist's patients. And he had always made it a point not to mix business with pleasure. Still she had caught his eye. And now, thanks to an incredible stroke of luck, he found himself assigned to her rehabilitation.

"See you Thursday?" he asked, trying to sound objective.

Pamela nodded her consent. As she watched him walk toward his next patient, she smiled. *I hope he's dropped some of his formality,* she mused, as she overheard him introduce himself to his next patient, using a familiar line.

"Hi, I'm Brad Aikman. You must be Mr. Amos Turbull Mintz, III," he said loudly enough for Pamela to hear.

His surreptitious glance in her direction caught her smiling. He was obviously teasing her again, because she had met Amos several weeks ago and knew Brad was his physical therapist. Amos was an extremely dignified-looking sixty-six year old Afro-American minister. He had suggested that she request Brad Aikman when it became apparent that her physical therapist was relocating to another city. Amos was robbed and beaten and his church burned by three teens several months before.

"They're in God's hands," he had said. "And the court's."

She discovered from one of the other rehab patients that he still prayed for the three assailants. She admired him for that, for his ability to forgive his enemies. That's a part of therapy she needed to work on, the part of her own rehabilitation she chose to neglect—the part called forgiveness.

Amos leaned toward Brad and whispered something in his ear. Then he winked at Pamela and gave her a thumbs up gesture. Brad was looking at her, too, smiling broadly.

Looks like they're up to something, she said to herself as she tossed a smile their way. She steadied her gaze on Brad. *I think he's going to be fun to be around.*

She decided to shower when she got home, so she headed to the door leading to the lobby. Just before she exited, she turned quickly, hazarding a final glance at the golden-haired merchant of rehab.

His slate gray eyes were trained directly on her.

CHAPTER FIFTEEN

amela winced as the razor-sharp pain flashed through her hips, legs, and elbow. It would be unbearable if it weren't for its laser-like brevity. Sometimes the pain forced her to stop exercising momentarily, until its lightning fast brutishness ended as quickly as it came.

Some breaks in her routine were longer than others, as she attempted to work her way through the slashes of cutting pain. She would fume inwardly at the prickly tormentors. Occasionally she would curse the treachery of her body, which she felt had betrayed her at a time when she needed, most desperately, to feel stable and in control. It had been four months since the accident and she was impatient to get on with her life.

Though Pamela was unable to completely put the past out of her mind, she found she could contextually compartmentalize it. Fear and pain were giving way to laughter, a therapy all its own.

A major source of that laughter was Brad. He was a consummate prankster, and kept her spirits lifted with his uproarious stories and good-natured teasing.

He tried to treat her like any other patient, but found he was not quite as impersonal with her. Lately his hand burned whenever he touched her to steady her progress or supported her as she braved each new tentative step. He had not allowed himself the luxury of these feelings before, but now he made no attempt to excuse himself for his quickening interest.

Brad couldn't keep his thoughts off her. She was a beautiful, confident, tough woman. He had seen that plainly the first time they met. In spite of her youth, she had a delicate toughness that was magnetic.

His compassionate, therapeutic side was making room for passionate, personal feelings. He wanted to discover more of her than Pamela the patient, Pamela the broken one. At first he thought he could bridle his feelings and remain professional. Now he knew all too well these intense feelings had slipped up on him, and that it was a little late to think about censuring what had now become yearnings.

I've got to get a hold of myself, he thought. *She's my patient. She's forbidden territory. I'm jeopardizing my career if I mishandle our involvement. Collateral damage. Isn't that what Amos called it when I mentioned my growing interest in her?*

But, damn it, I'm attracted to her. I feel like an irresistible force is pulling me steadily toward her. Therapist and patient may become lovers. What am I going to do then? If the association finds out it'll be the end of my career. And I hate to think what my family and friends would say if I throw my career away.

His thoughts were interrupted when his watchful eye suddenly became aware of a sudden break in her routine. Pamela had hesitated abruptly in the middle of one of her routines, paralyzed by a stab of acute discomfort. She held on the railing to steady herself, waiting for the streaking torment to subside. Then she lowered herself to the floor.

"Here, let me take care of that," Brad volunteered, as he placed his hands on her shoulders and began to massage her back.

Pamela inclined her head in a gesture of thanks. She was still reeling from the bothersome stab of pain that had migrated from her right triceps up to her shoulder and down to her lower back.

Brad moved his fingers rhythmically down her back and began a systematic treatment of rubbing each side of her back, focusing on her shoulder blades. Then he took his methodical kneading up her neck and down again to the middle of her aching back.

She groaned appreciatively with the relief of it.

She stood there, putty in his strong grasp as he worked her muscles free of the shooting pain. She yearned to lean back against him, have him cradle her in his strong arms. She wanted to nestle for a while, instead of having to pull away as soon as he separated her from her discomfort.

"M-m-m-m. That feels wonderful," she cooed softly as she tilted her head.

Brad smiled his appreciation.

"Simply wonderful. You've done this before."

"A few times," Brad boasted. "But only for my very special patients."

"Well, you sure know what you're doing!"

Sometimes, when he stood near her, poised to prevent her from taking a tumble, she wanted—even planned—to take an intentional stumble to send herself rushing into him. Other times, she plotted to use fatigue as a scapegoat to manufacture a sudden decline in her strength, compelling him to hold her close. Yet something within her, a force of will perhaps, or her independent spirit, would not let her use weakness as a tool to build an intimate relationship.

She smiled, the right side of her mouth upstaging the left side with a quick jerking motion, almost imperceptible, as she turned her head toward him. Her flush deepened as she glanced up into his penetrating gaze. *There is desire there,* she thought. *I can feel it in his touch.*

The faint smile lingered around her restive mouth, curving the line of her lips with just enough play to invite an admiring comment from Brad.

"Feels good, huh?"

"Oh ... h ... h, yes ... s."

"The stabbing pains will diminish after a while, and then they should completely disappear," he encouraged. He granted her a few more pokes and prods before his hands left her shoulders. "You probably have scar tissue forming," he added, "which affects the circulation. It'll cause you some pain and discomfort for a while, but it'll pass."

Pamela closed her eyes, enjoying what she knew were the finishing touches of his scintillating massage.

"Ah, that feels so ... o ... o good," she reveled, hoping to buy more time.

"You still feel a little tense," Brad commented, wanting to give her an extended reprieve. "Here," he emphasized as he pushed and kneaded an area near the nape of her neck, "and here," he accented, migrating a little to the left. "How does that feel?"

"Wonderful! Absolutely won ... der ... ful!"

"Then you don't mind if I spend a little more time here," he said as he pressed behind her ears.

"Oh ... h ... h ... h. I think I'm in heaven."

He ached to draw her near, to hold her, bury his head in the sweet fragrance of her shoulder-length hair, to cover her with desperate kisses. He wanted to sweep her hair up from her neck and kiss her very softly and deliberately, first drifting, then nibbling, up and down the base of her bare neck, occasionally extending the tease of his warm moist lips to her shoulders, and then up to the nape of her neck again.

Each day he steeled himself, bridling his desire, reminding himself for the thousandth time that she was his patient.

"Oh, yes—rub there some more. Don't stop."

He wondered, increasingly dissatisfied with his inability to stay objective, how he had permitted himself such a trespass in the first place. He had allowed himself to fall for one of his patients against his better judgment and the rules of his profession.

"A little more to the right. Ah ... h. There! Oooh ... I could get used to this."

"Spoiling you, am I?"

"It's the least you can do for making me ... work ... so hard ... That feels wonderful," Pamela murmured, as she leaned her head forward so that her chin touched her chest.

Brad smiled in appreciation. "There now, I don't want you going to sleep standing up," his voice rose, sounding more official. He squeezed both her shoulders one more time and then released her.

Pamela looked mournfully grateful as she brought her own hands up to her holders and rotated her neck a couple of times in a symbolic loosening up gesture, verifying the success of his on-the-spot massage. She drew in a deep breath and exhaled slowly, satisfied that the last remnant of her tension had melted away.

Brad tilted his head in the direction of a piece of exercise equipment.

"That's next. We need to do ten."

Still enjoying the effects of relaxed, pain-free movement, Pamela turned her head slowly, trailing his nod. Her voice was confident when she found it.

"Oh, we do, do we?" she teased. "Well, why don't you go first?" she ordered sarcastically, poking her forefinger into his chest. "You do fifty and then I'll do five."

"Beauty before age," he rallied, reversing the standard order, hoping she would catch the compliment he tossed.

The lift of an eyebrow told him she caught his improvised compliment, as they walked shoulder-to-shoulder toward the armchair.

Still searching through the multitude of reasons why he was crazy to fall for her, he settled on the only one that made any sense, the only sane excuse of the lot. He was falling hopelessly in love with a woman who came with baggage, the emotional and physical scars of a terrible life-threatening accident.

He longed to banish her fears, to sooth her hurts, to kiss the pain away, but he knew he didn't have the right. He wanted to help end the nightmares she confessed plagued her since the accident. The little signals she'd sent, he felt certain, were 'flyers' to tell him about the accident.

He sensed she had come close to telling him many times about her ordeal. He was sure of it. But he would wait until the time was right, when she was ready. *Or perhaps,* he thought, *when I'm ready.*

He eased himself out of his own thoughts and watched her squeeze a few more repetitions out of the next set of exercises. *Her courage is matchless,* he praised, watching her in respectful silence. *She's amazing. She refuses to quit.*

Her determination to recover and her refusal to give up or give in amazed him. He had helped many people who sustained far less immobilizing injuries than Pamela take much longer to work through the rehabilitation process.

It is her will power, he reasoned, *that commands her broken body to heal itself, to resurrect itself from the deep abyss of physical trauma.*

He was pulled out of his thoughts by Pamela.

"Half way there. I'm halfway there."

"What?"

"Five. Five more lifts to go. Are you impressed?" Pamela huffed, at the same instant she exhaled.

"I'll be impressed with ten." Brad recovered, dismissing her jubilation lightly. "Five is good, ten is impressive."

A light defensiveness pinched her face. Her mouth was arranged in a smile, but the steel in her eyes spoke differently. She wanted his praise, not his indifference.

Okay, she thought to herself, *you want ten, you'll get ten.*

Brad was both impressed and leery of her determination. She had not mentioned anything specific about the accident, but he felt it was one of the motivating factors that drove her toward a speedy recovery.

"Six!"

"Four to go," Brad encouraged, realizing she would get to ten without him.

"Seven. Eight."

"Awesome," he shouted, admiring her guts.

"Nine."

Even from the beginning, she had insisted on partnering with him in establishing her rehab schedule, the pace and intensity of the workouts, and the number of bonus exercises to celebrate her cumulative successes. She had been aggressive in both her planning strategy and implementation.

She thrives on challenge, he reflected as he watched the sweat trickle down her face, *and the tougher the goal, the more competitive she gets.*

"Ten!" Pamela's triumphant shout broke into Brad's reverie, forcing his thoughts back to the present.

He laughed heartily. "Yes, looks like we did ten."

"What do you mean, we? I don't see you sweating."

She joined him as their rising decibels of laughter filled the room, causing dozens of pairs of eyes from the other patients to descend upon them, wondering what all the fuss was about.

Pamela and Brad steadied their gaze on each other after completing a celebratory high five. Neither wanted to miss the praise that danced in the other's eyes. Unwilling to break the connection, both therapist and patient sensed that there was more to be expressed, more to be experienced between them than the smell of sweat and groans of exercise.

"This is your next to last week in rehab, you know," he stated, expressing the obvious.

Pamela nodded slowly.

"Your progress has been astonishing."

She nodded again.

"I read in your book that people and organizations should celebrate their successes, that they should find at least one tiny event to celebrate each week," he intoned, referring to the book

Pamela wrote several years before on cross-functional teams. She had presented him with an autographed copy after her first month of physical therapy in appreciation for his tutelage.

A smile curved her lips. *He's leading up to something,* she mused, enjoying his friendly, extemporaneous tussle with provisional foreplay.

"According to your book, it can be someone's birthday or personal accomplishment outside of work. But preferably, it should be some positive accomplishment at work."

Get to the point, Brad, she said to herself, her impatience mounting.

Mindful of her impatience, he decided to shorten his lengthy recital.

"Setting a climate that focuses on positive reinforcement will bring positive results. So, I thought a proper celebration was in order."

Pamela was bursting with anticipation. She could sense he was about to ask her out.

"Brad," she paused, smiling broadly, "the closer you can link performance to rewards, the better."

He tried to catch the thought he just lost. Her quickness had confused him.

"So?" Pamela was intentionally brief.

"So ... " He seemed hesitant, throwing her a blank stare.

"So, you want to buy me lunch?" Pamela enticed, seizing the opportunity to shorten his invitation.

"I'd love to," he rejoiced and then added quickly, "I thought I'd never ask."

"Well, you were setting the climate," she rescued, smiling again.

Her acceptance cheered him immeasurably and he felt himself relax a little. This time he settled for a smile, not wanting to oversell something that was already sold.

"Give me a few minutes to get out of these sweat clothes and shower," Pamela announced, cheerfully squeezing his arm, "and I'll be ready for some positive reinforcement."

He watched her disappear through the women's locker room door.

I hope you know what you're doing, he cautioned himself. *You're playing with fire, ole boy.*

§   §   §   §   §   §

His lunch was not impaired in the least by all of the undivided attention he gave Pamela, who looked positively radiant. The flush of her workout was gone from her face, replaced now by a more natural color, accented by mascara-lined eyes and just the right amount of soft pink blush on her smooth, well-formed cheeks. Her voluptuous lips, moistened by the sip of water she had just drunk, were covered with a light shade of berry-colored lipstick.

Pamela marveled, caught somewhat off guard, that this golden-haired rehabilitation therapist could suddenly mean so much to her, could have become, in so short a time, so essential for her recovery. He took precedence over things she thought were important. She had sensed his interest in her in a thousand ways, the longing in his eyes which he failed to conceal, the vulnerability, the warmth and strength of his touch, his infectious laughter, his uncommon sensitivity, the lightness and smoothness of his movements. And his awkwardness was perhaps the most endearing, whenever he tried to dodge embarrassing moments. But she adored his sense of humor the most, and his expressive, penetrating eyes, which were dark gray beacons of hope.

Brad and Pamela watched in silence as a stout middle-aged waitress arranged glasses, napkins, and utensils at appropriate intervals on the table. She placed a small basket containing an assortment of breads and a cup of lime wedges on the table between them and then handed each a menu, stating that she would return momentarily to take their order. Her manner was jovial, and her perception keen, as she gave the distinct impression that she would honor their privacy as best she could while performing her wait staff duties.

"This is one of my favorite restaurants," Brad declared. "The food, the atmosphere, the service are all excellent."

"What do you recommend?"

"It's all good," he raised his pitch slightly, and looked up from his menu directly into her eyes. Her look told him he needed to be more specific. "The chicken and turkey croissants are very good, and filling, yet light. The onion soup is delicious. If you're into pasta any of the pasta plates will satisfy your tastes. Their vegetarian plates are excellent, too."

Pamela studied her menu. "What's the difference between the house garden salad and the vegetarian salad?"

"Besides the price?" he teased, pausing to catch her raised eyebrow. "I believe the vegetarian salad has both lettuce and spinach leaves, loads of raw veggies, and comes without croutons."

"Um, okay. Thanks."

Their perusals complete, they only had time for a quick exchange of flirtatious small talk before they were interrupted by the waitress.

With a mental apology to herself and to all of the health and nutrition gurus who preach both abstinence and moderation, Pamela ordered something that surprised both of them. "I'll have the dish of vanilla yogurt with a spoonful of chocolate chips on top. No whipped cream, please. And a glass of sparkling water." *I'll seek penance later,* she thought. *Much later.*

Brad grinned. The look of mock astonishment vanished almost as soon as it appeared on his face.

"I'll have the luncheon special number two. I'd like to substitute a sweet potato for fries though. That all right? Sour dough bread. The house salad with light Italian dressing on the side, and a glass of sparkling water also." Then he shot a quick whimsical look at Pamela and added. "We're having our dessert later."

The waitress smiled and glanced inquiringly at Pamela. "Would you like anything else, Miss?"

"No, thank you."

The waitress politely took her leave again, without notepad committing everything to memory.

"I'm still impressed at how they can do that," Brad admired, tilting his head at the waitress. "Especially when they wait on another table or two before they post orders in the kitchen."

Pamela nodded her agreement. "Yes, it requires a good memory." And she then thought to herself, *I hope he remembers that positive reinforcement should be gradual with periodic increases in intensity.* She surprised herself by harboring such intimate intentions.

The unceasing buzz of the muted conversation around them and the vociferous merriment of a dozen or so college students who had joined several tables together in a corner of the restaurant provided a festive backdrop with its soft, but alluring invitation to gaiety. She noticed another waitress, a little dumpling of a woman, as tall as she was horizontal, make her way across the area between them and the college students. She wondered, *what do they feed the waitresses around here, they're all so heavy?* She quickly dismissed her appraisal of the physical attributes of the waitresses as she centered her attention again on Brad.

Her thoughts worked rapidly, hoping to channel their conversation toward him, his background, his interests, his dreams.

"I find myself at a considerable disadvantage, " she started, as she leaned back in her chair.

"Oh? How so?"

"It appears you know much more about me than I know about you," she said, leaning forward. She placed her elbows on top of the table and clasped her hands together so that she was able to rest her chin on them.

"You know most of my medical history, my home address, my work. You've read my book."

"And a good one it is," he interjected.

"You've met my sister and my grandparents. And you know that I have a craving for vanilla yogurt and chocolate chips. So ... tell me about you." She smiled, catching him a little off guard.

He hesitated slightly, then responded, "Actually there isn't much to tell."

Pamela separated her hands long enough to take another sip of her water and then reunited them as before.

"I was born in Durham, lived there most of my life, graduated from the University of North Carolina at Chapel Hill. Then worked a couple of years and went to grad school part time. I came into some money and decided to work part time and go to school full time. I graduated with a Masters Degree from Duke in 2002, and have worked at the clinic ever since. See, I told you there wasn't much to tell." He looked up in time to see the waitress place their orders in front of them.

Before she left, the waitress dutifully refilled the water glasses and then retraced her steps to a table near the door.

Brad raised his water glass and offered a toast.

"To your complete and absolute health."

Their water glasses met with a gentle clink, and separated, but their eyes remained glued to each other. Each knew the toast was a prelude to intimacy.

Pamela was the first to recover.

"UNC and Duke, huh?" Pamela teased, trying her best to appear serious. "I won't hold that against you."

Chuckles erupted from both their faces.

"Let's not over-look the ACC's NCAA dominance," Brad pleaded, lightheartedly. "The NCAA tournament is over for this year and, as I recall, both our schools made it to the Final Four."

Pamela smiled her agreement.

"There's one thing you can depend on in collegiate sports, there's always next year," he emphasized.

Pamela sipped her glass of sparkling water, wishing she had remembered to add a wedge of lime. She quickly sipped another taste, which she found positively refreshing, and then reached over to pluck one of the lime wedges out of the dish. She decided she had procrastinated adding it to her drink long enough.

Although she was fond of college sports, she agreed they wouldn't pursue a discussion on the topic.

Collegiate sports has become big business and not character development, she reminded herself, *and this last couple of years I've lost interest.*

She hadn't watched professional sports like football, basketball, and baseball for the same reason, although she did enjoy watching Kobe Bryant play. She had another reason for not wanting to watch professional football. The thought of seeing number eighty-four snag a long catch was positively revolting to her. Every applause Clarence got from admiring fans, unaware of his unethical conduct off the field, fueled his self-absorption and seemed to make him even more egotistical.

It's unfortunate, she thought, *that most people idolize professional athletes no matter what kind of person the athlete turns out to be.*

She decided to add another wedge of lime to her water, more as a diversion from her current thoughts than anything else. Then she looked at the glass of carbonated water with its perfectly-cut wedges of lime. It sat prettily on a brightly flowered cloth napkin.

That's how athletes like Clarence look in public, she analogized, *all spruced up in their uniforms, looking so noble and powerful. Their off-court behavior is just as important as their game-time behavior if you ask me.*

Her next compensatory look was at her own legs, which she considered fairly slim until she compared them with the fabulous slimness and lengthiness of the ones on the young woman who had just glided so majestically by their table. She regretted ordering the large portion of vanilla yogurt with all those delicious chocolate chips piled on top. Her sudden depression surprised her.

Come on girl, she encouraged herself, *give the new Pamela a chance.*

The warmth and gentle pressure of Brad's hand on top of hers evaporated her self-conscious thoughts.

"Pamela, is everything all right?"

She blinked her eyes a couple of times to re-focus, and breathed a sigh of relief.

"Yes. Sorry. I was just asking myself why I ordered the chocolate chips and yogurt."

"You have my permission, no, my blessings, to order something else."

Brad's boyish laugh, accompanied by another light squeeze on her hand, was just what she needed.

She reciprocated with a smile and then added, "Lots of people take the time to count calories, and they've got the figures to prove it. My motto is: Nothing tastes as good as thin feels."

"Is that so?"

"You can bank on it," she grinned.

"So that's why you look so marvelous."

Pamela blushed and then separated her eyes from his gaze only long enough to realize he'd placed both hands over her hand. As she enjoyed his warm touch, she wondered if he could feel evidence of her racing heart in the pulsing of her blood. His touches, no matter how slight, had that effect on her. She darted her eyes away again, finding the top of his left hand. He was wearing a Duke University class ring, its dark blue setting glistening under the overhead lights.

"Suppose we order something else for you."

She took another sip of water for courage, peering above the rim of the glass to catch a glimpse of his face. His eyes were riveted on her. She took a tentative swallow, and then, absolutely inspired, wet her lips with another.

"No, I think I'll stick with the yogurt." She played with several of the chocolate chips, using her spoon as a scoop to separate them from the melting yogurt. "I'll leave these on the plate."

He rubbed her free hand lightly with his hand and felt a flush migrating up his neck to his face. His heart began to beat more rapidly and there was a slight ringing sensation in his ears. He found his fingers inching clockwise around the top of her hand to her fingertips. When he reached the underside of her hand, he squeezed her hand gently and felt her tremble. His eyes shot up to meet hers. Impulsively, a smile creased his face. He started to speak, but couldn't find the words.

She started to withdraw her hand, but decided to allow his advance.

They sat in wordless anticipation, momentarily held captive by each other's penetrating gaze and the warmth of each other's touch.

Her eyes, Brad admired, *are radiant beams of light, as if frozen in time by an infatuated painter who has captured her arresting beauty on canvas, but can only manage a sophomoric attempt at the changing moods and elusive expressions that grace her remarkably beautiful face with joy or sorrow, envy or confidence, interest and even dismissal. And certainly no painter can blend oils enough, or poet bend words enough to capture her quick wit, piercingly sharp mind, undaunting courage, or relentless determination that contrasts so dramatically with her image of innocence and vulnerability.*

He continued with his amorous train of thought. *Such qualities make her admirers, myself included, remember her determination and integrity long after they've forgotten the precise shade of green in her emerald eyes, or the exact shade of polish on her long fingernails, or the bearly noticeable, tiny white scar that identifies the injury at her hairline. Her eyes are beaming with happiness. I'd like to think I had something to do with that.*

Entranced as they were in their expectant, yet reluctant foreplay, heads spinning and hearts whirling, neither noticed the amused waitress who placed the check on the table near Brad's elbow.

Pamela's face went suddenly somber, causing the curve of her lips to droop.

"I need to talk to you," she forced words that were difficult to fall from her lips. "But not here."

A serious expression enveloped his face. Pamela's sense of urgency had caught him off guard.

He released her hand to find his wallet and then quickly placed an Andrew Jackson on top of the luncheon bill to avoid having to wait for a credit card receipt.

"I know just the place," he exclaimed confidently. "It's a beautiful park not far from here."

Her despondency seemed to lift at his decisiveness.

He escorted her quickly out of the restaurant, neglecting the usual courtesies of waving at friends and chatting perfunctorily with business associates on the way out. His attention was drawn to Pamela's cry for help, and he was not going to deny her solace. He was in love with her, and that meant falling in love with all of her: her despondency, the mixture of competitiveness and vulnerability evident during her workouts, the career which consumed her at times, her guardedness when it came to intimate relationships, and her past, even the accident which had brought them together.

"Pullen Park," Pamela guessed in a level voice that indicated her familiarity with the park.

Brad remembered she was an N. C. State graduate. "Yes, it's the perfect place to talk, don't you think?"

Pamela agreed, knowing some of the most private places were in the middle of crowds.

A short walk back to their cars produced a plan. They would take both cars. She would follow him.

During the short drive to the park, Pamela planned what she would say.

Brad wondered what she wanted to talk about and readied himself for his input.

There were people in the park enjoying the sixty-degree weather. Quite a few were riding on the train that circled the park, others watched their children riding on the locally famous carousel, which remained a magnet to attract children every summer since its restoration. Some walked hand-in-hand, oblivious to others who were jogging past them or sitting on benches near well-trimmed beds of multi-colored impatiens, pansies, vinca and iris, resplendent in their floral coats of red, pink, yellow, bronze, purple, and white.

Holly bushes speckled with red berries were escorted by rows of azaleas that sprawled their massive flower-enhanced foliage across lawns. The sidewalks were lined with an extravaganza of hues ranging from red, tangerine and purple to pinks, plums and whites, with bursts of variegated Formosa petals that complemented their neighbors, adding a touch of integration to the mix.

All around them, the park was ablaze with a medley of polychromatic splendor, surrounded by pink and white dogwoods that spread their canopies of color overhead. The sun had assumed command of the flawless pastel blue sky, bathing everything in radiant sunshine.

Dowsed with the mild aroma of mingled scents and soothed by the melodious serenades of robins, cardinals, and finches which filled the afternoon air, Brad and Pamela sat facing each other on one of the painted park benches.

"You're sure you don't have to get back to work?" she asked enigmatically, knowing full well he could have excused himself before now.

"I decided to take the rest of the day off. Besides, right now, you're more important."

She allowed him to take her hand, and remained still while he inched himself over closer to her. She kept her eyes on their joined hands and then found his compassionate eyes. The slate color of his eyes had deepened to a dark ray, making him appear less clinical and more wise.

Faith supplemented the distress in her eyes. Painstakingly, in slow and deliberate detail, Pamela told Brad about the accident, the early morning jog, meeting Geoffrey, the bitter coldness of that fateful December morning, her break-up with Clarence, the black Mercedes speeding out of control, the horrifying moments just before impact, the push by Geoffrey as he sacrificed himself to save her.

Brad squeezed her hand.

"You don't have to ... " he petitioned softly.

"No, I want to. I need to," she interrupted.

She recounted the awful feeling of being crushed beneath the underside of the car. She described her loss of consciousness, Geoffrey's paralysis, the torturous hospital stay, including her own coma. She told him about the surgeon's intention of amputating her arm. She related how she had screamed out at them from the silence of her coma, pleading with them not to amputate her arm. She described her feelings of powerlessness as she fought to climb out of her extra-sensory abyss.

"My last thoughts to myself before I fell into some other corner of darkness," Pamela said as she shivered, "before I lost all sense of myself, of what was happening to me, was ... " She could only manage a whisper, "Oh, my God, I'm going to die."

When she finished, she saw that Brad's eyes were closed. His lips were sealed. He held her right hand, rubbing her thumbnail with his thumb, lightly and rhythmically. He was otherwise motionless. The silence fused them, binding them in a shared reality of revisited pathos.

Finally, he opened his tear-filled eyes and shook his head slowly. He looked at her soberly, compassionately, wordlessly. He lifted his free hand, wedging it under the strands of hair that bordered her face and cupped her soft cheek, pink now with the blush from her agonizing confession.

"Forgive me," he asserted, allowing his eyes to drop. He returned his gaze to meet her confused look. Then he tenderly pulled her hand up to his lips and kissed her palm. Leaning forward, he kissed the tiny scar on her forehead and sat back straight.

"Forgive me ... " he repeated, pausing for the longest time. His face took on a most serious look. "Because I put you through ... " He hesitated only slightly, "such tough workouts." He forced a quick smile, and then added, "You have been through enough pain. You're way over your quota. You don't ..."

Pamela placed her fingertips over his mouth, affectionately cutting him off. Her soulful eyes remained glued to him.

"I wanted you to know about my accident because I had to tell someone outside of the family. I trust you, Brad. I've never told anyone what I've told you about the accident. Not even my closest friends. I knew if I didn't tell someone, I'd explode."

"I feel honored that you've told me."

"I wanted you to know because I feel safe with you," she said softly, trying to appear confident.

Brad pulled her closer and put his arm around her shoulders so that her head rested on his shoulder. He squeezed her hand and then loosened his pressure a little. He decided he would encourage her to talk more if she could.

She needs to let it out, he thought to himself, *and I want to be here to help her.*

And let it out she did. She told him about the Asheville police efforts to find the driver of the car, of how Jake Detrick saved Hans, of her grandmother's refusal to allow the surgeons to amputate her arm. She spoke softly as she canonized her parents, telling him about their untimely deaths and of her and Karen's subsequent adoption by George and Constance.

Brad listened, nodding his understanding every time he sensed she needed it, squeezing her hand occasionally and smiling whenever he deemed those gestures appropriate. He shepherded her through what turned out to be three hours of catharsis. During their intense dialogue, the park swelled with hoards of people who came to enjoy the rides and take advantage of the extra hour of sunlight.

"Thank you. You don't know how much this means to me," Pamela smiled, as she gave him a quick kiss on the lips.

Surprised, Brad hesitated a moment before he spoke. "Anytime you want to ... " he cut into his own sentence, not liking where it was going, thinking that ending it with the cliché 'bend my ear' was not a dignified enough closure.

He began again, "I would feel privileged to be your confidant—any time you feel the need to talk. I'll be there for you."

Pamela gave him an appreciative smile, "Thank you. Your friendship means a lot to me."

He looked down at his watch. "Can you believe it, it's four-thirty?"

"Oh, looks like I've monopolized our entire afternoon. I'm sorry."

"Don't be. I wouldn't have wanted to spend it any other way," he said, smiling broadly.

She squeezed his hand tighter in response to the subtle pressure he had just applied.

"Look, I have a proposal to make!" he exclaimed, in an attempt to change the subject and keep things on the light side.

His exuberance seemed to lift Pamela's spirits. She gave him a whimsical look.

"Why don't you monopolize my evening as well?"

She broke into a smile. "Your whole day?" she asked, trying not to seem over-anxious. "I should think you've had enough of me by now."

"Too much of ye? Never, me lass," he bantered, in a poorly contrived Irish accent. "Say ye will have a wee bit o'dinner with me and agree to a movie to round out the evening," he entreated, still attempting to sound Irish. Then he slid off the bench and onto one knee and placed his hand over his heart. "I promise to be a perfect gentleman, me lass, and on me best behavior." He threw her a quick wink and ended his proposal with a playful close. "Say yes, and make this laddie happy."

Pamela hesitated, not sure whether to laugh or take him seriously.

"Ah, ye drive a hard bargain, I see," he pressed with another embarrassing attempt to sound even remotely Irish. Changing back to his natural voice, Brad continued, "Why don't we each make a quick trip home, freshen up, and relax a little. Then I'll pick you up, say around seven for dinner and we'll decide on a movie or whatever then. What do you say?"

A broad, slowly forming smile came to her face. She preempted what she was going to say with a head nod, consenting to his offer. "Yes, Mr. Aikman, I would like to monopolize your entire evening."

He was on his feet instantaneously and with a small flourish, bowed elaborately, kissing her hand in the process.

Pamela's radiance had returned and she seemed to enjoy his dramatics with childlike excitement.

Brad took Pamela's hands and lifted her gently to her feet, pulling her affectionately a few steps away from the park bench. He pirouetted her gracefully across the sidewalk, circling the small waterfalls that led to the parking lot. Then he waltzed her playfully around and around, delighting exuberant children, surprising attentive parents and students, and scattering scores of pigeons.

Pamela's happiness had returned. *This man,* she thought, as he spun her across the park, *is good for me.*

CHAPTER SIXTEEN

"Who's there?" Pamela raised her voice as she tossed her house keys and purse on the sofa.'

She looked in the direction of the kitchen.

"Gramma? Grampa?"

She continued her advance toward the kitchen, but stopped when she heard what sounded like a drawer close in her bedroom.

A smile radiated across her face.

"Gramma, I told you not to bother cleaning my bedroom. Remember?"

She reversed her steps and threw her jacket on the chair next to the sofa as she headed toward her bedroom.

By the time she saw him, it was too late.

His head was covered with a ski mask and he was dressed in black from head to toe. He was on her instantly, muffling her scream with one of his gloved hands while he brandished a knife in the other.

"Please don't hurt me," Pamela pleaded even though he kept his hand over her mouth.

His momentum carried them into a framed painting on the living room wall, sending it crashing to the floor. The force of his knee in her groin when he pinned her to the wall took her breath away.

"I ... I can't ... breathe," she protested.

Keeping his weight against her, he lowered his glove slightly allowing her to breathe through her nose.

"If you holler out or make one sound, I'll kill you. Do you understand?"

Her eyes darted from his masked face to the knife he eased up to her cheek.

"Yes," she muffled through his gloved hand.

"I'm going to take my hand off your mouth. If you scream, I'll cut your pretty little throat. Do you think you can be a good little girl and be quiet?"

Her widened eyes gazed frantically at his, as she nodded slightly. She could feel the cutting edge of the knife lift slightly from her cheek.

"Good," he said menacingly, as he lowered his hand to her neck and pressed his thumb firmly against her jugular.

When Pamela coughed, he slid his hand into a light chokehold and pressed the edge of the knife against the underside of her jaw.

Although she tried her best to control her breathing, Pamela began to hyperventilate. Her knees felt weak and the pounding in her chest escalated to her throat and ears, making it difficult for her to swallow.

She glanced to either side, wondering if there was anyone else in the house.

Her panicked surveillance amused the assailant, and he laughed as he jerked her slightly to his left.

"I prefer to work alone," he said gruffly. "I like to keep things simple. Don't you?"

When she didn't respond immediately, he squeezed her neck.

"Don't you?" he repeated sarcastically.

Pamela gagged and brought one of her hands up to his wrist.

"Please, you're choking me."

He forced her to take a couple of steps into the hallway before he loosened his grip on her throat.

Pamela worried more about his emotionless eyes than the knife.

"What ... what do you want?" she gagged out her inquiry.

She felt his fingers stiffen around her throat.

"Take your sweat pants off."

"Oh, no, please."

"Do it!" he shouted.

Pamela started to cry as she loosened the tie at the waist. She considered kneeing him as she lifted her leg from the nylon clothing, but censored her own counterattack.

He's too strong, she told herself. *He'll kill me.*

The assailant gave her just enough room to lower her sweat bottoms before he placed one of his knees between her thighs.

"I don't like surprises, darlin'," he said calmly. "Lift your legs out slowly."

She unzipped her cuffs and climbed out of the bottoms, letting them fall onto the carpet.

"Please don't do this. If it's money or jewelry you want ..."

"Now, take your panties off," he hissed.

Pamela's sobs caused him to grow impatient.

"I said take your panties off!"

She shook her head.

"All right then, bitch. I'll do it."

He eased his knife between one of her panty legs and her thigh and cut through her panties.

Pamela screamed, but was too frozen by fear to move.

He kept his hand on her throat and moved the knife to her opposite thigh. He severed her other panty leg and watched her silk panties fall beside her ankles.

Resigned to her fate, Pamela couldn't control her sobs. In a silent act of defiance, she closed her legs and covered herself with her free hand.

The assailant raised his knife to her cheek again and laughed disapprovingly.

"That's not gonna help."

He tilted his head back and taunted her with another hideous laugh.

Suddenly he used the hand he held around her neck to force her off balance and pushed her toward the bedroom. She hit the door facing, reinjuring her right arm and she winced as she back-peddled, ramming herself into the corner wall of the hallway. She glared at him, too frightened to speak.

"So you wanna do it right here, do you?" he hissed as he started toward her.

Pamela screamed.

"No! No, please. Get out of here."

Before she thought about the knife, she kicked at him, trying her best to postpone the inevitable.

Surprised at her courage, the assailant angrily kicked her several times.

"You want play rough?" he teased. "Okay. Let's play." He kicked her a few more times with his brass-toed boot.

Flailing her arms and legs for all she was worth, and absorbing his harsh kicks, Pamela held him off as long as she could.

When one of his kicks broke a rib, she cried out in pain and waved off his assault.

Realizing he had kicked her into submission, he canceled his attack and squatted beside her.

Pamela pulled her knees toward her chest, groaning painfully from her wounds. Her emerald eyes were filled with anger as he squared off in front of her.

"That's the first part of the message, Ms. Justice."

Pamela's eyes widened as she stared at him. "You ... know me?" she asked, as confused as she was surprised.

"My employer wants you to know he can get to you anytime and anywhere."

"What?"

"Do you understand?" he teased, touching her ankle then moving his hand up her leg to her knees.

"No, I don't understand. Understand what?"

"My employer wants me to assure you that my next visit will be, shall we say, less hospitable."

"Who? What are you talking about?"

"Where are they, Ms. Justice?"

Pamela squinted her befuddlement.

"Your copies of the medical and police reports."

"My medical ... why do you want them?"

"The reports, Ms. Justice. I'm growing impatient."

Pamela attempted to improve her sitting position, but her broken rib prevented it.

"I don't understand. Why do you want ... ?"

She cut herself off when he drew his hand back to slap her.

"Okay! Okay, you can have them. I don't care."

"Thank you Ms. Justice. You've saved us a lot of trouble. Now where are the reports?"

"In my office. I keep them in my office."

Before she could protect herself, he grabbed her arm and lifted her to her feet, sending a horrible streak of pain through her side and chest.

She bent over double and was unable to resist his pull as he led her toward her office.

"Please," she cried out, halting their advance. "It hurts so badly. Let me catch my breath."

When he yanked on her arm again she was forced to stumble after him.

"Why ... Why are my medical records and copies ... of my ... police reports important to you?"

"Where are they?" he growled.

Pamela nodded in the direction of the file cabinets.

He released her arm and motioned for her to retrieve the reports.

"What are you going to do with me once I give you the reports?" Pamela arched her eyebrows and glared as she asked.

"I'm growing impatient again."

"Okay. Okay."

"The reports! Don't push my generosity," he threatened.

"They're here," she whispered aloud, "in the top drawer of this cabinet. They're ... they're in the file marked ... accident investigation."

He pushed her closer to the file cabinet.

"You'll have to get the reports. I can't lift my arm. You've broken my ribs."

The assailant lifted the file from the drawer and glared at Pamela, who leaned against the floor-to-ceiling bookcase behind her.

"This all of it?"

Pamela nodded.

He took a menacing step toward her and held the knife blade up under her chin.

Pamela stood very still.

"You've just saved your life," he said, pressing the blade against the underside of her jaw for emphasis. He lowered his eyes and brought them slowly up her exposed thighs and tummy, before he reestablished eye contact. "It would have been such a pity to dump you in Falls Lake. Of course, I would have enjoyed you first."

He licked his lips as he ran his gloved hand along the outside of her thigh.

"Oh, here's the second part of the message."

Pamela remained silent, calculating her next move if he became violent.

"My employer wants you to forget all about the accident. That's all. Do you think you can do that?"

Pamela struggled to maintain her balance. She was becoming nauseous. The aching in her side and chest was becoming more pronounced.

Her assailant grabbed her arms and shook her, causing her to cringe with pain.

"I said, do you think you can do that?"

"Yes. Yes." Pamela screamed. "If you let me."

"Oh, ho! You're a feisty little thing, aren't you?"

"You stay out of my life, and I'll stay out of yours. Isn't that what you want?" Pamela whispered.

"What my employer wants, Ms. Justice, is your silence. Either you guarantee it or I will. Oh, you need to talk to that crippled friend of yours in Asheville. Both of you need to realize how lucky you are. You know what I mean? Neither of you wants to have another accident, do you?"

Pamela sucked in a sharp breath, causing her to wince in pain.

"Oh, sorry about the broken ribs. You really ought to get that taken care of."

He lowered the knife and patted her firmly on the side of her face.

She held her ribs as he vanished through the bedroom door and made his way through the house. She hesitated long enough to hear him leave through the kitchen door.

I've got to get to the hospital, she instructed herself. *And I've got to call the police, and Brad, and Geoffrey. Oh, God what am I going to tell them, and my grandparents?*

She pulled the afghan off the back of one of the office chairs and draped it around herself. Then she dialed her grandparents' number.

"Oh, darn. I forgot. They're out of town." When she dialed Brad's number she had to leave a message.

"Hello, Brad. Something's come up ... I'll have to ... take ... a rain check ... on tonight. I'm sorry. I'll call you tomorrow."

I guess I'd better spend the night at the hospital, she convinced herself. *I won't be able to sleep if I'm here. Damn it! I don't deserve this. I've got to call Geoffrey, too.*

She dialed 911 and calmly told the dispatcher about her predicament.

Before she called Geoffrey, she took time to slip into her sweat bottoms and pack a few essentials for an overnight stay at the hospital.

She moved gingerly as she doubled-locked the kitchen door. Then she dialed Geoffrey's number.

"Hello."

"Geoffrey!"

"Hi, beautiful. What's up?"

"Geoffrey ... " Pamela repeated before she erupted into tears. "I ... " she attempted to continue, but started sobbing out of control.

§　　§　　§　　§　　§　　§

"Brad, you didn't have to come over," Pamela protested lightly.

"Of course I did. If you'd told me what happened last night, I'd have come then! But I'm glad you called this morning. I can't believe this happened! How are you?"

"Sore ... and lucky. He cracked two ribs."

Brad closed his eyes and shook his head.

"I thought he was going to kill me," she confessed as she backed out of the doorway to give him room to enter the house.

"Pamela, I'm so sorry this had to happen to you."

"Me, too," she agreed as she eased herself onto the sofa.

"Let me help you," Brad petitioned, intending to assist her to her seat.

"No thanks," Pamela raised her voice. "I'd better lower myself."

Brad hovered near her, but kept his hands to himself.

"Oops. Sorry. I might have hurt you intending to help you. I'm glad one of us is thinking."

Pamela tossed him a grateful smile.

"You could bring me another pillow from the bedroom."

"I'd be happy to," he said and started toward her office.

"That way," Pamela directed, pointing toward the hallway leading to the bedroom. "There are extra pillows on the top shelf in the walk-in closet."

He was back in an instant, and placed the pillow behind her back and shoulders.

"How's that?"

"Great. It feels fine. Thanks."

"Now. What can I get you?" he said, clasping his hands in front of him.

"Nothing. I'm fine."

"Are you sure?"

Pamela nodded.

Brad found a seat next to her at the opposite end of the sofa. He started to say something, but sighed instead.

He glanced at the painting that was propped against the wall. Then he looked at Pamela, who sensed the obvious question.

"It got knocked off the wall in the scuffle."

Brad shot another uneasy glance at the painting and quickly returned his sympathetic gaze to Pamela.

"When you called, you said the police were here."

"Yes, they just left. They got here a little after eight o'clock this morning."

"Then you came home last night?"

Pamela nodded. "I was going to spend the night in the hospital ... but the hospital is no place for a sick person."

Both of them smiled.

"When I found out all they were going to do was wrap my ribs, I figured my injuries weren't severe enough to warrant an overnight stay."

"Do you have anything for pain?"

"Tylenol."

"They didn't prescribe anything stronger than that?" Brad asked, throwing her a concerned look.

"Yes, but I haven't needed it. The Tylenol's just fine."

Brad's eyebrows rose with skeptical arches.

"Honest, if I needed something stronger, I'd take it. I'm not into sadomasochism, you know."

"Okay, okay. I'm just concerned about you," he said, surrendering to her agitated look. "I won't say anything more about it. Scout's honor."

She smiled as he held three fingers up, mimicking the Boy Scouts' pledge gesture.

"You told me on the phone that he wanted your medical and police records," Brad said, in an attempt to swing the conversation back to the police.

"I think his main objective was to scare me ... which was successful ... very successful."

"You said he told you to keep quiet about the accident?"

Pamela sighed.

"And that's what confuses me. I've hardly talked about the accident. And I certainly haven't been investigating it like Geoffrey. That's it! Of course! I don't know why I didn't think about that before."

"What?" floundered Brad, trying to catch up with her.

"When I called Geoffrey and told him about the break-in, he said he'd been investigating the accident since February."

"He's the one you told me about yesterday?"

Pamela nodded.

"You said he retired on disability from the Asheville Police Department."

"The accident retired him," Pamela nodded quickly. "He's like a brother to me ... and Karen. His father was a policeman, too."

"But that doesn't explain why your home was broken into," Brad interjected.

"Geoffrey thinks it does. Geoffrey said he and Ted—that's his father—must have uncovered something in their investigation that has made whoever hit us nervous. Geoffrey thinks the break-in was an attempt to frighten me. He says the intruder could have gotten the police and medical records any number of ways."

"Well, that's true, I guess ... "

"Whoever it is doesn't want his identity known ... "

"Or jail time for a hit-and-run," Brad added.

"That's true. But why now? Why does someone want to frighten me almost five months after the accident? And why me? Geoffrey's the one who's been investigating it, not me."

"Maybe he wanted you to call Geoffrey off, or ... maybe he's next."

"That's why I called him right away. He's a paraplegic. He couldn't offer much resistance to anyone. Although he still has his service revolver, as he so aptly reminds me."

"He's an ex-cop. I'm sure he can take care of himself," Brad encouraged.

"That's what he told me. But I still worry about him."

"Well, I'm here to take care of you. I don't like the idea of someone breaking into your house and assaulting you."

"That makes two of us," Pamela agreed.

"Have you asked for police protection?" Brad asked as he stood.

"No."

"Pamela!" Brad raised his voice.

"It wouldn't do any good, Brad. Besides, I'm staying next door with my grandparents for a few days."

"Good. At least you're doing something to protect yourself."

Pamela laughed, then held her side, reacting to a sharp spear of pain.

"I'm not going over there for protection," she recovered. "I'm going over there to get Grampa's help. We're going to do a little investigative work on our own, and try to find out who broke into my house ... and who hired him."

"Pamela, I think you should let the police do that," Brad warned as he sat on the floor beside her.

"Oh, I expect them to do their part. But I'm not sitting idly by, waiting for another unpleasant visit. I'm not going through that again. I'm going to be ready next time."

"You're serious, aren't you?"

"I was quite happy letting Geoffrey track down the ones responsible for running over us. It gave him a reason to live. And a part of me hoped he'd find him so we could put that horrible chapter of our lives behind us."

She clasped Brad's hand. "Before last night, all I wanted to do was get these in better working order," she confessed, patting her right shoulder and thigh. "Now I know there's someone out there that wants to hurt me again. Evidently he's too foolish to leave well enough alone. I'm not going to let him hurt me again," she said bitterly, "and I'm certainly not going to live my life in fear. He should have left me alone. He should never have come into my house."

Brad sat with his mouth hanging slightly open. His eyes widened with surprise.

"I can see that you're upset, but you've got to let the police handle this," Brad cautioned, squeezing her hand for emphasis. "I don't want you hurt again either."

Pamela's resolute smile was her only response.

"Well, what can I do to help?" he asked, elevating himself to his knees.

"You already have."

Brad tossed her a lightly confused look.

"Your being here means a lot."

He smiled boyishly.

"I still owe you a dinner and a movie," he rallied.

"What time is it?" Pamela asked as she rotated the watch on his wrist.

"Two-thirty."

"I'm due at my grandparents right now. Why don't you come with me? You can help us plan our counterattack and then stay for supper."

Brad hesitated while he allowed her to use him to help lift herself slowly from the sofa.

"You said you owed me dinner, right?"

Brad nodded, trying his best to hide his confusion.

"Then the pizza's on you tonight," she teased, "and so is the cheese bread."

His slate eyes met her emerald gaze.

"You're sure your grandparents won't mind?"

"They're expecting you."

He retreated half a step.

"I told them you'd probably come with me."

"Am I that easy to read?" he asked, allowing a smile to leak across his face.

"No. But I hoped you would come. I need you to be with me."

He slid his hand between her hair and her flushed cheeks and kissed her.

"I want to be with you," he said softly, and trained his eyes longingly on hers.

Pamela ran her fingertips along his lips and then yielded to another soft collision of their lips.

§   §   §   §   §   §

"Message delivered."

"Good. Any trouble getting the message understood?"

"No. I think she understands what's expected."

"She was there then?"

"Walked in five minutes after I did."

"Oh?"

"Nothing like being able to deliver a message in person. I was, shall we say, persuasive."

"You think she'll keep quiet, then?"

"I'd be greatly surprised if she didn't. You see, I had to put my foot down."

"What do you mean?"

"I had to rough her up a little."

"I told you to scare her, that's all!"

"Oh, she's plenty scared. I told you I'd guarantee her silence."

"What about the cripple in Asheville?"

"He won't want her to get hurt again. He'll back off."

"And if he doesn't?"

"Loose ends are my specialty. I'll handle it when you say the word. One of your concerns, as I remember, is making sure there's no connection between their fate and your future. Isn't that right?"

"I just want it to go away. You said you can guarantee that."

"One of the things that makes my job more difficult is the reluctance of my employers. Shall I refer you to someone else?"

"No. No, you come too highly recommended. I want you to finish the contract."

"I'll call you in a few weeks. In the meantime, don't worry ... because I don't want to have to worry about you. People who worry make mistakes. I was told you were the kind of man who expected results."

"Okay, okay. I get the point."

"What do you want me to do with the medical and police records I got last night?"

"Give them to me."

"Anything else?"

"Not now. Where can I reach you?"

"Use the same number I gave you."

"Who's the person that answers the phone when I call?"

"Let's just say she's my gatekeeper. She'll know where to find me. I like plenty of elbow room."

CHAPTER SEVENTEEN

*I*t's the flavor of beef that counts," Constance announced proudly. "It blesses the potatoes and onions and baptizes the carrots. That's what makes beef stew beef stew."

Pamela and Karen looked at each other and matched raised eyebrows. Then elfish smiles fell onto their mischievous faces.

Karen was the first to poke fun at Constance.

"I didn't know that, Gramma," she winked at Pamela, "I thought it was the preservative on the potato skins or the steroids in the beef."

"Or the number of rings in each onion," joked Pamela.

"You two run out of work?" Constance teased, as she busied herself peeling the potatoes and scraping the carrots to go with the chunks of onions and beef that had already been deposited in the roasting pot.

"Not me," Karen contrived, wasting no time exiting the kitchen. "I haven't finished folding the laundry." She pointed an accusing finger at Pamela to let her know it was her towels and washcloths she was folding.

Pamela threw her a kiss acknowledging her contribution, then turned toward Constance, who had just finished slicing the carrots.

"When should we start the rolls?"

"They'll only take ten minutes. We'll wait till the roast is almost done." *In spite of her flare for mesmerizing an audience or thoroughly captivating a client with her business acumen,*

Constance thought to herself, *Pamela's sure not at home in the kitchen.*

She shifted her train of thought to ask Pamela a question.

"Did you two enjoy your trip to Asheboro this week?"

"Who? Brad and me?"

"Who else, silly. You two have been inseparable these past few months."

"Yes, it was beautiful. The North Carolina Zoo has come a long way. They've added quite a number of habitats since I was there. And the weather was perfect," she added.

"Did you walk through the aviary?"

"Of course, but my favorite tour was through the African Pavilion. Did you know it is home to over two hundred rare and unusual animals, especially the gorillas?"

"I'm sure I did at one time, but it has been a while since George and I visited the zoo."

"And you can't see any of it in a hurry," Pamela noted, as she leaned against the counter beside Constance. "The hills themselves dictate slower, more leisurely walks through the park for most tourists." She paused, and patted her legs. "I guess that includes me right now," she confessed, "but Brad says I'll be running again by July."

"Your recuperative powers are amazing, honey," Constance praised. "Just don't ... "

"Overdo it," Pamela chorused, helping Constance finish her sentence in unison.

"You know I'm only saying that for your own good," she cautioned.

"I know, Gramma, and I love you for it. But I am really old enough to take care of myself."

"Yes, I know, but I'm your grandmother. One of my jobs is to worry about my granddaughters taking care of themselves."

Pamela kissed her lightly on the cheek, "Despite what's happened lately, you needn't worry so."

"Mail call," announced Karen as she sauntered through the kitchen doorway carrying Pamela's mail.

"Oh, thanks," Pamela said appreciatively, as she unceremoniously took the mail out of Karen's outstretched hand. "I like having you two around."

Constance and Karen gave each other a knowing look. Pamela was a master at delegating household duties when they visited. Her only salvation was that they both loved helping her stay ahead of the dust, cobwebs, toilet bowl grime, and food mold in the refrigerator.

Karen thought about her sister's business as she watched Pamela open her mail.

Her business was rebounding slower than she hoped. Her Brussels contract had fallen through. Some of her clients, unfortunately a couple of her large anchor accounts, reneged on their promises to invite her back with open corporate arms. She's had to rebuild her entire business almost from scratch. Five months without a paycheck had almost exhausted her cash flow. But thank God there have been no more threats or break-ins.

Karen's concentration was broken by the sharp wail of the phone. She watched as Pamela raced into her home office to answer the phone's summons. *What's a client doing calling her on Saturday?* Karen asked herself.

In a few moments Pamela reappeared, beaming. From the look on her seraphic face, she was the bearer of glad tidings.

"It was Brad. He called to say he'd be ten or fifteen minutes late for dinner, but that the wait would be worth it." She reported, not at all concerned about putting dinner on hold. "He said he has a surprise, but that's all he would say."

Being somewhat detached from the snares of blind romantic love, Constance was able to be a little more objective. "If he's going to be late for any meal, this is the one. It will keep pretty well. We'll wait until he arrives to put the rolls in the oven."

At the sound of another call on her business line, Pamela rolled her eyes and lamented, "I forgot to put the message service on." She wheeled around and sprinted toward the office again. As she flew through the threshold between the kitchen and dining room, she brushed past Karen, who averted a collision by anticipating Pamela's flight route.

"Whoa, slow down there girl," Karen chided good-naturedly, "the speed limit indoors is five miles an hour."

"Sorry," Pamela excused herself as she breezed past her smiling sister.

Constance had not witnessed Pamela's precarious exit, and thought Karen's comment about the five mile-an-hour speed limit was for her benefit.

"Well, there's really no hurry," she advised, as she made one more pass with the damp dish cloth across the counter top and then leaned down to do a proper job on the glass oven door.

Karen chuckled, "I was talking to Pamela, Gramma."

"Oh, I thought you were referring to these old vintage parts." Holding the dishtowel she had used to buff the counter top, she put her hands on her hips.

"I hope I'm in half as good a shape as you are, Gramma, when I'm your age."

"Careful," Constance teased, "a woman's age and looks are sacred possessions."

"Aw, Gramma, you know what I mean."

Constance shot her a quick wink and pretended embarrassment. She enjoyed receiving compliments that hinted positively at how well she had taken care of herself. She had always prided herself in staying physically, mentally, and spiritually fit. And she was especially pleased that both granddaughters had followed suit, by building daily exercise into their lifestyle.

If I've given them the keys to health, she complimented herself, *I've given each of them quite an inheritance.*

Just then Pamela's voice sent a melodious ripple of joy throughout the house.

"Geoffrey! How nice of you to call."

"Yea, I've caught you home. Everything all right? No uninvited guests or things that go bump in the night?"

"I'm fine. No need to worry. Karen's visiting and Gramma is here cooking."

"Yes, I know. Well ... I know Karen's there. I'm keeping Hans for her. Say hi to them."

"How's my favorite law student?" she applauded in a voice filled with admiration.

She was so proud of him. He had retired from the police department on medical disability and was studying criminal law. He was taking a full course load, too many hours as far as she was concerned, but was doing extremely well. He seemed much more at peace with himself than the last time they had spoken.

"I've got a couple of things I'd like to tell you. You got a minute?"

"Of course, I've always got time for the man who saved my life."

"That's right!" Geoffrey confirmed in a jubilant tone. "You owe me big time, princess."

Pamela laughed, "And I'll gladly pay anything you want. Like I told you before, just name it." She meant it. Geoffrey was her best friend. He understood her better than anyone else.

"That's one of the things I want to talk to you about."

"Oh, so you're calling in favors, are you?" she teased, grinning in a decidedly conciliatory tone. She knew full well that he would never make an unreasonable request or ask her to do something she found objectionable.

"I haven't seen you since February," he pouted lightheartedly. "It seems a certain golden-haired boy has captured your fancy and ... "

"Geoffrey Collins, you stop that right now." Pamela interrupted, then continued hurriedly. "You know no one can ever take your place in my heart."

"Flattery will get your everywhere so don't stop," he said lightheartedly. "The reason I called is because I've got a couple of surprises for you."

Surprises, she thought. *I'm getting surprises from both of my favorite men today.* She didn't bother to mention that she had a surprise coming from Brad, too.

"You know I enjoy surprises."

"Yep, but you'll have to come to Asheville to see one of them," Geoffrey beamed triumphantly.

"To Asheville?"

Her pronouncement struck him as funny.

"Wait a minute. Let me take a peek outside. Yes, my house is still sitting on Oak Place in Asheville, North Carolina."

"Geoffrey?"

"In case you don't remember, it's a medium-sized city in the Western part of the state," he teased, trying his best to sound playfully magisterial. "The birthplace of Zebulon Baird Vance wartime governor of this fair state during the War of Northern Aggression, and the burial sites of Thomas Wolf and O. Henry.

"Geoffrey Collins!"

"It boasts a population of just under sixty-two thousand people and is surrounded by two gorgeous mountain ranges, the Smokies and the Blue Ridge Mountains. Divided by two rivers, the Swannanoa and the French Broad ... "

Pamela laughed heartily. "What do you suggest? Do I take a boat on the river or a horse across the mountains?"

"A plane from the Raleigh/Durham Airport will do."

"Oh, then you live in the civilized part of Asheville?" she taunted, enjoying the long distance reunion with Geoffrey, and in particular his good spirits.

"I see you've still got that Raleigh attitude," he ridiculed warmheartedly. "Are you civilized enough to enter a really civilized part of North Carolina?"

"I beg your pardon!"

"No, beg my forgiveness," he bantered.

"Okay. Okay. Forgive me for not visiting you this winter," she pleaded, feeling her way around his mild reprimand.

"It's almost summer, my dear."

"Geoffrey, I'm sorry."

"You don't have to apologize again. I forgive you, but I'd still like to see you and show you what I've done to the house."

"The house?"

"That's one of the surprises. I've remodeled the house. Well, I'm having a contractor remodel it. The interior is being re-designed to make it a more user-friendly home."

"You mean to make it more Geoffrey friendly?"

"Yep. For example, when you come—you are going to pay me a visit, aren't you?"

"My curiosity and friendship will get me there," she promised, sounding a bit philosophical.

"I'd suggest either a plane or automobile."

"You were saying before you interrupted yourself," she joked, unperturbed, overlooking the good-natured joke.

Geoffrey decided to abandon his sparring and be more specific about what he meant by a more user-friendly environment.

"I'm redesigning the place so it adapts to me rather than my adapting to it." He paused intentionally.

Pamela's admiration for him traveled through the phone.

"O ... kay. A new home for the new you," she stretched her reply.

"Yes, you've got it. I believe my favorite management consultant has got it."

Her eyebrows disappeared under her bangs, which she had just trimmed.

"There are practical ways to redesign every room, and even the outside of the house, to accommodate someone who uses a wheelchair or walker," he began. "I've widened all the doorways to give myself room to maneuver. The kitchen sink and stovetop have recessed fronts to I can pull my wheelchair close. I've also lowered the countertops to complement my sitting height."

"Geoffrey, that's neat."

"I've even installed a Highline Lite by Kohler ... "

"A what?" Pamela asked.

"A universal toilet."

"Oh, TMI," she mused.

"It's bowl height is seventeen and a half inches higher than the standard models like the one you have there in Raleigh, for instance. It allows me easier transfer from wheelchair to toilet and back again to wheelchair."

"That's incredible," Pamela interposed, genuinely impressed. "I want to see it."

"Good. I'm kinda proud of it."

"I can tell. Let me check my social calendar for the month of June."

"It won't be till next month, huh?"

"Geoffrey, next Thursday is June first," she said softly, speaking in a half whisper. "Why don't we come ... " she paused checking her pocket calendar. "How 'bout next weekend, Friday through Sunday?"

"That's great. Uh, oh, you said we."

Pamela laughed, "Yes, we. Karen and I. As you know she's visiting here now and plans to fly back home by next weekend. Oh, you thought I meant Brad and me?"

"I heard we, so I naturally assumed ... "

"That I meant Brad. Well, Mr. Lawyer, detective, investigator, instigator. I'll have you know that Mr. Aikman will not be accompanying me to Asheville this trip. He's attending a rehab conference in Atlanta next week."

"Oh, I see. And you're not going with him?"

"No, smarty. He's one of the concurrent session speakers and is presenting his topic twice. He's also a local chapter officer and has to attend several associational and leadership meetings throughout the weekend. Besides, we don't do everything together."

"I'm glad you can accommodate me with your busy schedule."

She frowned her guilt.

"I truly am sorry, Geoffrey, for neglecting you these past few months," she apologized again for her negligence.

"That's okay. Just don't let it happen again, young lady," he teased, sounding more charitable than upset. "Oh, one more thing about the renovations and then I'll get off the subject."

Pamela waited, pleased that he sounded so excited.

"By the time you two get here, my brand spanking new transfer shower will have been installed and in operating order."

"What's a transfer shower?"

"It's a shower for wheelchair users. The shower seat is the same height as the wheelchair seat and makes transfer from one to the other a piece of cake. The hot and cold controls are low enough so I can reach them from a sitting position and grab bars allow me to slide into the shower with ease."

"I can't wait to see this."

"The bars and seat aren't stainless steel either. They're color coordinated with my bathroom décor."

"That's amazing. What will they think of next? What colors did you select?"

"You'll have to visit to find that out."

"You stinker."

"No, actually I'm not a stinker," rallied Geoffrey. "Thanks to a company that specializes in barrier-free environments for the handicapped. I'm the proud owner of a universally designed self-cleaning toilet."

Pamela's uproarious laugh intrigued Karen, who appeared wide-eyed at her office doorway.

Pamela made eye contact with Karen and motioned her into the office with a hand gesture. She cupped her hand over the beige mouthpiece and addressed Karen.

"I'll explain later," she said smiling broadly.

Karen shook her head from side to side and waved off Pamela's cordial appeasement. "I was just checking on you," she whispered. "Tell Geoffrey I said hello."

Pamela nodded her understanding and then took her hand off the mouthpiece so she could address Geoffrey.

"Karen says hi and to tell you she's looking forward to seeing you next Friday."

A look of surprise flew onto Karen's face. Looking directly at Pamela, Karen mouthed a silent reply as her lips formed the word Friday. Her hands flew out in front of her palms up, in a questioning gesture.

"I have no idea what you're talking about," she whispered to Pamela.

Pamela waved her off and broke eye contact to emphasize that Geoffrey needed her undivided attention.

Karen pointed toward the door leading from the office and smiled at Pamela, and then waved good-bye as she made her exit.

Pamela waved good-bye as well. Then she covered the mouthpiece with her hand again and whispered, "Later," to a retreating Karen, who had already entered the hallway leading back to the kitchen.

"That was just Karen leaving," she said, bringing Geoffrey up to date.

"Got a few more minutes?" Geoffrey asked, then continued quickly, "I'd like to tell you about the second surprise."

"Listen, any man who has a—what did you call it—a universally designed self-cleaning toilet, has my complete unadulterated attention," she assured laughing heartily.

"Every home owner in America oughta have one," he chuckled. "Make a deposit and let the toilet bowl do the work."

"Geoffrey, I think we need to change the subject."

"You're right. Looks like our discussion has gone a bit ... "

"Geoffrey!"

"South?"

Pamela sighed.

"You're letting that new toilet go to your he ... ad," she stuttered the last word, realizing she had just given him another opportunity to elaborate on anal retention.

Geoffrey let out a devilish howl. "Well, since you brought the subject up again," he said evenly, deliberately pausing to provoke her objection, which he knew would come.

"You're so bad," she blushed.

"I bet your face is flushed."

"Geoffrey, stop it right now or I'm going to hang up. What's gotten into you?"

"I guess I'm being a little too cavalier, aren't I? But I'm really feeling good. I think I'm on to something, Pamela. Have you ever heard of Police composites?"

"What?"

"Composites," he repeated. "Electronic representations of people's facial features squiggled on a computer. That's the second surprise."

"You are, of course, going to elaborate."

"After what happened to you a couple of months ago, you know, the break-in. Well, you haven't had any more trouble, have you?"

"Only a preponderance of hang-ups. Other than that nothing."

"Good. Anyway, after you called and told me what happened, I decided to step up my efforts to identify the hit-and-run driver. I keep remembering more and more about the accident. Bits and pieces are coming together in my memory.

"I'm working with Galen Harris, the department's computer composite artist to complete a composite of the driver of the car that hit us."

"I'm impressed. I'm sorry I haven't followed up from my end."

"The Asheville police have not been able to make any appreciable progress. Over five months. Can you believe it? The only evidence they've been able to compile is a few bits of broken glass and paint from the accident scene and my brief description of the nineteen-eighty or eighty-two black Mercedes, with three, maybe four passengers. Pamela, I really could use your help on this. I bet you can remember more than you think you can."

Pamela sighed heavily. "I've already told you I remember the decorative hood ornament perched prominently on the hood. My only other recollection is the glare from the windshield just before the car plowed into us. But that's it. Everything else is a blur. The best term I can think of to describe my impressions of that day is frozen driftage."

"Frozen driftage? I like that. They certainly 'drifted' into us. They left us to die. The people, and I use that term lightly, in the car ran for cover like a bunch of cockroaches frightened by the light. That's why we've got to find them. They didn't care what happened to us."

"I know ... I know," whispered Pamela.

"I wasn't going to take you back there. Physically, mentally, or otherwise. But things have changed. Your house was broken into and you were assaulted. And you've just admitted you've gotten threatening phone calls ... "

"Hang-ups," she interrupted.

"Too many hang-ups. That's unnerving in itself. Has the phone company been able to help?"

"No ... I haven't called them."

"Pamela!"

"I guess I should have."

"You guess you should have. What am I going to do with you?"

"Be patient. You've got to be patient with me."

"Okay. But don't give up on me either ... or yourself. I'll never give up. Never give up."

"Yes, but it's been over five months now! And the only lead we've had is the attack on me," she raised her voice, sounding argumentative.

"And that's what caused me to accelerate my efforts here. We've got to find him before he tries anything else. That's why I told you to stay cool for a while, so he thinks he's scared you off. I'm beginning to get a picture, a faint image of what the driver looks like, so it's not hopeless. Don't you see?"

"You've what!" she asked from the depths of her gloom. "You think you may know what he looks like?"

"Almost. Galen and I've produced a draft of a composite of the guy I think hit us, but there's something about the face that isn't right yet And for the life of me, I haven't been able to figure out what it is."

"Who's Galen?"

Realizing that Pamela had completely missed his reference to Galen a few minutes before, he reiterated relevant fragments of his prior conversation.

"I want you to take a look at the composite and ... "

"Geoffrey, I can't do it," she sheared off the end of his sentence. He had pushed her panic button.

"You've got to," he blasted, raising his voice in anger for the first time. He caught himself, amazed that he had reacted so caustically. He had never raised his voice at her before. Never. His frustration at her squeamishness dissipated as quickly as it came.

The sharp edges of his voice were supplanted by softer tones of empathy and love as he began again, this time speaking in a more apologetic voice.

"I'm sorry. I shouldn't have said that. Do you forgive me? Please say yes."

Pamela hesitated only because she found it difficult to translate her thoughts into words.

"If you think it'll do any good, I'll take a look at it," she spoke softly, although her voice was a shade cooler than she intended.

"Are you sure?" came Geoffrey's eager reply. He knew she would remain true to the fidelity of her beliefs. She had never shirked from responsibility. He was pleased that she wasn't going to now.

"Yes."

"You know I wouldn't ask you to do anything I felt you couldn't do. You know that, don't you?"

"I thought so until you asked me to do this," she mildly protested. "But I know you're right in asking me to help, although I don't know what good it'll do. I didn't see anything."

"Maybe you saw something, maybe you didn't," he accommodated, trying to sound as objective as he could. "But it's worth a try," he added. "And you may be surprised."

"What do you mean?"

"You may have seen more than you think."

Pamela shook her head. "I don't know. It happened so fast. And I don't remember seeing anyone in the car."

"Don't sell yourself short, princess," he coaxed, protesting mildly. "You have a remarkable ability to pick up on nuances, to see the subtleties in things. That's what makes you such a good consultant. You have a way of seeing order in the midst of chaos."

His words settled around her like a familiar sweater, warm and protective.

At that particular moment, Constance appeared. She was concerned about the length of the call and a bit apprehensive at the sullenness that seemed to envelop Pamela, making her appear almost mournful.

"Is everything all right?" she whispered.

Pamela nodded and mouthed a silent, "I'm okay," in her direction.

"Are you sure?" whispered Constance.

Pamela nodded. When it appeared that Constance had more on her mind, Pamela spoke into the mouthpiece for Geoffrey's benefit.

"Hold on just a minute. Gramma is trying to tell me something."

"I'm sorry to interrupt you, honey. Tell Geoffrey hello for me," she stopped intentionally to allow Pamela to relay her greeting.

Pamela quickly proxied Constance's greeting. Then she lowered the phone as she met her grandmother's gaze.

"Everything is all right, isn't it?" Constance reiterated.

"Yes, Gramma," she allowed a tentative smile to edge across her face.

"Everything is fine. I'll only be a few more minutes." She raised her eyebrows lightly giving Constance an opening to say what she had come to say.

"I'm preparing Karen and myself a snack. Thought you might like to join us." Her eyes searched Pamela's for any flicker of interest that might help justify her impromptu visit.

Pamela's eyes brightened and a wide smile sprouted on her face, sending sparkles of light dancing in eyes dimmed just a few moments ago. She gave her Grandmother an affirmative nod, sending Constance hurriedly toward the doorway.

Before she got there, Constance turned toward Pamela again and held up her hand, extending all four fingers and thumb toward the ceiling.

"Five minutes?" she whispered, hoping to leverage Pamela's time. Then she motioned toward the kitchen.

Pamela nodded again and gave her a thumbs-up sign indicating her agreement. As she watched her grandmother disappear, Pamela brought the receiver back to her ear.

"Sorry."

"That's okay."

"Where were we?"

"I was just about ready to fax you a copy of the composite."

Pamela's mouth suddenly went dry.

"I'd like you to take a look at it as soon as you can."

Pamela swallowed several times, trying to get her mouth in working order.

"Is that okay? Pamela, are you with me?"

"Right. Okay. But I don't want you to be disappointed if the composite doesn't' mean anything to me. I can't promise anything."

"I understand. And Pamela, darling, it's all right. If you can help, great. If you can't, that's okay, too."

"All right," she surrendered, then she raised her voice, "You have my electronic fax number. Right?"

"Yep. And if it triggers any memories, any recollections ..."

"Geoffrey," she pruned his sentence, showing mild irritation. "It'll definitely trigger memories."

"I know, I know." He agreed. "I appreciate this, doll. I want to put this thing behind me as much as you do. I can't see letting that irresponsible jerk get by with vehicular assault. I'm chained to a damned wheelchair because of it."

"I know," Pamela winced, "I know."

Constance poked her head through the doorway and held out a small plate of sugar cookies she had just rescued from the oven. She wore a pleasant smile on her face and held the plate at arm's length with some premeditation.

Karen appeared beside her, holding two glasses of skim milk, one for herself and the other for the sister she hoped to pry away from the phone. As a further inducement she took a sip from her glass, making sure enough milk stuck to the area just above her upper lip to paste a white mustache above it for comic relief.

Pamela's blank look at both solicitors yielded no reaction other than eye contact that told them their timing was off, way off. Almost simultaneously, they ducked back out of the room, giving the appearance of having choreographed their speedy exit.

"I think we'd better leave well enough alone," Constance summarized, "she appears to need a few more minutes."

Karen nodded and tightened her lips slightly. "Our next challenge is to see if we can save her any cookies." She chuckled as she leaned over and bit off a section of cookie Constance was holding in her hand.

"I'm lucky I have any fingers left," Constance whispered, somewhat amused but mostly surprised at Karen's unscrupulous antics. "Here," she pushed the rest of the cookie toward Karen's mouth, which has just been emptied of its sugar-coated contents. Still handcuffed by milk glasses in each of her hands, Karen opened her mouth wide and willingly accepted the punishment, enjoying the exquisite taste of the other half of the warm sugar cookie.

One look at Karen standing there with two milk glasses in her hand, what was left of a sticky white mustache above her top lip, and the pilfered cookie, was more than Constance could take. She let out a robust laugh that sent the two of them scurrying down the hallway toward the kitchen in an attempt to take their noise to the other side of the house.

"Look, I've got to go. Gramma and Karen have made a snack of sugar cookies and milk and want me to join them."

"Sounds yummy. Any of those calories I can help relieve you of, just let me know."

"Fat chance. There's three women in the house who crave homemade sugar cookies fresh out of the oven. I ask you, what chance do you think you have of ever seeing any of these tantalizingly delicious cookies?"

"Don't save me any then. See if I care," he pouted good-naturedly. "I think I'll just pull some vanilla yogurt and chocolate chips out of the refrigerator and have me a party."

"You stinker! You know that's my favorite dessert."

"Stinker? Here we go again."

"No! Oh, no, we don't. We're not getting started on that again."

"Good-bye, love."

"Bye." Pamela laid the receiver on its cradle and then picked it back up, punching in the codes to activate the message service. Before she left the office, she looked at the office that had once been the epicenter of her life work. It didn't have the same feel to it now. Her relationship to work was different. She felt a growing distance between herself and the work that had occupied so much of her time for the past twelve years.

Unconsciously navigating the two-step rise that took her out of her office, she wondered, *What if Geoffrey's right? What if I subconsciously saw more than I realize? Will the composite sketch trigger my recognition of the driver, too? What memoires will it dredge up? I'm still having horrible nightmares about it. What if ...*

She stopped her train of thought and mentally chided herself for her reluctance to take control. *You cannot manage yourself unless you manage your choices,* she reminded herself. *I must deal with it now. Geoffrey's right. I want it out of my life, out of my present. The past doesn't have to be a life sentence. I can, if I choose, move beyond its pain and horror and demons— to find peace and love and joy. It will only seem like a bad chapter in my life if I continue to turn the pages fast enough. I can't rewrite that horrible chapter, but I can change the ending. One day it will seem like something I read in a book and then put away. I made it through those chapters. I can make it through the new chapter, and the next one, and the next. The book on me is not complete. Tomorrow will see a new improved me. A more determined me.*

Her natural pragmatism had returned. It was a personal characteristic that had defined her for many years, particularly since her parents' deaths.

She walked confidently into the kitchen and was immediately bathed in warm smiles and showered with cookies and milk.

CHAPTER EIGHTEEN

A combination of aborted plans had sent her to the beach. Geoffrey called on Monday to cancel her trip to Asheville to visit him. He was experiencing some complications, and had to spend a few days in the hospital for tests. Then a client in Greensboro called on Tuesday to postpone the scheduled training for Wednesday to the next month. So Pamela decided to use the free time for a mental health break at the beach. The business postponement was a relief. Geoffrey's cancellation was more of a concern.

Karen's polite refusal to accompany her was met with Pamela's shrewd pretense at disappointment. Pamela suspected that Karen wanted to get back home anyway. She had been in Raleigh for a week and a half and was anxious to see Hans.

Since Brad was in Atlanta and her calendar had cleared, Pamela decided to go on the spur of the moment and was proud of herself for her spontaneity.

Karen prefers the stability of the mountains over the transitoriness of beaches, Pamela thought, allowing a slight smile to overtake her face. *Karen is more centered and grounded than I am right now. I'm in transition. That's probably why I prefer the beach to the mountains.*

She laughed out loud. The pitch of her voice scattered a half dozen or so sandpipers, sending them scurrying as fast as their thin sticks for legs could carry them beyond her sudden outburst. She watched them as they stopped several feet away and began their methodical retreat and advance up the beach.

They managed to stay just ahead of her and in concert with the ebb and flow of the tides, as they searched for their breakfast. She was impressed with the sandpipers' ability to stay clear of the next salty installment of inexorable surf.

"Why can't I be in sync like that? Why can't I accept the ebb and flow of life? What do I need to learn from these simple merchants of the shore?" she asked herself aloud.

She was seeking firm ground in this transitory period of her life and was beginning to think she had found it in Brad.

"Oh, how I miss his caress," she addressed the wary sandpipers. "You would like him. You'd say he's good for me."

She drew a deep breath of freedom and started jogging quickly under a cloudless canopy of Carolina blue sky. It felt good to run again, to feel her heels lift and the pressure of the balls of her bare feet push off against the surface of the damp sand as each foot left its imprint on the beach. She held on tightly to her running shoes, each stuffed with a pink athletic sock. She carried the shoes like batons, and chased her shadow down a wide stretch of beach.

Two passers-by, an older couple, walking hand in hand on the beach a few paces from her, caught her jubilation as she pirouetted a couple of times in quick succession at the thought of Brad's name.

She smiled broadly as she whirled, her outstretched arms terminating with the running shoes she still held in her hands. Her smile lingered as she remembered the look on his face when he showed her his purchase, a 1988 Confederate gray Mercedes 560 SL convertible, his dream car.

She chuckled when she recollected how Constance summarized Brad's purchase: The bigger the boy, the more expensive the toy.

She was right, of course, but now I'm enjoying his toy.

Brad had insisted on her taking the car to the beach since he was in Atlanta. He justified it as a way for him to remain close to her. Although she was reluctant to drive a classic, he expressed his complete trust in her driving ability.

"It's not my driving ability I'm worried about. I'm concerned about the thousands of careless drivers who occupy the same roads I do," she said aloud, as she dodged a piece of driftwood.

Brad's promised me that when he joins me later this week, he'll cruise around the Outer Banks in the car of his dreams with the woman of his dreams. I like being called the woman of his dreams. With such a romantic overture, how could I refuse? she thought happily as she renewed her jog up the beige beach.

She let the tide wash over her feet whenever she ventured too close to the water's irregular, but relentless pilgrimage to claim more sand. She was hibernating in the open, distancing herself from the pressures of getting her business up to speed and from the worries of the past. The sense of freedom, no matter how abbreviated, felt wonderful.

Shortly after she tested her legs with a sprint, she was startled out of her reverie.

Just behind her someone had shouted a warning. She turned in time to hear the warning repeated.

"Geoffrey! You're much too far out. Come back toward the beach this minute."

Pamela watched as the youngster waded slowly to shore, resentful of his mother's intrusion. She smiled as he moseyed toward his concerned mother, who stood at the water's edge to show her impatience.

"Geoffrey! Oh, no," Pamela whispered aloud, as she clapped her hand against her forehead. "I forgot to open the fax after I said I would when Geoffrey called Monday. This beach trip came up so suddenly I completely forgot about it."

She breathed heavily, more from the troublesome hindsight than her physical exertion at the moment.

"Nothing I can do about it now," she whispered between labored breaths. She quickened her pace again, more determined than ever to isolate herself from the worries that brought her here. The beach was her centering spot, her public sanctuary.

The opaline morning mists that blanketed the beach had lifted, unveiling bleached stretches of sand and promising another gold-toned day. The dissipating mists pledged a rolling cinema of clouds and moved wistfully in white, fluffy caravans along the perimeter of the beach. They played dutifully to the metronome of the surf, assuring a miraculously new nautical concert.

"Today adagio, tomorrow, perhaps vivace," Pamela thought aloud as she watched the shoreline disappear, then reappear in rhythm with the advancing waves.

Broken shells speckled the beach under her feet. A gull first quickened his step, then stalked away arrogantly as she approached. Sporting a scallop shell in his beak, he glared back at Pamela over his feathered shoulder, spiteful of her unsanctioned intrusion on his stretch of bleached sand.

For the next week Pamela divided her time between the beach and the beach house she had rented. She lived in the moment, refusing to entertain thoughts about her past life, except for the phone calls each night from Brad. She kept her head buried in the stack of suspense paperbacks left at the cottage, discarded by previous tourists who used their salt soiled and sun lotion spattered pages as a momentary escape from their own harsh business or social realities.

The only interruptions to her hermetic routine were a quick visit to the sculptured nail shop two blocks away to repair a broken nail, and a trip to a cosmetologist for a haircut. Both outings confirmed her belief that people couldn't come to Emerald Isle or any North Carolina beach without having their personal idiosyncrasies pampered in one way or another.

These should last at least another week, she reminded herself, as she glanced at her fingernails.

As if to confirm her judgment, she lightly applied pressure to the tips of each fingernail, pressing down on each end to gauge the integrity of its bond to the base of the nail. Satisfied that all were securely bonded, including the recently repaired thumbnail, she turned the next page of the paperback she was reading, intent on finishing the chapter before she treated herself to dinner.

I love dining out at night at the beach. Everything is dark all along the coastline and harbors, except for the tiny pinpoints of light that dot the coastline or marinas.

"Why, they bring incandescent specks of artificial stars within human reach," she quoted a poet whose name she couldn't remember.

She nestled back into the deep-pillowed wicker sofa that cradled her, enjoying its plush softness.

The novel she had started to read was about a young ballroom dancing instructor who was being stalked by an ex-boyfriend. Suddenly she was haunted by the break-in and assault in her home. She quickly tossed the paperback on the end table.

A shiver shot through her, causing her to sit upon the sofa and close her eyes for a moment.

"That could just as easily happen to me. It *has* happened to me. The past two months may be a calm before the storm."

Now, you don't want to become paranoid over this, she cautioned herself.

Her depression caused Pamela to seek the safe harbor of an afternoon nap. Once she settled back into the soft cushions, she immediately fell to sleep.

She awoke several hours later to find the afternoon had slipped into darkness. She stretched and extended her yawn as she ambled into the kitchen to grab something to eat.

§   §   §   §   §   §

Geoffrey had met with a psychologist friend over the weekend, who hypnotized him and shepherded him through a series of subconscious recollections about the accident.

Memories had surfaced. Horrible memories. But he dredged up more of the facial features of the assailant and believed he had enough of a composite to show the police.

The whole composite-producing process, combined with the hypnotherapy sessions, gave Geoffrey an unforgettable glimpse into the science of traumatic memory impairment. His thoughts digressed to the conversation he'd had over the weekend with Samuel Weinstein, his hypnotherapist friend.

"Short-term memory normally holds only about seven items, give or take a few," Dr. Weinstein had summarized. "Any new item coming in randomly displaces one already there. The more compelling, as in the case of traumatic information, the more displacement."

"Then short-term memory is a sort of scratch pad where we store information temporarily?" Geoffrey asked, trying to grasp the concept.

"In a manner of speaking, yes," agreed Dr. Weinstein. "It is then filed in long-term or reference memory."

"Then are images, facts, sounds, for example, associated with my accident listed in my long-term memory now?"

"We have already dredged up some of them, my friend, through hypnotherapy."

Geoffrey nodded his understanding.

"Traumatic events leave a deep imprint on the mind. Cerebral circuits sizzle with current when we face danger, risk of the unknown, anything which threatens our survival. We have found that amygdala, that's Greek for almond, the lump of tissue tucked deep inside our brain, helps preserve memories of highly emotional situations. Stress, particularly severe stress ..."

"Like my accident," Geoffrey interrupted.

Dr. Weinstein nodded and then continued. "Severe stress causes a gland near the kidney to secrete adrenaline which stimulates the vagus nerve, which in turn sends a signal up the spine to the amygdala ordering it, in effect to save this critical information because it's important to this entity's survival."

"So hypnosis actually accesses this information and brings it to the surface," Geoffrey commented with enormous interest.

"It's all there," his therapist agreed, "and much of it is saturated with as much emotional pain as the body was damaged with physical trauma. The body, mind, and soul are interconnected in ways we are only beginning to appreciate."

"Then our minds are constantly finding connections between the pieces in our memories, both long and short term, like a certain police detective trying to find the pieces to build a composite of the face of a hit-and-run driver," Geoffrey guessed, confident that he understood.

"That's right. Thanks to powerful new tools for studying what goes on in your head," his friend blunted his own comment. "Well, we may not have discovered the tools yet to find what you've got missing in your head."

"Funny, Sam, real funny," Geoffrey scolded, issuing a good-natured reprimand.

"Techniques such as magnetic resonance imaging and positron emission tomography," Dr. Weinstein continued, "are helping us understand how memory works."

Geoffrey smiled as he thought about that last recollection. Positron emission tomography. Magnetic resonance imaging scans. Fancy tools for uncovering the brain's secrets.

And then another thought struck him, causing him to wheel his chair to his newly renovated desk. Fancy tools may unravel the brain's secrets and excavate facts from memory, but only love and compassion can penetrate the heart.

Nostalgic thoughts took him back to the early weeks and months of his recovery. He remembered his erratic mood swings, times when he plunged from tear-filled relief that he was alive, to anger and hatred toward the driver responsible for his broken body. Other times he was numbed by depression and despair and self-pity. He had seriously considered suicide. He fondly thought about the times when Pamela tried everything she knew to bouy him up so he could tread emotional waters.

He spied the framed photo of Pamela and Karen on his desk. It was one he'd taken of them several years before. His attention was drawn to Pamela. To her smile. To the resolute lift of her chin. To the confident gleam in her emerald eyes.

"The credit goes to you, babe. You cajoled me. You challenged my despondency. You insisted that I climb out of my self-imposed tomb of darkness."

His admiring eyes moved to Karen.

"You threatened me with sunlight every time you opened the mini-blinds I intentionally left closed for days on end."

He glanced to his left at the open blinds and smiled.

"Your only psychological tool was your conviction that anything was possible as long as I put my absolute faith in God."

He fixed his gaze on Pamela again.

"You said once that I was trapped in the paralysis of the moment ... and that I could stay there if I wanted to."

He chuckled his understanding.

"You were relentless, my dears, in your harping tactics."

He wheeled himself back half a rotation from the desk.

"You said depression has centrifugal force," he spoke to Pamela's side of the photo. "Well, I've felt its inexorable pull. When I wake every morning, I feel its paralyzing influence. I feel just like Christopher Reeve. He said when he awakened every morning, he had to re-accept his condition."

He lowered his head and looked at the large wheels that flanked his chair before he trained his gaze on the photo.

"I remember pushing everyone away at first. Dad, Karen, the Lees, you. The fellas at the precinct. You said I settled for outposts of on-lookers instead of communities of supporters. And you were right. It was easier to isolate myself than feel sorry for myself in public."

He rested his elbows on the padded wheelchair arms.

"You know, I cursed God for abandoning me. Then I realized it was I who abandoned God. All struggle is liturgy.

That's the insight I got. Every life is sacred. Each activity is important. How's that coming from a small-town cop?"

He hesitated reflectively before he spoke again.

"To tell you the truth, I still haven't accepted my paralysis. Christopher Reeve did a better job at that than I am."

He wheeled closer to his desk and placed his forearms on its lacquered surface.

"I will never accept my disability. I may tolerate it, but I'll never accept it."

He closed his eyes to seal out the pain. He knew it was his inability to fully accept this condition that sent him into fits of anger. He felt in control most of the time, but his mood swings still troubled him, erupting suddenly, viciously, whenever he dwelled too much on the accident. And yet he knew he had to focus on the accident.

"How else am I going to bring that criminal to justice?" he raised his voice. "How can I even begin to accept my disability unless I know I've done all I can to find the one who took my legs from me?"

The shrillness of the phone brought him back to the present. He wheeled over to the cell phone on the dining room table and turned it on.

"Hello."

No answer.

"Hello," he repeated, sounding a little cooler.

There was a distinctive click, signaling the caller had terminated the connection.

Geoffrey raised his eyebrows and punched the "Off" button on his cellular.

"Wrong number," he announced to himself. "I don't know why I didn't let it go to a message."

He deposited the phone in his shirt pocket and wheeled into the open space under his desk.

He pulled his personalized stationery out of its compartment in the top drawer of his desk and scribbled a quick note to Pamela about his visit with the hypnotherapist. He included a few lines of appreciation for her support, elaborated on the positive results from his hospital tests, and then folded the stationery and placed it in the envelope along with a copy of the composite. Then he decided that when Ted dropped by that afternoon, he'd ask him to take the mail to the post office.

He 'pick-pocketed' his phone and dialed Pamela's office number.

"Hi, doll, it's me again. I forgot to tell you about my visit to Sam Weinstein, so I've included a few comments about it in the letter I'm sending you. Didn't want the information to catch you by surprise. It's in the same envelope as the composite update."

He looked at his watch and then glanced at the photo again.

"I suspect you're soaking up that Emerald Isle sun by now. Enjoy yourself and keep your promise to yourself. The three R's, remember: relax, read, and release. Call me when you can. Love ya."

§ § § § § §

She stretched out her slim, but muscular legs, luxuriating in the hot, heavily-scented bath water. Pamela closed her eyes and sighed, exhaling slowly through her nose, content with her stolen moments of respite. She felt languorous and peaceful, allowing herself to unwind completely from the activities of the day.

She silently chided herself for pushing her legs too far. They ached.

I'm not used to running barefooted on the sand, she reminded herself, smiling contentedly.

Pamela's drifting thoughts preoccupied her for the next several minutes while she surrendered herself to the warmth and soothing effects of the hot bath. Slowly, almost trance like, she reached over to the ceramic shelf that rimmed the Jacuzzi and retrieved the glass of wine she had placed there, anticipating just such a moment. Just before she brought the rim of the glass to her moist lips, she paused to toast herself.

Then, with measured slowness, she took a small sip and steadied her gaze at herself in the mirror. Her free hand reached up and her fingertips moved across the surface of the tiny scar at her hairline, visible now only because her wet hair was combed back exposing her forehead. Her emerald eyes glowing beneath curved eyebrows registered a hint of sadness as she thought about Geoffrey's message on the phone.

"I will not call home before it's time," she promised her double in the mirror, and then pressed the glass to her resolute lips.

"Ah ... h," she sighed out the word. "I could get used to this."

Her gaze uncovered something behind her in the reflection of the mirror. She made a half turn toward the object and discovered it was a large seashell, an absolutely perfect pastel-colored shell. She placed the half-empty wine glass on its tiled perch and retrieved the shell, holding it close for examination.

"What a beautiful shell ... and so large."

Pink and white and apricot, it curled in on itself like a miniature whirlpool of sunlight. She carefully traced its symmetrical whorls with her fingertips, dimpled now and pale from their extended residency in the hot bath water.

Ceramic-like, each opalescent whorl was silken smooth except for the tiny raised ridges that claimed the center of each unblemished curve.

"How beautiful," she repeated to herself aloud.

Struck by its perfect symmetry and chromatic folds, she rotated the shell, taking care not to let it slip from her wet grasp.

Each shell, like people, she reasoned, *has its own distinct personality, its own unique fingerprint. No two are alike, yet each is more alike than different.*

The smoothness of her finger caught a slight cut near the base of one of the whorls. A quick verifying look revealed a small chip in an otherwise perfect field of color and smoothness. One of her hands lifted itself, making an unconscious movement toward her forehead again, while the other sent two fingers across the evanescent slip on the underside of the shell.

"More alike than different," she repeated aloud as she connected consciously with an earlier thought. A wry smile creased her face, as if she were summoned by a prior memory.

We are constantly crafting ourselves, she thought, *concentrating on both the shell and her own forehead. Life is an extension, a reflection of ourselves through others. We are all interconnected, man, woman, animal, plant and shell.*

She rotated the shell again, admiring it.

There is a mosaic of community, of oneness at work here. The whole society suffers a wound to the soul if one member suffers. Scars and chips of pain and suffering and defacement are woven into the fabric of life.

She touched the small cut at the base of one of the whorls again. *There must be a universal memory that records all of this. There must be a collective human response to recognize the chips and heal the scars. What we do to one we do to all,* she summarized reflectively, as she placed the shell back on the tile.

Her thoughts settled once again on the concept of universality, on the interconnectedness of all things animate and inanimate, living or dead, victim and criminal. She hadn't ruminated long when her lips, bare of makeup, curved in a reverent smile across her angelic fact. She had come closer, much closer, to making some sense out of life.

Trauma is part of the alchemy of experience, she said to herself, the insight coming from some cavernous depth. *And experience mirrors the refinement of the soul. We don't really discover anything,* she realized, *we simply recover it!*

A long, extended sigh escaped her lips as she closed her eyes, enjoying the peace and serenity of the moment. She was content.

"Is that it?" she whispered aloud. "Is suffering part of the refinement process? If that's the case, I should be pretty refined ... and Geoffrey, too."

The soft whispers that fell from her moist lips were more like religious devotionals.

"So, how much refinement can I take? Geoffrey's injuries were worse than mine. Does that mean he needs more refinement?"

She massaged her kneecaps with the sponge she lifted from the ceramic disk next to her.

"My scars are really stars in the firmament of my being."

She was satisfied with that assessment, which sprouted from nowhere.

"My scars are stars in the firmament of my living, my self-discovery ... my self-recovery," she chorused confidently, jubilantly, beaming at her reflection in the mirror. She lifted the wine glass, and saluted her personhood.

"You've come a long way, baby. You're a survivor. Don't ever forget that. You're stronger than you think."

The smile that creased her face and remained there for the longest time was a benedictory hymn.

§   §   §   §   §   §

"I'm telling you, it was her. She was coming out of the nail salon."

"I thought she was in Brussels. Didn't you say she had a six-month contract over there?"

"That was before the accident, stupid. I'm telling you, I saw her!"

"So what's the big deal? She's here. You're here. It's a free country."

"You're right. It is a free country. So there's no law against old lovers seeing each other."

"Aw, no Clarence. You're not thinking of seeing her. She's bad news. You said it yourself."

"That's precisely why I've got to see her. She looked too good coming out of the salon for a woman who is supposed to be recovering from an accident. I'm the one who's gone through hell these past few months. Her injuries must not have been as serious as they told me."

He struck the cue ball forcibly, sending it crashing against the six ball wedged against the corner pocket.

"No woman has ever dumped me and gotten away with it."

"Aw, come on man. Ease up."

"Ease up?" Clarence hissed, censoring his next shot. "You're telling me to ease up? She strutted out of that salon like she owned the world. Like she didn't care what happened to me. She's going to pay, Bo. You hear me? She's going to pay."

Clarence leaned across the pool table and lined up his next shot.

"You don't need her, man. There's plenty more women where she came from. Hell, we got 'em hanging around us all the time. You know that. We're football stars. We're celebrities. Remember the two we had last week? They maxed us out on pleasure. Why, the one you had ... "

Clarence aborted the next shot and glared at Bo.

"She's different."

"What?"

"I said ... you don't understand, she's different. She's ... she's different, that's all. Seeing her again made me realize we should be together. She was angry at me before. She said things she didn't mean. Awful things. But I know once she gives me a chance ... we can work things out."

"You're talking crazy, man. First you say she's gonna pay. Now you say you want to work things out."

Clarence looked menacingly at his muscled friend.

"She'll have to pay for her crime. I can't let her by with dumping me. After I'm through with her, she'll come crawling back to me. She'll beg me for forgiveness."

Bo lowered his head, breaking eye contact with Clarence.

"Bo, now don't do me that way. You know I've talked about her before."

"I know."

"I'm telling you right now. If I can't have her, nobody will."

"Clarence, why? Why are you so fired up about her all of a sudden?"

His demented colleague threw Bo a sinister smile.

"Absence makes the heart grow fonder. Isn't that what they say? She looked good, Bo. I mean ... she really looked good."

Bo cautiously nodded his agreement.

Clarence clapped his hands together, applauding his influence over his worried friend.

"Buy us a couple more beers," Clarence suggested, changing his whole demeanor. "I need to wet my whistle before I beat your sorry ass."

"Sure," Bo replied, relieved that Clarence had changed the subject.

Clarence watched Bo retreat to the bar.

You don't understand anything about women, my man, he said to himself. *They were put here to serve us. Pamela just needs to be reminded of that.*

CHAPTER NINETEEN

He was tired, bushed in fact, for he had not slept well again. Fits of insomnia, it seemed, had taken up permanent residence in his life, uninvited and unwelcomed. He would awake with a start in the early morning hours, plagued with images of the accident. Perspiring and anxious, Geoffrey awakened from his latest nightmare, reeling from the hideousness of the dredged-up memories.

He glanced at the digital clock beside his bed.

Two seventeen, he said to himself. *I'm right on schedule.*

Resolved to force sleep to overtake him, he buried his head in the pillow and turned away from the red glare of the electronic dial on the clockradio. The accident had left him partially deaf in one ear, so he turned his head on the right side, hoping to muffle the noises that announced the creaks and groans of a newly-renovated house at night.

"Damn the composite," he hissed to himself, punching the pillow he used as a buffer between his right hip and the bed. He had found that elevating his left side a little above bed level to offset the height differential between his left and right hemispheres enabled him to rest more comfortably.

Although he had taken steps to medically treat his insomnia, it was a condition that had become intolerable. He felt suffocated by his inability to sleep and humiliated by the paralysis that held his body hostage. Occasionally, his aching frustration would spiral into volcanic anger. He felt a shout of seething rage form on his troubled lips, surging upward from the depths of his tormented soul. And finally it came, full-throated and anguished.

"God help me!" he shouted. "Please don't let me go through the rest of my life like this."

His vocal ballistics filled the bedroom with the gut-wrenching wail of a man who was at the end of his rope.

"God, please," he moaned. "It's not right! What have I done to deserve this?"

His labored breathing settled into a more normal respiration as he lay on his back facing the ceiling. The decorative brass light fixture silhouetted against the white ceiling resembled a hexagonal-shaped island floating in a sky of ashen gray above him. Its quartet of faithful bulbs, tucked snugly in their sockets, waited for orders from the nearest light switch to illuminate the room.

"Poised obediently," he said aloud, admiring the patience of the bulbs. "Why can't I turn my own lights on and off like that?"

He closed his eyes again and began breathing rhythmically and slowly in syncopated, measured breaths as he attempted to clear his mind from all worries.

Sometimes this works, he thought, *maybe it'll work tonight.*

An hour and a half later he was still wide awake.

"I may as well study some more. Doesn't look as if I'm going to get any sleep."

He hesitated before he raised himself from the pillows.

Maybe my concern about the mid-term has caused my insomnia.

He quickly dismissed it, knowing full well it was his anxiety over the composite and the fruitless investigation that concocted the alarming nightmares. He closed his eyes and rested a while.

He looked at the clock again.

Five-twenty.

"Looks like I'm going to have to get up."

He slid out of his king-sized bed into the wheelchair and headed toward the shower. Once he cleaned himself up and pulled on his clothes, he wheeled into the kitchen.

"Another day ... another wheelie," he prophesied, and immediately tilted the wheelchair backward.

"There," he addressed the coffee pot, "a salute to the reality of handicaps."

After he poked the coffee pot on, he reversed himself and parked beside the cups that hung from hooks under one of the waist-high shelves in the redesigned kitchen.

He grabbed a clear glass mug and wheeled toward the coffee maker that was groaning its obedience.

"You, too, huh? Don't you wish you could make coffee on the run?"

Geoffrey waited until the pot collected enough of the black liquid to fill a cup.

You can fill the rest of the pot on your own time, he silently addressed the coffee maker, as he lifted the pot and filled his empty cup. He returned the pot to its thermal base and rotated his chair toward the kitchen window.

He looked at his reflection in the pool of coffee in his cup.

"I'm glad it's you in there ... and not Pamela."

Although he felt a tear inch its way down his cheek, he held the coffee cup still. When the tear fell from his chin into the cup, he watched the ripples distort his image.

He slowly lifted the cup and drank a few sips, realizing deep down that he must accept his own disability.

Feeling a bit more resigned, he lifted his coffee cup and saluted the diffused rays of sunlight that cut their way in through the kitchen window. A ribbon of golden light had found its way across the table and pasted itself along one arm and the back of his wheelchair, just missing his left arm and shoulder. In a few minutes it made its presence felt across his face and chest, causing him to reposition himself by parking the wheelchair at the opposite end of the table.

Ted offered to install a set of mini-blinds to block the sun in the mornings, but Geoffrey had politely refused, saying the minor inconvenience of the shooting golden-orbed rays was worth the temporary intrusion. The natural lighting bathed the kitchen with such warmth and brilliance that Geoffrey felt a sort of celestial companionship at breakfast.

"I know you're here," he whispered into the sunlight. "I can feel your presence. I know I'm not alone."

He closed his eyes and let the warmth of the golden rays bathe his face.

"Mom," he addressed her spirit, "ask the other angels to help Pamela. Tell them I'm okay. I'm worried about her. She needs their protection."

He took another sip of coffee and peered through one of the kitchen windows, void of window treatments but overflowing with soothing sunlight. His watchful eye caught the movement of his next-door neighbor as she retrieved the morning paper. She was wearing a pink flanneled nightgown and he could see that she had a cigarette in her mouth.

Geoffrey let out a mildly contemptuous huff when he realized she was carrying the nicotine-laced pacifier.

"What a crude way to start the day," he commented aloud as he watched her inhale a puff before she disappeared through the sliding door of her patio.

Then he focused his attention once again on his reflection in the now half-empty cup of coffee.

I've got a law exam to study for. I'd better get busy!

He took a large swallow of the decaffeinated mud and pronounced it delicious before he put the cup down.

§ § § § § §

The short drive back from the small airport at New Bern seemed long, much too far for Brad and Pamela as they pointed the convertible toward the beach house in Emerald Isle. Their love-making began shortly after they crossed the threshold into the screened porch of the beach house.

Their thirsty kisses at the airport and the seductive glances and covetous body contact on the drive home had heightened their desire.

Their intentions were clear by the time they hurried through the front door. He tenderly brought her hand to his expectant lips. Then he slowly and purposefully uncurled her fingers and kissed her palm, pressing it firmly against his waiting lips. Recognizing the familiar scent of the expensive perfume he bought the week before, he refused to leave her outstretched palm, drinking in the warmth and softness and intoxicating fragrance of skin bathed in Opium perfume.

He inhaled once more, filling his senses with the tantalizing aroma of her scent, willingly surrendering to a self-imposed entrapment.

Desire carried his lips up her palm and along the underside of her well-manicured index finger, momentarily pressing her inch-long fingernail against his lips, which parted slightly as he took her finger in his mouth.

A strangled cry erupted from Pamela's quivering lips. Her face was flushed and pink as she surrendered to his sensuous foreplay. Her free hand found its way to his neck in response to Brad's tenderness and her breasts rose and fell more rapidly under her souvenir T-shirt. Her eyes steadied on his. Her face was filled with both longing and consent.

"I love you Pamela. I love you Babe."

Her arms rose to encapsulate his neck, and her anxious hands, extensions of uncontrollable passion, tussled his golden hair violently, stopping only to press his head closer to her ravenous lips. Moving longingly down his back, her fingernails clawed at his shoulders through his cotton shirt, pressing him still closer to her.

"Kiss me," she ordered breathily. "Kiss me now!"

Her desire almost uncontrollable now, Pamela pulled him closer.

"Brad, take me. Please take me now!"

Her voice, accented with kittenish cries of passion, excited him even more, and her breathing was so rapid and hard that he wanted to squeeze her tighter just to feel her move.

Pamela clung tightly to him, her face aglow with rapturous anticipation.

"Oh, Brad," she breathed, deliriously happy.

He repositioned himself to lift her toward one end of the sofa in an attempt to annex the whole area for the love-making both knew would follow.

She buried her face in his chest and held on tightly as he lifted her gently across the mid section of pillows and deposited her gently, as the wicker creaked and groaned its support.

He smelled distinctly of Eternity cologne by Calvin Klein. *An appropriate choice,* she mused, *for the amount of time I want to feel sexually delirious.* She loved the smell of his laundered shirt and found strength in his raw masculinity. She could feel his heart pounding through his shirt, testimony to his heightened sense of her, to the delirious effect she had on him. She pulled forcefully on his neck again, raising herself to close the distance between them.

Another wild, passionate embrace held them there, stretched out over the sofa, intertwined, smothering each other once more with escalated desire, hot, expedient, unapologetic.

Another ravenous assault with his lips on her neck and throat produced a smothered gasp from her lips, and then her mouth opened in an unuttered plea. Each kiss, every caress deliberately maddening, spontaneously compelling, thoroughly intoxicating. She adored the teasing punishment he so freely gave, and submitted willingly to his sensual inquisition.

Desire possessed them, engulfed them, hurried them willingly into the soft, scintillating collision of their flesh.

An hour later, gloriously lit with the glow of their exceedingly erotic rendezvous, Pamela busied herself with the makeover every woman deems necessary before appearing in public: a warm luxurious bath, hair shampooed, perfunctory curling and feathering to add just the right amount of pouf, a touch of moisturizer and foundation to prepare the facial canvas for the accents of blush and eye make-up, topped off by the perfect shade of lipstick, waterproofed with lip gloss.

Satisfied her cosmetics project was superbly engineered, she glanced at the portable digital clock she always packed on trips.

Four twenty-five. Another hour and a half to dinner, she noted to herself.

Before she followed her impulse to dash out of the dainty little bathroom, with its floral towels and washcloths, wickered cabinet and laundry basket, and decorative, multi-colored fish and sea horse soap cubes cradled so adoringly in a white ceramic dish, she took one more look at herself in the mirror. Standing in her purple silk panties, completely made-up but braless, she gave herself an approving wink.

"You've come a long way, baby," she praised herself in a low, confident voice, and remained standing a short while appraising her looks, her vanity taking over.

A curvaceous smile crept onto her angelic face and her eyebrows lifted as a thought surfaced: *It's too early to get dressed for dinner, so why don't I slip into something comfortable while Brad showers ... and I know the perfect outfit.*

She jubilantly wheeled around and followed her smile into the hallway toward the bedroom, glancing at Brad on the way through. She could see the back of his head and the top of his shoulders above the low-backed wicker sofa. His stockinged feet were propped up on the glass and wicker coffee table. He was facing the doors leading to the deck.

He's evidently enjoying the oceanic view and sporting his own 'just-laid' look, she thought to herself, pursing her lips to conceal a small mischievous smile. *We are good together,* she reveled. *Very good!*

As she exited the narrow hallway into the bedroom, she adjusted her thoughts somewhat, in an attempt to justify their fleshy rendezvous.

Physical attraction is important in a relationship, she thought soberly. *Anyone who says it isn't is either lying or fooling themselves. But there's got to be more than smooth hands and good looks.*

She walked quickly over to Brad's hanging clothes, the ones he had carted back and forth from Atlanta. Two of his shirts were recently dry-cleaned, still bearing the small green paper tattoos of the dry cleaner stapled to the shirt tails.

"This one is perfect," she said softly, pulling one of the shirts off its hanger. "And I know the perfect man to try it out on—a man I can feel comfortable with, a man who respects me, who is sensitive and compassionate, who doesn't mind my getting into his clothes."

Her solitary monologue drifted off into silent thoughts as she spun herself into his white business shirt, which fell just below her knees.

A man who cares, who's protective, who knows how to treat a woman.

She rolled up the sleeves, with their monogrammed cuffs, above her elbows. Smiling sinfully, she negotiated the buttons only high enough to allow the shirt to hang open exposing the cleavage of her large breasts. She playfully fingered the open collar, appreciating her amorous arrangement.

As she paraded silently toward him, the thought occurred to her that he might want something more than a mere look. By the time she flanked the corner of the sofa and sauntered in front of him in her most sensual manner, she was flitting her long lashes with unrestrained abandon, and had placed one hand on her hip, the top of the other hand, palm facing out, on her forehead. Head tilted back, eyes trained on the ceiling, she waited.

Not getting the response she anticipated, she shoved her eyes in his direction.

Brad had fallen asleep.

Her mouth dropped in tolerant surprise, and then receded into a disappointed frown.

"My grand entrance was wasted," she pouted.

She recovered quickly and a devilish smile swept across her face.

"You snooze, you lose," she said, tilting her chin up.

Her thoughts fast-forwarded as she seized the covert opportunity to compensate for her disappointment. She decided to catch him at a disadvantage, to inspect him more carefully.

"I must have worn you out, poor baby."

She snuggled down on one of the wicker chairs parked a few feet away from the sofa with her back facing the sliding doors. The chair creaked its compliance when she repositioned herself by scooting up a little. She crossed her legs and pulled his white dress shirt higher, exposing her slender, well-formed thighs. With frivolous premeditation, she loosened all of the buttons on the shirt and flung it open slightly, letting it cascade across the top of her thighs so that it exposed much more than her cleavage.

Satisfied that her erotic presentation was choreographed to perfection, she purposefully squiggled, producing conspiratory outcries from the relatively stable wicker chair. She hoped to ease Brad into wakefulness.

"I'll have an audience yet. Come on, Brad, wake up! I'm afraid this chair is going to fall apart."

Her silent vigil combined with her playful antics only harvested a few twitches of his hips and a occasional movement of one foot or the other. His muscular arms were crossed over his chest, but she could sense the stalwartness under his shirt. One of the things that had attracted her to him in the first place was that his brawniness was not over-done. He had just the right amount of sinew to suggest invincibility but not enough to label him as narcissistic.

"Oh, Brad," she spoke softly. "Wake up."

She breathed heavily, partly in response to the emotional effect her admiring evaluation was having on her and partly to arouse him to wakefulness. Her lovelorn shenanigans paid off.

He blinked his eyes open and was startled for an instant at having awakened to so close of an inspection.

"Oh, hi, Babe," he greeted her softly, rubbing the corners of his eyes to adjust them to the outside light. "I must have fallen asleep."

"Yes, you did," Pamela agreed in her most sensual voice. She remained in her cross-legged pose.

Brad blinked his eyes a few more times before he became fully aware of the positioning of the beautiful woman in front of him.

"What a nice thing to wake up to," he announced. "You fill that shirt out much better than I do."

"I'm glad you like what you see," Pamela cooed. "It's called monogrammed foreplay."

"It's called gorgeous," he punctuated, as he rose from the sofa and extended his hands, inviting her to join him. "Babe, you are breath-takeningly beautiful."

Pamela smiled as she reeled in his adoration. She moved her lips closer to his, intent on a kiss that would be both passionate and consuming.

They fed on each other. Each welcomed the intensity of the encounter. He ravaged her mouth passionately, almost savagely. Pamela pulled him closer to her, so he could not stop.

His carnivorous kisses turned into hasty retreats as he pulled himself away from her slightly.

The pout on her face brought a compassionate smile to his face. He cradled her chin in his hands so that passionate gaze met longing stare.

"You know where this is going again, don't you?" he smiled his interest.

Pamela produced a succession of quick nods, and then wiped a lipstick smear off the corner of his mouth.

"We were going out to eat, you know," he pressed good-naturedly, trying unsuccessfully to conceal a smile.

Pamela let out a quick sigh that told him she had something else in mind.

"But you're all made up. We'll ... "

Pamela placed her fingers over his mouth, silencing his perjurious protest. "I'd rather make out!"

"You realize this will mess up your hair."

"I'd rather make out!"

"I'll have to cancel our dinner reservations."

"I'd rather have you for dinner."

"You are a persistent woman. You know that?"

Pamela burst out laughing.

"Then it's a good thing we had this talk," she rejoiced, loosening another playful laugh, as she allowed full reign to her uninhibited spirit.

"Talk!" Brad repeated.

"Yes. Talk," Pamela cooed. "Too much talk."

"Too much talk, huh," he mimicked, pinching her lightly on her upper arm, then her waist. He migrated his gentle pinches to her thighs, despite her attempts to intercept the methodical advance of his mischief-making fingers.

"Stop it," she giggled, as she managed to grab one of his wrists. "Stop it now. I mean it!" she howled, as she began an undignified retreat toward the bedroom.

"Oh, you want me to stop do you? But we're just talking, right?"

Another gentle pinch, this time to her buttocks, sent her laughter to a higher pitch, as she flew into the bedroom.

Overtaking her at the foot of the bed, Brad turned her toward him. Her radiant face indicated surrender and her breathing was rapid, accentuating the movement of her breasts.

He ran his fingers up the inside of the shirt, stopping teasingly on her heaving breasts. Continuing his advance past her shoulders, he stopped at the open shirt collar. His eyes were fixed on hers as he tenderly pulled the shirt off her non-resistant shoulders, letting it fall dutifully in a heap at her bare feet.

He hoisted her in his strong arms and carried her triumphantly to the side of the bed, lowering her ever so gently onto the floral covers.

"I love you," he confessed in a voice filled with affection.

"Oh, Brad. I love you so much."

Unsatisfied with the amount of titillating foreplay he had engineered, he launched another tickling attack.

"You're tickling me!" Her uncontrollable burst of glee renewed Brad's efforts to tantalize her.

"You mean you're ticklish here ... and here ... and here?"

Pamela's protests were smothered by her own laughter.

"I didn't know you were so ticklish. Here ... and there ... and here," he teased.

"Stop ... Stop it."

"Stop what? This?" Brad pretended innocently.

After a few more minutes of rapturous torture, he had the good sense to stop, allowing her time to recover before her ticklishness diffused her romantic mood.

"That's not fair. I'm ticklish and you're not."

"Did you say you're ticklish."

"Don't you dare start again. I'm all tickled out."

Pamela lay there, pleasantly immobilized. She panted heavily as she smiled between occasional bits of laughter that fell gleefully from her rosy lips.

Brad repositioned himself beside her, and leaned forward, kissing her forehead.

"I love to hear you laugh. And your smiles are symphonies," he admitted.

What a terrible loss it would have been, he thought, using a smile to conceal his regret, *if you had died in that accident. I would never have had a chance to know you. To love you. To be loved by you.*

Pamela opened her eyes and smiled at him. She turned slightly to find a balance in the bedding, which prompted her to send her hands up to the nape of her own neck. She flared out her hair, tussling it, enjoying the temporary respite.

"You're bad," she teased.

Brad smiled understandingly, and held fast to his sitting position.

"I guess you know I'm ticklish now!" Pamela admitted.

"I sort of figured that out."

"I don't know why, but I've always been ticklish."

"Oh?" Brad taunted devilishly, as he extended his hands menacingly toward her feet.

"Don't you dare, you heathen," came her quick reply, sounding more like an order than a request.

Brad launched a quick attack toward her vulnerable toes, but decided to abort the attempt about the same time she lifted her knees to avoid his advance. Her evasive action caused her knees to hit him squarely in the chin.

They both heard the crack, knee against chin, jaw against teeth.

"Ouch!" moaned Brad as he held his jaw, pretending he was more injured than he was.

"Oh, Brad, I'm so sorry," apologized Pamela, as she rushed her hands up to cover his mouth. "I didn't mean to ... I heard the crack ... Brad, are you all right?"

She looked into his eyes, hoping for a positive sign from him, but his eyes were closed. She leaned closer, growing more tense.

"I've really hurt you, haven't I? Brad, honey, I'm so sorry."

She pulled him closer and kissed the end of his nose. As she pulled away again slightly to fix her gaze on his eyes, she stumbled over several thoughts before she found one she could voice.

"Brad, darling, please ... "

"BOO!" he shouted, startling her so unexpectedly that she literally jettisoned herself backward against the headboard of the bed, causing it to smack against the wall with a thud.

"You animal!"

"First I'm a heathen, now I'm an animal?"

"An octopus that cries wolf is more like it."

"Oh, so you want more octopus, do you?"

"No, no! I'll behave—if you behave."

She giggled, making certain she held onto both his hands.

"Okay."

"Promise?"

"Promise," he agreed, and as he raised his hand in a scout's honor pledge, Pamela jumped, mistaking his clever conciliatory move as a counterattack.

"You promised!" she pleaded, trying to stop from giggling.

Brad straightened, holding his shoulders erect to complement his raised salute. "On my honor," he started. "I will ... I promise to do my best to please you and to take care of you and to ... ," he paused slightly, for emphasis, " ... tickle you only at your request." He smiled. "And to ... "

"And to stop talking at my request," she jumped into his noble pretense.

"I will do my best to stop talking ... "

"Brad."

"What?"

"Stop talking," she cooed, "and do your best to please me."

Her radiant smile and translucent eyes beckoned his immediate compliance.

He returned her covetous smile and paused just long enough to admire her scantily clad body.

He started to say something, but Pamela censored it by placing her index finger over his parted lips. Participating in his immediate disrobement, he positioned himself on top of her.

"Your pleasure is my pleasure," he announced, "I ... "

"Sh ... h.h.h," Pamela commanded, touching her index finger again tightly over his lips. "Sh ... h.h."

Brad nodded as his hands parted her unresisting thighs with a sensitivity and reverence she had come to know and respect from him.

"Come here," Pamela cooed. "Let's pleasure one another."

CHAPTER TWENTY

$\mathcal{E}$merald Isle's not that big a place. I'll find her."

"Let it be, man. She could be anywhere. You've got to ... "

"I told you. I'm going to find her," Clarence interrupted. "If I don't find her here, I'll find her in Raleigh."

"We've only got three more days on the coast. Let's not waste it looking for some broad who dumped you over six months ago."

Clarence grabbed Bo's arm and pulled him forward, knocking one of the beer bottles over.

"You think I'm wasting my time?" Clarence exploded. "I'll tell you who's wasting my time. These bimbos we're with tonight, that's who's wasting my time."

Bo jerked his arm away, infuriating Clarence, who shot him a fierce look.

"Keep your voice down, man. We're in a restaurant."

"I don't give a damn if we're in a cathedral. I'll say what I want," blasted Clarence.

"Come on. They'll be back any minute. They'll hear you."

"Let 'em hear me. I don't care," Clarence growled as he lifted his beer to his lips.

"Look, I'll tell you what. Let's show these two ladies a good time tonight. They wanna have fun, so let's keep the evening light. What do you say?"

A flicker of annoyance crossed his face, but Clarence ended his tirade with a bitter laugh.

"Not much use looking for her tonight, is it?"

Bo shook his head.

"She's not the kind of woman to stay in hotels at the beach. She'll stay in one of those beach houses that line the shore. That's where we'll look tomorrow."

"Good. We'll look tomorrow. Wait a minute, I'm not going with you."

"What do you mean you're not going with me?"

"There's no way, man. I'm not going to drive around all day looking for your long, lost love."

"Then I'll look for her myself. Who the hell needs you?"

"You do ... I'm the one who has the car."

"Look here, Bo, don't be pulling that stuff on me. You'd better damn sight let me use your car."

"Why can't you leave well enough alone? She's trouble for you, man."

"You gonna let me use your car?"

Bo sent him a disapproving stare.

"Clarence, I ... "

"You owe me."

Bo sighed heavily.

"Okay ... okay. But you've got to have the car back to me by one o'clock ... whether you've found her or not."

Clarence chuckled, amused at Bo's gullibility.

"Sure. I've only got a few more places to look. You want it back by one. I'll try to have it back to you by one."

"Clarence," Bo challenged.

"Ease up man. You'll get your car back."

Bo's attention was drawn to the women they had picked up earlier at the beach. He winked at his date, who had just squeezed past the first set of tables.

"They're back," he announced, pushing his chair back so he could stand. He motioned for Clarence to follow suit. "Don't spoil this evening and you can have the car all day tomorrow if you need it."

Clarence smiled obstinately as he stood to greet the women.

§　　§　　§　　§　　§　　§

The sunset was so outrageously beautiful, full of mauve and lavender, bordered by golden rays that stretched across the evening sky, that they found themselves lost in it. They stood trance-like on the sun-bleached deck. She was cradled in his arms, leaning securely against him. Neither wanted to spoil the mood. Only partially distracted by the evening's peacefulness, each was fully aware of the other's presence.

Pamela wondered silently which color would dominate the evanescent sunset before it made its appointed departure, allowing the blue-black cloak of night to reign until morning.

Tonight she had given him pleasure.

Tomorrow he would give her historic Beaufort and the charm of the Outer Banks, from Cape Lookout Lighthouse to Ocracoke, where the houses are laid out with old world irregularity along sandy streets overhung with moss-covered oaks and yaupon. Long believed to be the hangout of Edward Teach, better known as Blackbeard, Ocracoke is reached by taking a ferry from Hatteras.

"We'll have dinner tomorrow night in Hatteras," Brad said softly, jolting Pamela out of her swoon.

"What? Oh, dinner ... yes ... and more pleasure," she predicted as she reached up behind his neck with her hand and pulled his head closer to hers.

"We'll go to the Outer Banks on Sunday," he continued, as he kissed her shampooed hair.

"Do you think we'll see any Bottlenose dolphins?"

He kissed the top of her head again.

"I sent them special invitations. I told them you'd be there."

Pamela smiled contentedly. She loved to watch dolphins in the wild as they escorted sailboats and catamarans along coastal waters. She admired the playful courage of dolphins as they expertly glided, cut and surfaced dangerously close to boat hulls which made a habit of churning aquamarine water into white froth in their wake before the ocean reclaimed itself.

"If my memory serves me right, Cape Hatteras Lighthouse, barber poled and proud, was built in 1870, the same year General Robert E Lee died. It's the tallest such brick structure in America."

"I didn't know you were a history buff, Brad."

"I minored in history in school, but I've studied American history on my own since I was a boy."

"Oh."

"Did you know the lighthouse has been moved and renovated?"

"No."

"Well, it has ... and it overlooks Diamond Shoals ... "

He pinched her side playfully.

"Oh, so you're a closet historian, are you?"

"Not really," she replied coyly, as she smiled her way out of reach of his soft jabs.

He clasped both her hands in his, wanting to make some degree of physical contact.

"Are you ready for the two-hundred and seventy-some step climb to the top of the lighthouse?"

Pamela nodded angelically.

"I'm not exactly sure how many steps there are to the top, but there will be enough steps to test our stamina ... "

"Or our stupidity," Pamela inserted.

Both of them laughed.

"Being in good physical shape isn't stupid," she reminded him. "We shouldn't have any trouble climbing a few steps."

"What's stupid is to go to a beautiful place like that and not be able to enjoy the gorgeous panoramic view at the top of one of the most historic lighthouses in America," Brad chorused.

"I agree. And what's stupid is to waste this beautiful sunset thinking about tomorrow."

Brad pulled her toward him, rotating her slightly so that her back touched his chest. As he cradled her, he kissed the top of her head, lingering long enough to smell her scented hair. The shining rivulets of silvery light accented the blackness of her silken hair and complemented the glistening lights that danced across the ocean expanse just beyond them.

"Isn't it beautiful?" Pamela swooned, taking in a long measured breath and squeezing his arms tightly.

"Yes," Brad echoed softly. "It is quite beautiful."

He kissed her on her temple through her hair and then quickly moved down to grace her neck with thirsty, but respectful kisses. He felt her shiver ever so slightly in response to his innocent overtures.

"Are you cold?" he wanted to know as she rubbed her arms lightly.

"No," came her soft reply. "Only deliriously happy."

"That's what's beautiful."

"What?" she asked.

"Your happiness."

"Oh," and then she added, "Our happiness."

She turned her head toward him, pivoting her face so their eyes met. Locked in romantic worship, the lovers stood in statuesque poses, basking in the ozone of love.

Not a word was spoken. Finally, she raised her arm and gently hooked her hand around his head. She negotiated a half turn in his arms and brought his lips to hers. As their kiss continued, she completed an abbreviated spiral so that she faced him. After an extended passionate kiss, the lovers breathily paused to look longingly at each other.

"Remember the first time I ever kissed you?" he romanticized, as he leaned forward and planted the most tender kiss on her forehead. Then he kissed her again, this time on her eyebrow. "You were so surprised," he elaborated and kissed her lightly a fourth time in succession, only this time his lips barely brushed against hers, a preamble for the next kiss which came with a little more force and lingered much longer than its predecessors.

"Surprised?" Pamela challenged. "I think you were surprised that I let you."

Brad howled with delight.

"Relieved is more like it," he countered lightheartedly.

Pamela shot him a knowing look. "I think we both were," she agreed, pausing to clear her throat.

"It's like you hope someone you feel attracted to feels the same way, but you're not sure."

"And that first kiss seals your fate," he added quickly.

"It certainly does," agreed Pamela. "It certainly sealed ours." Her words settled around him quickly, the intensity catching him off guard.

"Isn't that what kisses are for?" he blunted his own question.

Pamela's eyes opened wider.

"To seal lovers' hearts?" he answered her inquisitive stare, as he placed his hands over each of their hearts. "And destinies," he added, lifting his affectionate gaze from her face to the night sky. He lowered his eyes, peering into the darkness that blanketed the ocean, and focused on the silver ribbon of moonlight that stretched out toward them from the glittering surface of the water, bringing the moon to earth.

Pamela followed his lead and pulled his arms around her midsection. She felt the strength of his embrace and the faint scent of his after shave came to her for a brief moment, competing with the gentle breeze which caressed her like the brush of angel wings, and the crystal clear image of the moon above.

"Oh, Brad, I don't want this to end. I feel so at peace."

She closed her eyes and faced directly into the wind, letting the cool summer breeze blow her long hair into her eyes and then out again as it obeyed the wispy commands of each small gust.

Lately everything had speeded up under her initiative, not his. She selfishly usurped as much of his time away from work as she could. She was addicted to his touch, his smile, his boyish charm. She reminded herself that he wasn't complaining.

Maybe he's the one guilty of encroachment on my time, keeping me from work. Maybe he's more in control than I realize. Or, perhaps destiny is in control of our lives.

She nestled back against him, pulling his arms more tightly around her.

Fate has brought us together, she assured herself. *And our love will keep us together.*

They huddled silently, entranced by the ocean's long dark cobalt swells and dwarfed white caps, whose rhythmic whispers of spray, muted by the darkness, lapped lazily toward the wet sand which reclaimed more of the beach when the tides retreated.

Her thoughts about fate and destiny revisited her just as a huge renegade cloud, hardly visible except for its massive silhouetted invasion across the face of the moon, neutralized the moon's silvery radiance.

For some reason, she suddenly remembered Geoffrey's phone message. A sudden pang of conscience overtook her as the memory intruded on her happiness.

Brad felt her tighten as her tension built, and opened his mouth to ask if she were okay about the same time she spoke.

"Brad."

"You okay?"

"Yes ... No." she see-sawed, wrestling with her conscience. She could tell from his tone that he was mildly apprehensive.

"Babe, what's wrong?"

He moved from his supportive position behind her and orbited in front of her, leaving his gaze glued on her.

Pamela flushed with embarrassment, trying her best to smile. "It's nothing, really. It shouldn't ... be anything upsetting," she acquiesced, searching for a more coherent succession of thoughts.

The clinical glint in his eyes told her to try harder.

Not knowing exactly what to say, she tossed her next thoughts out, hoping Brad could rescue her.

"I'm okay, really. I ... it's ... Can we go inside?" she stuttered, trying to find the control she needed to express her anxiety.

The short drive back to the beach house found Pamela silent and reflective as she cuddled next to Brad.

Brad put his arm protectively around her shoulders and, when they reached the beach house, gently escorted her through the sliding glass doors and into the living room.

"How 'bout something to drink?" he asked, as he seated her on the sofa, and then leaned down to kiss her on the forehead.

"Water would be fine."

"Good. That's all we've got," he confirmed, remembering they had consumed the wine at dinner a few hours before.

He re-entered the living room, strolling noiselessly across the thick beige carpet, and handed the drink to Pamela.

She watched the sparkling water fizz for a moment, while she summoned her courage to speak. Finally, she raised her head and made eye contact with Brad, who waited patiently for her to speak.

"This is so silly," she started. "I really am quite embarrassed that it's had this affect on me."

She took several sips of the hyper-active water and breathed a long sigh.

"Just take your time. There's no hurry," he encouraged.

When she started, the words fell from her mouth like dominoes, their cathartic affect more pronounced with each explanation she gave as she carefully spun her story. She told him about the phone call she had gotten from Geoffrey the same day he surprised her with his new car. She mentioned the barrier-free environment Geoffrey's renovations produced, and how proud of him she was for staying proactive and positive in spite of his disabilities.

Brad saw her eyes well up with tears, so he encouraged her to take another sip of water. His sensitivity reassured her, and her tearing, which had barely begun, subsided quickly.

"Geoffrey and I have always been friends. And I don't believe he would ask me to do anything that I couldn't handle, but ... "

"Tell me what's bothering you," Brad interrupted in a voice that sounded firm, but empathetic.

Pamela sighed.

"Ever since you picked me up at the airport this afternoon, I've sensed that something was bothering you," Brad admitted.

She bit her lip and then closed her eyes, opening them to his inquiring gaze. She took another sip of courage.

"Geoffrey thinks he knows who the hit-and-run driver is."

A noticeable gasp escaped Brad's lips.

"Or at least what he looks like," Pamela added quickly.

"How ... how did he ... does he know for sure?" Brad stuttered excitedly. "That's ... that's terrific."

Brad's excitement energized her. She took a deep breath and exhaled fully.

"He's pretty sure he knows what the driver looks like. He went to a therapist who specializes in hypnosis ... "

"Now wait a minute," Brad cut in. "A hypno-therapist? Hypnosis?"

Pamela waved off his impassioned entreaty. "Yes, let me explain."

She described Geoffrey's visit with Sam Weinstein and how he was able, through hypnosis, to see more of the driver's facial features. Then she explained his collaboration with a police composite sketch artist to develop a facial composite of the driver of the black Mercedes that hit them. She told him of her promise to look at the likeness of the composite, and see if it brought back any memories for her.

Brad could tell she was unsteady, and he wanted to embrace her, but he knew if he did that she wouldn't finish her story. A slight tension was building in his neck and shoulders, but he, too, held fast, offering gestures and other non-verbal cues that made it easy for Pamela to continue.

She enjoyed the refreshing bite of another sip of carbonated water and proceeded to tell him more about her relationship with Geoffrey. She described her early childhood, her school days with Geoffrey, and her life-long friendship with the man who saved her life. She elaborated about how well they knew each other and could read each other's thoughts. Her admiration and love for Geoffrey was evident as she shared story after story about their adolescent exploits and adult friendship.

A quick reflective glance from her tear-rimmed eyes prompted him to leave his seat and move beside her on the sofa. He remained silent, but took her free hand in his and waited for her to speak.

"I promised him I would take a look at the composite," she lamented, "to see if I could recognize the driver." She looked sorrowfully at Brad, who had the most woe-be-gone expression on his face.

He appeared about to speak, but waited for her to continue.

"I told Geoffrey I would take a look at it," she repeated herself. "But I'm not sure I can." She lifted her hand to wipe back a tear with her finger.

Brad rose from his seat next to her, retrieved a tissue box from the bookshelf behind the television and returned, setting it beside her.

After doing a proper job on her eyes, Pamela continued. "I really didn't see anything or anyone inside the car. The glare was so bad. It prevented my getting a clear look. It all happened so fast."

Brad squeezed her hand, and was content to remain dutifully silent.

"I agreed to look at the composite because I want to find the jerk who hit us as much as Geoffrey does. Before the break-in at my house, I had decided to let Geoffrey do what he could to bring closure to that chapter of our lives. I wanted to forget about it."

She took another sip of the sparkling water. "I wanted to get on with my life," she punctuated, as she lifted her hands from her lap, causing Brad to release his hold.

When her hands returned to her lap, he reached over and gently squeezed them again.

"Decisions like that are always tough," Brad consoled, "especially when people want to move beyond the limitations of the past."

Pamela nodded her agreement as the tiny curve of her lips hinted at a smile that never fully developed.

"I'm just glad you weren't injured any more than you were."

Pamela breathed a sigh.

"I don't know who he is. I don't know why he didn't stop to help us. All I know is he made a big mistake sending someone to my house to frighten me. Geoffrey's right. We've got to get to him before he gets to us. So, I've got to help him find the driver. I've got to force myself to look at the composite."

She looked at Brad pleadingly.

"It's the right thing to do, isn't it?"

Brad patted her hand and stared directly into her melancholy eyes. "That, my dear, is a decision you're going to have to make yourself. No one, including me, can make that one for you."

"I know you're right," Pamela admitted, somewhat apologetically.

"It's not a matter of what's right—or wrong, Babe. It has to do with where you are in the context of living and where you see yourself, or want to see yourself."

He brought his hand up to her cheek and held her chin in his palm.

"You don't have to give in to the past or give up on the present. I seem to remember a quote in your book, let's see, oh yes, it went something like: 'when you're faced with challenges in this life, you can sit, walk, or run, but don't vacillate.'"

"There's nothing worse than having something you've written thrown back at you," Pamela replied. She smiled as she siphoned the wisdom out of the comment. "I've certainly been vacillating around the composite issue. And I'd better find some balance before we get home because the composite will be there waiting for me when we return."

Brad looked truly concerned, and hesitated ever so briefly before he opened his mouth to speak. When the words finally came, his voice was at variance with his air of self-confidence.

"If you decide to help Geoffrey," he started, concentrating his gaze on her eyes, "I want to be there when you open the drawing. I don't want you going back into the pain of the past without my being there."

Then, after another brief hesitation, he relayed the substance of a just completed thought. "I want you and Geoffrey to deputize me. I intend to help you two find him. You did say it was a man that hit you, didn't you?"

Pamela shook her head in a way that confirmed his perception. "Yes, Geoffrey thinks it was a man."

"I've got friends on the Asheville police department," Brad announced quickly. He steadied his gaze on her to emphasize his next point. "I want to help you put this thing to rest."

She visibly brightened, although tears began to form, captured in the rims under her eyes.

Brad rescued her by handing her another tissue, and then offered her the same glass of water she had nursed over the past hour.

She took a grateful sip and placed the glass back on its coaster.

"Thanks," she said softly. She raised his hand and kissed the top of it quickly, but affectionately. "But you don't have to put yourself in danger."

"Believe me when I say I'll help you put this thing to rest. You've been hurt enough," he punctuated.

She leaned forward to kiss him.

Brad met her parted lips with his own, then moved his kisses to her hands.

"Thank you for being here," she said softly,

Brad tightened his lips into a smile and leaned over to kiss her affectionately on the forehead. His lips came to rest on the slight scar at her hairline.

When he pulled back, Pamela could see a tear fall slowly down his cheek.

"You are so good to me," Pamela praised.

Brad smiled his appreciation as he lifted her to a standing position.

"Why don't you call Geoffrey tomorrow morning? Reassure him you want to help, and tell him you've added a new recruit. Then we can turn the fun light on ... and leave it on for the rest of this trip."

Pamela followed her smile with several quick nods.

"In the meantime, we've got a clear night to enjoy. Shall we?"

"Before we officially re-light the fun lamp, I need to warn you about something," Pamela cautioned, as she halted their advance.

"Sure, Babe. What is it?"

"The man who attacked me ... he ... Brad, he ... he enjoyed hurting me. I never felt such an evil presence before. I don't think he has a conscience. If we pursue this investigation on our own, he'll come to us. And he'll try to hurt me ... or anyone associated with me."

Brad cupped her face in his hands.

"I'm not going to let anyone hurt you ever again. I promise you that."

Pamela threw herself into his arms.

"And I won't let anything happen to you," she said, tightening her embrace for emphasis.

CHAPTER TWENTY-ONE

In the corner of her room an indefatigable CD player blared, exhorting her, in a voice sweet but adamant, to stretch a little higher, lift, push, bend a little more. The lively music was punctuated by an energetic, but regimented, female voice that encouraged her to tuck, crunch, and twist to reach generally inaccessible body parts with parts of the anatomy that weren't even in the same vicinity, let alone touch the designated parts.

Suddenly, the phone rang. Her look of surprise was followed by mild irritation and then nonchalance.

"Probably wrong number," she guessed. "Everyone important to me agreed to call in the evenings. So it can't be anyone I know." She decided to let it ring.

The aerobics portion of the workout led Pamela through a series of high-intensity moves that required a tremendous amount of stamina. The litany of instructions encouraged her to breathe properly, inhale on relaxation, exhale on exertion, raise, lower, groan, widen, bend, groan some more, check pulse, cool down, relax.

By the time Pamela crunched her way to a sitting opposition, the phone rang again, but she ignored its summons. She listened to the last selection on the exercise CD. Thoughts about the rest of her day flowed as freely as the remnants of sweat down her brow as she sat thoughtfully, enjoying the effects of the workout and the soft gusts of salty beach air that forced their way through the screen door off the deck. She could hear the rhythmic wash of the surf as it made its relentless pilgrimage inland to claim more and more of the beach.

Brad's on the beach jogging, she guessed. *He loves to run along the shoreline.*

She pictured him leaving footprints on the damp, permeable surface at the water's edge, where the footing was kept more sure by the ebb and flow of the chilly June surf as it spilled itself onto the shell and seaweed-strewn sands.

As she sat, cross-legged on the exercise matting she placed on the carpet, she marveled at the serenity-producing power of the beach. She repeated her breathing exercise of a moment ago, except she held her breath longer before letting it out.

The end of the exercise tape brought her to her feet and carried her through the patio door onto the sun-bleached deck. The sheer beauty of the beach nearly took her breath away. She swayed to and fro as she watched the waves parade ashore.

So, there is more, much more, than the simple geographic distance between Manteo and Murphy, the symbolic bookends of North Carolina, she told herself. *Just as there is considerably more to a human life than the biological space between a person's head and feet. That's what brings people to the coast,* Pamela realized. *Re-integration, no, re-identification with their Source, their connectedness to the universe, to each other.*

She lifted her face toward the golden sphere flung so majestically in the morning sky and breathed deeply, letting the soft breeze brush against her face, sending her hair in shimmering strands about her face. She stood there, peacefully, contentedly, a willing participant as nature unfolded its light far beyond the section of sand called Emerald Isle.

"Why can't life be this peaceful all of the time?" she questioned herself aloud. "Why do people have to make life so complicated?"

Pamela moved her penetrating gaze to the mighty piers. *Wooden peninsulas,* she thought, *jutting their sun-bleached and stained planking out far enough to bring fishermen and sea together.*

She admired the eolian lightness of the sand, rolling over itself, tumbling first one way, then another, prodded by its constant companion, the salty sea breezes.

She visualized the sun's movement across the entire state, linked by asphalt ribbons of interstate highways, stitched with rail lines and speckled with symphonies of Civil War sites, which rest on sacred ground, consecrating the land. The thought of the haze-capped mountaintops that sequester both visitors and residents in their vale like benevolent sponsors brought tears to her eyes. The interplay between the mountain heights and the depths of the valleys cradles the faith of the spiritual, corrals the non-adventurous, and mystifies the uninitiated.

Without warning, a thought about Geoffrey and the composite slipped into her reverie, but she pushed it back out, recognizing it for what it was: a sour note of music in the total composition of her life.

"I'm not my past," she defended aloud.

"And, like the State of North Carolina, I'm bathed every day, cleansed with the newness and vitality of the sun's crusade to overcome the darkness," she prophesied. "Every day is a blessing. Each day counts. I am in the light. I am enjoying the warmth.

"You do not play a sonata in order to reach the final chord," she announced to herself aloud. "And if the meanings of things were simply in ends, neglecting the means, composers would never write anything but finales."

Her eyes settled on the sandpipers some distance away, as they scurried along the perimeter of the tides, foraging for their breakfast.

They understand decrescendos and ritards, she reminded herself. *They always have.*

Her envy for their instinctive synchronicity with the environment was etched on her face. Her perusal ended when several children dashed toward the startled sandpipers, sending the winged beachcombers further up the beach, just beyond her field of vision.

One of the children stooped to pick something up from the beach, only to have an overly-protective parent intervene in time to shake whatever it was out of the child's hand. A lecture followed, instigated by the woman who seemed intent on pointing her finger at the adolescent while she scolded him. The other adult, probably the husband, escorted the younger child a little further up the beach, purposefully assigning disciplinary responsibilities to the other half of the relationship.

Pamela smiled wryly. *How to ruin a child's vacation. Slap 'em around a little. Curb their enjoyment. Refuse to let them explore.*

Then her eye caught the familiar outline of her roommate, as she watched Brad's red Chicago Bulls ball cap bob up and down in concert with his stride as he jogged toward her. Her thoughts returned immediately to the subject of children.

If we decided to marry and have children of our own, she mused, *I wonder what kind of father he would make? Or what kind of mother I'd be?*

She laughed heartily and then mildly chastised herself, surprised that she had even entertained thoughts about marriage.

There is still so much about Brad I don't know.

He was less than a hundred yards from her now and evidently saw her on the deck because he waved at her.

Pamela waved back and leaned against the Chippendale railing that framed the deck. Her thoughts fast-forwarded to the trip they were going to take up the coast to Beaufort and Ocracoke.

The thought of the drive up the coast rejuvenated her. The maritime forests thrived on the leeward side of the barrier island because they were removed from the shearing effect of the ocean's bombastic spray. She remembered that tenacious oaks dominated these forests and sprawled expansively with their thick canopies, speckled with leathery leaves, toughened by years of conflict with the elements. Sculpted by salty winds and slapped unapologetically by the fierce gales and hurricanes bent on severing their relationship with the trees, the limbs of these scrappy oaks were twisted and convulsed, forming impenetrable hedges, which served as buffers to filter the geologic brutality of the pushy winds.

As Brad ascended the half dozen or so steps leading from the beach to the deck, he was met with a teasingly romantic kiss from Pamela. She leaned back slightly and pulled the cap off his head, tossing it through the open patio door.

"What's that all about?" he asked playfully, surprised at her energetic greeting.

"I was just thinking about our trip to Beaufort and Ocracoke."

She tussled his hair this time and her face beamed with delight.

"What does a trip up the coast have to do with throwing my cap in the beach house?"

"I don't know. It has more to do with my enjoying your company."

"Oh," Brad replied, pretending he understood.

"Are we taking the ferry to Ocracoke?"

Brad squinted, mentally modifying his reply so he wouldn't embarrass her.

"Yes, of course, unless you'd rather swim."

Pamela smiled.

"They're calling for afternoon thunderstorms."

Brad tilted his head toward the morning sky.

"It's mostly clear now. I think we'll have top-down weather from here to my brother's house in Beaufort."

Brad thought visiting his older brother and sister-in-law would be the politically correct thing to do, since they were vacationing so close to his brother's home. Besides, his brother, Robert, wanted to meet her.

Her face was cool and reticent as she contemplated meeting Robert and Barbara Aikman. Her concern was mostly for Brad, who was reluctant to visit Robert.

"I know you're not particularly looking forward to it," Pamela predicted.

Brad raised his eyebrows and allowed a pensive smile to form across his face.

"My brother and I have never really gotten along. I limit my social contacts to holidays and special occasions. If he weren't my brother, I probably wouldn't even socialize with him."

"What do you mean?"

"He preens himself on his monumental egotism. He's too occupied with himself to be conscious of anyone else, including his wife. He's selfish. He's overbearing. He uses people. He's just not my kind of people."

Pamela pulled him closer to her as she leaned against the railing.

"We don't have to go, you know."

"I've already called. They're expecting us." Brad replied sadly. He followed Pamela's example and leaned against the railing. "We'll go, but we won't stay long."

"If you're sure that's what you want."

Brad frowned his decision.

"I don't think I've told you, he's a tobacco company executive who has political ambitions. He used to be a senior research scientist in one of their labs."

He lifted his knee to his chest and began untying one of his shoes.

"He spends most of his time now in Washington, lobbying for the cancer sticks."

"Sounds like you're disappointed with his line of work," Pamela interjected as she watched him lift his foot out of the shoe.

"Disappointment is too soft a word. Repulsed is more like it. He's adapted a smelly cigar as his constant companion. I haven't seen him without one since he turned twenty. That was twenty-three years ago."

Brad explained that his brother had become part of the elite texture of Coastal Carolina high society, particularly the business and industrial elite. Robert and Barbara were a glamorous couple, powerful social magnets, used to multiplied luxuries. Brad told Pamela that Barbara was always gracious and charming with everyone, while Robert was disdainful of anyone he considered as 'common clay.' Brad believed Robert saw Barbara that way, inferior, servile, expendable, someone to be used.

"Robert Aikman, pillar of the community, graduated summa cum laude from one of the finest universities in America, has been unfaithful to his wife, Barbara, from the onset of their twenty-four-year marriage," he continued.

Pamela's eyes widened into spheres of disbelief.

"Each affair is, by design, sporadic and calculatedly anonymous, to avoid any woman who wants more of him than he's inclined to give. Each encounter is engineered purely for its erotic benefits. There can never be sequels, I suspect. That would mean romance, and Robert doesn't buy romance. He buys pure unadulterated sex."

"Oh, Brad, you don't have to tell me this. I ... "

"I want to tell you. To prepare you. My brother is not a very nice man. I'm sorry. I told him we'd visit."

Pamela squeezed his hand. "It's okay, Really."

Brad bit his lower lip.

"If he's that unhappy, why doesn't he leave her?"

"Leaving Barbara is not an option. Robert told me one day. She's too well-monied. Robert is aware of my disappointment in his penchant for infidelity and for his lack of morality in general, but he also knows his little brother is indebted to him."

"Indebted? What do you mean?

"He loaned me the money to invest in some non-invasive medical technology several years ago. It's made me a rich man."

"Brad. Why haven't you told me this before?"

"Because I didn't want you falling in love with money."

"Brad Aikman!" she interrupted." What am I going to do with you?"

"And because I wasn't sure I deserved you," he continued, withdrawing both his hands from her grasp.

Pamela was flabbergasted.

"Deserve me ... you weren't sure if ... you thought I'd fall in love with you for your money?" she sputtered.

"The thought occurred to me," he admitted, looking embarrassed.

"Then you don't know me very well," she fired back, pointing at him contemptuously.

"I had to be sure. Can you blame me?" he defended, reaching out to her.

She slapped both his hands away lightly before he could embrace her.

He looked shocked.

"Can you blame me?" she countered. "I'll smack any part of you that comes close."

She glared at him self-righteously, determined to punish him for doubting her.

Brad sighed.

"Pamela, honey, I'm sorry."

She purposely turned from him and placed her elbows on the railing. Her anger carried her eyes to the shoreline. She flinched as Brad put his hands on her shoulders.

He withdrew his fingertips and stood wordlessly behind her. His reconciliation attempt was interrupted by some sea gulls overhead as they swooped in the direction of several fishermen. One of the fishermen sat on an upended bucket while the other two rested on foldout chairs.

"Looks like they're plying their rods," he stated softly, hoping to engage her in conversation.

"Or swapping stories nobody believes," she countered, "like how big the one was that got away."

Before he could think of an appropriate retort, they caught the movement of a lone sandpiper. His only entourage was determination, guts, and cunning as he wove his way under one of the chairs and then hurriedly retreated, carrying his prizes in his beak.

Brad understood her metaphor and decided to choose his next comment carefully.

"I hope you're not referring to yourself as the one that got away because you thought I thought you might steal from my bucket. I love you ... I don't want money to be a barrier. And I was feeling guilty about ... " he cut into his apology. "Looks like I'm taking a bath here. I might as well take a shower."

He sighed as he backed away from her and headed barefoot through the open patio door.

"If we shower together, we'll be able to save some time and see more of Ocracoke," she suggested, giving him a solicitous wink.

Brad stopped and smiled knowingly. "If we shower together, we'll make time and never get to Ocracoke."

"Now wouldn't that be a shame?" Pamela teased, as she eased herself beside him and stroked his stubble-roughened cheek with her hand. "You'll have to do something about that, too."

"Rough, huh?"

"Just a little."

"What a shame," he bantered using a previous ploy of hers.

"It will be a shame if you don't shave," she challenged, sounding mildly irritated.

"Well, then. It looks like I'll have to do something about my rough exterior."

She leaned forward to kiss him and then pulled back. "Ocracoke can wait, but this can't," she insisted, rubbing his stubble lightly again.

An amorous look from Brad told her she wouldn't have to wait long.

"Haven't I always been smooth?"

Pamela pursed her lips to conceal a small mischievous smile, sensing his overture.

Remembering the appropriate courtesies, Brad trailed Pamela though the main guesthouse room and relieved her of the damp hand towel she'd used to wipe the sweat off her brow during her exercises. Extricating himself from his soiled T-shirt en route to the bathroom, he stuffed it into the plastic laundry bag, then tossed the towel into the clothes hamper nestled between the shower and the mirror-lined sink.

Pamela traipsed into the bedroom to undress, while he shaved. In a little while he felt the warmth and softness of her flesh as she embraced him from behind. He could feel that she was completely naked.

"Is that what the body of a wealthy man feels like?"

"Is this what the body of a gorgeous mermaid feels like?" he reciprocated.

"It could be your catch of a lifetime," she teased as she ran her fingernails across his bare stomach. "I promise not to swim away no matter how poor you are, if you treat me right."

"Treat you right?"

"Now that I know you're rich, you'll have to shower me with money."

"I've got a feeling it will be my pleasure."

She let out a playful giggle as she retreated toward the shower a few feet away. Just before the burst of tap water drowned it out, Brad heard another one of her seductive giggles.

§ § § § § §

After taking a long refreshing shower, Geoffrey devoured the egg and cheese omelet he'd concocted and then decided to take a leisurely spin through the neighborhood in his wheelchair.

His next door neighbor was outside again, cigarette hanging from her mouth, as she waddled back to her dining room door. This time she was crowned in over-sized pink hair curlers and wore her husband's tan bathrobe, which gave her the appearance of a gigantic strawberry ice-cream cone with a smoking disorder.

Geoffrey chuckled, finding her habits amusing. She was a high school principal and was a pretty good one from what he had heard. She believed schools should exist for the benefit of the students and not the other way around.

His attention was diverted skyward as he saw a pouch of color ascend slowly above treetops and soar majestically toward him. A hot-air balloon hovered silently overhead, buffeted by an updraft that lifted its rainbowed canopy higher, separating it from the toils of increasingly busy Asheville streets.

"I'm going to take a ride on one of those things one day," he promised himself aloud.

Geoffrey watched the hot-air bag disappear past treetops, almost full now with their characteristic green and burgundy plumage, newly acquired now that winter decided to spare the city of its icy wrath.

He noticed several pigeons canvass the area around their favorite park benches for any morsel they could find. Promising allegiance with their coos, they hovered on the pavement or on the back of empty benches, waiting for passersby to add to the litter already discarded by incorrigible predecessors who, whether by their defiance or disrespect, left their trash on the ground.

"You fellas are as capitalistic as the politicians in this state," he addressed the wary birds. "And both you and your political cousins leave a bunch of crap wherever you go."

He laughed at the comparison as he saw another pigeon join the assembly.

After a brief hesitation, Geoffrey wheeled his buggy across the street, to the dismay of the mildly diplomatic pigeons. He picked up several empty coffee cups and shoved them into a half-full canister.

"Caffeine's not good for you," he warned the agitated pigeons.

He wiped his hands on the grass and wheeled back toward his side of the street, glancing at the disappearing ranks of pigeons that elected to campaign for food somewhere else in the city.

Typical politicians, Geoffrey mused, *compromising too quickly and leaving at the first sign of trouble.*

He scooped up the morning paper en route to the kitchen door and placed it on his lap. Then he wheeled himself effortlessly up the ramp and through the kitchen entrance. He had decided to write Pamela another letter, only this time it would have nothing to do with composites or accidents.

The two of them used to correspond frequently, until he became deluged in police work and before she became a successful businesswoman. The accident had interrupted their letter writing, too.

So I think I'll re-institutionalize the paper handshakes, to use Pamela's term for our written correspondence, he thought.

June 5

Dear Pamela,

Just wanted you to know how much you mean to me. Sometimes friends forget to say that to friends, so I thought I'd put it in writing.

I'm not as good a writer as you, but I hope you'll understand what I have to say.

There is a part of me that wants to walk again and a part of me that knows I'll never be able to walk again. I have given each part permission to express itself with the proviso that rationality takes the lead.

I recognize now that I live in the present, and that I will do what I need to do right now, like writing this letter, and not what I thought I wanted or what was best for me yesterday.

In my darkness I have found a precious brilliance, my own essential nature that has been distilled by depression and brought to life by melancholy. Something very essential has emerged from the depths of my saturnine reduction.

I will never be able to walk again, but I can move with grace. I may never fully accept my disability, but I can see my physical limitations as a lens which brings into clearer focus my relationship with the universe.

I rejoice in your happiness with Brad. I am able to dance through your happiness, leap high in your contentment, and pirouette with your joy.

Love always,
Geoffrey

He sealed the two-page note in an envelope, addressed it, and placed it in one of his law books on the table nearby. Then he closed the book on it so he'd remember to take it when he left for school.

"I'm glad I did that," he praised himself. "I must be waxing philosophical in my ... handicapped cage," he added, looking at the wheelchair.

He settled back in his wheelchair and took another sip of coffee, satisfied with himself for taking the initiative in resurrecting an old custom. Endearing recollections of his relationship with both Pamela and Karen began to surface. He remembered the concerts they had attended through the years:

the Eagles, Neil Diamond, Lionel Ritchie, Barbara Streisand, Dolly Parton, Garth Brooks, Sting, Bono. He smiled when his thoughts took him back to Boston five years before, to the Boston Marathon. Both he and Pamela had participated—and finished, although he couldn't remember their times.

"Slow comes to mind, very slow," he chuckled. "It took both of us a week to recover." He could still remember the fractured look in Pamela's eyes when she vowed she'd never run in another marathon.

And then there was the time I helped their girl scout troop clear a wooded area so the council could convert it into a campsite. All three of us, Pamela, Karen and I, contracted severe cases of poison ivy, he remembered.

He found himself unconsciously reaching down to scratch his foot as he sat reminiscing about the incident.

His nostalgic trip down memory lane was abbreviated when his thoughts were interrupted by the doorbell. He glanced at his watch quickly, surprised at the time.

"Dad's supposed to pick me up at eight-fifteen this morning, but it's only a little after seven. The old boy must want to get an early start."

Geoffrey wheeled his chariot toward the kitchen door. Then he remembered, "Dad mentioned something about grabbing breakfast at Millie's."

"Oops," he caught himself, realizing he had just eaten his breakfast. *I'll have to find room in my pallet. Millie's pancakes are too delicious to miss.*

As he negotiated the wheelchair smoothly down the hallway, he thought. *Wait a minute. What's Dad ringing the doorbell for? He's got a key.*

"Oh," he reminded himself aloud. "It's probably the lawn doctor."

He had called the lawn service the day before, asking them to take a look at the brown spots in his lawn.

The doorbell whined again as he sped expertly through the living room.

"Okay, okay. I'm coming. You don't have to wear it out!"

CHAPTER TWENTY-TWO

*B*rad was unable to dodge the fist that slammed into his face. It came at him too fast. The intruder had caught him off guard.

Brad landed in a heap just inside the front door. Unconscious and bleeding from his nose and mouth, he lay motionless on the floor as the assailant stepped cautiously over him.

Hearing the commotion, Pamela poked her head out of the bathroom and listened for any sound that would confirm Brad's whereabouts.

"Brad, honey, are you all right?"

She narrowed her mascaraed eyes when he didn't reply and gently placed the tube of lipstick on the sink.

"Brad!" she raised her voice.

She eased herself out of the bathroom and started down the hall leading to the living room.

"Don't you dare scare me. You know I don't like to be scared. Where are you?"

When she took several more tentative steps down the narrow hallway, she froze. She could see the bottom half of Brad's body lying on the floor in the living room.

Before she could censor it, a scream tore from her lips. One of her hands flew to her mouth as she back-pedaled a half-step. She didn't know whether to advance or retreat as she stretched her other hand out to the wall for support.

"Now there's no need to worry, beautiful. Nobody can take care of you like I can."

"What? Who ... who?" Pamela whispered aloud, reacting to the voice that came from the living room.

Her legs overrode her emotions and started her moving backward toward the guest bedroom, but her eyes were riveted straight ahead, held there by a line of fear.

When the intruder stepped into the opposite end of the hallway, Pamela shook uncontrollably.

"Clar ... Clarence?"

"I just want to talk to you," he announced calmly, as he inched down the hallway.

Pamela's eyes darted past him to Brad's upturned shoes near the front door. "Is that why you ... did you kill Brad?" she asked, moving back another step.

He tilted his head toward Brad slightly and came to a stop.

"He's not dead. But I nailed him real good. He'll be out for a while."

"Get out of here!" Pamela demanded, continuing her incremental retreat.

Gooseflesh rose on her arms and her breathing was becoming rapid.

"You don't look happy to see me!"

An unsettling chill knifed through her.

"Clarence. I ... we broke up."

"You called it off," he blasted, pointing an accusing finger at her. "I tried to make things work."

Pamela swallowed hard, realizing she couldn't disguise her fear.

"We've been through this before, Clarence. You know why I left you."

Pamela put a little more distance between them.

"No, I don't know why you left me. I told you I love you. I made one mistake and you walked out on me."

"Clarence, I want you to leave! Leave right now or I'm calling the police."

Her eyes darted past him again, in time to see Brad struggle to his knees.

"You're frightening me. I want you to leave ... right now!"

"Not until we work things out," he shouted, as he marched a few steps toward her.

"There's nothing to work out, Clarence. That fake suicide call ended it once and for all. I'm calling the police," she shouted caustically.

She backed herself against the linen closet door at the end of the hallway.

"You're not calling anyone until we've ... "

His threat was cut short by Brad, who tackled him from behind, sending them both crashing to the floor.

Pamela screamed her distress as she sprinted toward the phone in the bedroom.

"Why you little son-of-a ... " Clarence started to reply before Brad punched him in the face.

Enjoying the power of raw tonnage, Clarence leveled a brutal punch into the side of Brad's head. Then Clarence raised himself to his feet and began dragging Brad with him toward Pamela's room.

Brad struggled to free himself and at the same time compromise his adversary's forward progress. By the time Clarence dragged him to the bedroom door, he was tired of fooling with this pesky adversary.

"You asked for it, you little shit," growled Clarence as he raised his elbow. The singular blow came like a sledgehammer as his elbow opened a ghastly gash over Brad's left eye, hammering him to the floor.

Blood covered Brad's face like a mask, rendering him helpless to defend himself from the next installment of blows that smashed into his face and neck.

Pamela stood horrified by the bed, unable to rescue Brad from the football player's vigorous assault.

She nervously dialed 911 and waited for the operator to answer.

"Stop it!" she shouted at Clarence. "You're going to kill him."

Clarence looked at her after delivering another crushing blow.

"What are you doing? Put that damn phone down."

Pamela strengthened her white knuckled grip on the phone when she heard the first ring.

"Put it down, I said!" yelled Clarence as he kicked himself free of his embattered opponent.

"Come on," she said, as she listened to the second ring. "Pick up! Please pick ... "

She was unable to finish because Clarence knocked the phone out of her hand, sending it flying into the nightstand. Pamela was halfway across the bed when she heard Clarence smash the phone in his powerful fist.

"Stay away from me," she shouted through her tears. "Stay away from me!"

She bolted toward the patio door off the bedroom, but fumbled too long with the lock.

He was on her immediately and grabbed both her arms, pinning her against the sliding doors.

"Let ... please let me go. Clarence, you're hur ... you're hurting me!"

"Not until you hear what I have to say."

He picked her up when she didn't respond immediately and slammed her down hard on the bed.

"You're gonna listen to me if I have to ... "

"Beat me? Are you going to beat me, too?" Pamela interrupted, as she ceased struggling for a moment.

Clarence straddled her with his knees and held both of her wrists, pinning her to the bed.

"I don't want to hurt you. So help me, I don't want to hurt you. But you don't understand how much I love you. If I can't have you, nobody can. Do you understand?"

His subtle threat took her breath away for an instant.

"Wha ... what are you saying?"

He leaned down to kiss her, but she quickly turned her head and gritted her teeth defiantly.

"Don't do this, Pamela. Don't reject me. I ... can't live without you ... and I won't let you live without me."

Pamela's eyes widened in horror.

"You said you weren't going to hurt me."

Clarence stared at her grimly. A roguish smile cut across his face as he loosened his grip in response to her absence of struggle.

"You've come here to kill me, haven't you?"

"I wasn't going to at first. I mean, I don't know what else I was going to do if I couldn't have you. I don't know what I was expecting ... a miracle, I guess."

He looked at Pamela fretfully.

"I loved you. I really did."

Oh, my God, Pamela thought quickly, *he's speaking about me in the past tense. He's really going to kill me.*

"Okay, okay," she fired at him. "Let's talk. Okay?"

His assessing eyes surveiled her, but a flicker of contempt lit a corner of his dark eyes.

"Nice try, darling, but it's too late. Do you think I'm going to let you sit up so you can run? It's over. You know it and I know it," he crowed as he tightened his grip.

She wanted to tell him he needed help, professional help. But she knew that would detonate his anger. Her bickering thoughts worked rapidly.

"It's never too late," she countered trying to appear calm. "Have you ever given up on a game?"

The sinister lines around his eyes and mouth softened slightly. A faint smile eased on his lips.

"You're good. You almost had me believing in my miracle. Let's see if it's too late."

He lifted her arms and placed one of her wrists over the other and clamped them tightly to her chest with one of his huge hands.

"What are you doing?" Pamela asked unsteadily. A sudden tremor swept through her.

"Helping you save the game."

Using his free hand, he held her face toward him in his vice-like grip, and leaned toward her, forcing her to gasp under the full weight of his tonnage.

"Ple ... please ... Clarence ... you're ... too heavy. I ... I can't breathe."

Ignoring her plea, he lowered his lips onto hers, forcing his greedy kisses on her. His reckless brute strength caused their teeth to scrape, hurting Pamela, who was powerless to stop his brutal assault.

He attended deliberately to his excitement, forgetting about the suffocating effects of his weight combined with the invasion on her lips. Pamela's struggle for air went unnoticed as his frenzied kisses engulfed her mouth.

Her eyes widened as her lips skirmished with his relentless, abusive assault.

Suddenly he stopped his inquisition and raised himself above her, keeping her wrist pinned to her heaving chest.

Pamela gasped for air, realizing he had almost smothered her.

"Please ... I ... can't ... breathe," she whispered between gasps. "Please, give me ... give me a chance ... to catch my breath."

Clarence smiled triumphantly and remained on top of her.

"Asphyxiated from kissing. What a way to go," he boasted. "I've missed those lips."

Pamela was still in the business of catching her breath, but kept her eyes glued to him.

His eye caught the scar at her hairline.

"What a shame. Poor baby," he teased as he ran his thumb over her scar.

Pamela jerked her head away from his repugnant touch.

"Yes, that's right. The game's over."

She narrowed her eyes slightly at his pronouncement.

"You said you never wanted to see me again. Remember?"

When she started to speak, he censored her by holding up his index finger, palm toward her.

"So, now I'm going to give you your wish."

"Clarence, I ... "

He tilted his head and waved her off.

"I'm going to miss you," he said sarcastically, as he began unbuckling his belt with his free hand.

Pamela struggled against his grasp, but was unable to budge.

"Such a waste. We could have had a long happy life together. But you had to go screw it up," he raised his voice. "I'm going to enjoy you one more time before I send you to live with your parents."

He unzipped his pants and sent her a wrathful smile.

Pamela flailed her legs wildly and struggled to free her hands.

"No, Clarence. Please."

Just as a taunting laugh left Clarence's mouth, Pamela heard him groan.

He released his grip on her and slumped slightly to the right. He groaned again before he could get off her.

Pamela heard a thump before Clarence groaned a third time and her panicked eyes caught the flash of chrome as it ricocheted off Clarence's shoulder.

Clarence stumbled off her and turned to face Brad who had raised the golf club over his head ready to strike Clarence again.

Brad's face and clothes were covered with blood, but he stood ramrod straight over Clarence, blocking his exit.

"Thank God you're alive," Pamela whispered to Brad.

She rolled off the bed toward him and took her place beside him.

Clarence massaged his back and shoulders as he glared at his adversaries. His nostrils quivered with rage as he rose to a sitting position on the floor.

"Stay there, you piece of shit, or I'll wrap this two iron around your sorry face."

Brad staggered slightly, but was supported by Pamela, who couldn't keep the tears from flowing.

"Go next door and call the police," Brad commanded.

"No, I won't leave you," countered Pamela, as she steadied him again.

"Go!" Brad shouted. "Get outta here."

"You don't want to do that," hissed Clarence, as he moved to his knees.

"Go!" repeated Brad. "Go now, damn it! I don't want to have to worry about you."

Pamela threw Brad a worried look and released him as she started out of the room.

"I can't let you do that," Clarence shouted after her, as he lifted his right knee off the floor.

Brad swung the club at him and then swung a second time, barely missing his head.

Pamela darted out of the door in obedience to Brad's wishes.

Brad swung at Clarence again, keeping him a bay.

Clarence leaned back against the wall, growling his contempt.

"I'm gonna break you in half, boy," Clarence threatened. "You're swinging at me like a woman."

Brad steadied himself for the attack he knew Clarence would launch any minute.

"Brad," Pamela shouted through the open sliding door. "The people next door have already called the police. They're on the way."

Clarence let out a growl and showed his teeth, much like a cornered dog.

"Stay outta here," Brad warned. "Wait out there for the police."

"Pamela," Clarence shouted at her as he inched toward the sliding door.

Brad blocked his exit and swung at him, forcing Clarence to keep his distance.

"It ain't over yet, darling. I'm gonna keep my promise. I ..." Clarence canceled his next comment in response to the siren.

He growled like a frustrated grizzly at Brad before he backed himself up to the bedroom door leading to the hallway.

Brad advanced a few steps, still brandishing the two iron. Clarence sneered at Brad, who was staggering to stay erect. As Clarence calmly continued taking small, calculated steps backwards out of the bedroom, he growled his anger.

"You're dead ... and so is she," Clarence threatened, scowling at them.

Clarence raised his head when the siren sounded again, and took advantage of the moment. He sprung toward Brad quickly, knocking him off balance, and then shifted his direction toward the hallway.

"You're dead, you hear? I'm going to enjoy breaking you into pieces, both of you."

Clarence then ran out the front door and made his escape over a fence and down the street.

By the time Brad limped to the front door, Clarence had vanished.

"Brad," Pamela yelled. "Are you all right?"

Her frantic voice sent him back into to the bedroom, where he collapsed. Brad shouted. "He's gone," he whispered, realizing his energy was depleted.

Pamela sprinted into the bedroom and rushed up to Brad.

"Oh, honey," she lamented, shaking her head.

She helped him sit up and cupped his bloody face in her hands as she sat next to him.

"It's not as bad as it looks," he spoke softly.

"Yeah, right!" Pamela objected. "We've got to get you to a hospital. Let me clean you up."

As she rose to moisten some towels in the bathroom, she was startled by two policemen who stepped into the bedroom.

"We understand you've had some trouble," one of the uniformed officers stated, as he broke eye contact with Pamela and glanced at Brad who remained seated.

Pamela nodded.

"He went out that way," she said, pointing to the front door.

The officer nodded to his partner ,who started toward the escape route.

"He won't be hard to find," Pamela prophesied. "We know him."

"You've got to be kidding!" Brad blasted. "He broke into our beach house. He assaulted us!"

"I'm sorry, Mr. Aikman. It appears to be your word against his," the officer replied calmly.

"Our word against his? Officer, he was here. Who do you think did this?" Pamela shouted, pointing to Brad's face and the bruises on her wrists. "This is unbelievable."

The officer shook his head.

"It appears someone was here," his partner commented, in an attempt to appear reasonable.

"No kidding, Sherlock," Brad said angrily.

"I'm sorry folks, but Mr. Blount has an alibi, three of them to be exact."

"What? How could he?" Pamela asked, flabbergasted at the officer's comment. "He was here!"

"According to a football buddy and two young ladies, he was with them all day."

"Aw, come on!" Brad said sarcastically.

"They said he was on the beach with them all day and that they had lunch in the women's hotel room."

"And you believe that?" Brad raised his voice. "Look at my face. I've got sixteen stitches above my eye."

Before the officer could offer any kind of rebuttal, Brad reached into the closet and pulled out his bloody shirt.

"Look at this," he yelled, "look at the blood stains on the carpet. How do you think they got there? I sure as hell didn't cut myself shaving."

Brad threw the bloody shirt on the floor and glared at the two officers, who stood silently with their hats in their hands.

"What about the golf club blows to his neck and shoulders? Brad hit him several times with a two iron." Pamela reminded them calmly. "There should be bruises on his shoulders and neck."

"That's right," Brad agreed. "He couldn't hide those."

"We looked at those," the officer informed them.

"Did you hit him anywhere else, Mr. Aikman?"

"What?" Brad asked, blinking back his disbelief.

"Did you use the golf club to strike him anywhere else? His legs? Arms?"

"No, what are you talking about. I hit him three, maybe four times, on his back, neck, and shoulders."

"What are you implying, officer?" Pamela interjected, not liking where the conversation was going.

The officers exchanged sympathetic glances and the senior officer frowned his disappointment.

"The bruises on his neck, shoulders and back were all recent injuries. We could tell that. But ... "

"Of course they were recent," Brad declared impatiently. "I put 'em there."

Pamela signaled for Brad to be quiet.

"He also had bruises on his legs."

"What?" Brad asked. "That's impossible. I didn't ... "

"He said one of the women used a golf club on him when he got too fresh. According to Mr. Blount, she hit him half a dozen times before he could take the club away from her."

"That's not true ... That's just ... unbelievable," Brad stammered.

"All three witnesses verified his history. We believe you two, but all we could do was question him. He had three air-tight alibis. I'm sorry."

The second officer stepped toward Pamela.

"He's a clever one. He said he didn't know you were here. According to him, the last time he talked to you was on the phone, just after you got home from the hospital, four or five months ago. He said he told you he never wanted to see you again."

Pamela shook her head in disgust.

"Ms. Justice, we know what's going on here. But without more evidence, I'm afraid there's not much we can do."

"The people next door, Mr. and Mrs. Anderson. Couldn't they identify him?" Pamela ventured.

The senior officer shook his head. "They heard the commotion and knew something was going on, but they didn't see anyone."

"How about his car or truck or whatever," Brad guessed. "He had to drive some kind of vehicle here. Didn't they see that ... wait a minute. He left just before you came. Did you see a car or truck pull outta here when you came in?"

"Unfortunately, no on both counts. You said he ran down the street. He probably parked down the street or had an accomplice pick him up. If what you've said is the truth ... "

"Hold it. Time out!" Brad challenged, using the sports gesture to indicate time-out. "What do you mean *if* we're telling the truth?"

The junior officer sighed. "The suspect told us, Ms. Justice, that he was an old boyfriend of yours and that you threatened to make trouble for him. He guessed that you saw him here and used this opportunity to harass him."

Pamela's jaw dropped in amazement, as she divided her surprised look between the three of them.

"I'm only telling you what he said," defended the junior officer.

"He's going to get away with this, isn't he?" she hypothesized, tightening her grip on Brad's arm.

Both officers broke eye contact with her and then reestablished it.

"Without proof, there's not much we can do. We ... "

"Without proof! What about this proof?" Brad shouted, pointing to his head and bloody shirt again.

"We can't use that."

"What?"

"Please don't take offense, but you two could have had a fight and concocted this whole story to ... "

"Get outta here!" Brad shouted. "I don't even want to talk to you anymore."

"I didn't say we believed them."

"Please leave. Thank you so much, officers, for your concern," Pamela patronized sourly. "I think we can handle it from here."

She pushed Brad gently to the side to allow room for the officers to squeeze past them.

"Thanks for nothing!" Brad hissed as he watched the officers retreat down the hallway toward the front door.

"Wait. Please." Pamela shouted after them.

The officers turned part of the way toward her.

"What about the blood traces on his hands? He hit Brad in the face ... in his bloody face. Trace amounts of Brad's blood should be on his hands ... on some of his clothes."

The officers exchanged uneasy glances again.

"Didn't find anything, right?" Brad predicted, as he unconsciously raised his hand to feel the gash above his swollen eye.

"No need to check. He had alibis," replied the senior officer.

"He's done something like this before," Pamela raised her voice. She explained the San Francisco incident that happened months before and urged the officers to contact the police authorities there. Although the officers took the information Pamela provided, she could tell there would be no follow-up.

"Thanks for nothing," Brad repeatedhis indignation.

Both Pamela and Brad sighed as they watched the officers exit. When they disappeared through the front door, Pamela turned toward Brad.

"What are we going to do?"

"You're going to stay here. I'm going to kill the creep," Brad threatened as he started toward the closet.

"You don't mean that. Brad, tell me you're not serious."

Brad reached into his suitcase and brandished a 9mm pistol.

"Oh, Brad. No!" Pamela said, as her hands covered her mouth.

"The police can't help us. You heard them. What else can we do?"

"You can start thinking," challenged Pamela. "This gun's just going to get you in trouble. You said you wanted to protect me. Well, you did. He would have killed me if you hadn't been here."

She forced him to lower the handgun to his side.

"Some help I was. He beat the shit out of me."

"He's a big man. But you held your own," Pamela reminded him, as she pulled his head to her and kissed his cheek. "You backed him off."

Brad shook his head and threw her a brittle smile.

"The sirens backed him off. Club or no club, he would have killed me."

"But he didn't. And I don't think he could have. You fought him with a broken nose and a gash above your eye ... and you lost a lot of blood. Give yourself some credit."

She pulled the gun from his reluctant grasp while she planted another kiss on his cheek.

"I suppose you're right," he conceded, biting his lip for emphasis.

"Suppose I'm right again and agree with my next statement," she pressed, sending him one of her patented smiles.

He narrowed his eyes suspiciously but decided to wait her out.

"Let's stay in a hotel tonight. I know, we'll probably have to pay for two nights," she reasoned. "Stupid minimum stay policy here at the beach. But who cares? We won't have to worry about another unpleasant visit from that creep ... and we both could use a good night's sleep. I'm sore and I know you must be exhausted."

"I suppose you're right again," Brad surrendered, pulling her closer to him. He flinched as Pamela eased herself toward his lips.

"Better stay here," he pleaded, pointing to his cheek. "My mouth's pretty sore."

"I'll call the hotel and your brother."

"That's right. We were going to see them tomorrow. I can imagine how he's going to enjoy poking fun at my face."

"I think he'll be concerned ... and thankful that you're alive," Pamela replied as she placed his revolver back in the suitcase.

"I'm sure my sister-in-law will feel that way, but ... "

"He will, too," she interrupted. "He's your brother, for heaven's sake. He'll be proud of you for protecting a damsel in distress," she prophesied, arching her back in his arms and placing one of her hands, palm up, on her forehead. "My hero," she praised, "my knight in shining armor."

"It's more like dented and chipped armor," Brad lamented.

"No, it's shining, all right! Sir Aikman! And your Confederate gray horse is waiting to take us away," Pamela praised, referring to his vintage Mercedes Benz.

CHAPTER TWENTY-THREE

*T*here was a pause the length of two heartbeats while his older brother studied him.

"He sure messed you up, little brother. That black eye is a whopper," Robert assessed. His tone was mildly sarcastic as he reached toward the stitched cut.

"He's lucky to be alive," Pamela inserted. "He saved my life."

"Yes, I understand he did," Robert yielded to her enthusiasm.

"I'd like you to officially meet the young woman I told you about," Brad commented diplomatically, placing his hand on her lower back. "Pamela, this is my brother, Robert and his wife, Barbara."

Pamela shook Robert's hand confidently and firmly. "Pleased to meet you," she greeted him cordially.

"And I, you," he reciprocated.

His gaze chronicled her, documenting her features. He assessed the way she extended her hand and the firmness of her handshake. He noticed how she returned his penetrating stare. The lift of her eyebrows, the swell of her breasts accentuated by the cut of her blouse, even the color of her nail polish caught his sharp eye.

"So, you are the notorious Miss Pamela Anne Justice?" he beamed, releasing his handshake slowly. "We finally get to make your acquaintance."

"Notorious?" questioned Pamela. "Notorious?" she repeated, unsure how to respond to such a disarming greeting.

Barbara extended her hand, using her own hospitable handshake to rescue her guest.

"He's referring to Brad's campaign to keep you a secret."

"Okay, you two," Brad warned good-naturedly. "I told you why I postponed telling anyone about her."

"So you did, younger brother. So you did," Robert said playfully as he pulled his eyeglasses off to clean them. "I hope we'll get to know her a little better over the next couple of hours."

"That's something I look forward to, too," chimed Barbara. "I understand you are headed to Ocracoke this afternoon."

Brad nodded his relief.

"Yes, we have reservations."

"Reservations for going there or reservations for staying here?" Robert joked sarcastically.

Barbara shot a disapproving glance at her husband.

"Robert, these two young people have sandwiched this vacation in between both of their work schedules. I'm sure they would stay here if they could."

Brad winked at his sister-in-law and smiled at Pamela.

"As usual, Mrs. Aikman, you are the perfect diplomat," Brad said, complimenting Barbara's politeness.

Pamela watched her hosts during the brief confrontation.

There was something indescribably unapproachable about Robert. She felt it. An innate iciness that made any contact with him, no matter how brief, seem empty, devoid of the usual feelings associated with amicable greetings.

There was an undercurrent of ingratiation, of stuffiness, perhaps savageness that acted as a repellent, preventing anyone from getting too close to Robert.

Robert's deep-set eyes were notched under wiry eyebrows that seemed too large for his sunken eyes. His prominent nose was moderately hawkish, further accenting his recessed eyes, which appeared to be different colors. Closer examination told Pamela that Robert had one hazel-colored eye and one variegated, partially brown eye with a slight hazel coloration. A few strands of hair crossed his brow running sideways, terminating at each temple.

She had always found it amusing that some men meticulously combed these sparsely connected strands of vanity across the top of their heads as if to conceal their blatantly obvious baldness.

Why don't they just accept that they're follically challenged and improve their appearance by plucking the half dozen or so strands they have left? She quickly erased a smirk she felt coming, and hoped Robert hadn't noticed her indiscretion.

She felt uncomfortable with his protracted handshake and overly-penetrating gaze which seemed to place a dragnet of suspicion around her, probing for something he could use to assert his influence later. She couldn't help feeling he never looked at a woman without undressing her. Brad hadn't told her about that!

Barbara appeared to be Robert's polar opposite. Strikingly beautiful, she was poised and gregarious, offering a sense of refined grace. She was considerably more diminutive than Robert, who was six feet four or five inches, Pamela guessed. Barbara stood five feet one or two inches in heels. She was petite and had an isthmus of a waist that separated willowy thighs and legs from comely well-proportioned breasts.

Her face was square, framed by a gorgeous head of chin-length flaxen hair, accented with strands of platinum blonde pigment that set her hair aglow. Her rich brown eyes were lined with long lashes that bore the insult of two layers of black mascara, making the lashes appear like a bristling hedge above her pupils.

The most noticeable characteristic about Barbara's eyes, Pamela thought, was that they appeared official. They seemed poised to satisfy and implied compromise at their corners once eye contact was made. Pamela also saw goodness in her mildly sad eyes, and a slight transformative tinge of light that danced dimly under the protective mascara.

Pamela's assessment was terminated when she felt Barbara's tug on her arm.

"He is okay, isn't he?" Barbara asked Pamela, referring to Brad's head injuries.

Pamela nodded as she stole a quick look at Brad.

"I think so, Mrs. Aikman. He was so gallant. I'm surprised he's as energetic as he is today. He really took a beating."

"Well, I'm happy you're okay, too. And, please call me Barbara. I feel as if I've known you for a long time ... although we've just met."

"Brad says I have that affect on people," Pamela admitted, chuckling at herself.

Both women smiled at each other.

"Let's show you the rest of the house," Barbara said softly as she pulled Pamela gently toward the interior of the house.

"You have a beautiful home," Pamela appraised. "It's so elegant ... and spacious."

"Robert designed it and did most of the plumbing and electrical work."

"It's nice to have a man like that around the house, isn't it?"

Barbara kept her attention focused straight ahead.

The men lingered just inside the front door and when Robert saw Barbara escort Pamela toward the living room, he closed the door and motioned for Brad to follow them.

In a few moments all four were walking through the foyer and into the vaulted-ceilinged living room. The walls were a riot of color, hosting a variety of expensive oil paintings, mostly of pastoral scenes and landscapes. Next to the paintings were collectibles, ranging from life-sized sculptures and pottery to embroidered wall hangings and rare china—all housed in expensive cabinets or shelves or perched on elegant stands. The massive pieces of stately furniture were baroque and heavily carved.

"So you've known Brad several months now?" Barbara addressed Pamela, as she guided her down the two marble steps that led into the living room.

Pamela noticed that Barbara's heels clicked smartly as her hostess stepped cautiously across the smooth surface. Pamela nodded her head. "Yes, we met at the clinic."

"March, wasn't it?" Barbara's voice picked up speed, although her tone sounded natural.

"Yes, March 7th to be exact. But I had seen him before."

"Oh!" came Barbara's slightly petulant, but even response.

"You mean Brad didn't tell you?"

Barbara shook her had.

"Brad did keep me invisible, didn't he?"

"Invisible, indeed," Barbara agreed, launching a mild chuckle. "We didn't know you existed until last month." She shot Pamela a quick look. "I don't want you to get the wrong idea. We don't keep track of Brad's whereabouts and we certainly do not pry into his personal life. And it's not like we see him often, with him in Raleigh and us here. It's just that we worry about him when he ... " she paused, " ... well," she cleared her throat, "when he pulls something like this."

Pamela threw her a surprised look.

"What do you mean?

"You mean he hasn't told you?"

Pamela shook her head. "Told me what?"

Pamela's eyebrows worked but her mouth didn't. She glanced quickly at Brad, who had his back to her, engaged in a side conversation with Robert. She returned her wide-eyed gaze to meet Barbara's mildly surprised look.

"A few years ago Brad and several others from his sky diving team were participating in a Veteran's Day celebration at the Charlotte Motor Speedway. The team was supposed to skydive into the arena as the closing act." She paused, as if she were not sure how to continue. Then she closed her eyes, and sighed, finding the courage to continue. "One of the divers misjudged the entry pattern into the area and overshot the drop zone."

Pamela took in a breath of air and covered her heart with her hand, suspecting what Barbara was going to say next.

"She was killed instantly when she hit some power lines."

Pamela tightened her lips and moved her head slightly from side to side. "You said she?"

Barbara nodded.

Pamela looked intently into her eyes, not wanting to miss a cue.

"She was Brad's fiancée."

"Brad's fiancée," whispered Pamela, as she touched Barbara's arm.

At the sound of his name again, coming from Pamela's lips in what he judged to be distress, Brad was tempted to intervene in the women's conversation. He decided not to interrupt when the women seemed okay, although he did maintain his stare long enough to return Pamela's quick smile. He guessed that Pamela was pumping Barbara for personal information about him, and by the look in her eyes, was being enthusiastically indoctrinated.

Touché, Brad mused, contemplating Pamela's discussion with Barbara. *What's fair is fair. We'll compare notes on our way to Ocracoke later this afternoon.*

Barbara spilled the complete story of Brad's two-year relationship with Susan Ledbetter, a former Miss North Carolina and press secretary for the governor.

"She met Brad when he was part of a skydiving exhibition for the Governor's conference on business and education's hi-tech interface," she explained. "Susan got interested in Brad and then in skydiving. They were engaged to be married a couple of months before she died."

Barbara forced her lips into a taunt seriousness. "We thought he'd never get over her death. He really took it hard. He even gave up skydiving for a year and only went back then to mark the anniversary of her death." She gave Pamela a noticeably maternal look. "He surprised us with the news of his anniversary jump last October. If we had known he was planning to jump, Robert would have stopped him. Brad was so despondent last year that we feared he would skydive to his death."

"Suicide?" Pamela whispered, sending her disbelief at Barbara more poignantly than if she had shouted it out.

"It wasn't a suicide attempt. It wasn't like that at all! But we weren't sure, you know. People do strange things when their world falls apart."

Pamela nodded in agreement and thought to herself, *I certainly can identify with that. I've been in a totally different world myself since December.*

A quick glance out the living room window told her the storm that followed them from Emerald Isle was being capricious, switching from drenching downpour to brief periods of sunshine with very little warning.

Tentative blue skies prevailed now. She could see that clearly through the open mini blinds. Her eye caught the brown and rust colors of a bird flash across the yard, evidently on its way back to its nest of fledglings to satisfy their constantly empty palates.

A light touch on her arm from Barbara pulled her back into the conversation.

"So you didn't know about Susan?" Barbara asked, hoping to redirect the discussion.

"No. Of course, there isn't much I do know about Brad."

"He's a pretty private person. Almost monastic. He lets few people into his world," Barbara said, using a slightly journalistic tone. "So he must really care for you."

"I think he's special, too."

Pamela thought of something she wanted to ask Barbara about Brad, but an anxious look from her hostess censored it.

Barbara had just made eye contact with her husband who, along with Brad, was on his way over to them.

"I'm going to apologize in advance for my husband for anything he might say this afternoon. Sometimes his conversations border on the rude, crude, or lascivious."

Pamela raised her eyebrows and forced a tight smile, a little surprised at Barbara's nervous disclosure.

"Although Brad hasn't said much about his family—or himself for that matter—he did manage to warn me about his brother on the way over here."

"Good. You've been prepared then."

"I hope so."

"Oh, please don't be upset. I don't think he'll do anything to embarrass you. After all, it's the first time he's met you. It usually takes him a couple of visits to get warmed up." She looked past Pamela's shoulder at the two men who were about to join them. "Just the same, don't take offense at anything he says. Just consider the source. And in this case the source is a pompous ass," she admitted, throwing Pamela a good-natured wink.

"Okay," Pamela agreed mechanically and joined Barbara in watching the men's approach.

Judging from his appearance, Brad seemed a little frustrated, even confrontive. Apparently the brothers had disagreed about something. Robert's expression seemed to suggest he was immune from the sparring and Pamela noticed the faint, bitter smile that lightly sculpted Brad's lips.

Both men seemed to change expressions, transforming themselves from angry combatants to hospitable relatives when they realized they had an audience.

Robert's voice was guardedly charitable. He spoke in a steady stream of exclamations as if to emphasize points that were not even in contention as they approached. Only a few feet away from the vigilant women now, Robert spoke to Brad, his comments arriving at the same time as the men.

"Without money you are vulnerable, used, susceptible to the whims of the rich and powerful. Or should I say the richer, and more powerful? He winked condescendingly at the two women, each mirroring the other's polite, but uneasy stare.

"Shame on you for keeping such a beautiful young woman a secret for so long," Robert addressed Brad, veering from his aloofness to a more rehearsed cordial warmth. Then he turned to address Pamela, who had just jumped, startled by a thunderclap which ripped through the mid-afternoon sky.

"Sorry, I don't know why I'm so jumpy," Pamela apologized.

"That's okay, honey," Barbara empathized. "I don't like these thunderstorms either."

"Those storms are all bark and no bite," Robert assured them. "Of course, next month they'll be all bite. Right, little brother?"

Brad nodded, knowing his brother was referring to the hurricane season.

"He hasn't mentioned much about you, young lady. Hardly anything at all," Robert announced as he winked at Pamela and then glanced at Brad, giving him a disapproving look. "Of course, I can see why you wanted to keep her secret. She's beautiful," he praised, addressing both Brad and Pamela, but allowing his eyes to linger much longer than comfortable on her.

"Yes sir, you can sure pick 'em." His voice sounded more flippant than admiring. Robert's whole facial geography changed, and settled into lines of harshness, which disappeared almost as fast as they came, giving him a somewhat comedic animation as his face adapted to his changing moods.

He wasn't finished insulting Brad and seemed to take immense pleasure in his public slights of people he considered inferior.

"I warned Brad not to leave me alone with you," he addressed Pamela. "I was afraid I might succumb to your obvious charms." He paused, preening himself on his ability to create awkward situations. "Of course, I perform very well under pressure."

Barbara laughed as she unconsciously used her hand to peel back her collar slightly, exposing more of her neck, and her stance became more rigid.

"About the only pressures you perform well under are your nightly constitutionals," Barbara said sarcastically.

Both Pamela and Brad held their reactions until Robert responded.

"One of these days," he recovered, making a fist at her. "I'm going to send you to the moon."

Pamela could see that the fire of contempt danced in their eyes. Robert shot Pamela a conspiratory wink, but Barbara's expression showed her resentment toward her husband's obstinacy.

Brad stayed diplomatically silent, then changed the subject quickly.

"Pamela has her own business. It's called Civilized Leadership."

"Oh, isn't that wonderful," chimed Barbara, clasping her hands in front of her. She threw Brad a quick smile, appreciating his steering them toward more hospitable territory.

"Civilized Leadership, huh?" repeated Robert, conscious of his brother's attempt to blindside his devilishness. "Is there any such thing as civilized leadership? Sounds like an oxymoron to me!"

Pamela noticed a slight stiffness overtake both Brad and Barbara, and quickly appropriated it as a warning to sharpen her diplomatic antennae.

"Only when leaders settle for an uncivilized work environment," she bantered good-naturedly, looking beyond him at the gray sheets of driving rain which lashed menacingly at the windows.

Robert's mouth surrendered mischievously into a slight curve, one of the few times he indulged himself in a grin.

He was so struck by the way she so adroitly lateralled the innuendo back at him that it took him a few moments to reshuffle his thoughts. He had not anticipated her level of confidence.

"Uncivilized or not, agreements are reached all across America, across the world, every day," Robert rallied, wanting to keep the conversation artificial.

"Those aren't agreements," Pamela pressed. "Many organizations confuse compliance with agreement and settle for something less than agreement. Agreement, true agreement, suggests commitment. Unless there is unequivocal commitment, organizations, corporations, countries, and even families generally end up with something bordering on grudging compliance or enrollment ... or tolerance."

Barbara thought to herself: *Yep. That about sums up my relationship with Robert—tolerance.*

Robert forced a smile. "Scuse me. I seem to have lighted a fire under our guest. Our very capable guest, I might add." He stuck his hand out toward Pamela. "Perhaps we can discuss agreements and commitments later," he said, squeezing Pamela's hand lightly. Then he addressed Barbara without looking at her. "Right now I'd like to negotiate a couple of civilized drinks before lunch."

Brad was amused at his brother's gallant capitulation, and openly cheered Pamela's successful skirmish with his brother.

"Looks like you have passed muster, Babe," he commented jubilantly. Then he tipped his head toward Robert. "I told you this guy was a bit feisty at times, but always the politician and ..."

"Usually a good host," Barbara interrupted, throwing Robert a scornful eye.

Robert clicked his heels and bowed slightly, signaling his agreement and surrender.

Barbara breathed a sigh of relief, pleased that Brad had averted another skirmish.

"Suppose we retire to the sun room and I'll prepare us something to drink," she suggested, glancing at Robert for approval and then at Brad for support.

Brad threw Barbara a quick wink and moved toward Pamela.

'Hold on there, brother," came Robert's retort, "you've had her all to yourself these past few months." He leveled his gaze on Pamela and took her gently by the arm. When he felt her recoil, a smile, hardly noticeable, cracked his face. "I don't want you slipping away before I get a chance to know you." He winked at Pamela, taking immense pleasure at forcing himself on her.

Pamela gave him a patronizing smile, and decided to employ silence as her chief conversational strategy with Robert.

"Why don't you help Barbara prepare the drinks and join us in the sun room?" Robert addressed Brad wryly, taking ominous pleasure in keeping the two lovers apart.

Pamela signaled a polite objection by hesitating before she allowed Robert to escort her through the house. Brad grudgingly acquiesced and then glided down the carpeted hallway to join Barbara in the kitchen. He engineered a backwards glance after a few moments and caught the fragile smile Pamela tossed at him. Her eyes looked intently into his for a few brief seconds, spilling their contempt for his pompous brother.

Contempt recognized contempt as Brad mirrored her displeasure. Brad's negative feelings for his brother escalated whenever he found himself too close in proximity to Robert's abrasive presence. The feelings were mutual he was sure. There had always been irreconcilable differences, unsettling scars of turbulence that marred their relationship, cutting a permanent wedge between them.

"Forgive my younger brother. He must have forgotten his pledge to share you with me."

"I think he's tired. He's had a headache all morning. I'm sure he's still hurting from his injuries."

"I have no doubt you'll be able to nurse him back to health," Robert teased.

Pamela hesitated before she spoke, not wanting to say what was really on her mind—that she thought Robert was a pretentious, obnoxious jerk!

Noticing her diplomatic acumen, Robert smiled as he seated her in one of the wicker chairs in the spacious sunroom.

"I meant that as a compliment. Sometimes I say things that put me in the doghouse. I hope I haven't offended you."

Pamela shook her head politely. "No, I understood what you meant," she replied confidently. "And thank you, I'll take very good care of your brother."

"He seems to be taking very good care of you. He says you've recovered from your injuries exceedingly well."

Pamela nodded, straightening herself on the cushioned seat. She crossed her legs and placed her hands comfortably on her lap while Robert fussed with his chair cushions before he sat.

She tightened her lips slightly as she watched him settle in his chair.

Maybe you're a reincarnated junkyard dog that's finding it difficult to acclimate to a human environment, she mused to herself as she raised an eyebrow, satisfied her suspicions were valid.

Sensing her introspective assessment, Robert made eye contact.

"Have I got a spot on my clothing or a hair out of place?" he challenged, frisking himself perfunctorily.

Pamela laughed to give herself time to think of a polite rebuttal.

"I was just thinking of how different you two brothers are."

"Oh! Are we really that different?"

"Most siblings are opposites," she said quickly, wanting to sound clinical instead of judgmental. "For example, you seem more bureaucratic and officious. Brad appears to prefer less formal environments. He seems to enjoy his freedom and gets his energy from being around people."

"That's a pretty good assessment. I'm impressed. Brad tells me you're a training and development consultant. Why don't you give me ten minutes of your best stuff?"

"I can give you ten seconds. I don't mix business with personal time," Pamela responded. She grinned at him dubiously and thought to herself: *This is going to be a long afternoon!*

§   §   §   §   §   §

With the exception of a few unpleasantries caused by the political brinkmanship of the brothers, the visit went relatively well, Pamela thought as Brad headed the car toward Ocracoke.

She liked Barbara's quiet reserve and was impressed in her ability to tolerate such an obnoxious spouse. Whatever Robert felt beyond his arrogance was masked by his cool, emotionless face and tight smile.

She glanced quickly at Brad, whose attention was focused on his driving. Since they left his brother's house, he had not spoken more than three syllables. There was too much to say. Pamela knew he was upset over the visit, so she opted for silence over idle chatter, to give him some decompression time.

I've never seen him so agitated, she thought. *He was right about his relationship with Robert—they don't have one. And by the looks of it, they aren't going to, not in this lifetime.*

She looked at the book cradled in her lap, *Lee, the Last Years* by Charles Bracelen Flood. Robert had given it to her to give to George. Despite her mild objections, he had insisted she present it to her grandfather as a gift from one Robert E. Lee admirer to another.

I don't know if grandfather has this particular volume. He's an avid Lee reader, so I suspect he already does, although I can't be sure. Nevertheless, how could I refuse a gift that was so willingly and graciously offered?

She was sharply conscious of Brad's disappointment at having included a stop at his brother's house on their jaunt up the coast, a stop she knew he didn't want to make from the beginning. Then she fielded a thought. *Oftentimes when people expect the worst, they get it! It's as if they magnetize it by sending negative thoughts out, attracting the very thing they say they are resisting the most.*

Her left hand found its way up the nape of Brad's neck and then migrated along the side of his head to the patch of hair immediately above his earlobe. She gently massaged the area over his temple and moved her fingers in measured strokes, combing his golden locks back over the top of his ear.

Her tactile entreaty was met with a slight curve of his lips as he tried his best not to smile, choosing to remain melancholy a few moments longer.

Sensing his mild arousal, Pamela moved the back of her hand over his mouth and nose, forcing him to smell the sweet fragrance that was distinctly hers. She purposefully lingered there, hoping he would respond favorably to her intimate cue.

His reaction initially came in the form of a kiss as he acknowledged the top of her hand, and then he surrendered to her fragrance by inhaling her sweetness slowly, bringing his free hand up to cup her hand. He gently incarcerated her hand against his lips, extending his olfactory pleasure.

"Uh ... mm. You smell good."

"Just wanted you to know I'm here," she acknowledged, smiling at her ingenuity.

Her affection commandeered him back to her, causing him to abandon his moodiness immediately and make amends.

"I'm sorry, Babe. It was such a miserable visit."

Pamela freed her hand and placed it on the back of his neck, massaging the base of his neck and shoulders.

"It wasn't that bad," Pamela consoled, moving her fingertips up to his ear again.

"You don't think so?"

"No. Not at all."

"I thought it was terrible. You didn't feel awkward at all?" he quizzed. "Or uneasy around him?"

"A little, but then both you and Barbara warned me about his philandering stares and off-hand comments."

"Barbara talked to you about him, huh?"

"His being a piece of work came up a couple of times," she responded nonchalantly. "After all, his obstinacy was hard to miss. And it made such interesting conversation." And then as an afterthought, she added, "I heard my name mentioned a number of times as you two hovered near the bookcase just before lunch. I felt roasted in an air-conditioned room," she teased, attempting to bring levity to a conversation that was becoming much too serious.

When he didn't answer right away, she continued, "What did you two talk about for so long, besides me?"

Brad started to speak but paused, trying to fit the right words together.

Pamela waited for his reply, but then decided to fast forward her critique.

"At times you looked so somber. One time in particular I thought you were going to strike your brother."

"I don't know which time you saw, but there were a number of times I felt like punching him out."

"Brad," Pamela raised her voice, flabbergasted at his admission. "You're not serious?"

He tossed her a look that said he was. He started to say something, then waited for his throat to clear.

Pamela followed his lead by clearing her throat. She was intrigued by a side of him she had never seen before.

He swept his hand through his hair agitatedly and then opened his mouth to speak, relaying the substance of his foul mood.

"I think Robert is leaving Barbara."

"Oh, Brad, no!" Pamela squeezed his arm, emphasizing both her surprise and sympathy.

Brad frowned, his eyes still trained on the road ahead.

"Something's happened to their marriage. They seemed like a different couple today. Now don't get me wrong, they've never been the perfect couple. Barbara left him for a while and lived with her parents in Maine last year. She came back after a few months to save what was left of the marriage. Unfortunately, or fortunately, depending on how you look at it, there isn't much left of their marriage to save."

Pamela remained silent. She couldn't see how Barbara could put up with such a pompous egomaniac. She liked Barbara, but four hours of Robert was all she could take. She turned toward Brad again and listened as he ventilated his disappointment.

Brad tucked his anger into his resolve to remain objective as he lamented his brother and sister-in-law's marital woes.

"What's amazing about their relationship is that by the time the summer festivities revive the Outer Banks again this year, Robert and Barbara Aikman will be the center of the coast's social activities, spinning days and nights of parties, receptions and grand openings. They are the perfect social magnets, beautiful, talented, and monied. And when they quarrel, they make sure they don't do it publicly."

"I'm sorry you're upset. I wish there were something ... "

Brad cut into her polite condolence.

"That's what is really upsetting me," he broke into a smile. "I'm upset that I'm even upset over it."

Pamela looked confused.

He chuckled. "I keep telling myself not to take responsibility for their unhappiness or for the lack of success of their relationship. Ba ... Barb's a great lady. She's the one that's held their marriage together all these years. And I love Robert, as crazy as that sounds. After all, he's my brother. But if it weren't for our blood connection, I wouldn't associate with him at all. He's not my kind of people." He looked to his left. "We're as different as that old pick-up truck and corvette we just passed."

Pamela glanced quickly behind her and caught a glimpse of the corvette trailing an old dilapidated green truck, loaded with pieces of household furniture, tied down but untarped. She quickly returned her attention to Brad, who brought her hand to his lips and kissed it affectionately.

"Thanks for understanding."

Pamela squeezed his hand.

"I hope the visit hasn't ruined your vacation."

"Oh, heavens no! I found it ... interesting."

He lowered his voice so that it sounded like a rumble of mild resentment. "I want to apologize to you for stopping there. I was ambivalent about it. When I called him yesterday I almost canceled our visit."

Pamela politely interrupted. "I'm glad we stopped. I've wanted to meet your family. You've not only kept me secret, you've kept them secret, too. Before this trip the only thing I knew about your brother was how he looked and that he is older than you."

"How'd you know ... ?"

"The picture on the wall of your condo. Remember? Your gallery."

Brad remembered the skydiving picture and white water rafting photos that included shots of his brother. "That's right! I forgot about showing you those."

"Brad."

The seriousness of her soft voice prompted a quick look in her direction.

"Barbara told me about Susan."

Except for the humming of the high-performance motor and the keyboard music of John Tesh emanating from the CD, the car bathed them in silence. Pamela almost wished she hadn't mentioned Susan, realizing she'd unintentionally pushed him back into the depression she helped him climb out of a few moments ago.

He breathed a heavy sigh as he started to answer, but the words fell away.

"Oh, Brad, I'm so sorry. You don't have to say anything about ... "

He reached over and placed his hand around the back of her neck and gently squeezed the top of her shoulder, preludes to his next statement.

"That's okay, Babe. I was going to tell you about Susan sometime. The right time just never came up. I would have eventually gotten around to it."

She shot him a mournful expression.

"No, really. I would have. I planned to tell you sooner or later. It just turned out to be later."

Pamela was about to offer an apology when he cleared his throat to speak.

"Everyone has baggage, the acts of a lifetime, done without thinking about the consequences," he said softly.

He sounded philosophical, almost reverent, as he explained his relationship with Susan, apologizing whenever he felt he elaborated too much or took too long to describe a sequence of events.

Until now Pamela was the one who had spilled out her life history. Now he found himself unable to arrest the flood of memories that fell from his lips in tidal waves of posthumous remembrance.

She pulled herself closer to him, silently resentful of the interior design of the car that compartmentalized them. Bucket seats kept them barricaded from closer physical contact, and the padded console was a cumbersome barrier preventing any sort of prolonged proximity.

Pamela was moved beyond words. Of all the men she had known, he intrigued her now more than ever with his many contradictions.

Pamela forced her buttock onto the console and cushioned her head on his shoulder, extending her arm around the back of his neck. Her right hand rested on his knee, just below the hem of his shorts, making her hand and wrist a peninsula of soft flesh against his tanned leg.

Brad felt her warmth through his shirt and the heat of her hand against his leg. He wanted to stop the car and hold her, to be held, to shut out the world beyond their tight embrace. He hadn't told Pamela everything.

There are some things best kept buried, he reminded himself.

The skeletons which were dredged up at his brother's had been dealt with now, at least most of them. The miserable visit was miles behind them and Pamela still seemed interested in him, in spite of what she had learned a few minutes ago.

He put his free hand on hers, gently wedging her hand between his palm and the top of his leg. Then he kissed the side of her head, near her hairline and felt the pressure of her hand as she squeezed his thigh.

"I love you," he said, half whispering.

"I love you, too," she cooed, squeezing both his neck and his thigh again.

"Thanks for listening."

"Aw, honey, I want to be there for you, too." Pamela encouraged. "If this is all we've ever got to worry about, we'll be fortunate. Fortunate, indeed."

"I agree."

Thoughts about Geoffrey and the composite leaked into her consciousness again, but she kept her recollections to herself. Somehow she knew it would turn out all right. The detour to Robert's house had brought her and Brad closer. Now she hoped they could manage the closeness.

"The bed and breakfast is just up ahead," Brad announced. Then he breathed a sigh of relief. "Babe, what do you say we forget all about Beaufort and concentrate on what's left of our vacation."

"Works for me," she said jubilantly, pulling herself away from him so that she sat straight in her seat. She slipped the compact from her purse and attended to her makeup, adding a fresh coat of lipstick to lips that would feel the strength of his kisses later that night. She gave her hair a few perfunctory puffs and smiled in the mirror. Her ritual complete, she settled back in her seat and looked for the sign that marked the location of the bed and breakfast.

"There. See?" Brad pointed it out, then looked at his watch. Four fifteen, he noted to himself. "The Silver Lake Inn," he announced.

"We have guaranteed reservations, don't we?" Pamela asked rhetorically.

"Yes. Late arrival."

"Then let's take a walk on the beach first. We can leave everything locked in the car and spend a couple of hours on the beach before we check in. Then we can freshen up. Do you feel up to it?" she asked playfully, raising her eyebrows and throwing him a naughty look.

"Insufferable romantic that I am," his voice lightened, "how can I refuse such a heated offer?"

"Take me to an isolated section of beach and you'll find out how hot the beaches get around here."

"Mercy, woman. What's gotten into you?"

"Disclosure."

"Disclosure?"

She nodded her head. "Painful disclosure."

Brad looked confused, but subscribed to her suggestion and headed the car toward the beach.

"Painful disclosure?" he asked, wanting clarification.

"Well, it's more what the painful disclosure means. What it does to people."

Brad was still playing catch-up.

"It brings people together," she explained. "It creates a common bond. It's a ... "

"Shared triumph over emotional adversity," Brad finished her sentence.

"Yes, that's right."

"But there are risks associated with it, too."

"I know, but the risks are out-weighed by the benefits."

"I hope so, because I've told you more than I've ever told anyone about myself."

"That's because you trust me."

"It's because I love you."

Pamela kissed him on the cheek. "I love you, too! I don't want anything to ever come between us."

Brad looked at her through his smile. "I don't either. I hope we can weather any storm."

CHAPTER TWENTY-FOUR

"Hi. We have guaranteed reservations for tonight. The name's Aikman, Brad Aikman."

"Yes, Mr. Aikman. I have your confirmation right here. Welcome to Silver Lake Inn," the owner greeted Brad cordially. "My name is Paul Bowers and I'm the owner. Your room is ready. Would you sign the register, please, and I'll get your keys."

Brad busied himself filling out the short registration form while the innkeeper retrieved the keys. The chest-high counter was an old converted post office lock box section. Its antique brass doors were splendidly crafted, decorative and polished to perfection, no doubt restored with countless hours of patient rubbing and buffing.

The inn had an air of timeless elegance. It seemed to tolerate the times instead of join them. The polished oak floor planks, gleaming with age and wax, were covered with islands of hand-crafted rugs.

The owner was squarely and non-apologetically built, wearing light gray slacks and a floral shirt that hung outside his pants. His partially gray hair was tied in a stubby ponytail and his face was etched with the tensions of a lifetime he had endured. His autocratic bearing was softened by a perpetual smile, exposing well-formed white teeth.

"Do you want to leave any collateral charges on your credit card?"

"We probably won't raid the mini-bar," Brad announced. "But just in case ... the card I reserved the room on is fine."

"Very good then. Here's the room key. Room number seven. Towels and toiletries are in there already. The queen-sized bed has been turned down. We adopted that practice for all our late arrivals." He smiled. "We even left a light on for you."

"Thanks, that's really nice," Brad replied as he accepted the keys and turned to go, but a sudden announcement from the owner halted his exit.

"Oh, Mr. Aikman. You have a phone message. The party said it was urgent. Let's see. Here it is. It's from a Mr. George Lee. It came in around four-thirty this afternoon."

Brad thanked him as he took the message in the same hand he was holding his credit card receipt.

"Do you need help with your luggage?" asked Mr. Bowers.

"No thanks. We can handle it."

The innkeeper nodded politely. "There's parking in the back and a few spaces on the side near the pool. You're welcome to use any available space."

"Thanks."

His next comment followed Brad to the front door. "Complimentary breakfast is served starting at seven. If you think you'll eat much later than that, let us know. Donna will be happy to prepare a couple of special breakfasts for you as long as you eat by ten."

At the sound of her name, his wife appeared from behind the swinging kitchen doors. She was a petite woman, around twenty-eight to thirty years old, wearing walking shorts and a red halter-top. Her shimmering blonde hair was full and stylish, framing a face that was square and tanned. She was an attractive woman and appeared to take good care of herself. Her eyes were so large that she seemed permanently surprised, or frightened, depending on the shape of her mouth.

"This is my wife, Donna. Chief cook and overall boss of the place."

Brad acknowledged her presence with a friendly nod. He watched them toss each other playful looks.

"Nice meeting you," Brad addressed the owner's wife. "A seven o'clock breakfast will be fine. We're early risers. Besides, we don't want to miss a ray of sunshine once it hits the beach."

"There'll be two settings for breakfast then?" Donna verified, using her most cordial business tone.

"Yes, ma'am."

"Hope you like cheese omelets and waffles smothered in homemade jam with a couple of patties of sausage on the side."

"You've definitely got two for breakfast."

Both Donna and Paul smiled.

Brad waved good-bye as he exited through the front door. He climbed quickly into his Benz, and as he pulled around to the back parking lot, he told Pamela about her grandfather's call.

"You go ahead and make the phone call," he instructed Pamela, handing her the room key. "I'll park the car and bring the luggage up in a couple of minutes."

"Are you sure?"

"Of course. The note says it's urgent. I wonder why he didn't just call you on your cell."

Pamela flew out of the car as soon as he stopped, leaving the car door ajar. In her haste, the Lee biography Robert had given her for George fell unnoticed out of her open purse, as she rushed up the steps to their second-floor room.

As she fumbled with the key in the lock, she thought: *I hope they're all right. What could the urgency be? Grampa would never call unless it was something serious. Come on lock, open! I don't have time for this.*

"Settle down, now," she chastised herself as she opened the door. "Finally! Jeesch! I don't believe how long it took me to open that door."

A dizzying wave of anticipation washed over her as she switched the lights on and put the cell phone to her ear. She allowed her anxiety to misdirect the number the first time, and had to hit the phone app again.

"Come on, Pamela, settle down!" she ordered herself.

She finally got her fingers working and touched the right phone listing on her droid. The familiar click after the fourth ring told Pamela that she would have to leave a message. The answering service announcement came at her mechanically as she listened to the obnoxious beep, which signaled the end of the taped instructions.

"Grampa, this is me. We didn't get your message until now." She reported, as she looked at her watch. Nine twenty-six. "We're in for the night. Call as soon as you can. We're in room number seven. Why don't you just call me on my cell? Anyway, like I said, we're in for the night."

She lowered the phone, but an afterthought pulled the phone back to her ear. And she added, "You've got me a little worried. I hope everything's all right."

As she ended the call, Brad appeared in the doorway, sandwiched between both sets of luggage. One look at her somber face prompted him to set the luggage down while maintaining constant eye contact with her. His inquisitorial gaze hinted at cross-examination.

"Babe, what's happened? You look so distressed. What is it?"

Pamela frowned and shook her head.

"I got the answer phone. I still don't know anything." She attempted to camouflage her concern by throwing him a fractured smile, but a growing sense of trepidation was beginning to pale her face. "Grampa would never call unless there were something terribly wrong."

Brad was at her side now and embraced her, cuddling her in the tight but gentle coil of his arms. He waited for his throat to clear and then, sharply conscious of her anxiety, kissed her on her forehead.

"Babe, I know you're concerned but let's not think the worst until we know what's happened. Maybe it's not as bad as you think. It might even be good news."

Pamela looked at him suspiciously, hopefully. Her emerald eyes narrowed, temporarily considering the merits of his logic, then widened to more pronounced ovals as she allowed her intuition to rule.

"It's not like Grampa to call," she repeated, looking at Brad pleadingly.

"Before you get yourself all worked up, consider this. George may be calling to tell you that a client needs you right away."

Pamela's eyes brightened a little, but dimmed again quickly.

"He knows there's been a downturn in your business and probably has some good news to share with you."

Brad wasn't sure he believed that, but bringing her spirits up a few notches couldn't hurt, particularly since they didn't know why George called.

Pamela sighed, responding to his logic.

"The note only said urgent," Brad punctuated.

But his simple explanation wasn't enough. There was a growing sense of uneasiness, of some unpleasantness heading their way. Both felt it, but neither could explain it nor admit it, out of concern for the other's feelings. The gnawing feeling of foreboding thickened the air in the room.

In the brief moment after the consolation Brad had so confidently manufactured, they let the silence of the room surround them. They heard the sound of a car go by and listened as the noise vaporized in the night air.

"I forgot to close the door," Brad confessed, releasing Pamela's hand. He threw her a reassuring smile as he walked slowly over to close the door. He stepped around the luggage on his way back to her, but then decided to retrieve the bags. Just as Brad reached for the suitcases, the room phone rang.

Pamela jumped off the bed and stood beside the nightstand, staring at the ringing telephone. They shot each other simultaneous glances as Brad followed her over to the phone, which sat, ringing ominously on the small cherry table next to the bed.

The third ring hammered her ears before she extracted it from its base. Her heart was pounding so fast that she thought it would explode. As she pulled the phone slowly toward her, she trained her nervous gaze on Brad, wanting to siphon all of the support she could squeeze out of his slate-gray eyes. His intense stare and go-ahead nod helped her lift the receiver to her ear before the fourth ring ended.

"Hello ... "

"Mrs. Aikman, this is Paul Bowers."

Her confused silence greeted him.

Unaware of her dilemma, he continued. "Your husband left his car lights on. The car was locked so I couldn't get in to turn them off."

She motioned to Brad that it wasn't her grandfather. Brad's puzzled look forced her to speed up her response. Pamela snapped her composure into place and politely replied, "Oh, thank you, Mr. Bowers. I was just expecting someone else to call. The car lights, you said? We left them on? You couldn't get in to turn them off," she summarized mechanically. "Thank you so much. We'll attend to it. Thank you again."

Brad retrieved his car keys, but elected to stay in the room until she completed the call. Pamela smiled wryly. A low, broken laugh escaped her nervous lips.

"He's probably wondering about us," she began, chuckling at the innkeeper's apology.

"Both of us had better calm down now," Brad reassured her. "Each of us is feeding off the other's anxiety. We're going to feel a little ridiculous when George calls to tell you that one of your clients wants you to fly to Dallas or Boston or Atlanta to help them whip one of the teams into shape."

She unwound her tightness a little and looked at him appreciatively.

"I know you're right."

"I hear a but. I'm not going to allow you to get worked up over what-ifs. Getting wrapped up in worry is not the way to package time."

She threw him a knowing grin. "But suppose something is wrong?"

"If it is, we'll deal with it. If it isn't, all the worrying and fretting and prophesying in the world will have been unnecessary. Right?"

Pamela nodded, trying her best not to broadcast the grin she knew was coming.

"Good. Now you just stay put," he ordered as he walked toward the door. "I'm going to dowse the car lights while we've still got some battery left, and then I'll be right back."

He could see her tighten slightly and caught a hint of nervousness revisit her eyes.

"I'll only be a minute. I promise." He threw her a kiss and started out the door.

She started to say something, but blunted it back, covering it with a smile. She put her fingertips to her lips and returned his endearment.

For the first time, she noticed the sound of the waves as they brought the sea to shore. The night air was cool but accommodative, carried unapologetically into the room by the soft breeze, intent on cooling the room with its own natural air-conditioning instead of waiting for the room thermostat to jump to attention.

The serenity of the moment was broken by the sound of the car door closing. She wanted him in the room with her, to even up the odds, to keep the phone at bay.

She could hear Brad now. Evidently he is navigating the steps two or three at a time, judging from the way his feet are landing on them, she guessed.

She smiled as she remembered his antics every time they ate at Golden Corral. He would always leap sideways over the railing that herded the guests into the dining area. Then he would wait for her to catch up, beaming at her with childish pride, feeling pleased with himself for operating outside the rules.

Brad reappeared behind a wide grin as he leaped through the doorway. He was carrying the book Robert gave Pamela to give to George.

"You must have dropped it when you rushed up here to phone George," he guessed. "It was lying beside the car."

"Oops! I'm sorry."

Pamela smiled, extending her hand to claim it, and then unceremoniously placed the book on the bed."

"I'm glad you're back," she admitted. She extended her arm again, taking his hand briefly in her own. "Is the car okay?"

"Yes, the lights weren't on that long. I can't believe I did that," he chastised himself, allowing a quick chuckle to leave his lips.

Brad redirected their attention to the book.

"I hope it didn't get soiled. Are any pages bent?"

Pamela turned the book over and gave it a cursory examination, using her thumb to flip through the pages.

"Nope, looks fine."

"That's a relief. I didn't want George thinking he had gotten damaged goods as a gift."

"I'm sure it's okay," she assured him.

After a slight hesitation, she picked the book up again and looked at the cover. The picture of Lee was the reproduction of a photograph taken by Matthew Brady, shortly before Lee died. Even with the poor quality of the image apparent, she could sense the magnetism, the resolve, the strength of Lee's dark penetrating eyes. Mesmerized for a moment, she did not notice Brad placed both suitcases on the bed.

She also did not hear his comments about how large and nicely decorated the bathroom was with its oak towel racks and quilted shower curtain.

Pamela opened the book to Chapter one and read the introductory passage that described Lee's predicament on April 9, 1865 as he studied the situation he found himself in on that Palm Sunday morning. She read that the General had stood on a hilltop in the fog near the village of Appomattox Court House, contemplating the future of the Army of Northern Virginia.

She shivered as a lightning-fast wave of apprehension shot through her. It was so noticeable that Brad stopped what he was doing and came over to her.

"Babe, are you all right?" He sat down beside her and put his arm around her waist.

Pamela sighed heavily and offered him a rueful smile. She was too embarrassed to tell him about the memories the passage in the book has just culled up. The hilltop fog reminded her of that fateful Saturday morning in Asheville when she met Geoffrey on the bridge. She knew how General Lee felt. She could sense his alarm. She imagined the faint crack of musketry, punctuated with the heavy dullness of exploding artillery fire, corrupting the morning stillness with its shattering, impersonal barks of destruction.

Her thoughts returned to her own accident. Her ears rang with the sound of metal scraping against cement, glass exploding as it scattered, sending hundreds of irregular specks of glass raining down on the bridge. Like General Lee, she knew about collisions. And like Lee, she felt she was a victim of circumstance, horrible circumstance.

"Yes, I'm okay." She looked at him and smiled through her reminiscence. Her eyes found the book cover again and she slowly ran her fingers over Lee's eyes in the photograph. "I just realized I had something in common with General Lee."

Brad's surprise took his lips to her as he leaned forward and kissed her lightly on her temple.

"And what might that be?"

She stared at the image of Lee again, focusing on his noble countenance.

"We both faced something that came at us from out of the fog." She looked up and turned her face toward Brad, meeting his steady gaze with her own.

"And we both knew it would force its will on us. Look at his eyes, darling." She held the book up so he could see it. "He knew his best was not going to be good enough. He knew he was going to receive a crushing blow."

She blinked back the tears that moistened the rims of her mascara-lined eyes.

"He knew there was no escape. He was surrounded. Cut off. Vulnerable."

"Babe, I know how difficult it must have been."

Pamela laid the book down and grabbed Brad's hand, bringing it to her lips, kissing it. Then she held his hand against her cheek, seeking his strength.

"I need to tell you this."

He nodded his consent, resting his gaze on her face with great intensity. His gentle squeeze on her hand announced his willing compliance.

"We experienced ... General Lee and I experienced the same overpowering menace that came quickly out of the fog. For General Lee it was the terminal velocity of the Union Army. For me ... for Geoffrey and me ... it was an out-of-control piece of metal."

Brad closed his eyes.

"Pamela, you don't have to ... "

"No, I want to," she insisted and emphasized her intention by squeezing his hand again.

He closed his eyes again and let out a heavy woeful sigh. He nodded his consent grudgingly.

"Geoffrey tried to push me clear."

Brad squeezed her hand tighter, but did not look away. Her recollections sped him to the horrible accident scene with her. He was caught in her story of survival.

"I knew that whatever happened ... " Pamela stopped in mid sentence, then gave Brad the most horrified look.

"What is it, Babe?" he raised his voice. "Tell me. You're beginning to frighten me. What's wrong?" His sentences were clipped, demanding.

Her mouth flung open, sending her lips into an oval curve of pink lipstick.

He moved closer, and cupped her cheeks in his hands.

"Pamela!"

Her faraway look, combined with her astonishment, commandeered an anxious response from Brad.

"Babe, talk to me. Don't do this to me."

Pamela shook her head as if to bring herself back to normal consciousness.

"Geoffrey was right," she whispered, staring at Brad but not seeing him. Then she blinked a couple of times and raised her eyebrows, sending a sigh from her lips. "He said if I tried hard enough, I might remember something about the accident."

She tightened her grip on his hand and looked at Brad intently. Her face was a shifting landscape of changing emotions, first surprise, then recollection. Then she seemed to move into agitation and finally to anger by the time she spoke again.

"Brad," she steeled her gaze onto his, "I remember something on the back of the mirror."

"What?" he asked, his excitement building.

"The mirror. I saw a sticker, or a patch," she corrected herself, "with red lettering, red numbers on a white background, I think."

"Red numbers?" Brad repeated. "Are you sure?"

Pamela shook her head, indicating she was certain.

"I remember a red letter—a capital A. And the number 240." She smiled, pleased with her discovery.

"240?" came Brad's query.

"Yes, Two hundred forty. A-240."

She raised herself off the bed and squealed with delight. "It was stuck to the back of the mirror. What do you think it means?"

Caught off guard, Brad hesitated, unable to make his lips move.

Pamela became more animated, her movements contrasting sharply with Brad's look of mock astonishment.

"It's probably a parking sticker, or club membership decal of some sort," she turned to Brad again.

His piercing slate eyes swept over her in a quick but thorough reconnaissance, moving with her as she slid next to him.

Pamela met his gaze head-on.

"I think I've got something here."

"Maybe ... But Babe, you were about to be hit by a car! Do you really think you would be seeing a sticker?"

The pout of her lips told him she was disappointed in his reaction.

"Now it's my turn to ask what's wrong," Pamela announced, unconsciously tightening her grip on his arm. "I thought you'd be pleased that I remembered something about the accident."

He sighed, "I am. I am pleased. It's just that ... "

"What?" She pierced his eyes with her stare. "What?"

He steadied his gaze on her, contemplating her, admiring her.

"It's just that I don't want you to get hurt."

"I think you know what I mean," he inched into his explanation. "I have dried your tears many times these past few months, whenever you felt pressured by Geoffrey to help find the hit-and-run driver, remember?"

Although his criticism sounded a little parental, she knew he was right. The thought of dredging up memories about the accident had traumatized her in the past, disabling her at times, and it had been Brad who had pulled her out of it.

"Yes, darling. I remember. You have been so good to me, for me. I don't know what I would have done without you."

"You've been assaulted in your own home and warned not to investigate the accident."

"But that's just the point," Pamela countered. "I have to find out who the driver is. He sent someone to scare me off. I'm not going to live my life in fear."

"I know. And that's my point. I want you to be careful. And I say that selfishly. I don't want to collect stitches or have my nose broken every time I open the door."

The sharp ring of the phone cut into his plea, and sent a chill up Pamela's spine.

A quick pleading look at Brad, followed by her hesitance to close the distance between the phone and herself, prompted him to answer the phone.

He caught it on the third ring and lifted it to his ear.

Pamela stiffened, remaining where she stood at the foot of the bed.

"Hello."

"Hello. Oh, hi, Brad. This is George Lee."

"Yes, George. We've been expecting your call."

"I'm sorry to have to call you under these circumstances." His voice sounded tired, and too melancholy for good news.

Something is terribly wrong, Brad guessed.

"Do you want to speak to Pamela?" Brad asked, thinking Pamela ought to be the one to hear this.

There was a slight pause. Brad could hear George let out a labored sigh.

"Yes, son. I need to talk to her."

"Just a minute and I'll put her on."

Before he handed the phone to Pamela, Brad motioned for her to sit on the edge of the bed.

Pamela's face flushed. Her confidence of a few moments ago vaporized, replaced now by nervous anticipation sending her heart racing through her chest.

"Babe, I believe there is something wrong. George does not sound like himself."

She started to tear up, but resolutely wiped the tears away, as she reached for the phone. Her voice was soft and brittle as she spoke.

"Grampa?" She started to say something else but her voice was leaden, dropping the words away. Conscious now of the growing alarm rising in her throat, constricting her speech, she decided to wait for her grandfather to speak.

"Pamela, honey." George began slowly. "I've got ... some terribly distressing news ... " he forced the words out. "I want you to be strong, my dear."

Pamela stiffened.

"It's Gramma, isn't it?"She barely got the words out before a sudden tremor swept through her, sending goose flesh up her arms. She reached out to grab Brad's hand, thinking she was going to faint.

Brad inched up beside her on the bed and cradled her securely in his arms. His eyes, narrowed and anticipatory, were focused on the minutest movements of her facial geography: an eye twitch, a quiver of the lips, the tear-filled rim of an eye.

Pamela's emotional antennae readied itself.

"No, honey. It's not Gramma. It's Geoffrey. He's committed suicide."

CHAPTER TWENTY-FIVE

*I*t had been three torturous weeks since Geoffrey's funeral and she had not plugged herself back into life yet. Not allowing anyone to dislodge her from her grief, Pamela chose instead to remain surrounded by the leaden silence she manufactured for herself, refusing to be pulled from her self-imposed emotional sarcophagus.

Her only occupation was the business of grieving, coping with the suicide of her dear Geoffrey. Karen came to her rescue again, assuming administrative responsibilities for her business. She canceled or rescheduled Pamela's business engagements, a task she had become quite familiar with the Christmas before, when she'd notified clients of her sister's accident.

Everything was an effort. Pamela would focus on taking a cap off the toothpaste, getting the toothbrush to her mouth, and rinsing her mouth with mouthwash. Flossing was out—it took too much energy.

Karen, her grandparents, and Brad collectively conspired to schedule their visits routinely to force her to eat properly. Only once or twice had she allowed any of them to coax her out of the house to a nearby restaurant.

She lay face-up on her bed, looking at the ceiling fixture which resembled a brass island in a sea of white plaster.

The funeral was beautiful, and horrible, she reminisced. *I've laid a dear friend to rest. Except for the thunderstorm, the service was just the way Geoffrey would have wanted it— reverent, highly personal, but sprinkled with moments of levity.*

He had written his own memorial service and the Unity minister honored Geoffrey's request by organizing the message, scriptural passages, and music just the way Geoffrey had specified, including a rendition of Dixie that brought tears to her eyes again. It was the one she'd had professionally arranged just for him when he had returned from a two-year assignment in Philadelphia with the narcotics division. He missed North Carolina so much that she wanted to make his return special, celebrating it in a way that would honor his love for the South.

A slight smile creased her face as she remembered the mixed expressions on the mourner's faces at the interment service.

"To live and die in Dixie," she whispered, quoting a line from the Southern tune.

"I promised myself I would climb out of my despondency ... Reclaim my life ... feel human again ... Put the past behind me, didn't I?" she had confessed to Geoffrey.

She let the tears trickle down her cheeks.

"Why, Geoffrey? Why?" she raised her voice. "You told me after the break-in that you'd find the driver. You said he wouldn't be able to hurt me again."

She closed her eyes and sobbed uncontrollably.

You lied to me, she pined bitterly.

"Damn you! You lied to me," she shouted. "You took the easy way out."

She rolled onto her side and stuck her thumbnail in her mouth, biting the polished surface.

I thought you were the strong one. Oh, Geoffrey, what a waste. You had options. Damn you! You could have figured something out ... You could have called me.

She buried her head in the damp pillow, moistened with her tears.

You could have called Ted ... or Karen, she thought. *You didn't have to handle this thing alone.*

Her grip on the pillow tightened, sending her face deeper into its folds.

We loved you. When people love you, you don't trash them, she reprimanded mentally. *You weren't helpless. You were more than your disability. You let your paralysis disable your whole body and your mind.*

Pamela pulled herself up higher on the pillow and popped her arms out from under the blanket, folding them over her chest. She slipped into one of Brad's old T-shirts, royal blue except for a small splash of color denoting the name, in gold lettering, of a sport parachute clinic he'd attend some years back.

"Oh, Geoffrey," she said at the end of her sigh, "you're going to make me find him on my own, aren't you? And I don't know what he looks like. I never got the composite."

She sighed again to emphasize her disappointment and anger.

"Maybe the mailbox vandals stole it ... or threw it away. Maybe it got lost in cyberspace."

A quick glance at the lighted dial on the face of the digital clock on her night stand told her it was ten-twenty.

Brad will be here shortly to pick me up, she reminded herself.

"He said he'd be here at eleven," she reminded herself aloud again, sighing heavily. But she made no attempt to move, her sense of urgency long since deflated by weeks of bereavement.

Brad had persuaded her to go to Linville falls for the weekend. He originally planned to take her spelunking in New Mexico, but Geoffrey's death changed that. Linville Falls was a worthy compromise. Both of them knew the healing properties of the mountains with their breathtaking scenery, cool mountain lakes, and majestic waterfalls. Their timeless heights and naturally air-conditioned forest floors pulled tourists and lovers alike from cities characterized by traffic exhausts, urban noise, and twice-breathed air in stuffy office buildings.

She leaned on her side and extended her hand to turn on the lamp. Like a custard thickening, the heavy sediments of golden lamplight jumped on her face and collected in the corners of the bedroom.

Sighing heavily again, she used her willpower to move. She laboriously put her bare legs over the edge of the bed and heaved herself up. Her joints cracked and groaned in lactic protest as Pamela moved toward the bathroom with a weariness that was leaden and stupefying. Conscious of her lethargy, she attempted a smile, but settled for a counterfeit grin. She was still not ready to forgive the world for taking Geoffrey away.

She was used to occupying herself with one crisis at a time. The present one, facing herself in the mirror, was all she could handle. The cool silence of the house wrapped itself around her, enveloping her in introspection and self-pity. Misery washed over her like dirty lake water, contaminating her thinking, muddying her judgment.

The expression on the face of her twin in the mirror came toward her, bearing a careful rearrangement of features that said: *Okay, kid, this is it! Snap out of it and pull yourself together!*

A slight eyebrow rise punctuated the necessity for a makeover. Pamela brought her hands up to her face. Her fingernails, polished Valentine red, contrasted sharply with her pale face. The tan she had gotten at Emerald Isle had disappeared from weeks of mourning.

"Yuk. Yuk!" she whispered, criticizing her looks.

She summoned the energy for a shower. Standing with her face toward the overhead spigot, she allowed the warmth of the spewing water to cascade over her face and hair, then on to her breasts and thighs. She stood motionless, eyes closed, hands at her sides. She felt enlivened by the chlorinated waterfall.

But the respite from her depression was short-lived as her thoughts transported her back to Asheville, to the cemetery with its heaps of bulldozed earth, evidence of the newly dug miniature mud and clay mountain. The exhumed dirt had rested silently beside its own rectangular hole before the remains of her beloved Geoffrey filled it depths.

Despite the rain, she had stayed at the cemetery long after the other mourners left. An inner urge, prompted by her abysmal grief, had kept her there to witness the last shovel-full of dirt that sealed the grave. She had insisted that it be her shovel-full. No one had objected, or even thought of objecting to such a sentimental request.

She remembered leaning heavily on her grandfather as they left the cemetery and she regretted that Brad was unable to attend the funeral. A sudden attack of flu had immobilized him.

She sighed heavily at the remembrance. Her ensemble of thoughts took her to the blurred images of thee other gravestones, blockish oblongs of marble polished to Methodist, or Presbyterian, or Baptist or Episcopal, or Catholic gloss. She wondered how Geoffrey's marker would look, resting one space over from his mother's grave. A morbid thought pushed its way into her consciousness, causing the ends of her mouth to turn upward slightly, almost unnoticeably.

One day Ted's body will fill that vacant space and the three of you will be reunited forever.

"Take care of him, Mrs. Collins. Your son is whole again. I hope you two won't hold that last thought against me. I want Ted to live a long time before he joins you."

Her thoughts returned to the cemetery. The afternoon sky had thickened and sunk lower with menacing clouds. It was ashen all day, insisting on staying gray, bulging with dampness. It was as if all of life itself mourned the passing of one so pure, so brave, so giving.

As she edited her thoughts, she found it odd that she remembered trivialities from three weeks before.

Her mournful eye had caught the tilt of the mailbox at the entrance to the cemetery as they drove past. It was inclined at a forty-five degree angle and the lid stuck open like a tongue begging for its cavity to be filled, but content to be neglected.

Recollections of her own curbside mailbox came to her as she quickly reminisced about her grandfather's enthusiastic commentary concerning its vandalism. While Brad and she were at Emerald Isle, vandals knocked down several mailboxes in the neighborhood, including hers, and scattered their contents.

He had not told her about it for several weeks. Geoffrey's death had taken precedence. George had repaired it, replacing and then repainting the broken post. He had even replaced the brass numbers corresponding to her street address.

She remembered that George wasn't sure if there was any mail missing, since a half dozen or so letters and several bulk mail pieces were strewn about. It appeared to be a simple case of vandalism, initiated by mindless students or bored drop-outs fueled by adrenaline instead of common sense.

"Sometimes people can be so common," she said softly. "It's a good thing I didn't see them. Oh, I couldn't have seen them. I was away," she corrected herself.

Her thoughts about the damaged mailbox caused her to bite her lower lip, sending a flush to her face that covered her paleness. A sudden prompting struck her.

"Geoffrey's letter. Dear Geoffrey—I need to read your letter again," she said aloud. At the memorial service, Ted had given her a letter he'd found in one of Geoffrey's law books. It was addressed, sealed and stamped, but had never been mailed. Suddenly the urge to read that letter one more time sent Pamela out of the shower.

"Think! Where did you put it?" she said aloud, grilling herself as she slipped a bath towel over her shoulders.

She spun around and dashed into her bedroom, becoming airborne as she catapulted across the bed and landed next to the night stand. A swift pull exposed the contents in the drawer, and she yanked out the envelope. It had an uncanceled postage stamp in the upper right corner.

"Here it is!" she exclaimed happily. "Sometimes I amaze myself."

She teared up as she ran her hand across the white face of the envelope. She knew what was inside and that she would open it, but she felt such reverence for its author that she needed a few moments to pay her respects. Finally, an exaggerated sigh forced her fingers to re-open the treasured envelope.

She trembled as she unsheathed the letter. After she placed the envelope on the nightstand beside her, she unfolded Geoffrey's last written correspondence.

The date at the top of the letter didn't come into focus at first. Her eyes were blurred with tears.

"June fifth," she whispered and then repeated it with an eveness that sounded more pragmatic almost investigative in tone. "June fifth!"

She was balanced on an edge of curiosity that could topple over at any moment into tears, or panic, or even denial. But the old Pamela, the resolute Pamela, the confident, willful Pamela was resurfacing. The corners of emptiness in her that needed to be filled were lined with a growing sense of foreboding, triggered by questions that were raining down on her. Why did Geoffrey commit suicide? What made him so desperate? Why would he write me such a sweet letter the same day he decided to take his life? Did I miss his cry for help? Why wasn't I more aware of his depression? Without the composite, how will I recognize the driver?

She flipped to the second page. Her eyes moved to the passage that read: *In my darkness, I have found a precious brilliance. Something very essential has emerged.*

She skipped to the last paragraph. Her eyes were glued to the page as she read tearfully the last words he had ever written:

I rejoice in your happiness with Brad. I am able to dance through your happiness, leap high in your contentment, and pirouette with your joy.

She wiped back a stream of tears with her fingers as she read his salutation: *Love always, Geoffrey.*

An agonizing wail left her trembling lips as she dropped the open letter onto her lap. She raised one of her hands to her face, covering her nose and mouth with her palm, and let out another mournful cry.

"Oh, Geoffrey, how could you leave me like that?"

The phone rang, sending a jolt through her as it sounded its shrill proclamation. By the time it repeated itself, Pamela was standing beside the bed, slowly folding the letter, intent on placing it back in its paper casket. Angered by the overlap in worlds, she made no attempt to answer the phone call that she knew would transfer into a saved message.

She threw a searing look at the phone.

"Apologize for your interruption or I'll deafen your tone!" she hissed, reprimanding it as if it were a delinquent juvenile.

She took several threatening steps toward it before she halted herself, satisfied that her indignation was justifiable, although she found herself a little embarrassed at having just chastised a telephone.

"What am I doing? I'm losing it."

A smile on her face would have lasted longer had it not been for another thought about Geoffrey. She closed her eyes, conjuring up the familiar lines of his handsome face, the prominent cheeks, the blue fields of his eyes, his golden hair and the extraordinarily warm smile that could melt any argument and cause admiring hearts to flutter.

Grief forced her to chronicle her memories of him—to waltz around his features long enough to fix them permanently in her consciousness. She would keep her photographs of him, but the images she wanted to be sure to keep would be the 'records' she kept hidden in her mental album.

Pamela lowered her gaze and examined the way Geoffrey had written her name in sweeping cursive strokes on the envelope. She admired his flair, the way he scripted the "P" so prominently, so stylishly.

His penmanship was more like a woman's, she thought, *than the jagged almost illegible scribbling most men claim as handwriting. It's too joyful, too flowing, too expansive to be a suicide note. But then Geoffrey brought a flare to everything he did. Why should a suicide note be any different?*

She closed her eyes again, reeling from the reality of it all. "Damn you, Geoffrey!"

She freed the letter again from the envelope and examined it thoroughly for any sign of depression, any hint of hopelessness in a "t" that wasn't crossed, or an "i" that remained unfinished. Her critical eye found nothing unusual about the letter, no grammatical inconsistencies, no sudden changes in handwriting, no incoherence in connecting thoughts to suggest self-destructive behavior, at least as far as she was concerned.

"I'm no expert in suicide diagnosis or prevention, but I know my instincts. And every fiber, every molecule of my being tells me you were not capable of self-erasure."

Her eyebrows plucked into skeptical arches as she completed her perusal of his letter.

"I can't believe you did it. I don't believe you could do such a thing," she repeated to herself in a low, methodical monotone.

She winced and pulled the letter to her chest, as she remembered the description the coroner had given in an attempt to autopsy the suicide. Geoffrey was found slumped over in his wheelchair near the kitchen table. His police revolver was lying on the floor beside him. He had shot himself in the right temple, just above the ear. There was no sign of struggle, no evidence of forced entry, nothing out of the ordinary in the room except the body of a young paraplegic who had just taken his life.

Floating lightly on waves of nausea, Pamela eased herself gently onto the bed.

"Suppose you did commit suicide?" she reasoned. *After all,* she thought, *you did mention something about your relationship to the universe.* "And you signed the letter 'Love always,'" she said aloud.

It was the addition of the word *always* that puzzled her. He usually polished off his letters with a simple Luv, Geoffrey or Luv, G.

"How could you say you love me and do something like this?" Pamela protested, throwing the letter on her bed.

Embarrassed at her tirade, she picked up the letter and placed it back in the envelope.

"Ted told me that when he picked you up earlier that morning, everything appeared normal. He said you ate pancakes for breakfast and then he shuttled you to and from school."

She remembered that Ted had found Geoffrey later that afternoon when he returned one of the textbooks Geoffrey left in his car. Ted surprised her when he admitted Geoffrey had mentioned suicidal thoughts during his horrible hospital stay.

Geoffrey must have kept those demons inside. I sure never guessed it.

Pamela bit her lip hard and the tears came, as she thought about Ted's daily pilgrimages to the cemetery since Geoffrey's death. Karen told her he sat for hours at the foot of the two graves in silent sentinelship, wanting to be close to the two people he loved the most in the world. Frequently he would speak to them, sometimes pleadingly, but more often descriptively, updating them on his daily activities or seeking their postmortem advice on both the mundane or unsettling circumstances he found himself in from time to time.

She was concerned about Ted. They all were. But she remembered that George Burns always talked to Gracie every day.

So maybe that's his way of coping with loss, she reminded herself. *Ted is sentimental, but strong! He'll pull through this. At least he's getting out every day. That's more than I can say for myself.*

With that realization she felt an odd sensation in her stomach. It produced a low groaning sound, which she quickly identified as hunger pangs.

"I haven't had anything to eat since yesterday morning," she reminded herself. "No wonder my stomach's growling."

She jumped up from the bed, feeling more energy than she had felt in a long time, and headed for the kitchen. Her bare feet moved across familiar tile and carried her from pantry to refrigerator, from stove to cabinet drawer, and back to the stove as she made short work out of breakfast preparation.

Suddenly she dashed out of the kitchen, moving lightly across the cool kitchen floor tiles to fetch the phone. She remembered she had not checked her messages. She located the phone and punched the app to retrieve any messages. It appeared that she had eight calls logged in.

As she waited for the first message, she stirred the cream of wheat, watching it simmer and then thicken. The flaccid bubbles rose out of the molten brew, releasing small puffs of steam, like boiling, bleached sand.

"Hello, Babe, it's me. It's eight-thirty-five. I don't know why I said that. Habit I guess. I know your phone records the time of each call. I wanted to tell you I'd be a little late getting back to Raleigh. I won't be able to leave Kinston until eleven, eleven-thirty at the latest. I'm already packed for the mountains, so I'll just drive straight to your place from here. I should be there by one or one-thirty, depending on when I leave. Love ya. Hope you're planning on taking that new bathing suit you bought at Emerald Isle last month. It'll be warm enough at the hotel pool for a swim. I'm looking forward to getting you back on the swinging bridge on Grandfather Mountain. I love you."

As she pressed the button to delete the message, she glanced at the clock on the nightstand. Eleven-forty. A sigh of relief escaped her lips.

I've got more time, she thought to herself and her eyes moved hungrily toward the shimmering cream of wheat. *I won't have to hurry through my meal,* she reasoned silently as she waited for the next message.

"Hello, Ms. Justice, we don't normally leave messages, but we thought you might be interested in our new line of ... "

As soon as she realized it was an obnoxious sales call, Pamela deleted the message with extreme prejudice. A smile creased her face.

That's one thing I can control, she thought to herself. I can delete those kinds of calls immediately.

The third message brought the familiar voice of her grandmother to her ears.

"Good morning, honey. Just thought I'd call to see if I could catch you before you left for Boone and Linville Falls. Looks like I missed you but I know you'll check your messages while you're on your trip, so have fun and be careful. Tell Brad I said take care of my granddaughter. Call me when you can. Your grandfather sends his love ... Oh, by the way, I don't know what made me think of this, George says he already has a copy of the Lee book Brad's brother gave him. He's going to keep it anyway though. He never returns gifts. Says duplicate gifts are double blessings. I meant to say something to you about it sooner, but you know how short-term memory slips when you get to be my age. Besides it wasn't something that couldn't wait. Call me when you get back. Let's see, you'll only be gone through the weekend, right? Call me to let me know how you're doing. Love you. Don't spend long in the sun. Bye."

The next call was typically Karen and it brought a smile to Pamela's lips.

"You know I don't like talking on these things. Call me when you get a chance. This is Karen. Bye."

The fifth call was a hang-up, so Pamela moved on to the next message that was also a hang-up. Then she quickly punched in the seventh call, recoiling at the sound of cool arrogance as Clarence's low, emotionless voice slithered into the receiver.

"Just heard about the cripple. Too bad. I always liked the guy. I still haven't forgotten you tried to frame me at the beach. God's punishing you for running out on me. You're gonna lose your current lover, too, 'cause I'm gonna ... "

Pamela deleted the rest of his call, screaming her disgust. It took her a few moments to compose herself before she retrieved the final call. She breathed a sigh of relief when the sound of Brad's voice slipped into her ear.

"Hi, Babe. It's me again. Add another half hour to my time. I'll be there around two o'clock. I promise. Sorry for the delay, but it can't be helped. See you soon. Love ya."

"I wish you were here now," Pamela pined. "I wish you could make Clarence go away."

§   §   §   §   §   §

The two of them followed the hiking trail toward Wiseman's View observation point on the west side of Linville Gorge, on a path cut through a vivid mosaic of fallen leaves, ferns and granite. Splashes of color caught their inquisitive stares and the pungent aroma of forest decay filled their nostrils.

The upper falls cascaded more than fifty feet over rocks and fallen limbs, disappearing briefly through a cleft in the mountainside, and then reappearing as the lower falls spewed its powerful spray down another sixty or so feet into the gorge.

Pamela breathed deeply, filling her weary soul with the timelessness of the forest, and the natural fragrances, and mingled scents. A remembrance of the funeral intruded as she slowly sucked in more of the forest. Unlike the natural mixture of scents around her as she stood in Pisgah National Forest next to a shimmering water fall, the air in the funeral home three weeks before was saturated with the stench of the competing aromas of perfumes as mourners descended into the mortuary to pay their respects.

She rationed a faint smile, as she thought about the symphony of sound and color and aroma which played itself out in natural, protected forests compared to man-made mortar and glass jungles, strongholds of the repugnant smell of greed and power.

A passage of sunlight, golden and intense, cut its way through a tiny opening in the trees that fringed the falls. She found herself relaxing again, completely spell-bound by the rural rapture of falls and gorge.

She reached over and took Brad's hand, squeezing it tightly, then released her pressure slightly, leaving her hand securely in his.

"It's beautiful, isn't it?" Brad marveled, responding to her affectionate touch.

Pamela nodded her agreement.

"Yes. Yes it is," she sighed heavily, as if to punctuate her affirmation. Then she released his hand and pulled herself around him, hugging him tightly. "Thanks for caring enough about me to force me out of the house."

"Healing takes time. I knew you needed to get out. I just didn't want to force you out before you were ready."

"I know."

"If I could have this year to live over again ... "

"It's okay," Pamela interrupted. "You couldn't have changed anything. It's not your fault." She squeezed him tighter. "I'm glad I have you."

Brad answered her with respectful silence. Then he reciprocated her hug and kissed her on the top of her head, lingering there to drink her fragrance as he breathed in her freshly-shampooed hair.

"You've been so patient with me, so loving, so understanding," she confessed as she clung to him. She felt her heart begin to race and wondered how much of its acceleration was due to gratitude or desire.

"Want to walk some more?" Brad petitioned, giving her a slight squeeze as he moved a halfstep away.

"Okay," Pamela agreed, stealing a quick kiss as they broke contact.

"How 'bout a closer look at the falls?" Brad suggested, pulling her in his direction, anticipating her immediate approval.

"That would be wonderful."

She filed in behind him as they began a skewed descent, characterized by frequent deviations and detours down rocky terrain.

As they made their way through the oaks and hemlocks and hickories, they came upon a beautiful cluster of gnarled rhododendrons, studded with white petals, cradled amidst jagged rock pinnacles. As they navigated the next assembly of moss-covered rocks, both fatigue and admiration halted their progress momentarily.

"Aren't they beautiful?" Pamela admired as she hesitated, catching her breath.

Brad used the opportunity to re-tie one of his shoelaces.

Less than twenty feet ahead of them rested more magnificent rhododendrons, some twenty feet in height, more resplendent than any they had seen. Wild grasses were escorted by water lettuce that clung to the peat-covered rocks nearby. Purple-fringed orchids and a tangle of moss-laden logs, neighbored by emerging hay-scented ferns and bursts of wildflowers—fringed phacelia, hepatica, phlox and white trilliums—formed multiple layers of lush forest ground cover.

"I've got to capture this digitally," Pamela announced.

The idyllic scene forced Pamela's phone into her hand. Her attempt to capture the rugged landscape with its colorful accents was complemented by the arrival of a pair of cardinals as they added their red plumage and orange bills to the variegated greenness of the gorge.

"They mate for life, you know," Brad spoke softly, waiting to speak until after she took the picture.

Pamela glanced at him, raising and then lowering her eyebrows quickly.

"Yes, I know. And the male has the brighter color of the two. The female's color is muted, sort of an orangish-brown."

"Why do you suppose that is?"

"I suppose it's nature's way of protecting the female, camouflaging her from harm so she can raise the young," Pamela said confidently.

"Interesting how it's the other way around in the human world," Brad interjected, volunteering an observation, but sounding a bit playful.

"Oh, you don't say!" Pamela countered, seeing where this was going, but not wanting to be reeled in so easily.

"Correct me if I'm wrong, but generally speaking, isn't it women who paint their faces with tons of make-up every year, douse themselves with buckets of expensive perfume, and jewelry, and dress in the most flamboyant and exotic clothing, strutting their stuff, all for the pleasure and enjoyment of men?"

Pamela started to speak but Brad waved her off.

"And after parading around, scantily clothed, and quite seductive, I might add, in the presence of men who become attracted to their sensuous arrangement of clothing, perfume, and flesh, these same women demand to be protected from the advances they set in motion in the first place."

"And your point is?"

" My point?"

Pamela stood there, allowing a whimsical smile to curve her lips. Holding her phone, she placed her free hand on her hip and decided to wait him out.

"Women could stay out of a lot of trouble if they would dress more like a female cardinal."

"You mean dress in more understated colors and wear orange lipstick?" Pamela teased.

"Not exactly. I mean 'yes' to understated, less flashy clothes, and 'no' to orange lipstick. I didn't mean that women should look like cardinals."

"That's a relief," Pamela exclaimed, sighing playfully. But she wasn't going to let him off that easily. "What, pray tell, should women look like?"

The look on his face told her that he knew he wasn't going to be able to climb out of the hole he had unwittingly put himself in.

"You mean women should take responsibility for how men feel about women?" she asserted, giving him a playful scowl.

"Oh, oh, I see. I'm sinking deeper into the hole I manufactured for myself," he admitted, smiling broadly.

Hoping to make amends, he threw her a quote he believed was from General Robert E. Lee: "I think General Lee once said that when you find yourself in a hole, stop digging."

Pamela laughed. "I don't think that came from the General, but unless I have your immediate and unconditional surrender, I shall move on your works," she gave him a confident wink. "That's a paraphrase from Lee's chief adversary during the Civil War, General Ulysses S. Grant."

"You not only have my surrender, but you also have my deep admiration and respect."

"But do I have your apology?"

"Most assuredly," came his quick reply. "I beg for mercy ... and plenty of justice—Pamela Justice, that is."

Pamela's smile curtsied into laughter. Her despondency had lifted, bringing a new radiance to her whole complexion. Brad's innocent awkwardness had always lifted her spirits, and this time was no exception. Out of appreciation, she decided to let him escape her superior banter.

"As a man, as a very special man, I want you to see me as attractive," she started, peering directly at him, her emerald eyes glowing with the rich greenness of the forest. "And I do care what you think of me, just as I hope it matters what I think of you."

By the time she finished her testimonial, her lips were inches from Brad's face.

"I care. And I want you to see me as attractive, too. I didn't mean ... "

Her lips covered his mouth, cutting off his sentence. When their lips separated, their eyes engaged.

"I love you," Pamela spoke softly.

"I love you, too. Suppose we continue our descent into the gorge. There's still plenty of day left for other things," he winked.

"Oh, I see," she replied, realizing what he meant. A smile slipped onto her face, covering her seriousness.

It was a steep downhill climb from the jagged cliff to the gorge below—an obvious statement where water is concerned, yet nevertheless an important point, for the two hikers knew the consequences of one false step. It was almost as if the gorge had compelled them on some symbolic subconscious level to sink to its granite belly, to experience its depth which would then necessitate a climb back up toward the light.

Geoffrey's death had plunged Pamela into an abyss of grief. A part of her sensed the metaphor. She was taking steps to extricate herself from its harsh subterranean depression by conquering a natural depression in the cliffs off Linville Gorge.

While the fissures, twisted spires, and serrated overhangs of miles of quartzite cliffs stood as powerful testimonies to the geologic experience of these mountains, Pamela's journey through the twisted hours of guilt and serrated days of anger and depression took her to the edge of deep remorse, and cut her off, slicing at her, rendering her helpless for a time.

She was becoming more aware of the psychic connection between healing woman and nurturing mountain. Her attention was focused on the steep, forested slope covered with sweet birch, sugar maples and chestnut oaks, bordered and infiltrated by Fraser magnolias, hemlocks and pine.

§   §   §   §   §   §

"Has Pamela Justice checked in yet?"

The hotel desk clerk scanned the register and then looked up at her.

"She's not listed."

"That's strange. She's not even listed for late arrival?"

"Nope. I'm sorry."

"Do you have a reservation for Brad Aikman?"

"Yes. As a matter of fact, we do."

"Has he checked in yet?"

"I'm sorry. I'm afraid I'm not at liberty to give out that information," the hotel clerk replied, using his most officious tone. "You're the second person who's asked about them tonight."

"Oh?"

"Some fella wearing expensive cowboy boots asked about them several hours ago. I distinctly remember the boots. They had brass tips."

"Did he say who he was?"

"Nope. He didn't stick around. Haven't seen him since."

"That's strange. I don't know who that could be. What did he look like?"

The clerk frowned. "I really didn't get a good look at him."

The look of disappointment that registered on Karen's face prompted him to attempt more of a description.

"He was tall, dark-haired. Well-built. Had a rain coat on." He nodded toward the front doors. "The weather, you know. They're calling for thunderstorms tonight."

Karen mimicked his nod.

"Oh, well then, may I leave a message for them?"

"Who?"

Karen's frown was followed quickly by a smirk.

The clerk nodded politely enough, but she could sense his irritation.

"What message would you like to leave?" He reached for a small pad of stationery and readied himself for her dictation.

"Before I leave a message," she began, "I'd like to have a room myself. Are there any rooms available?"

He instituted a perfunctory glance at the reservations screen and nodded nonchalantly, confirming that the hotel still had open rooms.

"I have my pet with me. Do you have any rooms available for vacationers with pets?"

"You should have called first," he reprimanded. "The State of North Carolina passed a law forbidding pets in hotels."

He followed his announcement with a doleful expression that cascaded quickly into sympathy when the pout on her lips registered her disappointment. Something told him to take a risk, to help her out.

"There are thunderstorms on the way. I'd feel guilty sending you back out into threatening skies. These mountain roads are treacherous when they get wet. Where ya from?"

"Asheville."

"That far, huh?" he joked, thinking: *help me out here. I'm trying to feel sorry enough for you to cut you some slack. You could have told me you were from Washington, DC or Los Angeles—anywhere but Asheville.*

He decided to discount geography as a disqualifying factor.

"What kind of dog do you have?" he raised his voice, trying his best not to leak a smile.

"Does it matter?" she asked, her surprise moving more toward agitation.

"Definitely."

"He's a German Shepherd. Why?"

"Oh, a big dog."

She shook her head up and down, indicating the obvious. "Yes, shepherds are usually pretty good-sized dogs."

A cherubic smile flashed across his face. "Oh, then he can definitely stay."

Karen shot him a confused look. Her face was a commercial of relief and surprise.

The clerk's eyes darted hurriedly around the room, and then back to Karen.

"I'm going to give you a room in the old section, room one twelve. I'm not supposed to do this, but you look so sweet and the weather is taking a turn for the worse." He leaned toward her. "Not a word about this to anyone, you hear, or it'll be my job."

Karen nodded quickly and smiled jubilantly, determined to conspire with him. She remembered another undercover canine operation earlier in the year when she had sneaked Hans into the hospital to see Pamela. She winked at the clerk.

"Thanks. You're terrific."

"Do you know in all my years in the hotel business, no German Shepherd has ever skipped out at night without paying the bill. No ma'am! And what's more, none has ever staggered back to its hotel room in the middle of the night all drunked up. They've never stolen a towel," he reported, obviously pleased with himself and enjoying the incredulous expression on her face, "and they've never taken a bedspread or picture. With the exception of an occasional howl, they've been perfect house guests." He paused again, but she could tell he wasn't finished. "And so, yes, he can stay. And if he'll vouch for you," he smiled broadly, "you can stay, too."

Both guest and clerk erupted in laughter.

"What's his name?"

"Hans."

"And you are ... " he intentionally abbreviated himself.

"My name is Karen Justice. I'm Pamela's sister. I thought I'd surprise her with a visit."

He smiled, showing a dentured set of teeth, and then pushed the registry toward her.

"I'm pleased to meet you, Karen Justice. Remember, not a word, not even a whisper. Not even a howl from your roommate," he grinned. "What method of payment will you be using?"

"Plastic."

"Oh, and what message would you like to leave the Aikman party?"

"Just say, Surprise—Karen is here in room one-twelve—with a guest." Then Karen added quickly, "thank you so much! You're terrific!"

"By the way," he leaned over and whispered to her. "They haven't checked in yet. They've guaranteed a late registration."

"Thanks."

He nodded his collusion.

"Where's the nearest fast food restaurant? I don't want my dog to eat alone." She smiled innocently, as a blush of embarrassment eased on her face.

"Back the way you came, about a mile down. There's a couple of them here. You can't miss 'em." He handed Karen the room keys. "The second key is for the convenience bar."

Karen shook her head and handed the bar key back to him.

"No thanks. I'd like to keep my room charges to a minimum." Then she threw him a quick wink. "Besides, Hans loves caramel candy bars. If he knows I've got the key, he'll want some."

His chuckle mirrored her grin as she walked toward the lobby entrance. A wall of light flashed in front of her.

"Heat lightning," trailed the desk clerk. "It's supposed to shower tonight. I think they said showers, accompanied by thunderstorms. Hope you brought your umbrella!"

Karen waved her good-bye, then disappeared out of the double set of doors which framed the front of the lobby.

§　§　§　§　§　§

Finding shelter from the driving tempest inside the lobby, Pamela stood, catching her breath and dripping small puddles of rain she brought in with her on the marble foyer.

The lobby's brightness contrasted sharply with the darkness outside, spilling golden light on Pamela's wet clothing. She smiled enigmatically at the hotel clerk, who lowered his gaze the instant their eyes met to continue his perusal of the evening paper, which had come to him in incremental sections from the hotel restaurant.

A flash of heat lightning followed Brad through the double glass doors and illuminated the awning above the outside doorway momentarily.

Pamela could do no more than smile appreciatively as she witnessed his sprint indoors.

Both Brad and the luggage were covered with speckles of sparkling droplets of water, remnants of the downpour which caught up to him in the parking lot.

A heavy sigh escaped his lips.

"It must have seen me coming," he smiled, stamping his feet to force the rain off his sweat pants and sneakers.

Pamela cupped his face in her hands and kissed him lightly on the lips.

"Thanks for letting me come on in."

"No sense in both of us getting drenched."

Pamela's gaze moved past Brad to the small gift shop nestled in one corner of the lobby adjacent to the restaurant and pool.

"Honey, why don't you check us in?" she suggested, then nodded toward the gift shop, "and I'll take a quick look in there."

Brad smiled, yielding immediately to the inevitability of Pamela's penchant for spending money on vacations, no matter how short the trip or how small the shop.

Pamela started toward the shop, leaving a trail of small droplets strung out behind her like liquid beads.

There was one important thing she had learned about herself throughout her own rehabilitation and now in the aftermath of Geoffrey's death. It was a coping strategy she intended to keep. Her depression took her to the malls and stores where her buying speeded up.

CHAPTER TWENTY-SIX

She drew on a lipstick mouth. Her rich emerald green eyes blinked under mascaraed lashes that accented the perfect curve of her lids. Her hair, blue-black and shimmering in the light, was mid-back length again, silky and light to touch. Her large square black onyx earrings matched the broach she wore on the new skirted suit she'd bought at one of the specialty shops during the weekend they spent in the mountains three weeks before. Pamela paused a moment in her make-up application to reflect on that weekend.

Karen had surprised her by showing up with Hans, and they had all relaxed and enjoyed the time together. Despite Karen having told them that a man who wore brass-toed boots had asked about her, their trip was incident-free. News of his presence worried her nonetheless.

She forced herself to censor her thoughts about the man who broke into her house, realizing she had a speech to deliver. Her thoughts returned instead to the weekend with Brad and Karen. Brad had commented that it was the first time he'd seen her so happy in a long time. He'd said that she and Karen giggled like schoolgirls while they tried on a variety of exotic and unusual clothing in the specialty shops.

In fact, that's where I ended up purchasing this very outfit, Pamela reminded herself as she gazed at her reflection in the mirror.

Karen was the one who discovered it, hiding among the other rather outlandish choices. The chic, collarless suit coat fit as though it were made for her, tastefully showing off her size six figure, wrapping her in her favorite color—purple. It was accented with a jet black V-neck trim that provided the verticality needed to suggest the right amount of symmetry and height.

Her slim legs, sheathed in stylish nylons, rested on feet encased in expensive low-heeled dress shoes, a shade slightly darker in color than her suit coat. Her long fingernails were Frenched and square at the tips, and her ring finger was adorned with a moderately-priced ring.

Pamela glanced at the tube of lip gloss, which was on the brink of obsolescence. Time for a replacement, she thought, and tossed it into the clear plastic bag that lined the small trash can under the bathroom counter.

Her public image complete, she dumped her room key into her handbag and started out of the door, pausing momentarily to deposit the DO NOT DISTURB sign on the outside door knob.

It was July eighth and she was staying at the Peachtree Hotel in Atlanta, preparing to give a speech at the National Association of Women Business Owners Convention. One of their national board members, a long-time client of Pamela's, heard about Pamela's accident and recovery, and thought she would be the perfect keynote speaker for their annual conference. Pamela accepted the invitation more out of her resolve to help other women see they could beat the odds than out of a motive characterized by hip pocket interest.

Her flight to Atlanta the night before had been full—overbooked, in fact, forcing some travelers to reward the ineptitude of the airlines by settling for food vouchers and pay-offs. She had arrived at the gate early enough to save her confirmed seat and was prepared to fight for it if she had to, particularly since she detested the airline's practice of overbooking flights. She had had confirmed seats bumped before and wasn't about to let the airlines abuse her again.

Part of the problem this trip was the increased traffic because of the largest 'Spiritual, Not Religious' conference in Atlanta's history. Hoards of New Thought people had descended on a metropolis, already overcrowded and ill-equipped to handle the enormous press of millions of tourists. Yet what city would refuse the honor of hosting hundreds of thousands of New Thought truth seekers, and the practicality of separating the spend-thrifty conglomeration of people from their hard-earned money?

She felt more like herself now. Her energy had returned and stayed. Her weight had stabilized, staying at one hundred thirteen pounds, and her stamina and strength were back, due largely from the disciplined workout schedule which she'd fully re-instituted in June.

As she moved past one of the hotel maids on her way to the elevator she was greeted cordially.

"My, oh my, girl. You look good!"

"Thank you," Pamela replied politely, surprised at the enthusiastic tone of the greeting.

"Purple must be your favorite color."

A pleasant smile jumped onto Pamela's face and she nodded indicating the maid's perception was correct.

"Have a nice day."

"Thanks, you too." Pamela broke eye contact when she heard the elevator bell sound. Someone was already a passenger and had pressed a floor button. Pamela punched the second floor button, where the meeting rooms and convention ballroom were located. She wanted to check out the microphones and room set-up before she presented at nine-fifteen. Since it was only seven-ten, she would have plenty of time to eat a leisurely breakfast and freshen up again before she spoke.

The woman beside her was pregnant with perfume, an odor of which spilled into the confines of the elevator so heavily that it made breathing difficult.

She must have fallen into the bottle of perfume, Pamela mused silently as she took several steps away from the woman, who seemed oblivious to her exaggerated stench.

Pamela pleaded silently with the elevator to close its doors, and then was relieved when it started its descent. Her eyes darted toward the lighted panel board as the doors opened to admit new passengers — and noticed the only floor selection was for the second floor, hers, and evidently the perfume factory's choice of floors, too.

That's it. I'm out of here, she encouraged herself, as she moved past the boarding couple. *I'll smell like a perfume warehouse myself if I don't get out of here.*

Out of the corner of her eye, Pamela caught both boarders' facial expressions in response to their recognition of the prolific odor emanating from the hydraulic box. She watched their smelly incarceration as the elevator doors closed, sending the metal cage obediently to its next recessed perch.

She visualized their chagrin as they struggled for clean air between floors.

I'm glad I bailed out when I did, she thought to herself. *The poor dears must be holding their breaths by now.* Waving her hand back and forth in front of her, Pamela made a superfluous attempt to fumigate her hair and clothing. Then she stepped back toward another one of the elevators. She made sure it was from a different port, then pushed the down button, waiting impatiently for a new carriage.

When the doors to the second elevator opened, she breathed a sigh of relief and entered, satisfied that her slight detour was worthwhile. The trip down two floors was uneventful and less toxic. She arrived on the second floor wearing a triumphant grin and her own perfume. Just before the elevator doors opened again, she raised her wrist to her nose and sniffed, verifying her decontamination.

Good, she smiled, *I'm still me.*

Pleased that her own preferred scent had survived, she moved gracefully out of the metal enclosure and proceeded toward Ballrooms A and B.

Her eyes caught the back of a tall man, dressed in a short-sleeved knit shirt and wearing a light blue University of North Carolina ball cap. Her heart skipped a couple of beats as surprise halted her progress. She had the greatest urge to run up to him. Finally, it occurred to her after a few anxious moments that those fragments of him—the tilt of a blue cap, the side of a face, the back of a leg, the ease of his stride, the fine blonde hair, the massive shoulders—all belonged to a man who, seen whole, was not Geoffrey.

She breathed in a nostalgic sigh, swallowed hard, and shook her head. *I've done it to myself again,* she scolded herself. Her rationality took over, having recovered from its temporary slippage, and she gave herself a few moments to regain her composure. *I've got to stop this. Geoffrey's dead. He's not coming back.*

Several people brushed past her in the hallway, setting her unconsciously in motion again. When she got to the ballrooms, she ran into a flurry of activity, which refocused her attention on her present surroundings. The banquet set-up crews were throwing the room together, ten chairs to each round dining table, each an island dressed in white cloth and accented with a floral centerpiece. Working alongside the hotel crew were several people who, upon closer examination, were completing each place setting by distributing the handouts Pamela had mailed to the meeting planner earlier in the week.

Good! They got here, she said to herself.

The meticulous part of her worried about things like that and was never quite satisfied until all her materials arrived. She always carried a camera-ready set, just in case something unforeseen happened. That way she would be ready for any contingency. Nevertheless, she was always relieved when her training materials arrived.

A huge twenty or thirty-foot banner was draped across the front of the room, advertising in large black letters the name of the organization: NAWBO. Beneath it was a raised platform burdened with a podium, surrounded on each side with oblong tables covered with lavender cloths and sprinkled intermittently with pitchers of water. The tables were connected with cloth streamers and each was decorated with a small vase of flowers like those placed on the hundred or so tables that dotted the ballroom.

Her attention was diverted by a young woman who had made her way onto the riser and over to the podium.

"Testing. Testing," came a meek, almost apologetic voice over the sound system. "One, two, three. Testing. Testing."

The woman fumbled with an on-off switch on the microphone stem and was finally able to silence it. She seemed pleased with her ten-second debut, although Pamela could tell she was nervous around a microphone.

Satisfied that the room was in operating order, Pamela ducked back out and headed toward the restaurant. It was seven-fifty by her watch.

Plenty of time for breakfast, she rejoiced. *Many speakers are too apprehensive to eat before an engagement, not wanting to take a chance at soiling their clothing with food stains before they speak. I've never had those reservations. Breakfast is my favorite meal.*

Remembering her experience in the confined elevator earlier, she decided to use the steps to go one floor down to the restaurant. She did not want to risk another toxic rendezvous with the woman who dowsed herself with liquid rose petals.

She walked hurriedly past the elevators and heard one of them groan its way past the second floor. An older couple had gotten there a little late and pushed the elevator button, hoping to catch the rising box, but settled for facing the doors, readying themselves for the next pass.

By the time Pamela got to the hotel restaurant, the morning crowd had descended and made seating difficult, but the hostess managed to find her a seat. The eating areas were well-foliaged, featuring hanging ferns, wandering Jews, holly and spider plants, all live and hanging in huge baskets. Magnificent arrangements of peace lilies, ficus and dwarfed trees of mixed varieties tastefully separated the tables, providing guests with both the privacy they needed as well as beautiful surroundings.

While she was eating her breakfast, she overheard the conversation at the table next to hers. Table talk conversations, strongholds of frivolous chatter, always amused her. And this one did not disappoint her. Both men were dressed in business suits, sipping coffee and putting on airs, each trying his best to impress the other. One of the men, bald and overweight, was doing most of the talking. He was clutching a folded newspaper and had evidently found something of interest, because he was half reading, half paraphrasing parts of the article, taking great delight in his oration. His voice was nasal and his manner jubilant as he launched his commentary.

Pamela could hear him clearly over the din of the restaurant. All the tables were occupied, and guests were busily engaged in their own idiosyncratic exchanges. Water glasses, coffee cups and juice glasses were being refilled promptly. Tables that were vacated by guests rushing off to meetings or workshops were cleared without delay and as quickly reset with teal cloth napkins and silverware that signaled readiness for the next occupants, who rushed through their breakfast as quickly as their convention-going predecessors.

The mention of Barack Obama's name brought her attention back to the two men who sat at the table adjacent to hers. The younger, more articulate of the two men referred to an article he'd read a few months ago about the President. Obama had lost his Democratic majority and there was talk of his being a one-term President. The two men laughed at that, and Pamela found a frown had jumped on her face.

Do they think they could do a better job? she mused to herself.

She lost interest in their conversation and busied herself doing a proper job on the two-egg omelet in front of her.

Both companions at the adjoining table howled again and accepted another warmer, as the waitress expertly refilled their half-empty coffee cups.

She grinned as she finished her breakfast. Her thoughts moved thirty-five minutes ahead as she wondered what type of reception she would receive as the opening keynote speaker for the National Association of Women Business Owners. There would be applause at her introduction, of course, but would there be applause at the end of her speech?

She signed the breakfast tab the waitress left on the table, wrote in her room number and then left the restaurant to freshen up before her speech. By the time she re-entered the ballroom, there were several hundred people there. Since her spot was clearly marked with a nametag, Pamela was able to find her designated seat at the head table.

The small talk at the head table was as boring as ever, accompanied by polite, but lukewarm eye contact, indifferent handshakes and politically correct, almost patronizing conversations.

Finally the woman who was to introduce Pamela lifted herself to the podium, having herself just been introduced by the conference chair. Pamela almost choked on the water she was using to moisten her throat before she spoke. The woman introducing her was the perfume factory she'd encountered on the elevator.

Terrific, she thought, *I'll spend the first half of my speech trying to breathe.*

The heavily scented lady read the prepared introduction just as Pamela had written it and then announced the speaker's name enthusiastically and with some pizzazz.

"And now women business owners, it is my privilege and considerable pleasure to introduce the speaker for our opening general session, Dr. Pamela Ann Justine."

She mispronounced my name. That airhead mispronounced my name!

Pamela groaned inwardly and smiled outwardly as she rose to take the podium. *First she fouls the air, then she screws up my name.*

The ballroom erupted with applause as Pamela took the podium.

She paused briefly and timed her remarks just after the applause settled.

"Women who attempt to run a business without a clear sense of vision, are practicing the concept of managing by stumbling around."

Pamela could tell by the audience's reaction that she had chosen the right opening line.

She continued her rehearsed opening statements. "One of the chief failures of any organization, large or small, woman-operated or male dominated is ... "

§   §   §   §   §   §

Long familiar with the logistics of carving, Constance ladled out the stuffing and dealt the slices of white and dark meat onto the platter.

George had called, using Pamela's phone, announcing that they were on their way home from the airport, and would arrive in less than fifteen minutes. He had already turned onto the Beltline and that meant they were only minutes away.

"Karen, would you give the gravy another stir and watch it for me? I've got to put the biscuits in the oven and then find the bun warmer."

"Sure. Was that Grampa?"

"Yes, they'll be here in fifteen minutes."

"Brad," Constance looked over at him. "Would you put the turkey on the table and fill the glasses with ice?"

Brad nodded and moved quickly past her toward the platter of sliced meat, rescuing it from the countertop. He weaved his way past Constance, who had just bent over to place the biscuits in the oven.

"This is Pamela's week for speeches, isn't it?" Karen announced, giving the thickening gravy another stir.

"When it rains it pours," came Brad's voice from the dining room.

"It's nice to see her at work again, and doing so well," Constance echoed, feeling both proud and relieved that her granddaughter was busy and productive.

"All we've got to do now is to get her fed and back to Research Triangle Park on time," Karen voiced the obvious. "It's a shame she has to go back out tonight."

"She wanted cooked food. Besides, she's got three hours before she speaks again. Don't worry. I'll get her there," Brad assured, gesturing as if he were driving a pretend vehicle by holding an imaginary steering wheel and pushing his foot on an invisible accelerator.

Both Karen and Constance smiled at his juvenile, but endearing antics.

"You won't have imaginary traffic from here to the Triangle, so you'll drive carefully, won't you?" Constance instructed, her gaiety adopting a slightly more serious tone.

"Gramma, you know Brad's a safe driver."

Brad winked at Karen and then drove over to Constance, applying his imaginary brakes when he got along side of her. His manner was jovial, but respectful as he leaned over and kissed Constance on the forehead. And then, not quite ready to put his playfulness aside, he added, "I promise to obey most of the traffic laws."

Constance raised an eyebrow and gave him a maternal stare, throwing both Karen and him into uproarious laughter.

The sound of a car pulling up in the driveway produced an uneasy question from Karen's lips.

"Should we tell her about the break-ins and the message on her mirror?"

Brad looked at Karen and then steeled his gaze on Constance, who seemed to be grappling with the question. He could tell she was deeply concerned underneath her polite response.

"No, honey, let's wait until after her speech this evening." Then after a momentary hesitation, she continued, as if to justify her unilateral decision. "She won't have time to go home first anyway. And there's no sense in upsetting her before she gives her speech."

Brad nodded his agreement and moved toward the front door.

"Constance is right," he agreed in the polite but authoritative voice he sometimes adopted. "Besides, it doesn't look like anything was taken, and George and I have already repaired the broken window and picked her car up from the shop. And the police have increased their surveillance around her place."

All three of their faces mirrored the same look of concern as they thought about Pamela's predicament. Each of them felt unsettled about the message scrawled in red lipstick, across Pamela's bedroom mirror. The note, all caps and in block-style printing had read: FORGET THE PAST AND YOU'LL HAVE A FUTURE.

The police were thorough in their investigation and wanted to ask Pamela some questions as soon as she arrived. Wanting to spare her the stress of an unpleasant visit with the police immediately before her keynote, George scheduled her for a visit to the precinct the next day.

Hans was the first to greet George and Pamela as they navigated the front steps. He was cradling a tennis ball in his mouth—the same tennis ball that George had tossed at him as a diversion to keep him in the yard when George left to pick

Pamela up at the airport. Now Hans was creating a diversion himself, blocking the entrance to the front door until one of them, preferably Pamela, accepted his invitation to play another quick game of fetch with the tennis ball.

"Okay, old boy," Pamela acquiesced, reaching down to pull the tennis ball out of his muzzle.

Hans obediently accommodated her gentle pull and released the wet game piece willingly, darting off the front porch, barking his delight.

She launched the saliva-coated sphere with an overhand toss that sent Hans scampering across the lawn, growling in anticipation as he followed the arc of the ball.

By the time he had skillfully retrieved it, pouncing on it ruthlessly, he heard the front door open and wheeled around in time to see his playmate and her grandfather disappear through the front door.

§　　§　　§　　§　　§　　§

"What? Forget the past and I'll have a future!" Pamela raised her voice in alarm. "That's the kind of thing you see in the movies. My God, Brad, he broke into my house ... and slit my tires."

Brad narrowed his eyes. "He? You sound like you know who broke into your house."

Pamela threw him a confused look.

"Yes, I think so. No. I'm not sure. It could be him ... or the creep that broke in before."

Brad narrowed his eyes again. "By 'him,' I'm guessing you mean Clarence?"

Pamela nodded as she repositioned herself in the car seat.

"It's either him or the low-life who threatened me before."

Brad gave her a worried look and then refocused his attention on the traffic, which seemed heavy for nine-forty-five at night.

"I figured as much—that's why I gave the police Clarence's name and told them about the incident at Emerald Isle. But if it's the guy with the brass-toed boots ... I think we could be in serious trouble."

"What do you mean?"

"We don't know what he looks like. He could be anywhere. He could get too close to you too fast. Babe, I don't like where this is going. We've got to get you some protection. You didn't have any trouble in Atlanta, did you?"

"No, not at all."

"Good. That means he doesn't know every move you make. But he sure knew you weren't home ... even though your car was in the driveway."

"What am I going to do?"

Brad shot her a sympathetic look.

"If it is Clarence, he's got hell to pay. He was there for one reason and one reason only. To show you he could get to you. He's still playing with you."

Pamela closed her eyes and reached out to take Brad's hand.

"Your office was a mess, files all over the place."

"Terrific!"

"Evidently he wanted to make it look like a burglary."

Pamela's incredulous look was all the answer he needed. She opened her mouth to speak, but only a sigh came out.

"Karen did the best she could matching contents with file folders," he continued. "All of your file cabinets were ransacked, including your desk drawers. It looks like he just wanted to wreck the place."

"It's like he took his anger out on my house because I wasn't there," Pamela guessed.

Brad raised his eyebrows.

"Could be," he agreed. "I never thought about that. But it's the message that concerns me. Whichever one of them it is, he's threatening your life."

"If it's Clarence, he's threatened both of our lives," Pamela reminded him, as she squeezed his hand.

He nodded and reciprocated her tight squeeze.

"I think it's Clarence," Brad said as he turned the air-conditioner up a notch.

Pamela steadied her gaze on him and waited for him to continue.

"Your house was a mess, Babe," he repeated. "It was as if somebody was in a rage. That sounds more like Clarence than the other guy."

Pamela shook her head, sighing heavily.

"By the way, your speech was wonderful," Brad spoke cheerfully, trying his best to fill the awkward silence by changing the subject.

"I just don't see how he expects to get away with it," Pamela exclaimed, bringing them back to the previous subject.

"Well, he's not going to get away with it. He's going to make a mistake. And that's when we're going to nail him."

Brad found himself offering lame reassurances.

"The local police have stepped up their watch in your neighborhood, and George stayed there last night, just to have someone there while you were in Atlanta.

"Gramps was taking a chance, wasn't he?"

"Well, yes, but not re..al..ly," Brad stumbled through the syllables. "Raleigh's finest did an excellent job with the increased surveillance. George saw them drive by a half dozen or so times before he drifted off to sleep." Brad reached over and gave her a light tap on the leg. "By the way, we ... well, you have an appointment with Raleigh's finest tomorrow at two o'clock. I'm going with you."

Pamela frowned her understanding. Then her face tightened. "Maybe I could borrow Hans for a couple of weeks. He never liked Clarence anyway."

Brad threw her a quick look and smiled broadly.

"His presence would certainly alarm an intruder, all right, particularly when he gives chase with that yellow tennis ball in his mouth."

Pamela laughed heartily. "Don't make fun of Hans. He's a good watchdog." She punched Brad lightly on the shoulder and then followed it up with another, more serious tap. "He's my protector. Remember? I told you. He wouldn't let anyone near me on the bridge after the accident. He ... "

She caught herself, a sudden rush of clarity hitting her.

"Brad, do you remember when we were at Linville Falls and Karen brought Hans to see us? Karen told us someone else had asked about us that night." She knew she was sounding rhetorical, but it was the only way she knew how to prerequisite what she was going to say next.

Brad nodded his head, indicating he was with her.

"I remember."

"Well, suppose this intruder wasn't Clarence? Suppose it was the brass-toed jerk!"

Brad scanned her face. The general content of her soon-to-be announced realization was about to jump from her lips.

"The composite!" she shouted, believing she had figured it out. "I never got the composite Geoffrey sent me!"

Brad kept his eyes on the road, realizing that the traffic, framed tightly in his windshield, was sending red brake lights in their direction.

"That has to be it! It's the only thing that makes sense." Pamela bounced in her seat, the adrenaline pumping as she moved quickly to her next thought. "And I believe the vandalism of my mail box was no accident. I bet it's linked to the break-ins. Suppose the vandals didn't find the composite in the mail box? That probably means Geoffrey didn't send it. And if he didn't, it's in Geoffrey's belongings that Ted packed in boxes and stored in his attic."

She trained her eyes on Brad, thinking only of her hypothesis and not realizing that the traffic had stopped.

Brad looked her directly in the eyes as he squeezed her hand. Pamela's expectant gaze told him she was waiting for him to reply.

"You may have something there," he stated charitably. "It does seem more than mere coincidence, doesn't it?"

"And it would explain the lipstick message on the mirror. The accident is in my past. I think the police should know this," she stated eagerly. "It might help them put two and two together."

"I agree, but ..."

Pamela resumed speaking. "Tomorrow, I'll call the Asheville Police Department and see if I can speak with the composite specialist who helped Geoffrey. He may have another copy he could send me. Let's see, I don't know if Geoffrey mentioned the artist's name on the phone or in a letter. I can't remember his name off hand." Then she added as an afterthought, "I know, I'll call Ted and ask him to look for the composite."

She switched her thinking again, this time cutting into something Brad wanted to say. "What was that artist's name?" She appeared to quiz herself more than direct her inquiry at Brad, who had just turned down the volume on the CD so the music wouldn't compete with Pamela. "What was it? Harridan? No, Harris! Officer Galen Harris, I think. Yes, that's it. His name is Galen Harris. Geoffrey told me who he was working with during a phone conversation. I think it was the same day you bought this car and had dinner at my house. Remember? It was on a Saturday."

"It'll be interesting to see what you find out, Babe," Brad interjected, offering her encouragement, although sounding a little too patronizing.

Pamela sat up in her seat and placed her elbow on the dash so that she could see his face.

He glanced at her and then looked forward again, concentrating on the traffic ahead, which seemed to be moving like stock cars, some drivers zigzagging, others speeding up then decelerating, waiting for the caution flag to lift as they jockeyed for position. He could see the strobing of blue lights near the Blue Ridge Road exit.

"Must have been an accident up ahead. See the blue lights?" he reported as he reached over and placed his hand on her cheek so that his fingers slipped between her silky hair and her soft skin. "It's not that I don't want you to find the guy who hit you. We've had this conversation before. It's just that I know what it does to you every time you think about it. I hate to see you so frustrated and upset." He sighed heavily. "We don't know at this point that it's not Clarence. He's part of your past, too. Remember?"

She cupped his hand in hers and pulled his hand over her mouth, kissing it and then lowering his hand so she could speak.

"I know, I haven't ruled him out, either. I'm sorry. I know you get upset when I get upset. But this time it's different. I'm not upset. I'm angry!" She paused, squeezing his hand for emphasis. "And feeling a little villainous myself."

The seriousness in Brad's eyes prompted her to elaborate.

"Don't look at me that way. I'm not going to do anything foolish," she promised, as she formed a tight smile. "But what if I'm right and there is a connection between the mailbox vandalism and the break-ins."

"I think it's a stretch," he tried to console her. "But if you're concerned about it, and your instincts are right, I think you should tell the police what you've come up with. I'm beginning to wonder about the connection myself."

Both Brad and Pamela were silent for a moment, realizing their differences were a matter of degree and not substance. Each focused on the traffic that snaked along the highway ahead of them. Interstate 40 was just like any other major highway, mile after mile of caution and utilitarianism, nothing but an asphalt ribbon of expedience, wrapping the Research Triangle Park and surrounding countryside in exhaust and litter.

Occasionally the congestion produced an accident that slowed traffic, and increased tension.

"Brad." Pamela spoke softly, almost in a whisper.

He tilted his head toward her but kept his eyes on the road with a sideways stare.

"I don't want to go home tonight. I don't want to spend the night alone."

"Okay." He spoke in a low voice. "Do you want me to take you to ... "

"I want to stay with you tonight," she interrupted, moving as close to him as the seat belt would allow. "I feel uneasy about the break-ins and I've had an exhausting three days on the road. I won't be able to get the rest I need at my place, worrying about my privacy and my safety."

"You won't hear any complaints from me! We'll drop by your place so you can get the things you need for tonight, then I'll take you to my place. You'll be safe there, I promise." He kissed her on the forehead. "You'll be able to relax there. And it's not too late for a luxurious bubble bath, if you'd like to soak the tension away."

Pamela smiled knowingly and rested her head on his shoulder .

"I think I know what you've got in mind, you conniving rascal."

"What? I've only mentioned extending you the hospitality of the Aikman Hotel tonight, with its spacious Jacuzzi and a suggestion of a hot, thoroughly relaxing bubble bath."

"Uh, huh." Pamela sounded playfully suspicious. "And what else is on the menu?" She sat up in her seat and punched him lightly on the arm and then the ribs.

"You suspicious thing, you," he bantered. "Are you suggesting that I have an ulterior motive?"

Pamela laughed good-naturedly, causing a chuckle to leave his lips.

"No, I'm not *suggesting* it," she teased as she started to tickle him under the arms, carrying her titillating touches across his abdomen and then moving down toward his thighs, which were covered by paper-thin dress slacks. "I *know* you have an ulterior motive."

"Now wait a minute, young lady," Brad protested, using his free hand to keep up with the mischievous movements of two faster and more determined hands. "I believe it was you ... who ... wanted to stay ... with me tonight." He had trouble holding a sentence together as he attempted to dodge Pamela's intimate pokes and prods.

"Oh, so you're blaming it on me, are you?" she teased, speeding up her solicitous play and flitting her long lashes with pretended innocence.

His counterfeit protests changed into a mild reprimand as he begged Pamela to stop her pleasurable assault. "Stop it, Babe. Stop it now. I'm driving."

She continued, taking delight in keeping him at a disadvantage.

"I mean it now!" he ordered, trying his best not to encourage her with his laughter.

She decided to give him a few more pokes just for good measure before she surrendered to his pleas.

"Okay, okay," he confessed, breathing heavily, enjoying every stimulating minute of her playful assault. "The thought of making love to you did cross my mind. After all, it has been a while."

"I know," pouted Pamela, "and I'm sorry."

"No, no. I didn't mean it that way. You haven't been able to since ... since Geoffrey's death. I understand that."

He caught her torturous expression.

"Really, Babe, I understand. I didn't mean for it to be a criticism. When a person goes through what you've just gone through, certain drives, certain needs give way to other needs. That's all I meant."

Her arms, automatically solicitous, hugged him. "Have I told you tonight how much I love you?"

He extended his embrace so that he was able to cup her head with the palm of his right hand.

"I love you, too."

She squeezed him tighter, in response to the affectionate pressure of his hand on the right side of her face.

Brad held her closely as he pulled the Mercedes into the familiar curve of her driveway.

"I'll only be a moment," Pamela assured him as she alighted from the vehicle. "I'm only going to bring what I need for tonight. I'm staying dressed in what I have on, so I won't be long. I'll change into something much more comfortable when we get to your place." She angled her lips with a smile that curved them provocatively.

"Wait. I'd feel better going in with you," Brad raised his voice, as he silenced the car and leaped out to join her.

Pamela smiled. "I'm sure I will be all right, but if it makes you feel better, come on in."

"Here, let me do that," Brad offered as he took the keys from Pamela and shoved them into the front door lock. As he skillfully swung the oak-paneled door open, he reached inside to turn the outside, as well as the inside lights on. Before he flipped the switch, his eye caught something move in the shadows. At first he thought it might be George, but he dismissed that thought quickly, remembering that the Lees were at Raleigh Memorial Auditorium attending *The Sound of Music,* and would not be home until around eleven.

He blocked Pamela's entrance by stepping in ahead of her and extended his hand to hold her away at arm's length.

Noting his alarm, Pamela wordlessly obeyed. She felt her own apprehension build, sending a rising sense of nausea to her full stomach.

Before Brad could clear the doorway and flood the room with light, he heard someone brush by a piece of furniture near him.

"Run, Babe, run!" He shouted as he started to close the door, forgetting all about trying to get inside.

Pamela bolted like a colt at the sound of his warning and streaked across the lawn toward the neighbor's house that she could see was still lit inside. She knew the hedge between the two properties was coming up quickly, but decided she would wedge herself between the nearest opening she could that looked even remotely passable.

She heard Brad let out a groan behind her as she chanced a panicked look over her shoulder, screaming at the top of her voice as she did.

Brad toppled down the front steps like a feed sack, landing hard on the liver-colored brick sidewalk.

Pamela penetrated the rugged interior of the hedge in full stride, finding little forgiveness in its tough freshly-pruned branches which scratched her legs and thighs, tattooing her with a patchwork of jagged cuts.

Two figures, dressed in dark clothing, stepped quickly past Brad's body and sprinted across her driveway, disappearing in the darkness beyond the dim glow of streetlights that lined the street.

Her neighbors, James and Kim Sanborn, a young couple from New York, had heard her blood-curdling screams and were already outside on their porch trying to determine the nature of the ruckus.

"Call the police," Pamela shouted. "This is Pamela, James. Someone broke into my house again."

Her fear detonated into tears as she spoke and her voice was laced with urgency.

"I think they've killed Brad!"

CHAPTER TWENTY-SEVEN

he investigation has taken much too long, Pamela thought.

An odd mixture of fact and conjecture had kept the detectives there until 2:00 a.m.

The thing that troubled her the most was that they had found evidence of an arson attempt. If she and Brad had not arrived when they did, her house would have gone up in flames.

The chief detective, a balding middle-aged man with rounded ears resembling dried apricots, was dressed in a suit characterized by mismatched plaids. Flesh had been added and had migrated to the middle of his body, collecting around his waist and stomach like a tubular mudslide. He had been obnoxiously thorough in his attempt to filter through the facts, but had redeemed himself by volunteering to follow up on Pamela's suspicion about Clarence and the connection between the previous break-ins and the mailbox vandalism. He promised to call Officer Harris of the Asheville Police Department to ask about the composite, and Pamela was relieved about that.

She had not mentioned to anyone her intention to call Ted, because she wanted to be the one to do that. Ted was outspoken in his fiery criticism of the department's lackluster investigation of the McDowell Street bridge accident. He was convinced that the inadequate investigation, plagued by delays, excuses, and missed opportunities led to Geoffrey's depression and ultimately to his suicide. He was in no mood to talk to colleagues he felt had betrayed him.

Pamela believed Ted's searing disillusionment with the department was getting the best of him. She worried about Ted, whose heart was flawed and in decline.

The sound of Brad's voice lifted her out of her melancholy.

"No, thanks, I'm fine. I'm not going to the hospital." He was standing in the living room holding his bandaged head that was wrapped in what looked like a white turban, giving him the appearance of an Eastern guru in Western Hemisphere casual dress. There were blood smears on his blue knit shirt and several more spotting his gray dress slacks across his right pants pocket and down his thigh.

"It's just a slight bump on my head. I'll be all right." Brad pressed, impatient with the over-enthusiastic care giving.

"Mr. Aikman," cautioned the paramedic, "you've got more than just a bump on your head. You have a mild concussion. And the blow re-opened that cut above your eye."

"What I've got is a mild case of anger," he raised his voice, looking at two of the police officers who unwittingly made eye contact with him. "You guys were supposed to be watching this place!"

Neither officer commented but both tightened their lips, looking down at the floor to avoid further eye contact.

Pamela edged closer to Brad and put her arm around him, feeling a need to hug him.

"You okay?"

He nodded, reciprocating her embrace by holding on to her affectionately.

The paramedic, his frustration toward Brad evident, directed his next comment toward Pamela, who seemed to respect his medical training more than the patient he had just treated.

"If he gets inordinately dizzy or nauseated or his headache continues, get him to his doctor."

Pamela gave him a fractured smile and answered with an affirmative nod.

"It would be best if he would see a doctor anyway," the paramedic continued, using Pamela as an intermediary. "But you probably already know how people in the medical profession are—they always make the worst patients for us." Then he added a wink, "Probably the only ones who are worse are paramedics."

"Thanks," Pamela whispered, prodding Brad with her elbow to help him show his appreciation.

"Thanks for the repair job," Brad obeyed, employing an economy of words.

The paramedic smiled wryly and drifted toward his medical equipment to finish packing it up so he could effect a speedy exit, leaving the police to continue their investigation.

"Well, folks, we've done about all we can do tonight," the chief detective spoke, clearing his throat as he approached them. "I don't think they'll be back tonight, but just the same, I've posted several officers outside. Ms. Justice, since the suspect may have been here before, I'd like you to be especially careful."

"We'll be staying at my place," Brad countered.

"Well, suit yourself," the detective responded, sounding a little gruff, and then directed his eyes toward Pamela. "I'll follow-up on the information you gave me. If you think of anything else, please call me. You have my card."

Pamela nodded and held up the business card.

"Mr. Aikman," he addressed Brad, "if you think of anything else, anything at all ... "

"I'll call you," Brad interrupted, finishing the detective's sentence and sounding a little agitated.

The detective averted his gaze from the two of them and addressed his colleagues. "Okay, fellas, let's wrap this up. These people need to get a good night's sleep."

He squeezed past them, making his way toward the front door, and disappeared into the early evening darkness without looking back.

In a few minutes they were alone again, the sound of the last police cruiser evaporating as it pulled away from the front of her house and turned the corner down the street.

The cool silence of the house wrapped itself around them as they stood there, like washed-out watercolor posters, next to each other.

§ § § § § §

She unwound her towel turban and gently shook out a beautiful tumble of jet-black protein, freshly washed and soon-to-be freed from tangles. Accented with glimmering blue-black specks of light, the strands shimmied past each other, producing a glow that radiated both elegance and sophistication.

The bubble bath was wonderful, she thought happily.

She had soaked in it for an hour, drawing more hot water occasionally to keep the temperature of the ceramic pond constant and hot. Normally, she wouldn't have bathed that long, but the events earlier that evening had kept her wired. The warmth of the Jacuzzi and the numbing effects of two glasses of white wine helped calm her nerves.

"Honey, are you okay?" she raised her voice as she stood in front of the mirror, blow-drying her hair.

When she didn't get an immediate response, she repeated her inquiry.

"Brad, honey. Are you all right?"

Silence greeted her again. When she started toward the door she heard his faint response that sounded a bit preoccupied and distant.

"Yes, I'll ... be there in a minute."

Despite his head injury, actually, because of it, Brad had elected to rest awhile. The extra-strength Tylenol mediated the effects of the pain only moderately and he could still feel the rush of blood every time his heart beat.

"You through with your bath?"

"Yes, and I'm standing here stark naked in front of the mirror, if anyone is interested," she teased, hoping to bring some sense of normalcy back into their lives.

He did not answer right away, but she saw his reflection in the mirror as he snuck up behind her. He was still bandaged and appeared tired.

Sensing she saw him, even though her back was toward him, he eased up behind her and threw his arms around her, one around her mid section, and the other expertly placed so that his hand cupped her left breast.

"Oh, Brad. I've wanted you to hold me like this all night," she whispered.

She quickly silenced the roar of the hair dryer, and laid it aside, as she leaned against him and placed her arms over his.

He could feel her warmth through his t-shirt and knit muscle pants that he wore in place of his pajama bottoms. He held her close, rediscovering how perfectly their bodies fit. What he couldn't capture in his embrace, he captured in the mirror: the sensuous curve of her parted lips; the mascara-less eyelids, although closed, sealed what he knew to be the most beautiful set of emerald eyes on the planet; and her gorgeous well-formed breasts that complemented her striking angular elegance.

His eyes were scratchy, salty from fatigue, but they did not fail to catch the smile that swept across her face as she raised her arms, wedging her hands around the back of his neck.

She felt his soft but hasty kisses on her neck and shoulders as he fed on her flesh, still pink from her bubble bath. The warmth of his breath on her exposed skin followed his kisses as his lips migrated across the back of her neck to one shoulder and then the other.

She moved restlessly against him, wanting more, but willing to sacrifice the pleasure of the moment to better her position. His hands divided their time between her heaving breasts and light strokes across her abdomen and thighs as he sought more of her. Desire engulfed them, obliterating their fears and easing his headache.

Finally, shared desire sent them into the bedroom where he forced their tightly woven bodies to a standing halt and ravaged her mouth passionately. He took his moist kisses to each of her fully stimulated breasts, lingering between each breast to plant a transitional kiss in her cleavage.

He could feel her long fingernails comb through his hair as he continued his erotic torture. He yielded willingly to her impassioned entreaty as he felt her firm grip on each side of his face. He allowed her to lift his ravenous lips back onto hers as they stood, locked in long, deferred desire.

He made another hungry pass at her parted lips and picked her up, carrying her to his king-sized waterbed. Their lips unwillingly broke contact as he leaned over and placed her gently on the rolling sheets.

Her hair fanned out like spangled threads of black silk across the mound of pillows. Pamela stretched her arms out longingly toward him. She wanted more of the faint scent of his aftershave, the crushing pressure of his lips. She pulled him to her, on her. Tonight, what was left of it, would be devoted to catching up on their pleasure.

§　　§　　§　　§　　§　　§

"I told you I didn't want any more screw-ups."

"We couldn't help it."

"What? You're supposed to be the best and you're telling me you couldn't help it?" He raised his voice, sending his spittle raining down on the mouthpiece. "What am I paying you for, you moron?"

"Her boyfriend was with her."

"Her boyfriend?" his accomplice hissed.

"We thought it was the old man at first, and before we could corner them inside, her boyfriend shouted for her to run."

"So?"

"So, we couldn't get to them fast enough. She was gone before we knew it, and he had started back out of the door."

"You imbecile!"

"I slugged him hard so he couldn't identify us and then we split."

"Is he ... ?"

"No, I don't think so. I didn't hit him that hard."

"Well, no matter. He's become as much a liability as she is."

"You mean you wanted us to take him out, too?"

There was a long pause on the other end of the line.

"Yes, I wanted you to take him out, of course," he replied huffily.

"What do you want us to do then?"

"Nothing!"

"Nothing?"

"You got a hearing problem? I said nothing. You've already done nothing too many times," he raved.

"We've delivered on everything you've asked. What are you talking about? What do you want from us?" he exploded, his vehemence sizzling through the phone.

"I've been very clear all along about what I want. And I'm tired of partial deliveries. I cannot risk any more of your screw-ups."

"Are you saying what I think you're saying?" he asked gruffly.

"I'm saying I'll handle it from now on, personally. Your slippage is causing me considerable grief."

"So you're terminating our services?"

"That's what it sounds like. Should I repeat it slower so it sinks in?"

"You still owe us the rest of our money."

"You'll get paid all that's coming to you. I never leave any debt unpaid."

"When do we get our money?"

"In two days."

"Two days!"

"I'm out of town. I'll be back in Raleigh on Friday," he clarified. His voice sounded harsh. "We'll settle up then."

"The usual place?"

"No. It won't be convenient there this time."

"Where then?" he asked, trying to hold his irritation in check.

"I'll call you when I get back to Raleigh. I'll let you know then."

"Don't be jerking us around," he announced in a voice laced with malice. "We like to keep things simple and uncomplicated. And we'd hate to complicate *your* life. You know what I mean?"

"Don't threaten me! I've been straight with you all along. I've used you before and I'll probably use you again. Maybe you're just having one of your unproductive periods, you know, like a batter's slump. Maybe time off will do you some good."

"We don't need ... "

"Let me finish, asshole," he sheared off his retort. "I think you need a rest because I believe you just threatened me. And nobody ... nobody in their right mind ... threatens me. Threats are very complicated things, with simple solutions, and threatening me is a mistake ... a BIG mistake."

"Holding out on us is a mistake, too."

"You're still having difficulty hearing, aren't you? I said I'll call you when I get back to Raleigh."

"Yeah, that's what you said."

"You just be at this number on Friday afternoon."

"We'll be here."

The accomplice hung up the receiver carefully.

"I'll make sure you two get what's coming to you," he said as a maniacal smile slipped across his face.

§   §   §   §   §   §

"Hi, honey. It's so nice of you to call."

"How are you?" Pamela asked, sounding cordial and enthusiastic.

"I'm fine," Ted replied, his voice low but well-modulated "How 'bout you?"

"Well, that's why I'm calling."

The sudden switch from polite lightness to seriousness was evident in her voice, which seemed mildly apprehensive.

Brad leaned over and kissed her on the cheek and then waved her a hurried good-bye as he started toward the door.

Pamela's affection gaze followed him to the door and her smile greeted his farewell glance, as he disappeared en route to a fast food restaurant. All they had on hand was stale bread, so Pamela sent him out for egg and cheese biscuits or croissants, whichever he could find.

"Is everything all right?"

"Yes, and no," she vacillated, trying to catch up to herself. "My house was broken into again last night. This time it was an arson attempt."

"Oh, no."

"I wasn't there, thank God."

"That's a relief," he sighed.

"But they were waiting for us," she corrected herself, feeling a little silly for adding to his confusion.

"Oh, no! Are you all right?"

Pamela was sitting in one of Brad's cushioned kitchen chairs, nursing her second cup of coffee. She took a quick sip and then spoke into the phone.

"Yes, I'm still a little shaken. But I'm okay."

Ted sighed his relief.

"Brad took me back to my place after he picked me up from my speech in Research Triangle Park last night. We stopped to pick up a few of my overnight things and when Brad opened the front door, we were attacked."

There was a noticeable gasp at Ted's end of the line.

"Are you sure you're all right? Are you both ... " Ted stuttered his way into the next sentence, his voice becoming increasingly higher pitched. "Of course you're all right, you're talking to me. Is Brad ... ?"

"Yes. We're both all right. At least Brad will be. He has a mild concussion and one of the blows re-opened the cut over his eye."

"What?" Ted sounded incredulous. "Brad was injured again?"

Pamela recounted the whole upsetting story, pausing periodically to reassure Ted that everything was okay and that they had the incident properly reported and investigated.

Despite her reassurances, Ted was not convinced everything was all right. His police instincts were still sharp, despite his retirement. He listened attentively while she described the violent episode and made certain she included every detail. Outwardly he was composed, but inside he was enraged at the intruders' audacity.

By the time she finished her story, he knew what he had to do.

"Pamela, honey, I'm coming to Raleigh ... "

"Oh, Ted. You don't have to do that. Really!" Pamela rebutted, sounding appreciative but not wanting him to go to such inconvenience.

"I'm as serious as a heart attack. I'll get there as soon as I can. Tell George and Constance I'm coming."

"Ted!"

"It's not open to further discussion," he replied. He sounded so resolute that there was nothing more to discuss except the arrangements.

"Okay," Pamela surrendered. "But are you sure you know what you're getting into? I mean the danger, the risk you'll be taking?"

"Honey, what I'm getting into is the space between you and whoever wants to hurt you. You're like a daughter to me. You and your family are all I've got now. I can't rest until I know you're safe. If it's Clarence, I want to be the one to punch his egotistical lights out. And if it's that hit and run driver, I want to bring him to justice."

Pamela's eyes filled with tears. She had told Ted of her suspicions about Clarence. It seemed Ted was taking up where Geoffrey left off, protecting her, making sure she was safe. She stood and pulled a tissue from the box on top of the refrigerator and blotted the salty rivulets from her cheeks.

"I love you. You're such a dear friend."

"I love you, too, honey. I'll call you and let you know the flight arrangements. I need to take care of some things here first, so I'll fly out there tomorrow afternoon, if that's all right."

"Yes, of course. Oh, I almost forgot the reason I called," Pamela raised her voice. "Before you fly out tomorrow, I've got a favor to ask."

"Just name it!"

She swallowed hard before the words came, but she was able to force them out.

"Do you still have Geoffrey's things in the attic?"

She winced, knowing her request might upset him, particularly since it related to Geoffrey's personal effects.

His pensive voice followed an awkward pause.

"Yes, I kept most everything but his furniture, books, and clothing. I kept some of his plants, all of his pictures, photographs, and police department memorabilia, especially his uniform and badge. Constance made me a patchwork quilt out of his flannel shirts. Remember? I'll always cherish that."

"I remember."

"I cherish that quilt and his photographs more than anything," he repeated himself. "It's like having him close to me, you know. Sometimes a flannel patch reminds me of the time we did something together when he wore that particular shirt."

Pamela bit her lip hard.

Ted's voice cracked as he continued. "It's a cloth masterpiece of memories. I'll always be indebted to Constance for having crafted it."

She decided to censor her request, but Ted pressed for her sensitive inquiry.

"Is there something else of Geoffrey's you want? I intend to keep my word. Remember what I promised you after the funeral? You can have anything of Geoffrey's you want," he repeated himself graciously.

"Yes, I remember. You're so sweet. I know how much his things mean to you, and I wouldn't be asking this if it weren't important."

Ted waited her out.

"Remember the composite of the hit-and-run driver Geoffrey and Officer Harris ran?"

"Yes, he worked several months on it with Galen, sort of on-the-sly. He finally came up with something he thought looked like the driver."

"Well, I never got a copy of it ... "

"I thought he sent you one months ago."

"He did. But I never got it." She explained her theory connecting the mailbox vandalism and the break-ins, including the last episode. Then she briefed him on her conversation with the Raleigh detective.

"I'll check with Galen," Ted volunteered, not wanting to chance the finer elements of the investigation solely to Wake

County law enforcement, especially since the evidence in question was at his end of the state. "I'll go through every box I have upstairs," he assured her, "and instead of taking the chance mailing, it. I'll just bring it with me."

"Oh, wait a minute, Ted. I'm, so sorry. I forgot to tell you."

"What, darlin'?"

"I have a three week team building session in Dallas beginning next week. So I won't even be here the day after tomorrow."

Ted hesitated briefly. "That's okay, dear. Actually, it's perfect."

"What do you mean?"

"You'll be out of Dodge and that's exactly where you should be until this thing is over. So, it's perfect timing for me to be there."

"Oh, Ted. I'm so sorry."

"No need to be. It's better this way, my being at your house instead of you ... or George. If these people are the ones responsible for your injuries, they're the same ones who caused Geoffrey's suicide. So I'm taking it personally—very personally."

"I don't want you getting hurt. I couldn't stand anything happening to you," Pamela responded anxiously.

"I'll be all right. I'm a tough old bird. They take another step in your house and they'll find more than they bargained for."

"Oh, Ted, I don't know about this. You're scaring me."

"Like I said, don't worry about me. I can take care of myself. You just go on down to Dallas and let us take care of things here," he encouraged, as he looked for Delta's 800 number. He chuckled nervously. "Geoffrey must have done a good job with the description or someone thinks he did."

"They're certainly trying to scare me off," Pamela interjected.

Ted switched to his official voice, and one that had a detached and investigative bearing. "Assuming all of this is related to the composite, how many people knew about it?"

"You mean the composite?"

"Yes, honey, the composite. Who knew about it?"

Pamela's head started to spin as her eyes strayed to her reflection in the sliding glass doors just off the dining room. Her voice tightened as the words fell out of her mouth softly, almost apologetically.

"Not that many people," she began, sounding unsure of herself. "Grampa and Gramma, Brad, and Karen. A few clients who are close friends of mine. The police. Officer Harris, of course. Surely you don't think ... "

"Honey, I just want you to be careful. It seems strange that this is happening all of a sudden. I've got the feeling it's someone who knows you or knows about you. And I'm not ruling out that sleazebag Clarence. He's no longer playing in the NFL. He's up on drug possession charges."

Pamela gasped, bringing her hand up to her throat.

"When did he ... How do you know that? Who told you? Is that for real?" she sputtered.

"I talked to Detective Carter with the Raleigh Police Department. He told me about Clarence. They're trying to locate him now."

"Couldn't happen to a more well-deserving jerk. But that means he's feeling pretty sorry for himself."

"And desperate to make someone else pay for his troubles."

"You mean me?" Pamela asked nervously.

"You ... Brad ... you said he threatened him, didn't you? And anyone else he might have a grudge against."

Looks like Clarence has gone off the deep end, she thought, as she waited for Ted to continue.

"It's definitely someone who knows your whereabouts, when you're home or away, your work schedule. All the break-ins occurred when you weren't at home. Right?"

Pamela shook her head affirmatively and then realized Ted couldn't see her nod.

"Yes," she recovered, "except for the break-in I walked in on."

"Who knows you're going to Dallas?"

Pamela thought quickly. "Everyone I mentioned before, except Officer Harris and my other clients," she answered, sounding a little irritated. "Ted, I don't like where this conversation is going."

"Neither do I," Ted confessed, but his voice sounded more authoritative than penitent. "Pamela, honey, I believe someone is watching every move you make. And I believe they're getting more nervous. When people get nervous, they get desperate. When they get desperate, they usually do something crazy."

"If you're trying to frighten me, you're doing a good job of it."

'I'm trying to get you to think like a cop. I don't want you to let your guard down for one instant. And I certainly don't want you to be another statistic."

"I understand."

"Do you?" he challenged, sounding mildly sarcastic.

"Ted, what are you talking about?"

"Who's going with you to Dallas?"

Pamela hesitated before she spoke.

"No one's going with me. It's a business trip."

He did not miss the acidity in her voice.

"Pamela, darling. Think! You've had death threats. Cancel the Dallas trip. You need to get to a safe house."

"That's the last thing I intend to do. I'm not going to live in fear. I'm not running away from this!"

"Well, my dear, whatever *this* is, it's coming straight toward you. And it intends to do more than frighten you."

"You're saying it's not going away."

"No, I don't believe it is. I think you're going to live under siege until this thing's over."

"You're not helping me feel any less frightened."

"Good! Turn that fright into caution and alertness ... and anger."

"Okay, okay. I'll be more cautious."

"Suppose I meet you in Dallas."

"No, Ted, no. I'll be all right."

"I wish you would let someone go with you. George? Brad?"

"The tickets cost too much. I'm not going to ask anyone to do that. I'll be fine."

"You're just like your father ... and Geoffrey."

"I'll consider that a compliment," she teased, laughing heartily.

Ted returned her laughter with sternness.

"Then stop leaving yourself open to attack. You're too vulnerable."

"What do you mean?" fired Pamela.

"Pay attention to your surroundings. Don't go anywhere alone ... you're about to violate that one already. You've got a registered handgun. Keep it where you can get to it easily. Don't stay home alone. Stay with someone else."

"I'm going to Dallas. I still have to make a living."

"Then practice a couple of evasive moves on the trip."

"Evasive moves?"

"Yeah. Now listen to me before you speak. Okay?"

"Okay."

"What airline are you taking to Dallas?"

"Delta."

"Is Brad taking you to the airport?"

"No, Grampa is."

"Okay. Ask George to drop you off at Terminal C."

"Terminal C?"

"That's right."

"But Delta's at Terminal A."

"That's right. And that's the point. Do you have to check any luggage? Of course you do, you're staying three weeks," Ted corrected himself.

"Yes, one suitcase. And I have a carry-on as well."

"When George drops you off at Terminal C, not Terminal A, take just your carry-on bag and proceed immediately to baggage claim."

"What?"

"If someone is following you to Dallas, they'll follow you into the Terminal. So you'll want them to follow you to the wrong terminal."

"Aren't we being a little melodramatic?"

"Probably, but appease an old retired cop who loves you."

Pamela smiled as she accepted a fresh cup of coffee from Brad, who had just returned with breakfast. He waved a bag of egg and cheese croissants under her nose to tempt her. Pamela licked her lips as she listened to Ted's instructions.

"Tell George to take your luggage to Terminal A and wait for you at check-in."

"Ted, do you think this is really necessary?"

"When you get to baggage claim in Terminal C, get a taxi."

"What?"

"And have him drop you off at Terminal A"

"Ted."

"Have your fare ready so you can make a quick exit from the cab and then meet George at the check-in."

"Ted. I ... "

"Do you see where I'm headed here?"

"Yes, I ... "

"I'd rather be melodramatic and foolish than read about you in the obituaries. If I didn't think it necessary, I wouldn't ask you to do it."

"Grampa's going to think this is strange. *I* think it's strange."

"That's not the first time someone called one of my ideas strange." Ted interrupted, sounding as if he had just received a compliment.

"Oh, Ted. I didn't mean it that way."

"That's okay. I don't care what you think of it, as long as you do it. I'll come to Raleigh as soon as I find the composite. Then I can be at the airport when you arrive for your Dallas trip. That way I can wait to see if anyone appears to be following you."

"Well, then, it looks like this cloak and dagger episode is on."

"Let's hope there's more cloak than dagger. I want your pretty little face around a long time."

"Me, too!" confessed Pamela as she caught her image in the coffee cup. Then she looked at him and said coyly, "Ted."

"What?"

"Thanks."

CHAPTER TWENTY-EIGHT

The Dallas trip went without incident.

Pamela confessed to Ted that she enjoyed the melodramatics he concocted at the Raleigh-Durham Airport both before and after her Dallas business trip. She felt like a celebrity intent on dodging the bothersome paparazzi.

Ted remained steadfast in making her personal safety his business, particularly since he and George had chased another intruder off Pamela's property while she was in Dallas.

With the Lees' consent, Ted and Brad devised a plan to get Pamela to a safe house at the beach once she returned from Dallas, until her stalker was apprehended. Using a series of diversionary tactics, the three men, aided by the police, managed to get Pamela safely to the coast.

It was mid-August and the Carolina coast was engulfed in ninety-degree heat, tourists, and seagulls.

She snuggled down into smooth, fragrant silk sheets, tucked beneath the folds of a light floral bedspread draped over a king-sized mattress that seemed dwarfed by the size of the spacious room. Then she took a deep breath, and allowed one leg to emerge, seeking her footwear. She poked a toe in her shoes and slid them closer to her beside the bed. Brad's absence propelled her out of the luxurious cocoon of covers into both of her sandals simultaneously.

"Got to get moving," she reminded herself. She was still wired, and her nervousness was evident in her hurried attempt to get her day started.

She crossed the room, wearing one of Brad's white dress shirts as a nightgown. Her soundless steps, accompanied by the musical jingle of the bracelets on her wrist, took her across the surface of the tightly-spun carpet toward the sliding glass doors.

A quick glance out the sliding glass doors told her that Brad was not sunning himself on the deck. So she wheeled around and headed toward the bathroom, where she splashed cool water from the sink on her face and flooded her mouth with mouthwash. With a sweeping motion that was both graceful and rehearsed, she raked a purple-colored brush a couple of times through her hair.

This morning she felt far removed from the dangers that had troubled her, terrified her back home. She was determined to take advantage of her privacy, hoping for some normalcy to return, resolved to take one day at a time.

Everything had come undone. While Ted was in Raleigh turning her home into a fortress, his beautiful home in Asheville was burned to the ground by an arsonist. He had lost everything except the few things he brought with him to Raleigh.

He surprised Pamela with a picture of Karen, Geoffrey, and her posed on horseback. It was one a classmate had taken when they were at a high school outing. All three were on separate mounts. Pamela was in the middle, flanked by Geoffrey, who wore the same light blue Tar Heel ball cap he had continued to wear everywhere, and Karen who was dressed in her fringed buckskin coat.

It was the first time he had worn that cap since buying it at the Student Center at the University of North Carolina, she remembered.

Ted found the picture during one of his tearful nostalgic trips through Geoffrey's things, and left it with Pamela for her to have copies made for her and Karen. His simple act of thoughtfulness spared it from a fiery demise.

One other thing caused Ted to count his blessings. The very day he left for Raleigh, he had taken the quilt Constance made from Geoffrey's shirts over to Karen's, for her to display at a showing of her special crafts and artwork. Ted was greatly relieved he was able to salvage these two treasures. Everything else was lost: his rifles, family picture albums, all of the police uniforms—his father's, Geoffrey's and his own—antique furniture, stamp collection. He lost a lifetime of memories. His entire past, except for the photo and quilt, had gone up in smoke.

But he still had his adopted family ... and a future. And he was determined that Pamela would have a future, too.

Neither Officer Harris nor he could come up with the composite. Officer Harris had deleted it from his file once Geoffrey had a hardcopy. Before the fire, Ted had rummaged through each box and searched in every crevice in the blustery attic for the composite, to no avail.

The police were still following up on leads and believed they had found both of the assailants who attacked Pamela and Brad the night the couple drove back from Research Triangle Park. Homicide fished them up from the muddy waters of Kerr Lake. Both had been shot in the head with a high caliber hand gun, gangland style, tied to cement blocks and dumped in the lake. The corpses had been left to the elements a little over a week according to the coroner, and were bloated beyond recognition.

One of the deceased malefactors was wearing expensive alligator boots with distinctive brass tips on the toes. Pamela confirmed the boots appeared to be the same ones on the assailant who broke her ribs.

They were the brass tips Brad remembered seeing when the two men stepped over him as they made their hasty escape.

Although it was dark, the streetlights had provided enough light to set the metal tips aglow.

The deceased's descriptions matched two smalltime criminals who had migrated to the Carolinas from Montana several years before. Both reprobates were well-papered, serving prison sentences at various times in their villainous careers, and had rap sheets as long as a giraffes' neck.

Brad had gotten permission from his brother to use one of Robert's beach-front properties as a safe house for her. Brad brought her to the largest and most expensive, and therefore the most remote of Robert's resort properties. It was in the village of Nags Head near Jockey's Ridge State Park. He knew she would be safe, and as an added precaution took a leave of absence to be with her.

She agreed to his beach house proposal after the disturbing incident at her house while she was in Dallas, when George and Ted chased someone from her garage and across the yard. They lost him when he disappeared behind the gazebo, making his escape through the woods.

The cottage was beautiful and was fully equipped, including a maid. It was when Pamela remembered they shared the cottage with a live-in maid that she caught herself at the bedroom door and closed a few more buttons on Brad's dress shirt so she could wander through the rest of the house freely. Having negotiated the last button up to her cleavage, Pamela entered the carpeted hallway and called for Brad.

"He's out jogging, Ms. Justice," crowed the maid, who saw her guest enter the hallway from the bedroom.

"On the beach?" asked Pamela, noticing that Brad's running shoes were not in their usual place near the dining room door.

"Yes, on the beach," she answered lightly, but scornfully, as if only an idiot would need to ask his whereabouts.

Pamela decided quickly, out of well-bred diplomacy, to put some energy into silence and resisted her impulse to level an insult at the recalcitrant maid. Instead, Pamela gave her a tight smile and paraded past her, altering her forward progress only slightly to swing past the coffee table that the maid had moved temporarily to ease her vacuuming chores.

The maid had not been particularly inhospitable to Pamela, although she had not made Pamela feel at home since she had arrived. Thinking the maid would eventually warm up to her, Pamela had not complained to Brad. However, Pamela believed there wasn't going to be any mutuality of warmth.

"Is there anything I can get you, dear?" the maid asked, forcing out a few syllables of politeness in Pamela's direction.

"No thank you. I'll help myself to the kitchen," Pamela countered, as their assessing eyes met, sizing each other up, searching for any sign of vulnerability that might give one or the other an edge in the politics of social intercourse.

"Suit yourself, dear. Fresh-squeezed orange juice is in the fridge and the English muffins are in the bread keeper."

Pamela threw her a gracious smile. "Thanks."

The maid moved her stout figure toward a wall outlet, intent on plugging the vacuum cleaner into the house current. "Waited 'til you got up to do this," she said loud enough for Pamela to hear, and then leaned over to engage the plug. She talked to herself incessantly while she cleaned the carpet, reminding herself of details and necessities. She worked at such a militaristic pace that Pamela stayed out of her way.

Although she made short work of breakfast, Pamela lingered long enough in the thoroughly modern kitchen, with its stove island equipped with a griddle and its walk-in freezer, to admire the centerpiece arrangement of dried fruits and vegetables on the table. Of particular notice were the gourds, practical vegetables gone chic, which Barbara used for so many different things—flower planters, water-dippers and birdhouses. She placed them in different habitats throughout the house and grounds.

Hanging from the vaulted kitchen ceiling were scores of reed and brass baskets bearing a profusion of exuberantly lush green plants undercut by dwarfed trees which rose up from the floor like potted stalagmites. Philodendrons, plumage sprays cut from pompous grass the year before, ficus trees sporting variegated leaves, spider plants resplendent with runners, ivies of all sorts, were all thriving under softly-focused light or placed near windows.

Carrying a half-full glass of orange juice from the kitchen, Pamela sauntered back through the living room, retracing her steps across the freshly vacuumed carpet on her way back to the bedroom.

The rippled ridges of the wicker sofa and chairs in the living room were softened with needlepoint-covered cushions, beautifully designed and skillfully executed by Barbara's craftsmanship, according to Brad. Pamela remembered that in one corner of the closet in the master bedroom, the one they were occupying, was a large crewel bag, a handmade repository of Barbara's unfinished needlework.

Barbara will probably reactivate that the next time she comes to Nags Head, she guessed.

There were other reminders of her penchant for stitchery all through the house: embroidered or creweled pictures, pillowcases, table covers, book marks. Everything in the house was precisely located, spaced with mathematical precision.

It needs some clutter, Pamela thought as she moved past a life-sized statue of what appeared to be a Greek or Roman goddess, coppery green with streams of black smears running down the hardened folds of its clothing like metallic blood.

There was so much artwork in the cottage that it could have easily passed for a museum. Some of the artwork was bizarre, not easily recognizable, and painted or cut in such a way as to warrant calling it nothing else but junk—expensive junk, but junk nonetheless.

Art is what you get away with, she remembered someone saying once, *which makes it sound more like stealing or some other kind of expecting-something-for-nothing crime. And maybe that's all certain kinds of so-called art are, a form of theft. A hijacking of visual imagery.*

A profusion of new metaphors came to her. *Much of it borders on piracy,* she concluded. *Profanity and pornography, under the guise of art, should not be protected as freedom of public speech.*

The artwork at the cottage was in good taste, except a few pieces that were just plain weird, no doubt placed there due to Robert's egocentric tastes.

Brad returned from jogging with reports of a Category II hurricane brewing in the Atlantic. Some locals on the beach told him about the embryonic storm. Hurricane season was in its third month and most of these people had a healthy respect for Mother Nature's summer tantrums.

"I need to show you the rest of the property and take you to Kitty Hawk before the weather goes sour on us," Brad told Pamela, as he finished getting dressed.

She gave him a collaborative smile. "Good. You know, I've lived in this state all my life and I've only been to the Outer Banks a couple of times," she lamented.

"You're kidding."

Pamela shook her head and part of her lips disappeared into a tight grimace.

"Well, we'll have to change that today," he stated reassuringly and then tilted his head, acknowledging her underdeveloped state history. "With the storm coming, we'd better make a quick visit to Kill Devil Hills first. I can show you Robert's beach front property when we get back."

Brad was referring to the sixty acres of beach property they were enjoying as guests of his brother. Pamela had already seen the cottage and indoor pool, but she had not gotten a cook's tour of the rest of the resort: the boat house, the brothers' private car collections, and the maid's quarters—which Pamela assured him was not high on her list of priorities.

"Have you had breakfast yet?"

"No. Only this," Pamela said, holding up a half-empty glass of orange juice.

"Let's grab something to eat and then we'll head toward Kitty Hawk," Brad petitioned.

"Okay. I could use something to eat," Pamela gave her cheerful consent, planting a euphoric kiss on his lips and then walked arm-in-arm with him toward the kitchen.

Brad broke open a couple of hot wheat and raisin muffins and lavishly buttered them, as Pamela poured juice into two large glasses filled with ice cubes which crackled as she flooded them with juice.

§ § § § § §

The park ranger covered a lot of ground in the closing minutes of his presentation.

They were standing at the marker that showed the distance Orville traveled during the first four sustained flights by a heavier-than-air powered machine across dry land.

She squeezed Brad's hand as the ranger explained more of the etiology of the historical flight. "On or about August 18, 1900, a thirty-year-old North Carolina fisherman named Bill Tate wrote a letter to Wilbur Wright." The ranger smiled, already tickled with what he was about to say. "Thrilled with the prospects of watching a glider fly high in the Carolina blue sky, Tate wrote the history-making epistle, over-stating the suitability of Kitty Hawk for flying experiments."

Pamela glanced at the dunes, drinking in the panorama.

The ranger smiled broadly as he put his hand to his hat rim for emphasis. "Tate understated the always-steady winds here," the ranger continued, becoming more animated and using more expansive gestures to complement his narrative. "Tate's report was so engaging and positively stated that the Wright brothers could not resist considering North Carolina as their flight laboratory."

He placed one hand on the huge stone marker adjacent to him.

"A few years later the Wright brothers, Orville and Wilbur, two pretty decent bicyclists, would make aviation history. At 10:35 a.m. on the morning of December 27, 1903, Orville Wright would man the first motorized controlled-flight machine in unrestricted flight."

He referred the tourists to one of the photographs he had shown them in the museum a short while before. "Perhaps the best-known photograph in aviation history was the one taken by John T. Daniels, who caught Orville's lift-off seconds after he left the ground. John Daniels had never taken a photographic image before."

Almost everyone present, including Brad and Pamela, let out a small gasp.

"Amazing." Brad commented almost subconsciously.

"That's leaving history-making documentation to chance," Pamela added, looking slightly incredulous.

Brad looked at her and nodded.

"Of course, it all worked. Better done than perfect," she summarized, remembering a line she had heard from a teambuilding colleague in Raleigh.

When the ranger finished his historical appraisal of the first flight, he encouraged everyone to stay longer and tour the entire 431-acre site.

Brad and Pamela spent another half hour touring the grounds before they decided to head to Jockey's Ridge. On their way back along one of the walks, Pamela compared man-made flight with Mother Nature's version.

"I'll bet the flight of the Kitty Hawk was awkward compared to the agility and grace of the sea gulls we've seen today."

"I hadn't thought of it that way," Brad said nonchalantly. "Only you would think of something like that."

"We were learning how to fly," she voiced another thought and then followed it with yet another. "Humanity has defied the effects of gravity. We've conquered the skies."

"And we're still trying to learn how to fly," Brad interjected, thinking about the rash of recent airplane crashes that had killed hundreds of people.

Pamela let her silence speak for her as she remembered the airplane crash that killed her parents.

"Air travel is becoming more dangerous, like every other mode of transportation. And now," she said softly, "people aren't even safe in their own homes."

"We're trying to fix that. That's why you're here."

"I know," she agreed as she squeezed his hand gently.

"Give this thing a chance to play itself out in Raleigh. The police have set a trap for the bad guys," he reminded her lightly. "The police woman they've made up to look like you will draw him or them to her. You'll be back in Raleigh in a week or two. So let's enjoy our time together here."

"But she's putting herself in danger."

"It's her job ... Look ... She's a big girl. I'm sure she can take care of herself."

"Maybe so, but you know how violent Clarence can get."

Brad nodded reflectively. "You got that right. Look, the police know what they're doing. She's trained for this sort of thing. And she resembles you in appearance, although ... she isn't nearly as beautiful as you."

She tossed a radiant smile in his direction. "I decided to come here, didn't I? And to enjoy your brother's hospitality." She paused again. "And to get the most out of today. How 'bout we head over to Jockey's Ridge before lunch. I'm not that hungry now. Are you?"

Brad shook his head. "Nope! Let's see if we can work up an appetite running up and down those dunes."

Pamela threw him a conspiratory wink. "You run, I'll watch."

On the short drive up US 158 By-pass toward the once-popular hand-gliding spot, the two of them shared hurricane stories, prompted by the occasional broadcasts about the fifth hurricane of the season, three hundred miles or so south of Bermuda.

Both knew the coast of North Carolina has been battered by countless hurricanes throughout the years. Many have assaulted the Barrier Islands, wrecking the Outer Banks and playing havoc in coastal communities. Several rogues have beaten paths of devastation deep into the interior, penetrating as far west as Charlotte and Statesville. Horrific hurricanes, like Hazel in 1954, Hugo in '89, Fran in '96, and Floyd in '99 left legacies of destruction, reshaping the geography of both the coast and interior of the state.

Brewed out of the heat of tropical waters, these hydrothermal seizures spin sinisterly across the open sea, gravitating westerly out of troughs of low pressure in the upper atmosphere. The height of a full-fledged hurricane reaches up to forty or fifty thousand feet from sea level and can be over six hundred miles wide.

"Did you know, Babe, that the word 'hurricane' comes from the Caribbean Indian word translated as big wind of storm god?"

"No, that's interesting. How do you know these things?" she asked, without attempting to conceal her surprise.

"You can't have properties on the coast without knowing a little something about tropical depressions, storms, and hurricanes."

Pamela gave him an inquiring look, indicating her interest.

"How do hurricanes get their names?"

"Now that's an interesting story in itself!" Brad began, welcoming the opportunity to show off a bit of his knowledge. "In the 18th and 19th Centuries, very few hurricanes were given names. Monster storms were named for the islands and other land areas they destroyed, ships they gobbled up, or the religious holidays nearest the time of their visit."

"How 'bout that?" Pamela said innocently. She seemed genuinely interested so he continued.

"The Cuba Hurricane of 1811 and the Santa Ana Storm of 1825 were named accordingly."

"You really do know something about hurricanes, don't you?" Pamela's surprise turned to admiration.

"A little. Now, in the early days of tracking them, references to storms were made using their relative position at sea. The numerical tracking system proved to be ineffective after a while, when several storms were throwing water around at the same time."

"They do tend to do that. Throw water around," she teased, liking his description enough to repeat it.

"Eventually," he continued, accepting her ad-lib politely, "the military began to use code names for tropical disturbances in alphabetical sequence like Adam, Baker, Charley, and so on."

Pamela opened the plastic water bottle she retrieved from the back seat and offered Brad a drink. When he declined, she took herself up on her own offer and sipped the lukewarm spring water.

"In 1953, a system was adopted using women's names to identify hurricanes and tropical storms."

"It figures. Sexist perverts," she complained, although she wasn't really upset.

Brad smiled and held up his hand in a gesture that solicited her undivided attention.

"You're not the only one who felt that way! In 1979, women's groups from all over the world lobbied the World Meteorological Organization ... "

"Yes!" Pamela interrupted, gleefully shouting her agreement and then looked apologetic, remembering she had interrupted him again.

Brad threw her a comedic look, and then continued, "... lobbied to include men's names and names of international origin."

"All right!" she squealed. "Let's hear it for women's rights and men finally getting some common sense."

He ignored her intentionally, although his collusive smile gave him away.

"A complete list of names is now cycled through each hurricane season and repeated every six or seven years. Except for the names of significant storms like Andrew, Hazel, Hugo, and Fran, which are retired, never to be used again."

"Aw, too bad," she teased. "Let's see, I've retired a few names myself. Sidney the Drip, my high school prom date. He couldn't see past his SAT scores. And then there was Will the Whirlpool, the politically incorrect college class president who lobbied heavily for the Republicans, then did a 180-degree switch when he became a staunch Democrat as an adult. Unfortunately, or fortunately depending on your partisanship, he got himself into some hot water politically and slipped back into local politics."

Brad laughed.

"Both sound like drips to me."

Then he gave Pamela a look that came at her steeped in anxiety.

"You're not thinking of retiring my name, are you?"

Pamela could tell he was serious, so she decided to play.

"Well, that depends."

"Depends?" he sounded surprised. "Depends on what?"

"On how good you are."

She seemed pleased with herself. This was going exactly the way she wanted.

He gave her a knowing glance and then slipped his attention back on the road. They were only a couple of miles from Jockey's Ridge.

"Babe, you know how good I am."

"Oh!" she questioned, laughing heartily. "Are we changing the subject here?"

"You were referring to my performance in bed, weren't you?"

"Why, Mr. Aikman, you did change the subject." Her wide smile met his confused look. "Is that all you think about? I was referring to how good you are at telling hurricane stories."

Realizing she had bamboozled him, Brad decided to launch a counterattack.

"That depends on how good you are, Ms. Justice," he began, "at rewarding the storyteller."

Pamela curved her lips into a devilish laugh, fully appreciating his gamesmanship.

"You have a one-track mind, don't you?" It took her only a nanosecond to produce the next clever retort. "I don't think you can handle the reward I've got in mind," she teased as she playfully unfastened the top two buttons on her silk shirt. "Just call me Hurricane Pamela."

Brad laughed the way he used to laugh before they had been besieged by the troubles of the past couple of months. His gaiety was full-throated and confident, without the tightness that had narrowed his joy.

"If Hurricane Pamela promises to be gentle," he bantered, winking at her good-naturedly. "I believe I can spin a story or two for her."

Pamela raised her hands and rotated them in front of her in circular motions, mimicking a pair of vortexes, and produced a swishing sound with her mouth as she pantomimed Hurricane Pamela.

"Menacing," Brad joked, reacting to her impromptu charade. "Stay stalled on that side of the car until I finish the story. Then you can head toward this body of flesh."

Pamela swished him again, raising her voice and sending her hands about more agitatedly.

"I warn you to begin your first story or suffer a depression if I remain stalled too long."

Brad began quickly, not wanting her to downgrade her intentions of making an intimate landfall.

"It seems that in the spring of 1876 in the town of Swan Quarter, a small congregation of Methodists decided to build a new church near the center of town. The property they wanted was not for sale, and the owner, Sam Sadler, turned down every offer they made."

Pamela swirled her hands again, making her familiar swishing noise.

"Determined to build in town, the church members obtained another piece of property on the edge of town, several blocks from the Sadler property. Are you still with me?" Brad asked, knowing what Pamela's response would be.

She repeated her trite swishing and swirling ritual, but less exuberantly than before and more abbreviated.

"The new church was dedicated on September fourteenth, the same day a major hurricane was churning menacingly past Cuba on its way to the Carolina coast. The hurricane roared across Pamlico Sound and flooded everything in sight, including Swan Quarter. Homes and businesses were submerged under five to ten feet of water. The hurricane had served notice. But evidently, so did God."

Pamela stopped her swirling and adopted a more serious look.

"During the height of the storm, as it swept through Swan Quarter, the rising tides covered the streets of the town and lifted the small church off its foundation, floating it toward the center of town."

Pamela's eyes opened wider.

"When the waters receded, the flood waters had placed the new church squarely on Sam Sadler's property, on the exact spot the Methodists originally wanted."

"You're kidding!" challenged Pamela, finding his story both intriguing and hard to believe.

Brad continued as if he weren't interrupted.

"Sadler was so impressed that he signed the deed over to the Methodists, believing that if God wanted the church there, it was fine with him."

"That's incredible."

"It's also true."

"Aw, come on."

"Really, it's true. A sign stands in front of the Providence Church today, reminding visitors and tourists alike that it is the church that was moved by the Hand of God in 1876."

"Can a hurricane really do that?"

"Yes, are you kidding? I've heard stories of a large flock of seagulls becoming trapped inside the eye of a hurricane in 1960."

Pamela eyebrows disappeared under her bangs. "Inside the eye?"

"They were carried hundreds of miles northward by the storm and deposited near Wilmington when the eye distended to sixty miles or so in diameter, allowing them to escape."

"Amazing. Where do the other fowl go? Ducks, sea gulls, cardinals?"

"Inland," came Brad's immediate response. "They fly inland, staying just ahead of the storm. Venomous snakes are flushed out, too."

Pamela contorted her face.

"Yuck!"

"Rattlesnakes and cottonmouths are often found in houses, cars, and stores."

She wrung her hands several times and then tipped her fingers away from herself toward the windshield in a gesture that gave the impression she was shooing the reptiles away from her.

Brad laughed heartily.

"Where else are they going to go?"

"I don't know, but I don't want them around me."

Brad smiled his amusement.

"In one hurricane, a family was forced to flee their home and cling onto an oak tree to avoid being swept away by the rising flood waters. When they all found their perches in the tree, the family noticed the branches above them were moving strangely. They were horrified to discover that the branches were filled with snakes."

"Eeye-oo." Pamela squirmed in her seat. "No more snake stories. Okay?"

"Okay, how 'bout fish?"

"Fish are okay," she consented quickly, still writhing from the residue of nausea left from his telling about snake encounters.

"Schools of fish travel upstream so thick sometimes, accompanied by large fish like porpoises, that rivers near the inlets look like a slow moving stream of flowing ink."

Pamela threw him a look of disbelief.

"I've seen them myself," he reported. "When I was five or six years old."

Just then a news flash caught their attention:

Tropical storm Elsa has been upgraded to a Category III Hurricane with winds in excess of 120 miles an hour. It is moving 15 to 20 miles an hour with the eye located 225 miles southeast of Bermuda. Stay tuned for another special report on Hurricane Elsa at the top of the hour.

"Looks like she's headed this way," Pamela surmised, as they turned into the parking lot at Jockey's Ridge.

"Yep. Our decision to tour here today was a good one." He looked at the sun-drenched sky. "By this time tomorrow, those skies will show the effects of Elsa. Looks like rain's on the way."

Pamela grabbed her camera and was the first out of the car.

"What happened to the ink stream?" she asked as she tied the laces of one of her sneakers that had come undone.

"What! Oh, you mean the caravan of fish swimming inland?" he replied, catching up to her. "Many live to weather another hurricane. Others die. Most fish kills are the result of lowered oxygen levels in the water, which are caused by tremendous quantities of stuff like leaves, limbs, soil, trash, and other kinds of organic matter that were carried into the streams and lakes by the storm. Sometimes fish fall victim to large wedges of salt water that have been pushed upriver by abnormally-high tides, causing them to suffocate."

"I wish I hadn't asked," Pamela's nose wrinkled and carried her mouth into a smirk.

§　　§　　§　　§　　§　　§

Goose flesh rose on her arms. Pamela had been uneasy all day with news of the approaching storm and now, although snug in bed, she was both spellbound and petrified at being the sole beneficiary of another one of Brad's expertly woven ghost stories.

"Alexander Hostler sat in his library in Wilmington, grieving over the untimely death of his long-time friend Samuel Jocelyn. The young southern lawyer was thrown from his horse and suffered a fatal fall," he said, and then paused teasingly, "or so everyone thought. They buried him at St. James Episcopal Church. Distraught over Samuel's death, Hostler became a recluse, shutting himself up in his library."

Pamela waited patiently for Brad to take a breath.

"Two days after the funeral, it happened," exclaimed Brad, raising his eyebrows and widening his eyes so that his blue irises were islands surrounded by white.

No sooner had Brad employed his dramatics than both storyteller and admirer were startled. Something crashed hard against the sliding glass doors, causing Pamela to jump.

"It's probably the deck chairs, I forgot to tie them down," Brad confessed as he lifted his T-shirt over his head and advanced toward the glass door leading to the noise. "Hold on to the story. I'll be back in a minute."

"Be careful."

"I'll just be right outside," he assured her. Brad switched on the deck lights and disappeared through the open door.

Pamela could see the intermittent flashes of heat lightning erase the darkness momentarily as she stood peering out the sliding glass barrier.

Elsa was dumping the rain in sheets and pushing everything ahead of her with fierce winds.

Brad had guessed right. Several deck chairs had blown against the house and rested in a tangle, stuck to each other by their joint trip across the deck. He tied them securely, but left them wedged where they were.

Toweling himself dry after his serendipitous rescue mission, he settled back in a cushioned chair and faced Pamela, who had found shelter under the bedcovers again.

"Okay, where was I?"

"The funeral. It was two days after the funeral," she reminded him.

"Oh, yes. Two days after the funeral, it happened."

He paused waiting for another of Elsa's unannounced visual aids to complement his story.

A smile curved Pamela's lips. "You don't miss a trick, do you?" she teased.

He acknowledged her good-natured accusation with a grin and then continued.

"As Hostler grieved alone in his library, his brooding was interrupted by the sudden appearance of ... " he blunted his own sentence and then began suddenly by raising his voice, sounding ominous, "A ghost!"

He did not get the reaction he expected from Pamela, who remained perfectly calm and poised, as a spectator too used to his shenanigans to fall for every one of them.

"As you can imagine," he began, "Hostler was startled by his friend's ghostly figure. Suddenly, his dead friend said, 'How could you let them bury me alive?'

"'Bury you alive?' Hostler exclaimed, both terrified and horrified at the apparition's announcement.

"'Yes, bury me alive,' roared the ghostly figure."

Brad let out a long-drawn-out moan: "O-o-h-h-h."

"It's not going to work," Pamela commented lightly and followed it up with an admiring smile.

"Maybe I should switch to another story," he joked, pausing to catch her reaction.

"This one will do. Besides, if you switch stories, you switch rewards."

Brad took the hint and continued immediately.

"'Open my coffin and you'll see that I've struggled.' Then in a flash he was gone, vanished into thin air." Brad trailed off almost to a whisper and imitated the ghost's disappearance by throwing his hands up and outward to capture the effect. "Hostler rationalized the apparition away, believing it to be caused by a combination of shock over the loss of his friend and his own lack of eating.

"He was visited again the following night by the pesky corpse, who again entreated him to open the coffin to reveal his true fate." Brad dramatized the ghost's petition by sliding off his chair, ending in a kneeling position on the floor.

Pamela showed her amusement, but remained wrapped in the folds of the silk sheets on the waterbed.

"Shaken by the second visit, Hostler hid in his closet the next night, fearing another ghoulish visit. Sure enough, he had a closet-mate, but only for a short time, because he bolted out of the clothes-strewn closet and ran toward the door, only to trip over himself and land at the feet of the almost-transparent apparition. This time the ghost petitioned even more pitifully."

Both storyteller and enthusiast could see the gray sheets of rain lash at the windows. An hour earlier, the weather report announced that Elsa had stalled in the Atlantic.

It's the perfect night for ghost stories, she thought as she waited for Brad to continue his eerie tale.

"Hostler could not stand it any longer. He called a friend early the next morning and devised a plan to disinter the body the next night. The appointed night was stormy, much like tonight," Brad teased, using the latest flash of lightning to corroborate his last point.

"A dog howled ... " Brad continued. He paused briefly and then lifted his chin, sandwiching a howl just like the wail of a dog, between the first and last parts of his sentence "... causing the grave diggers to jump as they started to dig the soft three-day old dirt which covered the grave."

Pamela threw him an approving smile. "You howl really good."

Brad smiled, and then howled again before he continued his story.

"Hostler's shovel struck the top of the coffin with a thud. Carefully, the men uncovered it and raised the lid. The light of the lantern his accomplice was holding cast a golden glow into the open rectangular box."

Brad stood beside the bed next to Pamela.

"Hostler let out a blood-curdling cry. 'Ah-h!'" Brad shouted at the top of his voice, dramatizing his character's chagrin.

Pamela applauded Brad's theatrics, squealing in delight.

"There," Brad whispered. "There lay the body of his deceased friend, on its side. Evidence of a struggle was present: claw marks were on the underside of the coffin lid and one of the deceased hands was at his neck, clutching his open collar. Samuel Jocelyn had been buried alive!"

As the last words fell from his mouth, Brad straightened his posture and sent his arms up into a spread-eagle position as he tumbled onto the foot of the bed, sending subterranean waves of water rolling in each direction as the plastic pouch sought to stabilize itself.

Pamela's applause was enthusiastic as she laughed her way into his arms.

"I suppose you're expecting a reward for that fabrication""

"Fabrication!"

"Yes, fabrication. But a good fabrication. Who told you that story?"

She eased onto him, pinning his hands under hers over his head.

"Oh, I don't know. It's been around for a while. I think it's supposed to be true."

"You're kidding!"

Brad shook his head.

"I hope you weren't kidding," he petitioned winking at her.

"Not kidding about what?" she asked, pretending not to read the desire in his eyes. "Oh, I see. You're expecting some sort of reward, aren't you?"

"You promised," he reminded her, as he lifted both her hands and placed her fingertips in his mouth. Then he kissed them and placed her forefingers in his mouth again.

She glanced over at another flash of lightning, which yielded to the darkness as quickly as it had lighted it.

"Are you ready for Hurricane Pamela?"

Brad kissed her hands again.

"Come here," he said softly, releasing her and extending his embrace to pull her toward him. "Make landfall here!"

Their foreplay turned to unbridled passion as they stimulated each other in the usual ways. Finally, she stiffened, then spasmed, arching her body toward him as she convulsed again, flooded with desire. She let out a low series of kittenish cries, shuddering again, clawing rapturously down his back and sides.

He knew with absolute certainty that he thrilled her, that she experienced with him an ecstasy, a sexual fulfillment that was special. He arched, too. His strong arms, rippled and taunt, were braced on either side of her, grasping the rocking bed which complemented their movements, giving just the right amount of pitch and roll to increase their pleasure.

She arched once more and took him completely. Responding breathily and surrendering to the enveloping sweetness of her own orgasmic delight, she traced the length of his chest with her fingernails, only to fall limp onto the silk sheets, signaling her joy and her breathless confirmation of a body spent and at peace.

"It was perfect," she swooned. "The best yet!"

CHAPTER TWENTY-NINE

Elsa was just thirty miles due east of Frisco, a small village located on the Outer Banks between Ocracoke and Nags Head, known for showcasing the culture of the American Indians. Although still considered a Category III hurricane and well out to sea, Elsa was threatening the coast of the Carolina and was dangerous. She was stalled in the Atlantic according to the latest reports, undecided on which land area to molest first.

Brad decided they would be safer in Elizabeth City and managed to book them a room in a hotel there.

Pamela had never been in a hurricane and was relieved that Brad wasn't one of those die-hards who risked their lives by riding out storms like this.

She'd wanted to leave earlier that morning, but understood that Brad had certain housekeeping responsibilities as a guest of his brother. Both she and Brad had made phone calls earlier to their respective relatives, informing them of their intentions to vacate the premises.

Brad was boarding up the place and she was carrying anything inside that wasn't fastened down. The maid had left an hour earlier at Brad's insistence, so that she could help hurricane-proof her sister's house in Manteo.

Although Pamela was happy to be rid of her, she could use two more hands to help her extricate the heavy gas grill that had toppled over and lodged itself between a large wooden planter and the deck. She was particularly upset because she had broken two fingernails in an attempt to get the grill into an upright position.

The poncho Brad had supplied her earlier, designed to keep her dry and protected, wasn't doing either. The surface area of the poncho acted like a kite, catching gusts of air, and suddenly lifted her off her feet as if she were a toy doll, sending her airborne over the grill and into several bushes that bordered the deck. Common sense, accompanied by desperation, took her back into the house as soon as she recovered from the surprise lift-off.

Now I know how Orville felt, she said to herself, remembering the Kitty Hawk's wind-aided flight at the turn of the century.

Discarding the poncho as soon as she was inside, Pamela unwrapped herself completely and headed toward the bedroom. She could hear the fierce tropical winds carry the rain against the windows, lashing at them, chucking debris against them. Elsa's brutish winds held at bay by the cottage's well-fortified beams and rafters of oak, wanted to follow her inside to rearrange the furniture and artwork somewhat differently than the maid had done.

She poured herself into her purple wet suit, considering it the only practical apparel for Elsa's visit, and braved the slanting rain again as she ventured back outside.

It came at her from all directions, in aggravated sheets, stinging an exposed flesh with its liquid missiles.

She decided to forget the grill, which seemed wedged securely enough, book-ended by the deck and wooden planter, and looked for Brad.

The unforgiving downpour carried her toward the building where the brothers kept their collection of cars. Some were restored antiques, others classics. Some were simply the idiosyncratic preferences of two brothers who had more than their share of discretionary income.

She had seen the cars yesterday, but only from a distance, although she understood why Brad was so concerned about protecting them. All of them were expensive and none of them seemed replaceable. Brad's collection included several MG's, an Austin-Healey, and a couple of vintage Mercedes. Robert's interests were a bit more extravagant and matched his ego: a couple of Rolls-Royces, one gold, the other white; a very old red and white corvette sports coupe, and three thunderbirds which must have been the first ones made, because she recalled having seen pictures of them in some old magazines in her grandparent's attic.

"Babe!" Brad shouted at her, realizing she had joined him.

Pamela saw him motion toward her with a hand gesture. He shouted her name again, but the driving wind and rain carried anything else he said away from her.

She moved in his direction, leaning forward to keep her balance. Her purple wet suit appeared black since it had gotten wet, making her hard to see until she stepped into the light near the entrance to the warehouse.

"Babe, you okay?" Brad shouted.

"Yes, I came here to see what I could do to help you," Pamela raised her voice, cupping her hands around her mouth so she could be heard.

"Good, I can use your help."

Pamela stood for a few moments, anticipating his instructions.

"Come over here to my left and hold this side up," he yelled, "so I can screw this side in."

Pamela grabbed the weathered piece of aluminum and held it snugly against the window. Judging from the condition of the piece of aluminum shielding, she guessed that it had been used in many a tropical storm. It was spotted with dark-rimmed screw holes that showed the wear and tear of coastal storms.

"You all packed?" Brad asked, turning toward her so he could shield his face from the whipping rain.

Pamela nodded, ignoring the pelting rain.

"Everything in the car?" he quizzed her again, running through the logistics of leave-taking in his mind.

"All except for us," she responded, smiling as she cleared the water off her brow.

Brad returned her smile with one of his own, appreciating her humor and objectivity.

"I'm almost finished here. I need to get a couple of more sheets."

"Babe," he was shouting again. "I've got enough to finish this window and the next, but I'll need one more for the window on the north corner. The sheet I'm looking for has a large black number three painted on it." He hesitated. "Oh, I'll need some more rope."

He ducked as a huge tree limb blew into the side of the warehouse, just missing him.

"The rope is inside," he shouted, but then halted his instructions, realizing she hadn't heard him. *I'm not surprised,* he said to himself. *I can hardly hear myself think.*

He started again for her benefit. "The rope is inside on the bottom shelf next to the Austin-Healey. Can you hear me?"

Pamela nodded.

"The last piece of window shield is just inside the door. You'll see it as you go inside." He paused to clear his throat. "Meet me on the other side of the warehouse. Okay?"

Pamela nodded her agreement and started past him. As she did so, he pulled her to him and planted a wet kiss on her lips.

"I'd much rather be ravaged by Hurricane Pamela," he joked, smiling broadly.

"If we live through this, that's a strong possibility," she yelled, wanting to make sure he heard her. "Nothing like a little excitement to get the adrenaline flowing."

His smile preempted another hasty kiss as he escorted her through the warehouse door.

Once inside, Pamela moved past the silver Mercedes and slid beside the Austin-Healey to retrieve the rope. As she turned to reverse her steps, rope in hand, she tripped over the edge of one of the boxes on the floor adjacent to the cars. Her arms flailed out as she unconsciously grabbed for something to break her fall. The rope slipped out of her hand, as she tried to regain her balance. Her other hand had knocked several gallon paint cans off the shelf, sending them into the side of Brad's silver Mercedes.

She watched helplessly as she followed the cans onto the floor, hitting the cement hard with her knee, the same one she had injured before on the McDowell Street Bridge.

"Damn it! Damn it! Damn it!" she cursed, reeling more from embarrassment than pain.

Memories of the way she had injured her knee on that fateful day last December flooded through her head. She sat on the floor, rubbing her knee through her wet suit, feeling more emotional pain than physical trauma.

"I'm not going to do this to myself," she said aloud, refusing to allow the past to inch further into her present.

A quick look at the paint cans, scattered on the floor, and the rope lying next to the front tire of the Mercedes, prompted a glance at the warehouse door. Evidently Brad had not heard the ruckus, because the door was still closed, shutting out the pounding rain and sealing her mishap inside.

I've got time to clean up this mess before Brad sees it, she schooled herself. "What a klutz I am."

She raised herself onto her hands and knees, and then lowered herself down on her midsection as she assessed the area under the cars, hoping she had retrieved all of the paint cans. Satisfied that she had, her next move was to fish the paint cans from the floor and set them back on the shelf before Brad discovered the reason for her delay.

As she bent down to grab the second can, her eye caught a mark on the door of the silver Mercedes—a scratch mark!

Her hand covered her mouth as she straightened, forgetting all about the paint cans on the floor.

"Oh, no!" she let out a horrified gasp. "Brad's going to kill me."

She leaned down toward the scratch and ran her fingers over it.

"Damn it!" came another expletive as she started to get upset with herself. "He's outside trying to protect these things and I'm in here destroying them."

Her apprehension lifted her eyes from the damaged car to the shelves nearby. She spied a can of rubbing compound and quickly pried it open with a screwdriver. Another anxious glance at the door, which was still closed, prompted her to use a rag she found nearby to begin buffing the dark scratch, which wasn't coming off as easily as she had hoped.

I thought this stuff was supposed to work, she tried to console herself.

Another frenzied attempt to erase the scratch yielded the same result. Just as she was about to confess her clumsiness to Brad, a ghastly thought leaped into her consciousness.

This scratch hasn't cut through the silver paint deeply enough to expose metal. There is an undercoat of black paint showing.

She stood motionless, mouth hanging open, eyes squinting. She was crackling with adrenaline. Disbelief took over, then bowed to skepticism, which gave way to a growing sense of alarm. A rising sensation of nausea washed over her.

She stepped back a few steps to collect herself before she leaned toward the car and ran nervous fingers over the blemish. She retreated a few steps, taking her puzzlement with her. Her fingers traced the contours of the metal surface of the car as she moved slowly to the front of the hood. Her trembling fingers came to rest on the stainless steel hood ornament that identified the make of the automobile.

A searching expression eased onto her face and morphed into rigorous analysis, as her eyes combed the expensive piece of metal parked in front of her.

Pamela tried valiantly to still the shaking sensation that seized her, convulsing her insides. She became aware of the involuntary twitching that pulsated at the corner of her left eye, a telltale sign of her growing nervousness.

Now that she was alerted, there was something awfully familiar about the lines of the dark contours of the hood, the slant of the windshield. And then there it was! She had not seen it earlier that day on their perfunctory tour of the car collections. She had not looked for it. There was no reason to. Its relevance had not registered. After all, she was only touring a warehouse full of empty cars. She had entered the warehouse with a veneer of presumption, disinterest. She had only consented because Brad wanted to show off his collection of cars.

On the backside of the mirror, between the mirror and the windshield, was a red and white sticker. She had seen it only once before in her life, when Geoffrey had pulled her to him to face the oncoming car, seconds before impact.

The fall on the cement just moments before, re-injuring her knee, caused a flood of memories to resurface. Horrible memories. Memories she had kept buried out of self-preservation, out of anger, out of guilt.

"This is the car!" she raised her voice defiantly.

Her tight lips and tear-filled eyes were torn between suspicion and trust, yet her heart was beginning to harden with a thick layer of ice. She examined the sticker again. *A-240,* she repeated to herself, reading the information on the decal.

Fury propelled her. She circled the car, her eyes gleaming with a mixture of betrayal and rage. When her tears gushed, washing away the months of happiness and joy she had found with Brad, her malice doubled.

"This is the car." She repeated angrily.

She raised her hands, palms up, beside her in a gesture that symbolized the surrender of disbelieving heart to rational mind.

"Oh, God, please no. Don't let it be Brad."

She vacillated between suspicion and desire, as her heart pounded in her head, pleading for Brad's clemency.

Maybe he bought the car. Yes, that's it, she tried to convince herself of his innocence. One torturous thought followed another as the vortex of uncertainty spiraled her into the dizziness of despair.

"Then why did he paint the car silver?" she agonized out loud. "He's the driver?" A new flood of tears found their way onto her face.

Maybe the driver painted it and then sold it to Brad, her heart spoke, still bargaining for acquittal.

Then she began to replay the little inconsistencies, the subtle nuances, the slight oversights throughout their relationship that had escaped her. She remembered their first meeting at the clinic when he seemed troubled about her medical history, but had offered a reasonable explanation, justifying his concern for his patient from a clinician's point of view.

She remembered something else he'd told her which had surprised her at first, and seemed to be an odd thing for him to say at the time. During one of their trips to the beach, he said that shadows crossed his path and no matter how fast he ran he knew he would never outrun them.

A heavy sigh escaped her lips. Her heart did not want to admit what her mind knew.

Another disquieting thought surfaced. Ted was responsible for putting it there when he had suggested the person responsible for the break-ins was someone who knew her.

She shivered with realization. *Every time there had been a break-in, I was away on business or vacation. Brad knew my schedule.*

"No! No!" she fought herself aloud. "Brad was almost killed several weeks ago when he took me home from Research Triangle Park ... and he fought Clarence to a stand-off."

She breathed a sigh of relief as she leaned back against the car. But then her inner voice refuted her previous thought.

He could have staged one of the break-ins. Except for the altercation with Clarence, his head injuries weren't serious. The last time he rescued me, he was certainly healthy enough to make love to me later that same night. Is Clarence the driver? Are they connected somehow?

The downpour seemed to worsen outside. She could hear it pelt the roof and lash at the aluminum siding as brutishly as her suspicions lashed at her. The aluminum protecting the windows reduced the flashes of light to rectangular slits around the perimeter of the shielding.

Her battered heart skipped several beats.

Any suspicions, she told herself, *are entirely fabrications of my own deluded mind.*

"Brad couldn't have been the driver" she spoke aloud, the words sounding strangled, causing her to cough. By clearing her throat, she hoped to clear her mind. "Or could he have been? There must be a reasonable explanation," she choked out a tearful defense. She wiped back her tears, wanting to compose herself, needing to gain a modicum of control.

She took another spiteful look at the car.

Regardless of whether Brad is innocent or guilty, she silently addressed the car, *you are guilty and Brad is guilty by association.*

A destructive impulse caused her to circle the car much like a wolf circles its prey. She retrieved the large screwdriver she had used to open the rubbing compound and freed it from its slot on the pegboard against the wall.

Glowing with vindictiveness, she edged the blade of the screwdriver along the surface of the hood, scraping it hard enough to produce thin black streaks of indignation. As the sharp edges of the screwdriver exposed more of the original black undercoating, Pamela went into a rage, applying more and more pressure, quickening its defacement, cutting through both layers of paint down to the bare metal.

Revenge in her eyes, she spied a sledgehammer leaning against one of the shovels next to the wall and swooped upon it, lifting it.

The sound of sledgehammer hitting metal filled the warehouse. Despite the car alarm sounding, she took an enraged tour around the vehicle, leveling violent blows each time she took a step. The third frenzied attack on the windshield sent the hammer into the vehicle's interior, as she lost her balance and stumbled against the car.

Unrepentant and seething with volcanic wrath, she crawled through the opening that had held the windshield in place to rescue the sledgehammer. Her outrage incomplete, she let herself out of the car, intent on renewing her attack.

She took a few more swipes at the defenseless vehicle before she saw Brad standing just inside the open warehouse door. She did not fail to notice the hammer he held in his hand. She watched, standing ramrod straight, her emerald green eyes turned forest green in anger, as the hammer slipped slowly from his grasp. The indomitable set of her mouth, amplified by the pugnacious tilt of her chin, signaled a woman who was fortified by revenge.

Loyal still in her outrage, Pamela searched his mournful expression for the slightest sign of innocence, for the tiniest hint of confusion as to why she would inflict such a vicious attack on the car. She concentrated her full attention on his face. To her total dismay, she got her answer. His silence was consent.

You even had the audacity to show me your collection yesterday, she thought angrily. *Arrogance seems to run in your family.* She glared at him as if she were going to loosen her rage on him at any moment.

Brad stood frozen in the midst of her menacing presence. His eyes were wary and his manner cautious, as he tried to accelerate his thinking.

The painful look of defeat in his fretful stare spoke volumes. His eyes were not the eyes of a collector upset at finding a prized possession destroyed. They were weakened by remorse, not fueled by anger. He wore the expression of one whose trespass had been discovered. The sorrow that caused his shoulders to sag was his own indictment.

Pamela slowly backed away from the pulverized vehicle that resembled one of its past incarnations of twisted metal and broken glass.

She stood stiffly, her eyes filled with anger, her hands grasping the ten-pound sledgehammer, holding it at her waist in front of her.

"Why?" she erupted as seething anger fed her tears. "Why, Brad? Why? Damn you! Why?"

CHAPTER THIRTY

$\mathcal{H}$e felt exposed and clumsy. He met her fixed stare with the silence of remorse.

Her anger was visible in the tight corners of her mouth, and he could plainly see glimmers of resignation and sadness as she released her grip on the sledgehammer, sending it with a dull thud to the cement floor.

He witnessed a kaleidoscope of her emotions as they squared off at each other, letting silence speak for them. The expression on her face changed again, moving from somberness to grief, sending her lips quivering uncontrollably, forecasting the flood of tears that he knew would erupt down her face.

He stood dripping wet. The driving rain, which had drenched him, ran in tiny rivulets down his poncho, ending in puddles of water on the floor. Shifting nervously on his feet, he allowed the words to tumble from his lips.

"I wanted to tell you from the start," he lamented, "but I didn't want to lose you."

Pamela was too overcome with shock to speak. Her eyes were riveted on him, glaring at him.

"I almost refused to take you as a client after I knew who you were. When I looked at your medical history ...," he proceeded slowly, gauging her reaction. "When Amos told me you requested me to fill in for your old therapist, I should have declined to add you to my case load. It would have been easy then to have referred you to another physical therapist."

His voice sounded weak, almost raspy, as apprehension pinched his throat. A long sigh drifted from his unsteady lips.

"But you didn't," her contempt came at him like a bullet.

He shook his head slowly, despondency etched clearly on his face.

"No, I didn't," he murmured.

"Why?" she raised her voice. "Why did you go through with it? You led me on all this time."

He tried to meet her gaze, but his eyes wandered.

"Look at me, damn you!" she shouted. Her voice was filled with indignation. "I want to know why you didn't have the guts to tell me in the first place." She paused, then quickly continued. "I know why! I would have had you arrested. You'd be in jail. And I'd have seen to it that you rotted there. How could you do it? How could you let me fall in love with you, knowing what you did to me?"

All of the pent-up emotions associated with the abuse she had taken at the hands of Clarence, and her anger at Geoffrey's death erupted, putting a scalding edge on her words.

"We've been a lie!"

"It wasn't a lie! We weren't a lie," he snapped, his eyes coming to rest on hers in an urgent appeal. "I loved you the first time I saw you." He took a half step toward her, feeling his way around her anger. "That's when I ... "

Pamela went ballistic.

"The first time you saw me, you indecent son-of-a-snake, was when you ran over me on the McDowell Street Bridge."

Her face was contorted with fury. She managed to keep a safe distance from him, but her anger pushed her several steps closer so that she was standing at the back of the Mercedes.

"I meant the first time I saw you in the rehab center," he explained, but the steel in her eyes rendered his rebuttal meaningless. He knew full well what she was referring to. And she was right. He had not made any attempt to help her as she lay unconscious and bleeding to death on the icy bridge.

Before he could say another word in his defense, she lashed out at him.

"You didn't stop to help us," she screeched, as the tears fell unchecked down her cheeks, dissolving into her wet suit. "You left me to die! You left us both to die," she added, thinking of Geoffrey.

He closed his eyes, feeling hammered by her accusations.

"I'll never forgive myself for that." His voice faltered as he said it. He took several more apologetic steps toward her, backing her up.

"You won't find forgiveness here, either," came a low guttural indictment from her quivering lips. "I tried to put the past behind me, to move beyond the pain, even to forgive the driver, which I know now was you. You knew who the creep was in the brass-toed boots all the time. You even hired him. I wish Clarence had killed you."

"It's not what you think, Pamela! You've got to let me explain," he interrupted, closing the distance a little more between them. "There's something you've got to know. I ... "

"I know all I need to know," she screamed sorrowfully.

Pamela mirrored his advance with her own retreat, except this time she moved counterclockwise behind the Austin-Healey.

"How long were you going to string me along?" She glared at him scornfully. "Did you think I'd never find out? You hoped I wouldn't, didn't you?" She silenced her lips for the briefest of pauses and stared at him. "It was your picture on the composite, wasn't it? It must have been."

He stood silently, helplessly, withering under each of her angry salvos, the last one coming as a threat.

"You don't understand," he wailed.

Her grief, aided by the fury of the storm, drowned out his petition so that she did not hear it. She sprinted toward the open door which he had vacated moments before in his attempts to confront her disbelief and anger.

She was through the door and out into the storm before he could catch her. The storm slowed his pursuit by tossing a limb at him again, causing him to trip as he attempted to hurdle it.

An inbred wariness made her censure her flight into the house. She remembered that Brad had pulled the main power switch and that the house was cloaked in darkness. If she remained outside, she would at least have the benefit of the lightning flashes to illuminate the way with their pyric displays of electricity.

She fumbled with the lever on the garden gate just long enough to lose the time she had gained. Through it now, she scrambled toward the convertible, which was packed with their overnight bags. She flung open the door and climbed in hurriedly, as she heard Brad's wind-muffled voice behind her.

"Pamela, wait. Don't do this," came his pathetic entreaty.

She heard his cry distinctly, but busied herself locking the car doors by pushing the driver's side door lock, which automatically secured both doors.

Sharply conscious of his whereabouts, Pamela let out a nervous yell as she reached frantically for the keys that she knew were in the ignition. Her eyebrows curved into panic-filled arches as she looked for the keys that were nowhere to be found.

"They've got to be here."

She jerked herself back upright in the seat at precisely the same time she saw Brad's weathered face in the driver's side window. A scream left her lips as she reacted to his threatening presence.

Fear gripped her, paralyzing her momentarily as she saw the keys Brad rattled against the driver's side window.

The keys, she screamed in silent terror as her internal alarm sounded. *He's got the car keys.*

She moved to the passenger's side now with her back to the door, widening the geography between them.

Brad was half pleading—half shouting as he addressed her.

"Babe, this is ridiculous. You've got to let me explain."

He lowered the keys and Pamela heard them jingle their arrival in the lock.

She was breathless now and opened her door only seconds after he gained entry. Fear jettisoned her out of the car at the same time he torpedoed in for her.

"Pamela! Pamela!" he shouted after her. He decided to give chase, but was yanked off his feet when he closed the door on his poncho.

He lay on his back in utter disbelief, looking at the disheveled sky above him. The cool water soaked through his already-wet clothing.

"First tree limbs and now this," he bellowed, as he struggled to free himself from the snared poncho. Growling his frustration, he pulled hard on the wet poncho. Unable to negotiate his freedom, he wobbled closer to the car and jerked the door open, freeing the poncho and doubling his anger.

Pamela cleared the security gate and was headed full gallop down the long driveway that led away from the cottage. In her several panicked looks back, she had not seen or heard Brad, but she knew it was only a matter of time before he would catch up with her.

Exhaustion overtook her as she rounded the bend in the driveway. The main road was only a couple hundred yards away. Her legs felt rubbery and the wet suit was heavy, having sponged up its weight in water. She stopped and placed her hands on her knees. Standing bent over in the middle of her escape route, she looked back toward the cottage. Still no sign of Brad.

Her quick reconnaissance was aborted when the macadam beneath her feet was suddenly bathed in light, indicating the glare from a set of headlights. Pamela wheeled around, almost losing her balance as she pivoted.

Headlights approached her from the main road, their beams on high. She could see the slanting rain dance past the beams as she ran toward the two spheres of light.

"Help! Help!" she shouted, raising her arms in a flagging gesture. 'Please help me."

The car slid to a stop beside her. Just as she placed her hand on the door handle, the passenger side window lowered, half of it disappearing inside the door.

Desperation, combined with relief, threw her mouth open. "Help me, please. Someone's after me."

"Pamela, is that you?"

She squinted, placing her hand above her eyes as she peered cautiously into the dark interior of the car.

"It's me. Robert."

"Robert?"

"Come on, get in."

"Oh, Robert, I'm so glad it's you," she said breathily. "It's Brad. You've got to get me to the police."

"What on earth is wrong?" he quizzed, giving her his full stare. "Is Brad hurt?" He started inching the car towards the cottage.

"No! Stop!" yelled Pamela. "Don't go that way. He's not hurt. Just get me out of here."

Robert stopped the car.

"What is it, Pamela?" his voice sounded gruff, a little too gruff to make her comfortable. "I get a phone call from my brother telling me you two are headed to Elizabeth City. I drive up here to stay with my place. To protect my interests. There are expensive automobiles here, you know."

She nodded uneasily. He was taking too long to justify his concern. Brad would be on them any minute.

"And I find an hysterical woman—a woman whom I've only met recently—in the middle of my driveway, running away from my brother, telling me to take her to the police." He looked at her guardedly as if trying to figure her out.

"I'm not taking anybody anywhere until you tell me what's going on." He smiled wryly, his eyes straying to the set of headlights approaching them from out of the darkness.

Pamela moved nervously in her seat, giving Robert a horrified look.

"He's the one. Please get me out of here," she begged. "He's ... "

"I don't understand. What's Brad done to get you so upset?" he interrupted, sounding a little condescending.

"I found out he's the hit-and-run driver," she blurted out.

"What?"

"He's the driver of the car that hit us, Geoffrey and me, in Asheville." She hurried her words, seeing Brad's car pull along side of them. "Please don't let him hurt me."

When Brad's car came to a stop, Robert lowered his window in response to Brad's having lowered his.

"I've got her. What's going on?"

Brad glanced past Robert's emotionless face and looked directly at Pamela, who seemed frozen in her seat.

"Pamela, get out of his car and come get into the car with me," Brad instructed. His voice was laced with urgency. "Pamela, now!"

She stared at him. Her apprehension, combined with confusion, glued her to her seat. Something about Brad's voice, the look in his eyes, his nervousness, caused her to automatically place her hand on the door handle. She hesitated just long enough to hear the door lock mechanism activate.

Robert had locked the car doors and had now grabbed her wrist with his free hand. His fingers, vice-like, bit into her flesh, hurting her.

"Let me go," she screamed. "You're hurting me!"

A smothering feeling of panic enveloped her. Goose flesh speckled both her arms, then migrated over her entire body.

"Follow me back to the cottage," Robert ordered Brad, with such iciness that her defensive instincts were alerted.

Pamela struggled to pull on the door handle to no avail, while Brad shouted a reminder at his brother.

"You gave me your word you wouldn't hurt her."

Pamela's eyes widened when she saw the concern in Brad's eyes as the water-coated window on Robert's side closed, obscuring Brad's image.

"Let me out of this car," she demanded, more out of fear than anger, although her voice bordered on defiance.

"You've presented me with quite a dilemma, Ms. Justice," he answered, as he glanced into the rear-view mirror. Brad had circled around behind him, making a motorcade of two as they drove back to the vacant cottage.

She stopped struggling against his vise-like grip and gave him a horrified look. Paralyzed by the icy detachment in his voice and the sinister glow in his deep-set eyes, she sat motionless, helpless, feeling like a caged animal. She waited for the words she knew she didn't want to hear, although she didn't know exactly what would come.

"Have you been looking for this?" he asked coolly. His voice sounded antiseptic as a conniving smile twisted his face. He handed her a folded sheet of paper.

Her fingers trembled as she slowly shook the folds out.

"Oh, my God," she whispered aloud as her hand covered her mouth. "The composite! It's ... you!"

"A rather nice resemblance, don't you think?" he announced coyly, seeming to take immense pleasure in witnessing her distress.

She tucked her anger in, but only for a moment. In that split second of chilling awareness, she wanted to smash his face, kill him, for all of the pain and suffering he had put her through the past six months. She was pregnant with malice.

"You! You're the driver!" she bellowed again and attempted to strike him with her free hand.

Robert blocked her fist before it came crashing down on the side of his face. His eyes were glazed, hollow, maniacal. His fingers clamped tightly on both her wrists, his superior strength evident.

"And I don't intend to pay for a mistake that was unavoidable." He looked at her, his face porcelain, immovable. "It would have been less complicated if you two had just died on the bridge."

The words hit her as if she were slapped in the face. She couldn't believe his callousness, his insensitivity.

Making sure he had restrained both wrists with one hand he accelerated the car slowly, deliberately.

She felt hemmed in by his derangement and by the car's steady forward movement. She experienced a choking sensation, the kind people get when exposed to the stench of evil. She tried to wrench her wrists from him as if he was contaminated, but his strength preserved the flesh against flesh handcuff. His strength surprised her. Horrified her. She was shaking, sealed in her fright.

She glanced behind her. Brad's headlights were tailgating them, sending their beams into the car windows.

Her eyes darted back and forth in their sockets as she contemplated her next move. She thought again about Brad's culpability or innocence. Why did he have the car if he wasn't involved in some way? What did he mean when he told Robert not to hurt me? Why did Robert come here tonight? Oh, my God? Brad has kept me close so they can kill me. Ted was right. It is someone close to me.

Pamela considered her next reaction foolish, yet a chill knifed through her as she attempted to shake off its morbidity. She had to confront Robert and learn the truth.

"Then it was *you* who knocked down the mailboxes and stole the letter containing the composite," she gave him a scornful look.

"I had it done," he spoke coldly.

Pamela did not respond outwardly to his harsh admission, but compressed her lips tightly, nervously biting them on the soft inside tissue, causing them to bleed.

"You may as well know," he paused as he pulled the car up to the circular part of the driveway in front of the cottage. "I orchestrated the threats—the break-ins—the fire. And Jason tried his best to kick your ribs in."

He smiled when she glared at him.

"Fire? You had Ted's house burned down? Why? Why?" she screamed, attempting to free herself.

Robert simply tightened his grip on her wrist and laughed demonically at her pain.

"Easy, you might hurt yourself."

Still unable to free herself, Pamela leaned as far away from him as she could.

"Because I couldn't take any chances on copies of the damned composite surfacing," Robert sneered. "Actually, my dear, you were quite lucky. If those idiots I hired hadn't messed up, your house would have been toasted, too."

Pamela glared at him through gritted teeth, yet remained silent, waiting for his next maniacal confession.

"You should have left well enough alone. But you stuck with Brad, had fun in the sun—and in the sack."

Robert gave her wrists an extra squeeze as she tried to break his hold. He used both his hands now to hold her wrists and continued calmly, as if they were discussing the weather over coffee on the verandah.

"Brad told me about your flashbacks—about your determination to do what your precious Geoffrey had asked you to do. For all I knew, you might have remembered my face, too. I couldn't risk that, you see. So you became a liability I couldn't tolerate any longer. Why couldn't you have just let well enough alone?"

"I did! I was piecing my life back together when you sent that maniac to my house. That's when I decided to find you. *You should have left well enough alone, you monster!*" she screamed. "You poor, pathetic monster!" She made no attempt to disguise her volcanic rage.

Brad was standing at the car door waiting for Robert to unlock it. The agonized look on his face was evidence of his concern as he saw her struggle to free herself.

"Robert!" Brad shouted. "Let me in. Unlock the door." He moved to Robert's side of the car, considerably upset with the way things were going.

Oblivious to his brother's pounding on the window, Robert slowly turned toward Pamela.

She wisely sensed a macabre change in Robert's demeanor and held her spiteful tongue, choosing instead to launch a rather chilling glare of her own at her abductor, who appeared impervious to her anger.

His face was emotionless. He appeared determined to force his will on both her and the exasperated sibling pounding angrily on the window inches from his ear. The rigidity in his neck and shoulders conveyed a sociopath gone berserk.

"The biggest mistake I made was letting my little brother ..." he severed his own explanation. "Brad! Stop beating on the window," he yelled, adding his spittle to the rain-soaked window. "Stop it! Stop it now!"

Brad stopped, showing his obedience.

Robert renewed his stare at Pamela, who realized how puppet-like Brad was.

"The biggest mistake I made," he repeated, "was allowing Brad to protect you. If it weren't for him, you'd have been dead long before now."

She shivered involuntarily, violently, as she glanced at Brad, who resumed his hammering on the window.

Her eyes moved down to Robert's strong hands. His knuckles were white and protruding sharply as he held her. The veins in his hands were puffed up, resembling the burrows made by moles in their subterranean exploits across lawns. They were cutting off the circulation in her wrists. She could feel her heart pound more pronounced now, flooding her ears and chest with bursts of tension.

"Too bad the old cop wasn't in it when it went up in flames," he stated emphatically. His detachment was amazing. His voice, flat and devoid of expression, had a dark, ruthless edge to it.

The glare of her eyes and the tightness of her lips, accompanied by hands formed into fists, demonstrated her contempt.

Having been ignored so expertly, Brad tried all of the doors, ending his futile attempts to gain entry by appearing again outside her door.

"That stupid composite. I was sure Geoffrey had given his old man a copy. Couldn't find it—couldn't take any chances. And I sure couldn't let you see it! Too incriminating, you know." He fixed his demented gaze on her.

Pamela was as motionless as Brad was animated.

He pounded heavily against the roof and kicked the car door, spending his energy in frustration.

"I have a career to protect, a reputation and wealth to preserve, a public image to uphold." He looked directly at her, but his rationality was lost in his plaintiff stare.

"So I couldn't let them live, you see. They were liabilities, which made it necessary for them to be erased." When he finished his sinister recital, his lips closed, forming a slippery, deceitful smile.

The words leaked out of her mouth before she was ready.

"They? Who?"

"My poor unfortunate accomplices, of course. They decided to take a swim in Kerr Lake."

Pamela suddenly remembered the two men the police found in Kerr Lake.

"You killed them?" she asked rhetorically, knowing his answer, yet hardly believing it.

"Some things you've got to do yourself. Ask Babs."

"Who?" she repeated cautiously.

"Babs. Barbara to you. You wanna ask Babs?" A roguish smile creased his porcelain face as he depressed the automatic trunk release, popping the trunk lid.

Out of the corner of her eye, Pamela saw Brad disappear, his attention now diverted to the rear of the car.

Suddenly it occurred to Pamela that Robert, in his gloating endeavor to pop open the trunk, had inadvertently unlocked the doors and loosened his iron hold on her wrists. Her razor-sharp instincts reacted to the improbable escape opportunity before Robert could recover in time to snare her.

She quickly raised her right hand and in a lightning-fast karate move that would have made any Sensei proud, swung her arm high in a sweeping motion and delivered an open-palmed blow directly to Robert's right ear. The force of her blow slammed his head laterally to the left into the driver's side window. Her surprise attack was the advantage she needed.

She wheeled around quickly and jumped against the car door, pulling the door handle as she did to extricate herself from the metal prison.

Brad heard the car door open and aborted his interest in what the open trunk revealed. He rushed to the passenger's side door the instant Pamela flung it open.

The force of her escape slammed the door into him, knocking him down. Pamela rushed by him, reinvigorated by her newly-acquired freedom. As she rounded the rear of the car on her way toward the cottage, she chanced a glance into the trunk.

Her scream drowned out Robert's expletives as he fell out of the car in an attempt to pursue her.

There was a body in the trunk. And by the looks of it, the blond-haired woman was dead, lying face up in the trunk.

By the time Brad reached the rear of the car, Robert was pointing a revolver in Pamela's direction.

POW! The first round went off.

"Robert, stop! What are you doing?" Brad shouted as he cleared the back of the car, failing to notice the body inside. "I'll be damned if I'm going to let you kill her," he yelled as he sprinted toward Robert.

When the second round went off, Brad slumped to the pavement, and lay motionless at his brother's feet.

Pamela heard the second shot from her position just outside the house. Frantically, she ran around the porch to the kitchen door and reached for the cell phone in her wet suit pocket. It took her a second time to punch in 911 correctly.

When she heard the monotone voice of the policewoman at the other end of the phone, Pamela hurried her plea.

"Please help me. Someone's trying to kill me. I'm at ... "

She stood in abject horror when she realized Robert was less than ten feet from her. Panic propelled her over the porch railing and into the wrath of the hurricane. She heard another gunshot, but didn't look back.

Her escape route took her past the warehouse where she reversed her direction and headed toward the boat house. Thinking he wouldn't look for her there, Pamela made a beeline through the trees. She needed time to think, to stop her head from spinning.

She knelt in the shadows inside the boathouse, trying to slow her breathing, fearful it might give her away. The sailing paraphernalia in front of her offered little protection, but she had the advantage of seeing him first if he should come that way. A quick look around convinced her that the door she entered was the only way out.

Terrific, she thought nervously. *I may have backed myself into a corner.*

When the door swung open, Pamela let out a gasp and jumped back, burying herself in the shadows.

The wind had taken part of the corrugated roof off the boathouse, leaving a long rectangular slit in the ceiling, the length and width of one of the panels. When lightning streaked across the troublesome skies, a rectangular patch of light would illuminate the floor and then extinguish itself.

Shortly after the next thunderclap, Pamela saw a figure silhouetted against the vaporizing light. It was Robert!

"They're all dead now, my dear," he announced proudly. His voice pitched, and his words were like fingernails scratching a slate chalkboard, grating at her. "You may as well join them," he hissed ingratiatingly, and with growing unpleasantness.

She remained hidden, silent, steeling herself against his demonic invitation for her to reveal her whereabouts.

"Brad is waiting for you, too," he teased, his spiteful mouth taking over.

Pamela renewed her intense stare at him at the mention of Brad's name. He was trespassing now, into her confusion between disappointment and desire. Brad's betrayal had wounded her deeply, irreparably, but she didn't want him dead.

So, Brad's dead, too, she surmised remorsefully, as salty tears made their way to her eyes and dropped unabated down her reddened cheeks.

"And Babs," he whispered, giving in momentarily to artificial melancholy. "She liked you from the moment she saw you. It's your fault, you know—that she's dead. That's her in the trunk. She wanted me to turn myself in. Can you imagine that? Turn myself in. Lose everything. That's what she wanted me to do—over two people I didn't even know. I couldn't do that. It would have been my Chappaquiddick."

Pamela's gasp was too loud.

He heard it and turned in her direction.

"Oh, hi there," he said carelessly, a touch of his patented arrogance evident in his tone. He moved a couple of steps in her direction. His towering figure was illuminated through the rectangular opening in the roof. His dark eyes swept over her in one concentrated disapproving glare.

"You may as well come out. It's time for you to join the crippled policeman and the others."

Pamela was seething in anger behind the cartons and lifejackets that shielded most of her from his evil gaze.

"Should I let you continue to believe his pitiful death was a suicide?" he teased, "or shall I tell you I had him erased? Yes, I think I shall tell you that. He was such a pesky cripple."

He said this with such heinous arrogance that the chuckle he thought would come to his lips leaked out as a snort.

Pamela lost herself in anger. Fury compelled her to stand.

"Oh, you've decided to make it easy for me?" he addressed her sarcastically, and brandished the revolver he held in his hand.

"I'm going to kill you for killing Geoffrey," she spoke evenly, but her tone was unmistakably callous. Her defiant stance was frontal and unapologetic.

The renegade winds and rain of the hurricane plummeted the boathouse, hurling debris indiscriminately all around them. In front of her were clusters of fishing tackle and rods, hanging above scores of crates scattered throughout the boathouse, and Robert's menacing presence.

"Go ahead. Shoot!" Pamela yelled. "You'll have to because I'm going to kill you."

"I was surprised to hear how calm he was before he died. He really loved you, you know. So I thought I'd put him out of his misery."

"You piece of garbage."

The sinister smile left Robert's face.

"Say a quick prayer, you little hussy."

Robert raised his handgun and pointed it directly at her. Until that moment, there had been perfunctory stumbling, recoveries, and clutches for an edge, any advantage that one might gain over the other. The half-crazed man who stood before her now, blocking her exit, was hell-bent on her destruction.

"I would have let him live ... live ... ten seconds longer if he hadn't spit in my face. I don't think he liked me."

Revenge, not fear propelled her toward him. All balance was lost. Reason forgotten. Her own safety set aside, she lunged at him, her only weapon her searing rage.

When the gun barked she wondered how she was still able to take hold of him as she fought him to the floor. She landed on top of him, her hands at his throat, fire in her eyes. She heard him groan and drop the revolver.

Why isn't he trying to stop me? she wondered, as she tightened her stranglehold.

All of the strength she possessed was focused on one point of contact, the soft cylinder of his neck. She would stay there until she had taken all of his air.

"I'm going to kill you! I'm going to kill you!" she screamed tightening her stranglehold.

She wasn't sure how long she struggled on top of him, but suddenly she felt hands, strong hands, pull at her. Her first reaction was to strike back. She adopted Robert's insanity as she twisted herself away. Scooting across the planked flooring, she took up a defensive position some distance away, thinking it was Brad coming to help his brother finish her off.

"Pamela, honey, it's me."

Heart pounding, her self-preservation antennae operating at full intensity, she vacillated between defiance and recognition.

"Pamela, it's me, Ted. You're safe now."

§   §   §   §   §   §

She packed the last of Brad's things in cardboard boxes and had George deliver them to Brad's house. It was Pamela's intention never to see Brad again. And now the last of her sentimental deliveries had gone to him—shirts, photographs, letters, jewelry, and other gifts—were on their way back to him, thanks to her grandfather.

Brad was still recovering from the gunshot wound inflicted by his brother. While his injuries were healing, his heart was not. In spite of heroic reconciliation efforts on his part, Pamela had not spoken to him since the day Robert died.

Clarence had been arrested in Florida after fleeing Texas on drug charges. Some poor woman of low self-esteem, his latest sexual toy, had called Pamela a couple of days before on Clarence's behalf to ask if she would loan him bail money. She had given the woman the best piece of advice she could: ditch Clarence. Don't walk away—run! She could tell the woman couldn't comprehend the quagmire she was in, so Pamela wished her the best and hung up the phone.

One of the most touching consequences of her ordeal with Robert was a letter she received from Polly Holcum, a nurse living in New York. The letter was an epistle of gut-wrenching apology, seeking absolution. She was Brad's companion, the fourth person in the car that had plowed into her and Geoffrey. Frightened of Robert, she had fled to New York and tried to begin a new life there. Plagued with guilt, she'd re-established contact with Brad and poured out her anguish on him.

It was Brad who gave her Pamela's email, suspecting Polly would eventually want to contact Pamela about the accident. His instincts were right. Her guilt forced a lengthy confession.

Pamela's ability to forgive Polly on the spot sent the poor woman into a Niagara of tears that lasted close to ten minutes on the phone when she called Pamela to thank her for responding to her email. Both women wept unabashedly: Pamela for a truly repentant nurse who needed to be cleansed from her guilt, and the nurse for herself as she crawled her way back up to some semblance of decency and self-respect.

Pamela sat contemplatively on the side of her bed, stroking the quilt made out of Geoffrey's flannel shirts that Ted had given her. Besides the picture of Karen, Geoffrey, and her on horseback, it was the only thing spared from the fire.

She smiled radiantly as she caressed the squares, some of which had been sewn with the pockets of Geoffrey's shirts still intact. It was in one of the pockets that Karen had found a copy of the composite.

Ted had acted on instinct when he refused to wait for Pamela's return from the coast to Raleigh. He thought she should have the composite as soon as possible. Hurricane or no hurricane, Ted had driven to Nags Head and arrived just in time to witness the death of the man responsible for four people's deaths, including his son's. Fortunately, Pamela wasn't his next victim.

When she leaped on him in the boathouse, he had fallen backwards and was impaled on a piece of debris the storm had blown in. Pamela hadn't realized it until he pulled her off Robert.

Pamela remembered the family's assessment of what had happened. Evidently Geoffrey had been wearing one of his flannel shirts when he worked on the composite. He must have placed the completed drawing in his shirt pocket for safekeeping and forgotten all about it.

Surprisingly, Constance hadn't noticed it when she cut up the shirts and created that beautiful quilt for Ted. Ted's charity toward Karen, wanting to show his support for her craft show just before the fire, had spared the quilt and preserved the evidence it had kept hidden from going up in smoke.

Geoffrey, you had something to do with this, Pamela thought as she stroked the photo once more.

She looked at her watch. Time to go.

§   §   §   §   §   §

Shortly after her arrival at Karen's house in Asheville, Pamela found herself at Geoffrey's graveside.

"You can rest in peace, Geoffrey," she proudly told him as she petted Hans, the loyal canine at her side. "You protected me even from the grave."

As she jogged back toward Karen's house, past the spot on the McDowell Street Bridge where the Mercedes plowed into them nearly a year before, she paused and ran her fingers over the still visible gouges in the cement abutment.

A brittle smile leaked across her face.

I know you hear me up there, Geoffrey. Thanks for saving my life; Hans says thank you, too. He wants both jogging partners back ... But I told him you're off on your next assignment.

She kissed her fingers and touched the deepest gouge.

I will always love you, Sir Galahad. The rest of my life shall be your grail. As God is my witness, I shall make something of myself.

Pamela knelt beside the faithful German shepherd.

"You're going to hold me to it, aren't you, fella?"

Hans barked his obedience and sent his tail wagging.

About the Author

Bil Holton has been writing, speaking, teaching, coaching, and publishing for over 30 years. He brings quite a background of experience and depth of knowledge to his work. In 1984, he and his wife, Cher, founded The Holton Consulting Group, Inc., which is still alive and well today! They work with clients in the U.S., Canada, Germany, England, and South America, with a mission of leading, guiding, and inspiring people and organizations to live productively and joyfully at the speed of life … one choice at a time. Their impressive client list includes Fortune 100 companies, healthcare facilities, universities, associations, and government agencies.

In addition to Bil's novels, Bil and Cher have authored and co-cuthored over 50 titles, including *The Manager's Short Course to a Long Career,* which was selected by SoundView Executive Summaries as one of their Top 30 Business Books, and *New Metaphysical Versions of Matthew, Mark, Luke, John,* and *Revelation*—the first ever verse-by-verse metaphysical interpretations of these books.

When he isn't involved in work and research, Bil enjoys golf, travel, jigsaw puzzles, the theatre, and landscaping. The Holtons like to push the envelop and maintain their zest for life by taking what they call "Indiana Jones Adventures," such as white-water rafting, sky diving, and fire walking. American-style ballroom dancing is also in their DNA. Although they have retired their competitive dance shoes, Bil and Cher love to perform ballroom showcases and exhibitions. Their two sons, beautiful daughters-in-law, and incredible grandchildren all live nearby. Their visits are always joyful.

To learn more about Bil and contact him for speaking appearances and book signings, visit his website, BilHolton.com/ (Remember—it's Bil with one L)!